I Can't
Stop Tomorrow

Sara Powter

ISBN: 9780645441598
Paperback

Pacific Wanderland Publications
ABN 99 768 734 831
Kincumber NSW 2251

saragpowter@gmail.com
www.sarapowter.com.au

1st edition 2024 printed by Kindle, an Amazon Company;
available on Kindle Unlimited & KDP

Artist: Francis William Topham c. 1845
Medium: Watercolour on paper Accession #: 2018.3
This work by British artist Francis Topham shows a group of pilgrims
at the base of a large stone cross at the monastery of Clonmacnoise.

The cross featured in this work is **The Cross of the Scriptures.**
It is 4 meters high and one of the most skilfully executed of the high crosses that survive today in Ireland. It is particularly noted for its inscription, asking a prayer for Flann Sinna, King of Ireland, and Abbot Colmán, who commissioned the cross. The cross was carved from sandstone taken from County Clare. The three distinct sections of the body of the cross show the Crucifixion, the Last Judgement, and Christ in the Tomb. The Cross of the Scriptures remains one of the steps in the modern-day pilgrimage tradition.

Australian Historical Novels

(All stand-alone books)

A First Fleet Story (1788)

Gentle Annie Soames
Paternity Unknown (2026)

The Hunter to Macquarie Collection (1795-1822)

When Upon Life's Billows (2025)
Saddler's Song (2025)
Tuppence to Pass (2025)
His Majesty's Pageboy (2025)
Fist Full of Holey Dollars (2026)
Far From the Whispering Sheoaks (2026)
Bound Down in Iron Chains (2026)

Unlikely Convict Ladies Trilogy (1792-1840s)

Dancing to her Own Tune
(co-authored by Sheila Hunter & Sara Powter)
Amelia's Tears
A Lady in Irons

The Lockleys of Parramatta (1800-1900)

Unshackled Lives - *Prequel novella - free with newsletter signup*
Hands Upon the Anvil
Out Where the Brolgas Dance
Diamonds in the Dirt
The Earl's Shadow
Once a Jolly Swagman
Jonty's Journey

The Convict Birthstain Collection (1820-1840s)

No More, My Love
The Vine Weaver
Scotch at The Rocks
Waiting at the Sliprails
Convict Shadows of the Past
In Defence of Her Honour
I Can't Stop Tomorrow *(2024)*
Madeline's Boy *(2024)*
Jam or Marmalade for Tea *(2025)*

Shelia Hunter's
Australian Colonial Trilogy (1840-1850s)

Mattie
Ricky
The Heather to the Hawkesbury

Historical Notes

The Irish potato blight did not just affect Ireland
but Scotland, as it also spread into the Highlands.
Somehow, many of our poverty-struck antecedents survived.
Some ended up in Australia as convicts, as they stole food to survive.
How our ancestors then coped as convicts still leaves me in awe!
They each had scars on their hearts.
So, to all those who have gone before us, thank you!

The Potato Famine in Ireland 1840s

Potato blight hit hard in Ireland in the mid-1800s.
The population fell by over one million in ten years.
Not all died; many emigrated.
Four thousand female orphans were sent to Sydney in 1848,
and this is the romanticised story of two of the orphan girls.

You will need tissues for the first three chapters.

**John Moore's story of Avoca Beach is at the back of the book.
Born 1803, Co. Wicklow Ireland - died July 1865 East Gosford NSW.**

Thanks to my husband,
Steve, thank you for all your support in my writing.
He's my Alpha reader.

To Roby Aiken
for your patience in correcting my punctuation
and to my Beta readers
Noreen Robertson, Linda Upcroft, Lee Boehm & Anna Marie Leffew
for doing the final read-throughs
& Anna Marie Leffew for the wonderful advertising she does for me.
And…
Rebekah Robinson for my cover.
Cover by Beckon Creative
beck@beckoncreative.biz

Acknowledgement of Country:

In the spirit of reconciliation, I acknowledge the Traditional Custodians of country throughout Australia and their connections to land, sea and community. We pay our respect to their Elders, past and present and extend that respect to all Aboriginal and Torres Strait Islander peoples today.

Table of Contents

The grammar and language in this book are
Australian English spelling.

KEY

~ Time passing in the same locality

- Different locality/country

<u>Two Gaelic names that are difficult to pronounce</u>

Gráinne pronounced *Graan-ya* (means grace & love of my heart)

Shéamas pronounced *Shaé-mu*s (Irish Gaelic for James)

Chapter 1   Babes and the Blight

*K*ieran O'Shane looked over to his lovely wife. She had recently given birth to their latest child. He said, "April 1847 will be seared into my mind forever, Gráinne, my darling love." He was holding their youngest child, gazing down at him adoringly. The baby boy was weak but breathing.

Thirteen-year-old Clare had helped her father deliver the baby as she had done many times before. At eleven, Kerry, her next sister, looked after the other little ones while their mother travailed in childbirth.

Kieran cradled the babe, waiting for the afterbirth to come. He knew Clare could cope with the bloody mass when it appeared. He would then return his son to his wife for his first meal. The grin on the young father's face showed his contentment. The farm looked good; they had a small cottage he had built from the rocks in the fields, and they now had six wonderful children. This year looked to be a bumper crop, and on the strength of a good forecast, he had purchased a new pick to dig the soil and plant more potatoes. Six shillings was a lot of money for the new tool, but it meant they could increase the size of the cropped area. He was not afraid of hard work, and now, with two sons, he would need to work hard to increase the size of the arable land. Their four daughters would also need some dowry money, but that would come later. For now, he had to open up more areas to farm. He looked down at his dozing wife. Gráinne had suggested that they plant a few other small areas of different crops, but Kieran had said that potatoes were going up in price as some areas had blight and their crops had failed. On the far western coast of Ireland, the potato blight had not bothered them too much. They did not have to buy seed potatoes as they had kept ones from last year. There was little chance of the cursed disease spreading as far west as their farm.

Father Patrick Murphy needed to be told that they had a new child and that he would need to be Baptised as soon as it could be arranged.

"Sweetie, how about Patrick Anthony for this little mite?" Kieran saw that his child had his mother's dimple on his cheek. "Paddy, my little Paddy. Yes, I like that." He handed the baby to his mother for her first proper cuddle.

~

Eight weeks later

Liam O'Shane, the nine-year-old son of Gráinne and Kieran O'Shane, was laid to rest in the small churchyard of Tarbert Catholic Parish just before sunset. The June day had dawned bright and sunny, and as most of the children did each morning, Liam had decided to go for a morning dip to clean up. Why he had risen so early or how he'd been caught in the strong current, no one knew, but he had drowned. His body was seen floating in the lapping waves when the other family members arrived for the morning swim. Ten-year-old Sean O'Day, Liam's best friend, was missing too, but after an hour's search, he was soon found further down the bay. Apparently, the two boys had decided to go for a dawn swim but had been caught by a rogue wave and dragged out into the deep water. Sean had been able to tread water, but Liam couldn't swim. The tragedy was compounded as Paddy, who had never thrived, was only buried the week before. Both sons were now dead.

Kieran, Gráinne, and the girls somehow made it through that week. To lose both boys was terrible enough, but the potato blight had been found on the O'Day's farm the month after Paddy was born. It had been in other counties for the past two years, but being so isolated, their farms had escaped.

The day after Liam's burial, Kieran had been unable to sleep. Creeping out of the tiny cottage, he checked the crop. The new shoots of their enlarged crop stood nearly a foot high, and as expected, it should be enough to sell and enlarge the cottage. Walking along the mounded ground on the newly tilled paddock, he checked as he was the closest to Anthony's contaminated crop. He saw a few leaves curling up and plucked off the stems. As he walked, he kept tweaking off the distorted leaves. He decided to burn these rather than dig them back in for some reason. As the sun rose, the extent of the spread of the blight through their potato crop was now visible. Most of his crop had leaves curling, and dark patches were now visible. The leaves of the plants showed the telltale dark blotches and curled edges of the devastating blight. Kieran had tried to get Anthony O'Day to dig and destroy the infected part of his crop, but they were so poor that it was just not feasible. Kieran knew it would spread, but he had no idea how to stop it. He fell to his knees and wept. "What more, God? Our two boys are gone, and now this?" He was not sure if he was angry or gutted, probably both. He had ploughed all his money into expanding the farm yield, and if the blight destroyed the praties, his family would have nothing. He had to return and tell Gráinne they needed to harvest what they could and sell any good praties. Hopefully, they could get some money to see them through the winter. Kieran's return home was met with joyous squeals from his girls. Clare and Kerry were a little less enthusiastic, but Mary and Kathleen mobbed him.

Gráinne noticed his face and waited until the four girls had headed down to the foreshore to see if they could find something to eat.

Gráinne watched them leave before turning to Kieran. "It's here, isn't it? I can tell by your face."

Kieran couldn't answer. He just nodded and drew her into his arms. His sobs made her cling to him. "I was so sure that it would not make it this far. Gráinne, I have put everything we own into that crop, and if it fails, we will have nothing left. Not one thing! I can't stop time, and I can't stop tomorrow. We have nothing to fall back on, not a penny."

Gráinne could feel his nails digging into her back. He was the strong one, the one everyone looked to when things went wrong. But to her, he was her childhood sweetheart and also the forbidden fruit. Kieran was Catholic, and she was Protestant; to them, it didn't matter as they both loved God. They had run away to London and married. Clare and Kerry had both been born there. Liam had been born only weeks after arriving on the Tarbert farm. Kieran's cousins, the Moores, had been good enough to supply shelter for months until Kieran found a farm. Now Liam was gone, and little Paddy was gone, and now their crop would be gone too. It could, and should, have been life-changing. It was undoubtedly going to be that, only for the worse. Kieran was shattered; it was just too much to deal with.

The following weeks saw the family digging every potato they could; their cart and horse carried load after load to market, but the blight had coloured many, and they needed to be eaten immediately. Kieran was exhausted. Usually, they would leave their crop and harvest it as required. This year, they needed to rescue everything possible.

~

Summer faded into winter; the huge crop had brought in a fraction of the cost. Even the horse now cost too much to keep. Kieran took it to Limerick and sold it. Father Pat gave him a lift home, but the journey back had been almost silent. Winter that year was particularly cold. Storms blew in from the sea, lifting the shingles from above, so now their roof leaked.

As fast as Kieran could do the repairs, more things needed fixing. First, Mary and then Kathleen died of winter chills. Mary was eight and so skinny that Kerry had easily carried her around. Then she was gone. Kathleen lasted until after Christmas. She had become chilled and coughed until she, too, was gone. She had just faded away. The cottage was now eerily silent. The joyous laughter was absent, and the four remaining occupants spent their days hunting for food. Their lines and fishing nets had been stolen. They had no way of catching fish. Hand-made twine didn't last. The nearby rocks had already been scoured for shells, and kelp soup became a staple meal. It tasted revolting and had little in it to sustain anyone, but it was better than nothing.

Both girls' healthy curves vanished. Their developing breasts had flattened, and their bones were easily visible. Hunger was a way of life, and survival was a day-to-day chore.

Gráinne was once again expecting a child, this time due in the

Summer. Surely, by then, things should be better.

Easter came and went unnoticed.

They walked to the small church each Sunday and visited the graves of their four children. Father Patrick Murphy did what he could, but the needs of the many stretched his finances to the point that he could no longer hand out money for food. One Englishman and one only was sending food, but it was nowhere near enough to stretch, yet he praised God anyway.

It wasn't enough. Soon after Easter, Anthony O'Day walked into the water and swam out to sea. All knew he was not a good swimmer. It had become too much for him to cope. His wife, Maeve, was left with Sean and Ciara in a cottage with no roof. Kieran sat on the beach in shock. How could his friend take his own life, leaving his wife and children to starve? How? On return home, Kieran realised that he needed to sell their remaining gardening tool. The wet summer brought more mould and more blight.

Mid-summer, Father Patrick had spoken to Kieran about them moving to Australia and that he knew of an English duke who was helping some families escape the famine. "Kieran, my half-brother, Hugh, is the Duke of Gracemere's minister. Hugh told me the duke has some Irish family connections and has just returned from the Antipodes himself; he's determined to assist where he can. His cousin is married to Sarah McCarthy as she was, but she is now known as Sarah or Sal Lockley. They have been looking for you." He noticed Kieran's interest, but it was more than that.

Kieran's rare smile was visible. "I knew my cousin Sal McCarthy while living in London before I married. I presume it was the same lady. You know Gráinne and I are cousins? We share great grandparents, Pat, as does Sal Lockley."

The young priest nodded. "It's why the duke wrote to me. He asked me to find you. He heard you had settled in Avoca in county Wicklow with the Moores, but they forwarded his letter to me as they were not quite sure where you had settled." He was not going to judge true love. The Roman Catholic Church had much stricter rules about cousins marrying. He knew that in England, even first cousins could marry. He was more upset about the bigotry of a Catholic marrying a Protestant. His own father was a protestant, so he had his own views about that. He had violated his mother, who was a maid in his house. To Pat, God was for all.

Kieran said, "Yes, we stayed in Avoca for a while, but when they discovered that Gráinne was not Catholic, we moved here. Sal's papa was Gráinne's uncle, and her mama was my aunt. Like us, they had to leave as her papa was a Protestant and her mama was a Catholic. We visited her mama a few times, but Sal was working somewhere. I met her only once, but I liked her immensely. If she's living in Australia, could you arrange transport for the four of us? There's nothing for us even in London."

Patrick was almost relieved. He was right in thinking that there was nothing left here. Kieran's friend Anthony's death had been the last straw. "I will do that for you, Kieran. I had already arranged for O'Day's to leave for Canada, but Anthony went and did what he did. Now Maeve won't go alone."

Kieran brushed away the tears and then nodded. "We'll go when this child is born. I'll go to Limerick and sell the pick, and we shall use that money for the journey. Maeve can have our house then, Pat. Can you see to that, too?"

Patrick nodded. He arranged to collect his friend for the trip. While in Limerick, he would confirm their passage to Australia. He had the letter ready to post. The Duke of Gracemere had written asking for a date. Finally, Kieran had given his okay.

Kieran woke at dawn the following week, kissed Gráinne and the girls, and walked into Tarbert. He had his nearly new pick slung over his shoulder and walked to Father Patrick's house. The trip from Tarbert to Limerick was spent in deep and meaningful conversations, from the meaning of life to their final destiny.

Their discussion about heaven left Patrick with his jaw-dropping open. "You have visions? Dreams of heaven?"

Kieran nodded. "Yes, Pat, I have done so since I was young. I knew something was wrong the morning Liam died. I woke and started running to the water's edge. There was no reason for it, but I knew that's where I had to be." The look on Father Patrick's face made Kieran continue. Kieran's conversation was depressing. They had lost so much, and grief nearly overwhelmed him. Kieran told Pat a lot about his ideas of bigotry, about religion, and how he felt it was confused with Jesus's true teaching of the faith. "I miss little Paddy and Liam, but then our little girls died. Unlike Job in the Bible, I felt God was closer to me than He ever had been. Having you close by was wonderful, too, Pat. You are non-judgemental." He glanced at the priest next to him. "Gráinne and I had wondered how you felt about us as what my father called a mixed marriage. My bigoted father died while we were in London, so we moved back to Ireland and finally settled here. This farm was as isolated as we could find. Mama knew where we were, and as you know, she regularly wrote until she died. Gráinne's family won't talk to her at all, so that's why I want to leave Ireland. Over there, in Australia, we should be able to start again. I have a cousin, John, out there somewhere, and of course, there is Sal. John is my closest male relative. Considering Gráinne and I are cousins, you would wonder about the antagonism over religion."

Their conversation continued until they reached the outskirts of Limerick. The thirty-five-mile trip had taken most of the morning. The market was still in full swing, but the early August market was half the size as usual. Kieran said his farewells and went off to sell his pick, and Pat to post his letter.

An hour later, Patrick was summonsed by a young lad. The boy had blood on his hands and could hardly speak. "Father Pat, they hit him and took his money, an' he's callin' for you. You gotta come quick 'cos he's bleeding real bad." The two hurried to the marketplace, and Patrick found his friend surrounded by an angry mob. A woman, who turned out to be the boy's mother, was attempting to stem the bleeding from a knife wound to the stomach. Patrick threw himself to the ground beside his friend. "Oh, Kieran, what happened?"

Kieran grabbed Patrick's shirt with both hands. "Mugged Pat; they took my money. It's all I had left for Gráinne and the girls. Make sure they get to Australia for me, won't you? Please send them to Sal. I won't make it, Pat; promise me you'll send them!" His breathing was getting shallower.

"I promise, Kieran; I'll ensure they get to your cousin." Pat drew his friend into his arms. "I'll tell my half-brother, Hugh."

Kieran squeezed his friend's hand, "Thanks, Pat!" His last breath rasped before he exhaled with a burble of blood.

Patrick let out a howl of grief. Kieran's death was pointless. The crowd that had circled around him slowly moved away. Four men were left. Two were the town's burliest men and held two well-known ruffians. One still held the bloody knife and had the three shillings in his pocket. Patrick waved them away, "Let the magistrates deal with them. Just get that money back for Kieran's wife." Some other unknown person had placed some coins next to his body.

While this occurred, Father Bartholomew had arrived from the presbytery in his cart. He had heard the scuffle and the boy's message. Realising something was wrong, he followed as soon as he could.

The two priests loaded Kieran's body onto the wagon. Patrick knew that he had to take him home and tell Gráinne.

The following morning, Kieran was laid to rest in the small cemetery. Gráinne and the girls were almost prostrated in grief. Maeve and the children stood at the cemetery's edge but refused to come closer. As Anthony had taken his own life, he had not been permitted to be buried on the church grounds. Father Patrick had a grave dug right on the boundary line for him but said all the same prayers. Maeve was often seen sitting next to it. It was where she was today. Patrick wondered if Gráinne would have the child early. She had refused a lift to the church, and as soon as the first handful of dirt was thrown in the grave, she turned on her heel with the girls following. Patrick let them go.

A week after the funeral, Patrick visited Gráinne. As he gave her the money with a few more coins that he had added, he told her of Kieran's last wishes. He told her the passage was already booked to Australia.

Gráinne's eyes held his as he spoke, and then she nodded with resignation that no matter where she went, Kieran would not be part of it anymore, but she knew they could no longer stay. They would leave as soon as the child was born.

Chapter 2   *Diggin' Praties*

Kerry's pointed stick dug into the earth. There was little hope of finding edible potatoes as the three children had searched the field numerous times. Kerry was about to give up when she felt the firm, rounded mound under her fingers. Carefully looking around to ensure they had not seen her, she eased the huge perfect pratie out from its hiding place and tucked it under her apron. Her two friends were having no luck finding anything. But secreting this meant that her mother and sister might live. Kerry feigned injury. "Ouch, I got a big splinter. I gonna go home and get Clare to fix it up."

Her friends waved a mournful farewell and kept digging. The enormous potato bounced against her knee as she walked. She dared not pull it out in case anyone saw her carrying her bountiful meal. She had no idea why she had decided to dig off to the side, but her hunch had paid off. Today, the three of them would eat. The thought of only Clare and her mama at home brought tears to her eyes.

Earlier that month, their father had died in a fight over a few shillings from the sale of the last item they owned. It was no use owning a pick to dig praties if there were no praties to dig. Kerry missed him so much. His joyous laugh had always made the tiny cottage a warm and loving home, even when they had nothing to eat. He had learnt to catch fish and source things to eat along the foreshore. He had always filled the house with laughter. Papa had made her a digging stick from a long, fat branch. He had smoothed the outsides and sharpened the tip. Kerry found that she could poke into the soil and feel if there was resistance. It was how she had found this juicy pratie.

Her joyous mood saddened when she thought of their four little brothers and sisters who had all succumbed to illness or hunger, and now only Mama and Clare awaited her at home. Mama was big with child, and Clare had stayed home as Mama was having back pains. Kerry wondered if the new baby would be a boy or a girl. Happy at that thought, she skipped, knowing a new baby could be awaiting her at home. She mustered the strength to pick up her speed and headed home. The small stone cottage was falling down around them, but it was a roof over their heads, albeit an earthen roof, and it kept off the worst of the winter winds.

Kerry rounded the last corner, and her heart sank. Clare was sitting outside on the log weeping. Something was wrong, seriously wrong.

Clare heard the footfalls of her younger sister as she crunched along the gravel pathway to home. Trying hard to put on a cheery face, she brushed away her tears and rose to meet her. How could life be so absolutely horrible? Clare took a few paces, then stopped; her shoulders dropped.

Kerry came running. She flew into Clare's arms, weeping. No words were needed as she gathered her sister into her arms. Kerry had not yet heard that they had both died, but she realised that Clare would not be outside unless this had happened.

They were now alone in the world with no food and little shelter. Clare would keep the promise she had just made to her mother. She would pack up what they could and leave. Five children and their parents were all gone in a year. It was more than Clare could cope with. As her mother had tried to push the child into the world, she cried out for her father. Clare knew he was not there to give them the strength her mother so desperately needed.

As her mother writhed in agony, travailing with the birth pains, she told Clare they had to find a way to get on a ship leaving Ireland. "See Father Patrick, Clare; he has made the arrangements. There's nothing here for you two. Go to Sal. John is there too somewhere." It didn't matter where they went, but they must go.

Clare remembered that her mother often laughed about the irony of her name. She knew that one meaning of the name was *grain of corn*. They didn't even have anything to eat. Kerry knew that it also meant love, as *Grá* means love in Gaelic. '*Grá mo chroí*' means '*love of my heart*' in English and was the meaning of *Grace*.

Clare quietly said to Kerry, "Mama died when the baby girl was born. She never breathed, Kerry, and it was as though Mama just gave up 'cos Papa wasn't there. Mama wanted her named Tara, but she never took a breath."

Kerry pulled back from her sister's arms. "What are we going to do, Clare? We have nothing."

Clare wiped away the tears from her cheeks and said bravely, "We're going to do what Mama wanted. We're going to pack what we can carry and leave here. I promised Mama we would walk off the farm and go where there's food. We will have each other, but as that's all we have here, we can't do much worse. Kerry, Mama made me promise we'd go see Father Patrick, and he has sorted our passage to a cousin in Australia." Clare's filthy face showed the channels where the tears had washed the dirt away. There was a smear of blood on what remained of her gown and more on her apron.

Kerry knew the day had come to leave, but she never expected that their mother would not be with them. When their papa had first suggested they go, Gráinne hesitated. Then Kieran was killed, and Gráinne cursed herself for not listening to him. Now, it was too late. Both parents were now dead, and the girls were alone.

Clare once again drew Kerry into her arms. As Kerry wept on Clare's shoulder, a lump bumped against her knees. "Kerry, what's that?" Clare could feel something pressing into her thigh.

Kerry pulled away and dug out her precious cargo. "I found one, Clare. A good one, with no blight. I told Sean and Ciara that I got a splinter and snuck off to bring it back home to you and Mama." Her voice broke as she mentioned her mother.

Their minute cottage was on the farthest outskirts of the small Irish village. No one was likely to come, but they carefully carried the precious bounty inside. Neither had eaten since the morning before, and seaweed soup was not filling. Clare's kelp and cockle soup contained a few tiny fish she had found in the rock pools. It tasted revolting, but it was something hot in their tummies. Now, even that was gone. Their clay cooking pot had broken in the fire, and the last of the kelp soup had spilled and extinguished the flame. There were enough dry peat blocks for one last fire.

The girls went indoors to cook their one colossal potato. With no pots or pans remaining, they encased the potato in clay and pushed it into the coals of the smouldering peat fire. They had long since learned that to put it in the fire uncovered meant they had less to eat as the outsides burnt. This way, the entire potato would remain perfect. While they waited for the scant meal to cook, Clare spread their last blanket on the floor and carefully placed anything usable into the parcel.

As Clare worked, Kerry stood looking at the still figure on the bed. Their mother lay on the small mattress off to the side, and Kerry pulled back the rag Clare had covered her face with and kissed her farewell. Gone was the well-rounded smiling face she knew and loved. Gone was the joyous laughter and big comforting hugs. The skeletal face that lay so still now had unseeing eyes and still arms that would hug no more.

As Kerry gazed at her mother's face, Clare's arm slid around her waist. "She isn't hurting anymore, Kerry." Clare leaned forward and pulled back her mother's skirt. It had been covering the almost skeletal body of the stillborn baby girl. "If Tara had breathed, she would not have lived long. Mama had no milk for her, and with no food, she would have died anyway. Kerry, we must follow Mama's last wish to leave here. We'll tell Father Patrick on the way out, but it will only be a pauper's grave with Anthony outside the cemetery."

Kerry nodded, sniffed, and then they recovered the two permanently sleeping figures. There would be no funerals. They cost money. The pair returned to scavenging what they could from the almost empty hovel. Pots, pans, blankets, and saleable clothing had all been sold long ago. The apparel they wore now was almost in tatters; there was one garment that they needed to take to make both girls decent. Their mother needed to be stripped. The piteously small bundle on the floor held little more than their shared hairbrush, a comb, and a few household trinkets their father had made for them to play with. A limpet shell on a handmade twine loop was the only toy they had. There had never been dolls or money for frivolous things. A small Bible with no cover was also included in the pile. With the cabin scoured, the girls knew what they needed to do. Soon, their mother lay in her calico undergarment. Both had refused to leave her there naked. Her chemise at least meant that she was covered; the dead baby was placed in her arms, and again, Clare covered her face with the rag.

Aware that time to leave drew near, they rescued their last meal from the coals and enjoyed their sumptuous repast. Knowing that eating something on an empty stomach was not too clever and not knowing how long it would be until they had access to more food, they kept half of the potato for later and nibbled carefully at their share of the delicious meal. It was the first solid food either girl had enjoyed for over a week.

As their infant sister would not need the small baby shawl Gráinne had kept for its use, Kerry wrapped that around the remnants of her badly torn blouse. She had no undergarments, and the torn fabric barely covered her developing breasts. To see the priest, they both needed to be at least covered. He would see to the burials.

Gráinne had told Clare to make sure she had to hand him the letter she had written. It also included the title of the land. As they would no longer need it, at least the English couldn't take it from the church.

The twelve and fourteen-year-old girls took their last look around their home. Clare had almost forgotten the letter for the priest and ran back to grab it before pulling the door closed behind them.

Now, their new lives were ahead of them. First, they needed to see Father Patrick, and then they would make for the harbour and see if they could find out where a ship was leaving for the new world. It didn't matter where they went as long as they could leave.

Kerry refused to cry; she had to make Clare proud of her. She carried their small bundle and traipsed along the dusty trackway towards the town.

Clare angrily brushed away her tears. She was glad that she had insisted that Kerry go and hunt for praties as it meant that she didn't have to witness the agony of their mother's passing. She had actually died before the child was born. It had its head out when her mother breathed her last. Clare tugged at the baby, hoping that it was living. It wasn't. The birth had taken too much of a toll on both mother and child. The day's occurrences haunted her, and she didn't want to tell Kerry about it. At fourteen, these were not the memories one wished to have about their home.

Kerry saw Clare's upset and silently slipped her hand into her sister's damp hand. "Sorry I wasn't there to help, Clare." She asked again, "Was it bad?"

Clare couldn't answer, so she just nodded.

Kerry gave her hand a gentle squeeze. Words were unnecessary.

Both girls had heavy hearts. Their walk into Tarbert would take half an hour. Father Patrick would hopefully let them stay on the church grounds for the night; then, they would have to walk to wherever the boat left from.

The road from their farm was just two-wheel tracks through the coastal foreshore. It was overgrown as Papa had sold their horse and cart last year. No one else had been to visit except the priest. He came on a horse, so it didn't flatten the bushes. The two girls had tried to avoid brushing against the prickly plants as they walked, as they knew the ticks that lived on them could make them sick. That was the last thing they needed.

Trying to keep their minds from what they had left and what was before them, they chatted about where they thought they would end up. They had heard their parents talking about two places where ships took emigrants, Canada or Australia. The girls knew that earlier that year, many had gone to Glasgow in Scotland to try to find work. Father Patrick had heard of the extreme overcrowding of that city and that there was no work, no money, and no food. Kieran and Gráinne had decided that they would head to Australia as they had family there. Both were foreign places, and they didn't really care where they went as long as they could stay together. Father Patrick knew they both spoke English, as well as Gaelic, so they figured either country would do. As the girls had been born in London, they learned English. Gráinne had also taught them to read and write in both languages.

By noon, the girls had reached the outskirts of the tiny hamlet. The houses in this area were scattered, and the church was tiny.

Father Patrick had charge of the Catholics in the area, and as many as possible would attend Mass and take communion as often as possible. He had minimal funds, as everyone in the parish was similarly desperate. He could point the girls in the right direction. But a roof over their heads would be good for tonight.

Tarbert was quiet as the girls entered the churchyard. Before seeing their priest, they visited the grave where their father lay. A small white cross marked his final resting place. Hopefully, their mother could join him forever, but they would leave that to Father Patrick. They paid their respects to their papa before heading to the residence.

The heavy wooden door was slowly pulled open. The young man saw the two girls standing there and realised precisely what had occurred. "Gráinne has died, hasn't she?"

Clare and Kerry nodded in unison.

"The child too?"

Clare confirmed that, too. "Father, we were wondering if you could

11

tell us how to catch a ship to leave Ireland. Mama made me promise that I would take Kerry and get out of here." As she said these words, she handed him the letter her mother had written. "Father Pat, Mama said you are to have the farm. It won't do you much good as the soil is bad."

The soil was bad throughout Ireland, as this was the second year the potato crop had failed.

Father Patrick took the letter and tucked it in his pocket. "Thank you, Clare; I shall put this with the others." He patted his pocket. "Now, girls, come inside." He led the way into his office and sat the girls down. "Your mama was correct about getting out of here. However, I have some good news. I have received a letter from my half-brother. He is a Church of England minister in Maidstone, and the Duke of Gracemere recently returned from Parramatta and knows the colony well. To cut a very long story short, one of the people he knew out in Australia has family in Ireland. It turns out his cousin is married to your cousin Sal. Therefore, I discovered that your parents are part of this family. Because of them, the duke decided to sponsor some needy families to go to Australia to live. In your case, your papa had arranged for the four of you to travel together. Your passage is booked already. Even though there are now only the pair of you, I must get you to Limerick to start the journey."

He waited to see if they would accept his offer. With their father dead, he was going to suggest that they travel with their mother. However, with Gráinne now gone, they had no choice but to leave. Death was all that would happen if they stayed.

The girls consulted each other. A raised eyebrow and a nod were all it entailed. They would leave. Both knew it was what their parents had planned to do.

Father Patrick nodded. "Stay here for a day or two; we'll bury your mama and the babe, and then I will take you myself on the first leg. Your father also has another cousin out there. I only know his name is John. He is your closest male relative, but I know nothing more about him."

The following day, they saw their mother and baby sister buried in the same grave as their father. It was more than they had hoped. There was no coffin for either of them and no shroud, but their parents would be together for eternity.

Both girls stayed and helped Father Patrick until the grave was filled.

The deed done, they were now ready to leave Ireland forever.

Chapter 3   In Transit

*T*he girls were soon *en route* to England; at least, they had done the first miles of the journey. As they passed through the countryside on the back of the priest's small cart, they saw the signs of famine everywhere. Their family at least had the foreshore to find food. They had occasional fish, kelp, and some shells, so they had not been as impoverished as many others. The walking skeletons they passed by only had shreds of clothing covering their nakedness but little else. Both girls gasped. They thought they were hungry, but these poor people were barely alive. "Father Patrick, where are all these people going?"

The priest passed by them without acknowledging their desperation. The cleric was not immune to the poverty, but he realised that to pick up one would start a crush for as many as possible to climb on board his already rickety cart. He had carried many of his own parishioners to their destination, and there would be more that would follow. These two girls were two of his flock and were getting his full attention today. He had to take them to Limerick. From there, the Duke of Gracemere would have his team take over care of the passengers.

Once the bedraggled group were out of earshot, he said, "Girls, they are heading to the workhouse. There, they will get two meals a day and, if capable, they will be asked to work to keep them occupied. Many will still die, but they will be under cover, fed, and buried with a modicum of dignity. It's more than what they have now." He fell silent as they were about to pass another group of walking skeletons. Once they passed them, he continued, "Earlier this year, a boatload made it to Liverpool. Because of England's poor laws, they were sent back as they did not have enough money to make it to America. I think some of them are in that workhouse."

The girls gasped. "Will that happen to us, Father?"

Father Patrick shook his head. "No, girls, you have the duke sponsoring you, and your passage is confirmed. You are being met in Sydney by your cousin. Your papa wrote to her." He knew that from Limerick, the girls would be put on a boat for Plymouth. In a way, the timing was good as the boat was leaving soon. The next one would not be leaving Ireland for some months, and by then, there would be no food at all, even in the workhouses. Patrick shot up a prayer of thanks for the duke's food donations. He knew that in Plymouth, they would join others heading to Australia. In the two days since they arrived on his doorstep, Father Patrick had taken time to write them a couple of letters, which Clare now had wrapped with her meagre possessions. One was a reply to the Duke of Gracemere, who would meet their ship in Plymouth; another was a character reference for both girls once they reached their destination in Australia. The way things were going, few parishioners would be left in his parish. He would stay until the last person had left or died, then move to Limerick with Father Bartholomew to help with his flock.

Once past the next dishevelled group, he continued telling the girls about what he had planned for them. "I knew that you would not be able to last long on your farm once your papa died, so I made plans with your mama that you were to leave. Unfortunately, you will need to travel alone with her now gone too. However, all the arrangements have been made. You will stay with Father Bart at the presbytery in Limerick as the workhouse is already overfilled. He and the sisters there have filled the presbytery with single girls. You won't have much room, but it will be safer than jammed in with the others at the workhouse. Father Bart here will ensure you get on the Plymouth-bound vessel when the ship comes into port. Once there, you must disembark and wait for the next ship to take you to Australia. The Duke of Gracemere said he would be meeting this ship in Plymouth, and you must give him that letter I have written, Clare."

Clare nodded. The girls were absorbing his words as he unfolded their future. She said, "Mama made me promise we would come to you, but I didn't know she had it all planned." It was too much for Clare, who looked away quickly. Tears slid down her cheeks as she thought of the last words her mother had said. Her entire life had been spent caring for her family, and her final thoughts were again to keep the girls safe. She had even made plans for their future. Clare was determined not to let her mother's memory down. She sniffed as quietly as she could.

Kerry had seen the action of her wiping away more tears. Without a word, she reached for her sister's hand and held it tight.

Limerick's presbytery was a small building surrounded by shanty hovels. It looked like many others had come for refuge. Father Patrick drove the small cart to the front of the building, and Clare hopped out and tied the reins to the hitching rail. The front door opened, and an old priest waited to welcome his guests. The jovial man said, "Father Patrick, welcome, welcome!

Come in and put your feet up. And, may I ask, who are these two lovely lassies you have brought me today?"

The three new arrivals were ushered inside before Father Patrick answered. "Father Bartholomew, these are the last of the O'Shane family. You know about Kieran O'Shane's death here last month. Unfortunately, their mother died in childbirth along with her child. Clare and Kerry will now travel under the protection of the Duke of Gracemere to Australia. Goodness knows what we would have done if it were not for his food shipments. Few Englishmen would stand against the authorities to break the embargo and send food."

Father Bart turned to his friend and nodded. "Father Patrick, things are so bad here now that the walking skeletons are digging their own graves and sleeping in them in the cemetery. They wish to be buried in hallowed ground and have no money to do so. The sisters and I check each morning how many have succumbed to the famine and bury them accordingly."

Patrick acknowledged the older cleric's plight and replied so the girls could hear. "Father Bartholomew, admittedly, I have done much the same. God loves them all. I don't ask questions. I, too, have had a few do something similar." Pat frowned at the memory of how skinny some of the dead were. They had perished in pain and anguish. He dropped his voice and said, "Bart, Shannon McCarthy's cousins are currently with the Duke in Kent; otherwise, I would have sent the girls to them. But they are better off going to Australia to make a new life. They have no one here now but us."

Father Bart nodded. Pat had already filled him in after Kieran had died, but it was good for the girls to hear the arrangements confirmed. As they were all still standing in the hallway, the older cleric merely nodded before saying, "Oh dear, that is very unfortunate for you both, dear ones." He scratched his head, then said, "Now, where will I put you two? I think in the dining room. There is a small area under the table where you can sleep. I only allow the younger girls in there so you can sleep unmolested, too." He shuffled a little further down the hall. He stopped and knocked on a closed door.

A girl opened it to his knock, and the first thing they all noticed was the smell. It nearly knocked them over. The stench of body odour and filth in the closed room was overpowering.

Kerry moved closer to Clare and took her arm with both hands, fear etched on her young face. Clare felt like turning around and running. They may have had no food, but their mother had made them bathe in the sea every day that they could. Even their clothing was as clean as they could possibly make them.

Father Bartholomew hobbled in and crossed the room. "Sorry, ladies, but we have two more to add to this group. I know it's cold outside, but this room could really do with some airing. Close the window before night, but you need fresh air." He threw open the window and drew a deep breath of fresh air. "Ahh, that's better! We may need to arrange a bath for these dear folk, Father Patrick. I know the ships will be in close quarters, but if they can arrive clean, that will be half the battle. Most of these folk only arrived this morning. I shall get the sisters from next door to arrange hot water for them. I'm sure Sister Mary and Sister Johanna will make a private area available for bathing and washing."

Father Patrick had not entered the room but saw that the only space left was quite literally under the large table. At least the girls would be safe from abuse, as Father Bart said. He had done the best he could for them as he had promised their parents he would. He was sad that they would need to make the journey all by themselves. Life was sometimes unfair, and he considered the deaths of their parents to be more than unfortunate. The sights he had seen over the past months had hardened him a little to the privations of his flock. It still hurt, but he and Father Bartholomew had met as often as possible to pray for the strength to cope with the months and years yet ahead of them. Tiredness overwhelmed him.

Occasionally, the three nuns from the next-door cottage joined them. Only by working together could they endure the gruelling conditions they were all now facing. Even with the funds from Rome, conditions were dire. Money could not buy what was not for sale. Shipments of food would have been more beneficial.

Patrick knew all this. Death came knocking daily, and with each one, Pat felt a part of him die. Kieran's death had hurt as he had been a good friend. He had passed away in his arms, and Pat had promised Kieran that he would care for Gráinne and the children. Now, she, too, was dead. He thought back to the cemetery; no sooner had the gravediggers dug one hole than multiple bodies filled it. Gráinne O'Shane had been lucky as Kieran's grave was still fresh enough for her to be placed with him. Many others who had arrived in Limerick from other areas were sadly only thrown into paupers' graves. He and Father Bartholomew had performed more than one mass burial. He hated doing this, but they had little choice; the bodies needed a covering. Neither priest asked questions about religion. Pat took a deep breath and moved down the corridor towards the kitchen. Even a cup of hot water would be welcome to his grumbling stomach. The door to the back cookhouse at the rear of the presbytery was closed, and he knocked before entering.

Sister Judith was stirring a cauldron over an open fire. The delicious smell of cooking stew met his nose. His mouth began salivating at the aroma. She called a greeting as he entered. "Afternoon, Father Patrick! Would you mind tasting this for me? The duke sent a barrel of salt beef, and I thought I'd make a good thick stew for everyone. I'll thin it down before serving to make it stretch, but the poor darlings are so hungry that they would bring it up again if they ate a full meal. A thin gruel is more than they will be able to cope with, but it will be nourishing."

Father Patrick willingly obliged. He hadn't eaten since yesterday, so he almost greedily took a bowlful of the stew she handed him. He almost felt guilty, but he realised the pot was so large that there would be enough for everyone. He knew he needed to eat to continue aiding his flock. Aware of eating too quickly on an empty stomach, he savoured each mouthful. It was plenty salty enough, and he said as much to the nun. "The split peas and lentils could do with a bit more cooking though, sister, but this is delicious; no more salt needed."

The elderly nun merely nodded. "That English duke friend of your brother's also sent onions, garlic, turnips, swedes and all sorts of other goodies. I have used all the wilted vegetables for the stew and put the rest in the underground larder for later use. I've also added some grain to thicken it. The rest of the delivery is in storage for the future. That duke may not be of the true church, but his heart is in the right place." She fell silent and kept stirring.

The quietness of the kitchen was a relief to the myriad of voices from the various rooms in the parsonage. He decided to stay to assist with serving the meal, and then he would wend his way back home at leisure. More death would await him there, and he was not keen to discover who would be buried next, possibly the O'Day's. Last night, while the girls slept on his kitchen floor, he had attended to another family and given last rights to the dying youngest child. He was, therefore, tired and thought he would catch forty winks while he awaited Farther Bart. He pushed his empty plate away and rested his head on the table, leaning on his folded arms. Within moments, he was deeply asleep. For once, others could deal with the world's problems.

Father Bartholomew entered and saw his young friend asleep on the table. Sister Judith had shushed him as he entered. She passed Bart a bowl full of her stew and whispered, "Happy birthday." Rather than drag out a chair to sit, he ate it while standing. Sister Judith knew that today he turned sixty. He felt old, really old, but the famine was the cause of most of his stress. He and Pat had commiserated with each other often.

When Bart heard of a fresh young priest moving into the area a few years ago, he had been worried that he would be one of the new breeds of radical thinkers. Thankfully, this young man's heart was faithful to the good Lord's teachings. He knew of some who abused their positions and the trust the families placed in them. He had even heard of rumours of inappropriate abuse inflicted on some of the children. When this horrific situation was first reported to him, he admittedly denied that that could possibly be true. However, more and more reports filtered through to him from the same area, and Bart realised that he must report the priest to Rome. He did, and the priest in question was just moved to another closer parish. Bart had revealed his dilemma to Pat, and they prayed about what to do. Both realised that they could only protect those that they could. Bart spoke to the priest and challenged him about his actions. The man had laughed at him and walked away. As Bart scooped the last few mouthfuls of stew into his mouth, he smiled at the memory of the said priest's demise. The cottage he slept in had been struck by lightning during a fierce storm, and the man had no hope of survival. Bart dared not call it divine intervention, but he was thankful it was one less problem the two faithful priests needed to deal with.

Patrick slept for over an hour. He had not heard his friends coming or going or the arrival of more hungry humans temporarily to the house. He had slept the deep, healing sleep he needed. He awoke refreshed, if somewhat groggy. Even in his tiny cottage, he had to sleep, aware that he was always on call. He rarely was able to have an unbroken night.

Father Bart had placed the new arrivals outside as they had males in their group. Indoors was exclusively for young female occupation. An elderly woman occupied his own bed. He had been sleeping on the floor of the food storeroom, off to the side of the kitchen. All of the visitors were kept from this section of the building as their food supplies from the duke were housed there. This food was more precious than gold, so he had moved a small mattress into the storeroom and placed it on the hatch of the underground cellar and larder, and he could rest whilst on guard.

Now refreshed, Pat had made his farewells to the girls before returning home to face whatever ordeals were before him. When he was ordained, he had no idea that his ministry would require burying so many of his parishioners in such a short time. He had hoped for a parish where he could sew the seeds of faith in the needy. Kieran had been a breath of fresh air for him. The family already had a strong faith, and they were even literate. He relished the visits he had to this impoverished family.

When Kieran was killed last month, Pat nearly resigned. It had been Kieran's prayerful support that had kept him strong. If Father Bart had not come across him soon after his friend's death, he probably would have just walked away from it all. Telling Gráinne of her husband's death had been horrible. He teared up at the memory of that. For her, Kieran's death was like the light had gone out in her life. If it had not been for the two older girls, he was sure Gráinne would have given up then and there. They had already lost four small children in a few months; he was not surprised when Clare said her mother had died in childbirth. Gráinne had mentioned to him when he had visited the week before that she had not felt the child move for some time. Her losses were just too much for her to bear. He had promised to care for the girls and get them to her family in Parramatta. It was all he could do for them now. For the girls to lose both parents in the space of a month, just hurt.

Chapter 4   Leaving Ireland

*T*he ship arrived in Limerick three days after the girls were incarcerated in the dining room. The vessel that docked in Limerick was soon overloaded with emigrants leaving Ireland forever. It was moored next to where the new floating dock was planned to be built. Clare remembered her father taking an interest in the project, and she had asked about it while walking around town.

The nuns had found the girls some decent clothing and even a blanket each. All the girls in their room had bathed before sleeping that first night. On this short voyage, everyone was crowded into one deck. Clare and Kerry had been allocated two hammocks side by side. They were thankful for small mercies but were frightened to leave their valuable possessions for even a minute, so they dressed in layers with the blankets around them as shawls. The tattered bible and precious letters were down Clare's bodice.

Father Bart came on board with the group that had been staying at his house to make sure they were settled. Beckoning the two girls, he introduced them to the captain. He knew the captain had a strongbox in his cabin and asked if they could store their valuable letters in it while on board. The safety of these documents was paramount, and the girls willingly accepted the captain's offer.

With the Bible and letters now secure, the girls only had their hairbrush and toys, which their father had made for them. Again, they were carried at all times. Sister Joanne had found them four new dresses from a charity box, and for the first time in a long time, both girls were decently clad.

Kerry had kept her shawl as it was the last thing that their mother had made.

Clare kept their hairbrush in her pocket as even such a thing was worth stealing. All they had of their home were now memories.

The ship weighed anchor at high tide and sailed westward down the long bay. The girls stood at the gunnels on the aft deck and watched the shore pass by.

After an hour, they neared the bend in the bay, and a familiar figure stood on the shore waving. Father Patrick had come to say his farewells. He stood waving both arms above his head, and they could hear his shouts of farewell as the ship sailed on.

The girls shouted "Thank you" back to him. They returned his waves and shouted until he was out of sight around the headland. They clung together as soon as their homeland faded from view. However, they had one particular place to see for the final time. Their farm west of Tarbert came into view. The two girls stood with an arm around each other's waist. They did not need to voice their feelings of fear, despair, and anxiety to each other as each knew them well. Both wiped tears from their faces.

The ship sailed on.

Their tiny home came into view, and both girls gasped at once. Their three friends stood on the foreshore waving.

Kerry still felt guilty about not telling her best friend about her potato find. Father Pat said he was taking some food and clothing back for them.

As Kieran and Gráinne suggested, Father Pat let the O'Day family move into their cottage. Kerry knew that their sod roof had fallen in on their friend's house. With no money to fix it, they moved homes. So their home had new caretakers. Sean and Ciara were jumping on the spot and shouting their farewells.

Their small cottage had been further along the foreshore, and the O'Days had also lived a little better than those who survived on potatoes alone. Hopefully, they could still eke out a subsistence from the sea. They were still hungry, but they had lost the youngest of their siblings and their father, Anthony. Maeve and the children would not leave.

Kerry spoke softly, "I'm glad they are using our house, Clare. They had so little; we at least had a roof over our heads. They didn't even have that. Ciara said that one wall was also in danger of falling in."

Clare nodded. She didn't trust her voice. Memories flooded over her, and she wanted to curl up and die, but she needed to look after Kerry. She had promised her mother that she would. She would get to this lady, Aunt Sal, and only then would she weep.

They waved until their house had faded from view. They walked to the stern to keep waving.

Then, as the ship rounded the bend in the estuary, the house and their friends faded from view. Both girls fell silent before returning to the bow to watch the familiar sights for as long as possible.

The next landmark they knew was the Carigafoyle Castle ruins. The craggy edifice was visible from their side of the ship. The girls had remembered going there for picnics when they arrived from England. They knew that other families had moved into the ruins when their crops had failed, so they had not returned for visits as the families occupying the building were very territorial. Smoke puffed from the remains on one of the chimneys.

Littor Beach was where Anthony O'Day had died. Neither wished to think back to that horrible day. It reminded them of Liam's death.

Knockbrack East headland faded from view as Beal Point was approached. Opposite that point, on the northern County Clare side, was Carigaholt Castle. The four-story high tower was just visible from the deck of the ship. They glanced across but didn't bother to cross to that side of the vessel. Both pairs of eyes were fixed on the known areas they would not see again.

As Beal Point and the flat coastline slipped past, the Hills of Dooneen approached. The cliffs signalled the exit from the wide mouth of the bay. The vessel sailed down the dividing line of County Clare and County Kerry, the areas both girls had been named after. This was a way to remember their parents' country of birth. They had no idea that they would grow up living within view of both counties.

Now, out into the bay, the seas grew rougher. They knew they had days ahead of them before they reached England's shores.

Father Bartholomew had pulled out a map and showed the girls where they would be going. Some of the families were heading to Canada, others to Australia. Clare and Kerry asked questions about their destination and found that the priest was a fount of knowledge. They were unaware that he visited the country some time ago. He had returned from the Antipodes to settle in Ireland. The girls that shared the floor of the dining room were all to join them on their passage to the other side of the world. All the others in the other rooms were to head to Canada.

At twelve, Kerry was the youngest of the entire group. Kerry was still talkative, but Clare realised it was more nerves than anything else. As the land was now just a line on the horizon, Clare was feeling a little better. They would probably never return to Ireland, never see their home again. They had gazed at the land for as long as possible; now it was gone. There was nothing for them there anyway; a new life awaited them with Aunt Sal, but they both wished they knew more of what was ahead of them.

Father Patrick had sought Clare out the night before they had left for Limerick. He had waited for Kerry to go to sleep, and he had woken Clare to tell her about his conversations with her father. They had sat chatting in front of the stove in the kitchen. He had made Clare promise to say nothing until they had left.

She now turned to Kerry and took hold of her shoulders. "Kerry, what do you know about our family? I mean, Mama and Papa's family?"

Kerry looked puzzled. "Not much; I think Mama and Papa were cousins, but there was more that they wouldn't tell me."

Clare sighed with relief. Thankfully, she knew that much. "Yes, they were related, Kerry, and as such, not supposed to marry. It was part of the reason why we lived here instead of near the rest of the family, but that wasn't really the problem. Mama wasn't a Roman Catholic. Father Patrick said Papa told him the story. Anyway, they were chased out of their homes when they ran away to London to get married. It's why we were born there. The church here wouldn't recognise the marriage as Mama's family was from the Church of England. Kerry, Father Patrick is sending us out to Aunt Sal, whose parents did much the same. Her grandparents are Eamon and Nioiclín O'Shane. They were also Mama and Papa's grandparents. So, Kerry, we're going to family." Clare was unable to keep the excitement from her voice. "I didn't know that this Aunt Sal had actually met Papa and that Papa had already made all the arrangements for our travel. We should all be going together. One of the letters Father Patrick gave me contains a letter from Mama to her cousin Sal. Mama gave it to him the last time he visited her. I didn't tell you as if it were known in Ireland that we had Protestants in the family; we could have been persecuted." Clare drew her little sister into her arms. "We have to stick together, Kerry. We only have each other, and we must pray that we can always stay together."

Kerry's head nodded against her sister's chest.

This new town awaited, and so did this mysterious duke. Clare knew him to be very distantly related by marriage to this mysterious cousin in Australia and that he had requested to meet them personally when they arrived. He had apparently been in contact with Papa.

The first night on board was a trial for both girls. Neither was too keen to sleep in a hammock, but that quickly evaporated as they discovered rats infested the deck. The hammock was harder for the creatures to get into.

As the seas quieted once they rounded the headland, they returned below and tried out their sleeping arrangements. The canvas hammocks didn't look very comfortable, but with full bellies after their onboard meal of fish stew and potatoes, the sleeping deck soon echoed with the mumbles and snores of the young female passengers as they all slept soundly.

On deck, the night watch sailors steered the small vessel towards England and a new life for all the passengers.

~

The passage to Plymouth in Cornwall took three days. On the third day, dawn brought the land back into view. They had been becalmed in the middle of the Irish Sea. Below deck, the girls heard waves crashing against rocks and quickly dressed to see what was nearby. They stood leaning over the gunnels and were chatting about what was before them when the captain joined them.

The cheery comment of welcome met their ears. "Good morning, girls! Thank goodness the doldrums are now behind us. Those rocks are called Ponds End, and the cliffs on the horizon are Land's End in Cornwall. We should be in Plymouth by nightfall if all goes well. Come and see me after the noon meal, and I'll give you your precious bundle."

Their meal consisted of two flat bread-like buns, a boiled potato and a cup of stew-like soup. Considering what the passengers had previously eaten, this was the food of kings. None knew where their next meal would come from, so the buns were pocketed for later consumption.

The girls wrapped their items in one of the blankets that Clare had tied around one shoulder. Kerry wrapped the other blanket around her like a shawl as a chill breeze blew the ship towards the shoreline.

Clare had been watching the captain. He beckoned her, and Clare tapped on Kerry's shoulder and went to collect their letters.

As the captain handed Clare her property, he said, "I had a spare oilskin pouch, so these letters should remain safe for the next leg of your journey. Girls, when the rest of the passengers alight, stay on board. The duke will come and collect you. I gather you have a mutual family. I had a quick conversation with him on my last visit, and he said something about his twins not liking travelling too much. I'm gathering he had little ones?"

Clare and Kerry glanced at each other. Clare said in English, "We have no idea, captain. We have not met him and don't know anything about him. Father Patrick, and Papa made all the arrangements. We didn't even know we had family in Australia. The duke is related by marriage somehow; we have no idea how. Our parents were supposed to be with us, but both are now dead. Father Partick's half-brother is the duke's chaplain."

The captain was impressed that their English was so good and said as much. Kerry answered this time. "Sir, we were both born in London. We mostly spoke English at home but are equally happy with Irish Gaelic or *Gaeilge*. Mama insisted that we read and write in both, too." Kerry was happy that she was able to read. Sean and Ciara had refused to learn. They had said it was a waste of time. Time will tell, as it may well be useful.

Rame Head Bay was now to their left. They could hear the waves crashing onto the shoreline. The flat dune-shaped hills surrounding the bay were almost treeless.

The girls stayed near the captain as the harbour drew closer.

The captain had moved them up to where he could chat whilst still steering the craft. "Girls, we're now in Plymouth Sound. The lighthouse on the break-wall is new. It was only completed five years ago. I believe there are even some mentions of new forts being constructed on either side of this bay. The navy often holes up here, as do many other vessels, as it's a good anchorage."

As they neared the harbour, a pilot vessel came to meet them to give directions for anchoring.

Even though they had already packed up their belongings, they had to wait until morning before they could draw alongside the dock. Once again, they settled for the final night on board.

It was nearing the end of August. So much had occurred in so little time that the girls were still numb with shock. That month had stolen both parents. Their family was gone, and others, even though friends, now occupied their home. Now, they had to meet a stranger and entrust their lives to him. Who was he, and why was he interested in two orphaned girls?

Clare slept with the pouch shoved down her bodice. On rising, food again was provided, and many thanks were, once again, given to God for the provision of sustenance. The girls on either side bunk to them were in gowns so threadbare that their breasts were not covered. Clare and Kerry relinquished their spare gowns to their new friends. They knew the indignity of being all but unclad.

The ship was towed to the wharf by a small steam tugboat. The unruly passengers were jostling to disembark as fast as they could. The two girls hastened to the captain's side as the rest of the passengers were ushered off the ship.

The captain chuckled, "I don't know why they are bothering; it's not like there is anywhere to go. They will be sleeping in one of the empty warehouses until your next ship is ready to board. The duke will probably take you two somewhere a little better. He's a trustworthy man from the reports I have heard about him. I believe he spent many years in Australia, so knows it well. He will probably have his wife and kiddies with him, too, as they like to travel together. I hope you are good with kiddies?" His offhand comments were almost relaxing. Although the captain didn't really want them to answer, both nodded.

Soon, the cacophony of noise died down as the straggling line of poverty-stricken young women and girls entered the barn-like building.

The gulls overhead circled, looking for a feed, but there was none to be had. The two girls were so busy watching the gulls' antics that they nearly missed the arrival of a fancy-looking coach.

The captain drew their attention to their visitors. "Girls, I think your ride has arrived."

They gazed at the most beautiful carriage they had ever seen. There was nothing like this shiny mahogany vehicle in Limerick. The door opened, and a tall, well-dressed blonde giant of a man alighted. He handed out his wife, and three small fair-haired children followed.

Kerry gasped and leaned over to Clare. "He's our cousin?"

Clare had no idea. "He must be, or why else would he want us?"

The fair-haired lady stayed on the wharf with the three children while the man walked towards the gangplank. In quick and sure strides, he almost bounced his way on board. As he reached the top of the walkway, he called, "Ahoy, captain, permission to come on board?"

The captain was waiting for his illustrious guest. "By all means, Your Grace." He bowed him aboard and then turned and beckoned the girls to his side. The captain introduced the girls as Duke Edward, Duke of Gracemere, and they each bobbed a curtsy but remained silent.

The duke frowned. He then addressed Clare. "Do you speak English?"

Again, Clare curtsied. "Yes, Your Grace, we both do."

Relief swept over the man's face. "You had me worried there for a bit. Gaelic was never my strong point, either Scottish or Irish. Firstly, we'll get the formalities out of the way. I believe Father Patrick said he would send me some information. Did he give you a letter? Are your parents below deck?"

Both girls shook their heads. Tears flooded their eyes and soon flowed down both girls' cheeks.

Before either could say anything, the duke realised what had occurred. "They are dead? Both of them?"

Both girls nodded in unison.

Clare then turned her back to the two men before retrieving the pouch from her bodice. She turned around and opened the case before perusing the letters. She pulled out the appropriate one and handed it over.

"You can read too? Really?" The duke had stood watching.

Kerry nodded. "Yes, Your Grace, mostly in English but some Gaelic too. Mama insisted that we needed to know both. Sir, we were born in London and spoke English there."

The duke accepted the proffered screed and flicked open the seal. He stepped away slightly and read the missive. They heard him say, "Tch tch," and then, "Oh, how tragic!" Before he turned back to them. He drew a deep breath and bit his lip. His frown worried them. "I gather you have nothing but what you stand up in?"

Both girls shook their heads again, then nodded. "We had one other dress each, sir, but others needed them more than us."

He blew out his cheeks and then smiled. Unexpected dimples popped in both cheeks. His grin was huge and made the girls relax even more. "Do you see that beautiful lady with the children?"

The girls nodded, seeing a tall lady he had arrived with.

The duke was still smiling. "Well, that's my wife, and she will take you two shopping, and to help us, you will have to help her look after the little ones. They are imps and will need all your vigour to keep up with them. The older twins are now five, Liam is three, and the younger twins are one, but they are asleep at the inn with the maid. You will have your hands full with the five of them. Do you think you can manage?"

The smiles on the girls' faces showed him they were delighted.

The duke said, "Yes, we have two sets of twins. It's in the blood, but don't worry, not your side, mine. Grab your things, and I'll introduce you. Oh, and you can call me Uncle Ned." He turned to the captain and asked,

"How many are awaiting me in the warehouse, captain?"

Captain liked this man. He had an easy way with him. Nothing ostentatious, and as he always travelled with his family, he was obviously happily married. "Seventy or so, I believe, Your Grace. There could have been more, but there was a vessel leaving for Canada, and many older ones chose to go there instead. I feel sorry for them. The ones I took to Liverpool in April were turned away, and I had to return them to poverty in Ireland. Some may be with this lot. Without your sponsorship, this group would have died by the end of the month. They have had more to eat in the last four days than in the last weeks. Thank you for providing the food."

The duke said nothing more but nodded in acknowledgement. He shook the captain's hand and departed with his new charges in tow.

The girls had managed a quick word of thanks to the captain before leaving. The three disembarked, and the girls turned and waved farewell again. Both greeted the duchess with a polite curtsey and then squatted down to talk to the children. The captain watched as the little girl threw her arms around Kerry's neck. The two little boys both hugged Clare but stood more aloof.

Within ten minutes, the duchess had gone with the five children. Duke Ned would walk back to the inn. The duke watched them leave and then introduced himself to those waiting in the large shed. They would have ten days until they could leave, but the new ship was to dock the following day. "Food will be delivered here tonight, and you will board the next vessel tomorrow. I will make sure there is sustenance and clothing available."

One of the attendants who were overseeing the group translated his words. One of the younger children tugged at his coattails.

The red-headed, heavily freckled lass looked up at the tall blonde giant and said, "*Go raibh maith agat.*" There was little more than skin stretched over her bones. Her clothing was filthy rags. Her body also had weeping sores, yet she had the grace and manners to come and thank him.

The duke knew enough Irish Gaelic or *Gaeilge* to understand her words meant *thank you*. He bent and tousled the hair of the skinny girl-child. "You're welcome!" The girl was supposed to be fourteen, as that was the youngest age Earl Grey and he would take. This child looked barely ten. She was so emaciated that he was surprised she had the energy even to walk, let alone smile. He found it hard not to weep at the state of the walking skeletons surrounding him. He knew the famine was terrible but had never seen such emaciation. Even the Aboriginal children in the colony were well-fed in comparison to these folk, and on the whole, the native children were healthy. He was determined to send even more food to Ireland and to Patrick in particular. If what his chaplain, Hugh, said was true, then the shipment of food the duke had sent to Limerick had given hope to the poor wretches, so he would send more, much more. Hugh said Patrick had passed it to his senior priest, who was feeding the most needy.

The state of these poor children was enough to make a grown man weep, and he did. The duke turned on the ball of his foot and left before his tears were noticed. He swiped them away before anyone noticed.

Ned served for over twenty years as Major Ned Grace in the 48th Regiment at Sydney Cove and Parramatta. He had arrived in Governor Macquarie's days and left when George Gipps was in charge; much had changed in those twenty years. He thought he was toughened by deprivation and adversity, but not so. Ned had seen privations and emaciated people, but he had not seen starvation on such a mass scale as this. His first two years in the colony were spent under Governor Macquarie's leadership. During that time, he was privileged to see Macquarie not only meet regularly with the local tribes but clothe, educate, and feed them, too. The governor encouraged monthly gatherings and had even learnt some of the local languages. Other governors followed, and most were caring and good. There were still skirmishes from many of the free settlers who had stock stolen or killed. But there were rotten eggs in all races. The convicts were, on the whole, a sorry bunch of no-gooders, worthless air-suckers, as a friend of his called them. Sam Corbett Garney had served time and included himself in that term. It was a term Ned had heard bandied around about when in Parramatta. Scattered amongst the convicts were those like Charles and Sal Lockley. There were others Ned helped through the years, those who had stood out from the rabble. Twenty years later, to find that Charles was a cousin amazed him. Then, discovering that Charles was an Earl astounded them both. Now Ned was sending these two orphans to Charles and Sal as they were the only family they had left who could look after them. Patrick had mentioned a cousin called John, but he knew nothing more about him.

Ned refused to wipe the more tears from his eyes until he was out of sight of the woe-begotten group. He wished he could do more, but at least he had saved this lot. He couldn't save them all, but he could do something for these girls. What he did was a fraction of what was needed. He had tried to pull strings in London and make the government help out, but they only sent food to the north of the border. He was livid. Even that was not what they needed. Turnips were no substitute for potatoes. At first news of the blight reoccurring a few years ago, he and his friends had planted as many potatoes as he could in whatever fallow land they owned. This bounteous harvest had been sent in its entirety in secret. It had been a mere drop in the ocean to what was needed. Hopefully, they would be ready to send over more food soon. He had chosen areas that were on the outlying fringes of Ireland, where little, if any, food was available,F and the English did not frequent. His chaplain, Hugh, admitted soon after he started in the role that his half-brother was a Catholic priest in the west of Ireland. Reverend Hugh Williams was the illegitimate son of a disreputable Earl of Weedham who enjoyed sowing his seed into as many of his maids as he could. That earl then delighted in having his illegitimate sons trained as clergy. Most were sent to the same college, where many became known to each other. Father Patrick Murphy's mother was one such maid and thus half-brother to his own chaplain, Hugh. But Pat had done most of his training in Italy. After college, quite a few of the half-brother clergy kept in contact with each other. It was through this connection that Ned had become aware of the desperate plight of the orphans in Ireland. However, he had been hunting Sal's relations to rescue them. He had brought her immediate family to stay at his castle until things improved at home in Ireland. Had it not been for the girls' unfortunate situation and the promise that he would send the family to Sal and Charles, they would have been brought back to the castle, too. Their situation grieved his heart but knew they would settle better in Australia than relocate with elderly and somewhat religiously biased grandparents in Ireland, or they would live at the castle indefinitely. Ned would do everything he could for them.

As he walked back to the inn, a thought occurred to him. He had friends near Plymouth, and their son was in Parramatta. They had over a week or more to wait before sailing, giving them plenty of time to go to Newlyn and see his friends. Jennifer could even write to her son, and the girls could deliver a letter or anything else they wished to send. Possibly, that would be cheeses. With this thought in mind, his mood brightened.

While Christina sorted clothing for the girls tomorrow, he would see to the waiting passengers. The day after that, they would embark on the eighty-mile journey south and have a late summer holiday by the sea with the Kellow and Williams families. A broad smile settled on Ned's lips, so much so that his two deep dimples appeared again.

On arrival back at their lodgings, Ned quickly penned a note and sent it to his friends, Jennifer and Billy Williams. He hoped Felix and Isla would also be in town as he liked catching up with them. Felix may well be fifteen years his senior, but he was the Duke of Shesham. Ned had turned to him for assistance when stumbling his way through the requirements in his new role as duke. Ned knew Felix had married a milkmaid rather than a society lady and that the milkmaid's sister had once been a convict and soon had put the two things together. He was one of the few let into the secret of the unusual relationship. Ned had been the soldier assigned to oversee Jennifer in Parramatta and during her time of conviction in the colony. During these years, Jennifer and her husband Billy became good friends with Ned. Jennifer's eldest son, Kit, had returned to the colony and ran a branch of the family dairy that was next to Government House in Parramatta. He also realised that Charles and Sal were also friendly with Kit Kellow, which would be another link for the girls. He also knew of a cargo vessel leaving for Sydney the following morning. Although it carried no passengers, it could take a letter to Charles telling him of the girls' impending arrival. With his notes sent on their way, he joined Christina in their rooms to tell her of his plans.

The following morning, the girls played with the five adorable children. The youngest twins were identical girls, Charlotte and Isabella, known as Charl and Izzy. They were almost inseparable, except one had a heart-shaped birthmark on her hand. By mid-morning, the dressmaker had taken the Irish girls' fittings, and by nightfall, two new gowns with new undergarments awaited them.

Ned had been busy, and the first of the seventy girls were settling on board the *Lady Kennaway*. They would have time to make themselves comfortable before the remainder of the passenger compliment arrived from other areas.

After a week in Plymouth, Ned and Christina's staff packed their luggage, which was sent off at dawn the following morning. The family and girls would travel together. They would stay at their friend's house for the best part of a week, and no staff would be permitted to remain with them.

~

The shiny, large ducal carriage was loaded with family and set off to Cornwall. Most of the staff were given the week off in Plymouth, and only the carriage driver was to accompany them.

After over twenty years in the colony as a major, Ned delighted in throwing off the trappings of society. He and Felix had that in common; neither duke liked the promiscuous society they needed to live in. Christina was a hands-on mother, and with the two girls' assistance, the five small children and two adults would relish the time that was just *en famille*. Once the family was delivered to their destination, the carriage drivers would be dispatched to Penzance to stay there until required.

Ned's family had made this journey a few times over the years, and it was as near to being in Parramatta as they could get. Felix always made them welcome, and Jennifer always greeted him with a big brother-like hug. Christina had met Jennifer in Parramatta before the Williams family returned to Cornwall in 1834. It was just before Ned met Christina, but they had mutual friends, and Christina wished to see how cheese was made. She had walked up from her new cottage, and she had stayed chatting for some time. The ladies' friendship was instantaneous and genuine. Jennifer and Ned were the same age, but their roles were vastly different. She was a convict, and he was her supervising officer. Christina was ten years their junior.

Duke Felix Shesham was the eldest of the immediate group of friends, and Billy was four years his junior and the same age as the eldest of Jennifer's brothers. Jennifer's younger sister, Isla, was six years older than Christina. So, Jennifer's ten siblings and their partners filled in the seventeen years between. The group with all their children was now huge. Children of all ages were everywhere, and everyone watched the little ones. The large party of over sixty gathered on the headland for an evening picnic.

The night they arrived was one of joy and happiness. The girls laughed for the first time in ages.

When Ned and Christina visited to Cornwall soon after their return in 1842, they were surprised to see that Jennifer's sister, Isla and Felix were expecting a fifth child. Isla had just turned forty, and therefore, her condition was unexpected.

Young Edward Felix was now six and the image of his father. He had his father's hook nose and dark brow. He could mimic his father's look of disparagement to a tee. His one eyebrow raised, and a nonchalant glare he delivered was enough to freeze a stranger. But he had also inherited his mother's sense of the ridiculous. The little boy was a joy and delight to those who knew him. As he was much the same age as Ned's older twins, they all got along well.

Jennifer and Billy's four children were now all grown. All had all made lives for themselves in the family business. Jennifer had a son before they married due to an assault, and Kit Kellow still lived in Parramatta. All the children worked in the vast dairy and cheese industry, as did their spouses. The cheeses were still all hand-rubbed weekly, and the business was easily large enough to support all those relying on their produce. Life here was good!

Only Jennifer's eldest son, Kit, had returned to Australia. He had met his father, a baron, only once. The man had assaulted his mother on their one and only meeting. Jennifer had conceived him. Acknowledging the child was his, the baron had ensured Kit had been given an excellent education, first in Sydney, then at Eton, followed by university.

Kit had wished to meet his father with the possibility of having a relationship with him. However, on meeting him, Kit punched his father so hard that the baron's nose never looked the same. When Kit reached maturity, he decided to return to the Parramatta farm and take over the family dairy there.

For the first time in a long time, Clare and Kerry relaxed. They were absorbed into the cacophony of noise and mayhem in such a wonderful family. Once again, they were surrounded by love, laughter, and acceptance.

The Duke and Duchess of Gracemere were soon Uncle Ned and Aunt Christina. Duke Felix and Isla were similarly given honorific titles. Jennifer, Billy, and all the rest were just first names.

Hugs abounded, and the girls did not realise how much they had missed receiving them. Both wept as everyone's love soaked into them.

Chapter 5   Lady Kennaway

*A*fter an idyllic week in Cornwall, where Clare and Kerry began to relax a little, the girls talked to Jennifer and asked what Parramatta and their cousin Sal were like.

Jennifer told them everything she could. She also told them of her son, Kit, and filled in the story of his unfortunate start in life. Being the victim of abuse, Jennifer conceived a child out of wedlock and delivered him the day Billy arrived in the colony looking for her.

Ned befriended their family and soon became a good friend. Over the last twenty-eight years, that friendship had grown. Ned had only been a soldier then, but he had seen the calibre of many people he saved or helped. He learnt to take people at face value rather than their birthright.

In those intervening years, they had all seen much of the murkier side of life. Ned had used his time there to rescue many of the more innocent convict girls. He placed them in various safe houses or with better-quality families. Sal had been his first female rescue, and that had been at Charles's behest. They had married only weeks later.

Ned needed to return home when he inherited the grand title of Duke of Gracemere. His role changed to getting the laws rewritten to protect the less fortunate before they were in trouble. Felix, Jennifer, and Charles were all instrumental in this work from both sides of the world. Clare and Kerry were two more girls who would find a safe home where they would find love. In the short time he knew them, Ned realised they were not young ladies of leisure. Although they were keen to babysit his five children, they were eager to learn about the dairy industry when the opportunity arose.

During the week in Cornwall, both had risen at dawn to help milk the large herd of dairy cows, and they had watched the rennet being added to the milk and the beginning process of cheesemaking. Both had milked before, but it had been a goat. Neither girl shirked the more unpleasant jobs, and both were as willing to muck out the dairy after milking as they were to enjoy the melted cheese on toasted crusty fresh bread eaten with a breakfast with creamy cracked wheat porridge. The girls also encouraged the three six-year-olds, Chip, Sarah and Felix's youngest lad, Edward Felix, to get their hands dirty and learn to milk. Much to everyone's astonishment, the three small children loved this work and soon were up each morning at dawn and waiting for the girls.

Sadly, the days of freedom and relaxation passed all too fast. The *Lady Kennaway* was ready to depart, and the Gracemere carriage needed to return them to Plymouth.

Upon arrival at their lodgings, a large travelling case awaited the girls. Christina's order of clothes and other accoutrements had arrived from the outfitter. Knowing what life was like in the colony and the future the girls were to have, she had purchased only one good gown each, and the remainder of their wardrobe was serviceable dresses. That said, these gowns were far better than any they had ever seen before. Each chose a reasonably plain cotton drill dress to wear to board the ship. The two hundred steerage passengers sponsored by Earl Grey had already boarded, and the orphan girls who arrived with Clare and Kerry had joined them. Only a few of the widows with children remained in the shed.

Ned arranged for them to travel in the next vessel, and they were assured that they would remain safe. The twelve remaining women were moved into better accommodation until the next vessel was ready. Ned, Felix, and Earl Grey were three of the commissioners who arranged the various consignments of orphans. This was the third ship to rescue these poor waifs. The previous two went to Sydney and Adelaide; this one would terminate in Melbourne.

Before permitting the girls to board the vessel, Ned insisted on meeting the other first-class passengers. They were Doctor Brock, the Surgeon-superintendent, Mr and Mrs Langland and family, Mr Palmer, Mr McKenzie, and Mr Lithman. Of these passengers, only the Langlands had children. Their eldest son, John, was eleven, and there was one more son and three young girls. The Scottish family was heading to Melbourne to join Mr Langland's younger brother. They intended to set up a store and promised to oversee the safety of the two Irish orphans.

Ned paid them for delivering them safely to Melbourne and boarding a steamer to Sydney. Captain Santray assured Ned that he would ensure the girls arrived safely. Ned explained to the girls that when farewelling their family, they were to call them aunt and uncle and hug them affectionately. This simple public display of affection would allow the crew and captain to ensure their safety. Chip, Sarah, and Liam needed no coaching as the three of them were in tears as the girls boarded. The entire family came on board and saw them settle into their cabin. They were introduced to Doctor Brock and the ship's maids. All were somewhat in awe of the fair-haired giant and his equally as awe-inspiring wife. The five small children behaved impeccably, as did the young ladies accompanying them.

The commodious cabin had a fitted ewer and washbasin that emptied when folded. The cabin was not far from the galley but at the far end of the vessel from the head. Christina explained that the term for the built-in chamberpots on a ship was called the head, and there were normally two of these, and they were on either side of the ship at the front of the vessel, hence the name. She recommended that unless the seas were smooth, they should not use them but utilise the chamberpot in their cabin. With only the two heads on board, the condition of the primitive facilities was often unsavoury at best. Christina helped the girls unpack and arranged for the large chest to be safely stored next door in the small sitting room Ned had booked for them. After an hour, the five small children were getting a little quarrelsome in the cramped cabin. After checking with the captain, the family decided to go ashore and say farewell on the dockland. They still had an hour until cast-off, and the venue would give the entire ship's complement a good view of the public farewell.

The youngest of the Irish orphans, the skinny, red-headed, freckled-faced girl, was fourteen, a bit older than Clare's age, and by their state, they had come from conditions that were far worse than the O'Shanes.

Ned and Christina visited the steerage quarters to check on the human cargo. They had so little that some were virtually naked. Thankfully, after the first two voyages, they were somewhat prepared for what they saw. Felix and Ned had seen them off and were aghast at the emaciated condition of the girls. He wondered if they would actually survive the journey. Somehow, they all had. Unbeknownst to the Colonial Land and Emigrations Commissioners, Ned had sponsored other Irish emigrating families. Some were sent across the Atlantic, and some to Australia. He, therefore, had many cases of clothing and other requirements awaiting these new girls. The purpose of the visit was to arrange for the distribution of new gowns and underclothing. More would be issued on arrival in Melbourne, but the girls would be decently clad and warm. There were more than enough to go around. And they had been instructed to wash regularly, both their persons and their attire. Three meals a day would be provided to all, and no hoarding was required. There was a long refectory-like table down the centre of the deck, and this was for eating and occupations like sewing and reading. Privacy was provided by sheets or blankets hung on ropes.

Christina wondered if any of them could read and doubted they could. There was a large box of books, including Bibles, and another of slates and chalk. She doubted they would be used, but they were available if required. There were also bolts of fabric, sewing notions, and needles. She had learnt that the long months at sea could be dull and could be used to learn something constructive. Hopefully, these girls would do the latter.

On their return to the cabin, Ned handed Clare an envelope. "Clare, this is for your use; half each for you. It's a small amount of money to give you a fresh start in your new homeland. Use it as you wish, but don't waste it."

"Thank you, Uncle Ned." With her back turned to him, Clare tucked the envelope down her bodice. She had nowhere else to stow it and would find a safe place later.

The two girls took the elder twins' hands and escorted them down the gangplank. Ned and Christina followed with the three younger children. Once on the dock, the three elder ones were permitted to let off some steam and run around.

Christina sat chatting to the girls about the orphans below deck. She mentioned the books, slates and sewing materials available for use and wondered if they would be interested in possibly setting an example for the older girls. From the smiling looks the siblings gave each other, she did not doubt that her idea had been planted in fertile soil. She discovered that Gráinne had taught the girls well, as both could read, write, and sew well. Neither had the need to do much of either, but they knew the basics. Christina had met Mrs Langland on the way back to the cabin and mentioned the fabrics. With nothing more she could do to assist her charges, she set about reminiscing with the girls. The more they knew about what the colony was like, the less fearful they would be. Having met Jennifer and knowing they carried not only letters but six large waxed cheese wheels, the girls felt they were being useful. They were not going empty-handed, as one of these cheeses was for Sal. This was a journey to a new life for them, and they knew they were unlikely to return.

Ned and Christina had only returned from Australia the year before. Izzy and Charl, had been born in Parramatta, and they had returned before they started crawling. The ducal family planned to revisit Australia and would ensure they met up again when over there. With that thought in mind, the call came for them to board. The tide was about to change, and the ship would be tugged out into the sea and be on its way. When the moment came to say their farewells, the tears were genuine. Christina clung to them both as a mother saying farewell to her children. Christina enfolded both girls before kissing them goodbye.

Ned, too, gave them each a big bear hug. After more cuddles from the children, they were walked to the gangplank and waved aboard. Halfway up, both turned and called farewell to their 'aunt and uncle.' No sooner than they were at the railing, the gangplank was hoisted on deck, and the ropes cast off.

The journey had begun.

Clinging to each other, the girls shouted more goodbyes and stood waving until the shore was out of sight.

They were alone. Fear of what was before them washed over them anew. Clare didn't wish to leave the gunnels, but Kerry nudged at her arm. "Clare, we have months on board, and Aunt Christina said it was up to us to teach the girls below. So come on!" Kerry noticed her sister didn't move.

Rather than harassing her, she slipped her hand into hers and stepped closer.

"We're leaving everything we hold dear, Kerry." Clare didn't look down at her sister. She couldn't, as the tears filling her eyes would have spilled down her cheeks.

Kerry tugged at her sister's hand. "No, Clare, they are always with us here." She put her hand on her heart. "There is nothing here for us any more." Clare's shoulders shook as she finally lost control.

Kerry dropped her hand and slid her arm around her sister's waist. "Clare, you have always been the strong one, and now it's time to rest. Aunt Christina told me I had to look after you, and I will, but you must let me do that for you."

Clare nodded; Aunt Christina had said much the same to her. But as the eldest child, she had always been the responsible one. "We'll never come back, though, Kerry."

Kerry's eyes lifted from her sister's sad face to the fine line of land on the horizon. "No, we won't, but Aunt Sal and Uncle Charles are waiting for us. They are our family now, Clare." She paused as she let her words sink in. "And what's more, we have a job to do for Jennifer and Billy. Kit needs us to deliver his letter and cheeses." She chuckled. "Do you think he would notice if a chunk were missing?"

Clare replied with a gurgle of her own. "I think we'd be in big trouble. Jennifer said one of the wheels of cheese was for the governor, and another was for Uncle Charles and Aunt Sal. But Kit needs them to take a sample of the new culture." She leaned over and kissed the top of her sister's hair. "Come on, sis; you said we have work to do."

They turned to go below, and Clare said, "Thanks, Kerry!" As they walked towards the hatch, she squeezed her sister's hand as they left the railing. No more words were needed.

~

The *Lady Kennaway* sailed on.

From the first day at sea, the girls had been busy. Rather than Mrs Langland looking after them, they took all their children down to the lower deck and asked for assistance from the orphans. As the girls were younger than all of them, they soon had more than enough assistance as babysitters. One thing led to another, and as Christina had told Clare about the box of books, she kept them entertained by reading. Soon, the group of seventy who had accompanied them from Limerick split in half, and Clare offered to teach the older Langland children to read and write while Kerry read stories. Some of the other girls watched on. They sat at the long table in the steerage section with some slates. Soon, more of the newer girls joined in.

The ship headed straight down the African coast.

By the end of October, they were nearly halfway and pulling into Table Bay, at the southern tip of South Africa.

After six weeks on board, many could at least write their names. It was still two months before they reached Melbourne, so others joined the classes.

Sewing was also done with gusto. One or two of the older ones could draft a gown pattern, and they willingly showed others how to cut out a pattern and sew a dress.

Christina had told Clare about the four hundred new gowns in the hold awaiting distribution on arrival, but it was better if the girls learned how to make their own clothing as this skill they would all need. It would at least pass the days for the two hundred orphan girls that filled the steerage deck.

By the time they arrived in the Cape Town harbour, the fabric stock onboard had been exhausted. Clare opened the sealed envelope that Ned had given her for emergencies. She knew it contained money and wondered if she should use any of it to buy more material. She would sacrifice some if it contained £10 to buy what she could. Clare opened the envelope and was stunned to see that it contained not just one ten-pound note but twenty of them. Uncle Ned had given them £100 each. She stood holding the enormous amount of money and giggled. There was more than enough to share.

Clare took one of the notes and folded the others to store away for use in the colony. She had no idea their future, but £190 would solidify it. Smiling at Uncle Ned's generosity, she safely stowed the remainder of their money and put the £10 note in her reticule to use while shopping. She was determined that the remainder of this money would become their dowries.

Having gained her sea legs, Mrs Langland was well enough to escort the two girls shopping. They would be in port for a few days to restock. Mr Langland and the majority of the orphan girls would remain on board and babysit the Langland's children.

One of the ship's agents in Cape Town escorted the three ladies to a fabric warehouse.

Clare didn't want good fabric for the girls but serviceable and hardwearing fabrics that would last them a while. She was thrilled when she came across many water-stained fabrics that would make very serviceable dresses for all the girls. Twenty-five of these damaged bolts were found, twelve of which were full, one-hundred-yard rolls, and the rest were fifty-yard bolts. This should allow about two more gowns each per girl.

Clare was pleased with her purchase, and all for a mere £8.

They were about to leave the warehouse when the manager beckoned them over. "Miss, could you use some badly stained lawn and poplin? We can't sell it. I have six full bolts, which will be thrown away if you don't want them." The look he gave the ladies made Kerry giggle. He hated to see good things go to waste.

They had discussed purchasing one bolt of white fabric so the girls could make new drawers for themselves, but it was too expensive. To be given such a gift was a delight. Even calico, which only came in a one hundred and fifty-yard bolt, was £2.50 for the roll. They didn't have enough money.

Clare willingly accepted the bounteous gift and gave thanks in her prayers that evening. All the girls would have new undergarments. There was enough for not only camisoles but drawers, too. All the females on board were busy cutting and sewing for the remaining eight weeks. They cut the bolts into lengths and boiled these in concentrated fresh urine collected from girls in steerage. The area stank of ammonia, but the fabric emerged white. Once dried, they cut out the clothing items from the clean white material.

Unbeknownst to Kerry, Clare had purchased some special fabric for each of them, and in the few precious hours Clare had to herself, she decided to make each of them a gown for best wear. They may never wear them anywhere else but to church services, but at least they would have something pretty. The two gowns Christina purchased were ball gowns, and they were too good, even for church. The ten metres of fabric she found was an off-cut with a pulled thread all the way through it. There was enough to make two gowns with matching reticules. It was of sprigged muslin and prettier than any fabric Clare had ever seen. The tiny flowers reminded her of the pretty flowers on the potato plants. She would cut the fabric so the embroidery would be around the hems. It looked like a potato field in full flower. Liam had been alive back then, and life was good, and even little Paddy was still healthy. The memories of their losses made her tear up again. After a few moments of melancholy, Clare shook away her tears. Kerry was right; the memory of their lost family would always remain in their hearts and memories.

~

Weeks passed quickly, and soon, the ship approached the headland to head into Port Phillip Bay and then to Melbourne. The last item of clothing from Clare's shopping trip was completed.

The two hundred now healthy girls below were excited to start their new lives. Earl Grey and his team had told them they would be met and soon placed in various positions and houses. All jobs and homes had been thoroughly vetted and deemed suitable abodes for an unmarried girl.

Tearful farewells were made by all below deck. The older Langland children did the rounds of most of their friends below deck. Captain Santray, Mrs Langland, and the two girls had their chests brought up from the hold, and each girl received two new gowns as they left for their new lives. From having no clothing at all, each disembarked with at least five dresses and new underclothing. Each had a calico bag to carry them in.

After a mere eighty-five days on their journey, Clare and Kerry were packed and ready to hear about the final leg of their journey. The *Lady Kennaway* was heading directly to Guam from Melbourne, so they needed to change ships.

Captain Santray oversaw the paperwork for the next leg of their voyage and sent a message to Charles Lockley on a ship departing that evening. There was no telegraph, so if the girls were to be met in Sydney, their guardians needed to know their imminent arrival. He yet had to transfer the girls onto their new vessel, but at least someone would meet them at their destination. This would give Charles Lockley a day to arrange transport to Sydney. He had been able to book the girls' passage on another ship.

As it happened, the coastal steamer, *Christina,* was in port and leaving for Sydney the following day. The girls' transfer was made after the other passengers alighted. As the *Lady Kennaway* had been pulled up on the other side of the same jetty, the two captains met as soon as the *Lady Kennaway* berthed. The *Christina's* captain, Captain Saunders, was overseeing the cargo loading, or they would have left already. There were five puncheons of potent rum, eight pipes and seven hogsheads of wine, twenty-two boxes of tea, and one hundred and forty-three bales of wool. This cargo took time to load, giving the two captains time to chat.

Captain Santray transferred care of his two special passengers to Captain Saunders and saw them settle into their cabin. He made the girls promise to lock their door each night and bade them farewell. As Charles Lockley was well known to the captain of the new vessel, their safety would be assured. Captain Saunders vouchsafed to deliver them into the company of the Lockelys personally, even if he had to take them to Parramatta himself.

The Langlands were the final group to depart the *Lady Kennaway.* Once the girls had settled into their new cabin, they came back on board to assist with the children. Mr Langlands had to arrange for their mountains of luggage to be unloaded, and then he had needed to find accommodation for them and arrange transport of their possessions. The girls saw how harried the mother was and went to her aid. The children eventually bade a tearful farewell, and soon Clare and Kerry stood alone on the wharf.

As the carriage departed, night descended, and the noise around them abated. They heard heavy boots descending the gangway. Turning, they saw the new captain approaching.

Captain Saunders walked to their sides. "Good evening, ladies; I have come to escort you aboard. The dockland is not a good place to be after dark. The evening meal is nearly ready." He presented his elbows to the girls, and they hooked their hands through his arms as they had seen Mrs Langlands do. As they returned to his ship, he chattered happily about how delightful the Lockley family were and how lucky they were to make their home with them. His chatter eased their loneliness.

The girls shared a glance and a smile. God was already preparing the path before them.

Chapter 6   A Letter to Parramatta

$\mathcal{A}$lthough still daylight, a late evening knock on the door of the small cottage was answered by a tall, willowy, faired-haired lady. Birthing six children had not marred her sylphlike figure. Her graciousness was more queenly than her countess status. Opening the door, she greeted the postmaster and handed him a jar of her preserves. "David, you really didn't need to deliver our mail personally. I'm sure this could have waited until Charles collected it tomorrow."

The postmaster smiled, "Normally, I would not have Mrs Lockley, but this one is marked *urgent*. I thought I'd drop it in myself as I was locking up. It came in with the governor's despatches from Melbourne."

Sal took the envelope from the postmaster and thanked him again. "David, the pickles are from today's batch. I promised Prudence I would send a jar when they cooled, but this is the half jar to see if you like it. I'll pack up your half of the batch when they are labelled. The pepper will make it hotter as it ages." As she spoke, she turned over the letter. Noting that it was addressed to them both, she opened the seal and pulled out the single sheet of paper. Perusing it briefly, she said, "Oh, David, thank you so much for bringing this down. You are correct; it is urgent. We need to go to Sydney tomorrow to collect my cousins. They are coming from Ireland and will make their home with us. I must tell Charles!"

David took the cue, bowed to acknowledge her thanks, and departed. He found it hard to believe this couple were the Earl and Countess of Coxheath. Lady Sal had told Prudence all about her Irish family coming to live with them. The family were victims of the Irish famine.

Sal heard her husband's gentle snores emanating from the sitting room. He had again fallen asleep on the big leather-winged armchair he had purchased with money Ned had sent him.

After so many years of living in the cramped inn with six children and numerous visitors, the two-bedroom cottage they shared with their youngest son was ideal. Luke had just finished his final year at The King's School and would be heading to Sydney after Christmas for the inaugural year of the new University that had been started. He would be living at Government House in one of the rear rooms. Sal wondered where she would place the family of at least five people just ten days before Christmas celebrations. They had received a letter from Kieran only last month. The extended Lockley family would descend on Parramatta, and every spare room in all the houses would be needed. She released a long and somewhat frustrated sigh, and this gentle sound woke Charles.

The debonair but rather sleepy gentleman asked, "Love, is something up?"

Rather than reply, Sal handed him the letter.

"Kieran and Gráinne are arriving tomorrow? Really?" His eyes dropped to the screed again. He noted a postscript on the bottom. Turning over the sheet of paper, he read it. Sitting up with a jerk, he exclaimed, "Oh, no!"

Sal did not realise there was more on the back because she had not put on her spectacles. "Charles, what is it?"

She met her husband's startled gaze. "Sal, Kieran and Gráinne are dead, and it's just the two eldest girls who have come."

Thankfully, she was near her chair and almost collapsed into it. "Dead?"

Charles nodded. "That's what the captain said here. The two girls are alone and are coming on the coastal steamer tomorrow with Captain Saunders. They have letters for us from Ned."

The room fell silent. Sal's lips wrinkled, and tears slid down her cheeks. "Oh, Charles, they are so brave making the journey alone."

Charles nodded but remained silent. He was deep in thought, but he reached out for her hand. Sal's family in Ireland had been on their minds for some time. Ned had written extensively about it on his return home last year. He had arranged a shipload of orphan girls to be sent out to Sydney, and they had arrived earlier in the year. Charles and Sal had taken it upon themselves to assist with finding placements for many of the poor, lonely waifs. The five youngest he sent to Jack and Bea Barnes on the Bathurst road. Many had since married and found good homes; the younger ones had found positions in various houses in and around town. Eight years before the cessation of convict transportation occurred. As the convict girls' terms expired, there was a sad lack of available maids and nursemaids. All the new jobs were paid ones, and the homes they were placed in were vetted and marked as safe houses for the girls. Sal, the ladies of their family and church, took it upon themselves to train the Irish girls and place them with lovely families. However, these two lassies were family, and their lives had yet to be planned.

Sal looked up and said, "Charles, we must keep these two close by. They have lost everything and will become like two more of our daughters. Liza and Anna can do with help in the house, and each could squeeze one more girl into their homes, or they could go to Charlie at the inn. However, I would like them to be nearby for a while, and I'll pop across the road and see Jenna."

Charles roused himself and rubbed his eyes. "I'll come too, love." He grabbed his walking stick and followed her out the door.

The middle-aged couple didn't need any coverings. The December night was hot, and they only had to walk across the road. Eddie was their second son, and he was a blacksmith. He had been born on Ned's twenty-second birthday and had been named after him. Ned was the godfather to all four of their sons. However, Eddie had always been special to Ned. He was like the son Ned never thought he would have. When Eddie married just a month before Ned, there was no gift. The duke's access to funds in the colony had been minimal. When Ned arrived back in England, he wrote with the news that Charles was not who he thought he was. Also, Ned discovered he was related. Charles was Ned's third cousin and held the title of Earl of Coxheath. Charles had never known. However, Ned's letter also contained a wedding gift for Eddie. £1000 was more money than the family had combined. Eddie was determined to share his good fortune. Not only did he build a house for himself as Ned had explicitly requested, but he moved his parents out of the inn and into one of the cottages in the row of three that Ned and Christina had lived in. Ned had owned the cottage closest to their inn, and Christina had lived in the top one.

Later, with money Ned had sent Charles from the duchy coffers, they purchased the centre cottage, and each was renamed. Ned's cottage became *Little Gracemere*, the centre one became *Coxheath Close*, and their top cottage became *Christina's Cottage*. And so it stayed. Eddie's house, *Bramblemere Close*, was diagonally across the road from the cottages.

Wills and Cathy had recently moved out of the lower cottage and moved further into town to *Roseneath* at the top end of town. This had been a house rented for the past few years by extended family. They had moved even further west to Emu Plains near Wills and Cathy's main home, and Wills had purchased it for a base in Parramatta. Harry and Vicky still stayed there with Wills and Cathy. The two couples were, thankfully, best friends as well as business partners.

Entering through the back gate, Charles and Sal went in through the kitchen door. Cara, their Irish cook and housekeeper, had retired for the evening, but Eddie and Jenna were up with little Christopher, also called Kit. He was their fourth child, and although twenty months old, he was a bad sleeper. As Jenna was expecting a baby, Sal and Charles spent much time helping with the children again. Their oldest children were twins born weeks before Ned's eldest pair. Ed and Jenna's next son, Kit, was born between

Ned's youngest twins, Charl and Izzy. The three were born on the same day in adjoining rooms. Christina and Ned were stunned that they had two sets of twins. Sal smiled as she thought of the twins in the family. Their eldest son, Charlie and his wife, Gracie, also had twin boys. So many small blonde children were around that it took many to watch them all. Names were often muddled, and they all learnt to respond to sweetie, poppet, or similar.

Eddie heard their entry and came downstairs in his nightshirt. "Hello, Mama, Dar, what's wrong?"

Charles waived the letter he held. "The O'Shanes are coming tomorrow, or at least, what's left of them. We expected the family, but there are only two girls remaining."

Eddie gasped. He knew that his mother's relations were having a tough time in Ireland, but they had been unable to find out more about them.

Charles continued. "Can they stay here until we sort them out? Your mother and I will go to Sydney to collect them tomorrow. Depending on their ship's arrival time, we may have to stay the night, but if you can get Cara to sort a room for them, that would be good." Eddie ran his eyes over the letter and nodded. Charles continued, "How about that small one behind the kitchen? I think there are two small cot beds in there."

"Sure, Dar, whatever you think is best. They can stay there over Christmas, too, as no one ever uses it." Ed yawned; he knew he should have been asleep as he needed to be up at dawn for work.

His parents had no intention of staying, so Sal kissed her son good night, and they left the way they had entered, through the kitchen.

Eddie stood watching their departure, his mind working overtime. Cara's two girls had slept in this room when the twins were tiny. They alternately attended to the babies' needs when they were firstborn. Eventually, one moved upstairs and slept in the nursery. With four small imps now up there, both girls had moved into the more spacious room beside the nursery. Having more assistance over Christmas may be good as more small children would be around.

Moira and Shauna were children of their Irish life-convict parents and were more than just servants. Eddie was paying for the girls to go to school. However, Cara and Paddy Connor were like family these days as their eldest daughter married one of Eddie's brother-in-law's brothers. The Connors lived in their own quarters behind the stable and shared the room with their two youngest sons, Shéamas and Liam. These two strapping young lads had worked up at the Government Dairy since they were old enough to work. In the early years, they had slept in the loft at the cottage next door to the dairy rather than trudge through the frosty mornings and start the milking at dawn. At fifteen and thirteen, they now shared the stables accommodation with their parents. Although they still milked the herd, they were often out on the farm. Shéamas stuck his head out the door and waved to them as they passed. "Just checking for strangers, sir," he called, lifting his hand in a salute before vanishing. He had not even waited for a reply.

Charles and Sal strolled back to their cottage with much on their minds. They would catch the first ferry to Sydney and return with the girls. Charles and Sal had met Captain Saunders a few times over the years. Charles first met him when he managed Government Stores from his inn. With the cessation of transportation, the Government Stores had closed, the barracks had moved further up the hill into a permanent sandstone group of buildings, and the old town was vanishing fast. Until his retirement, Ned had lived in a beautiful cottage he shared with fellow officers. Since Sal had first been assigned to him back in 1820, she had continued to do his washing and ironing. It was through that and Charles's first placement at Perry White's house that drew the three closer together. Perry had been a friend of Ned's from England and needed two servants. Ned had found Charles and Sal for him. Both often thought of *Glenmere House* at the end of their street and their happy first years there. The two eldest Lockley boys had been born in their rooms above the Glenmere stables. And when Perry had left, it had been Ned who arranged for the Lockleys to run Government stores and the Jolly Sailor Inn.

Charles opened the door for his lovely lady. "We'd better get some sleep, love, if we are to have a full day tomorrow." Twilight had faded to dusk, and the two headed to bed.

The morning brought a flurry of activity in the small cottage. Luke had missed all the activity of the evening before and groggily emerged from his room to the smell of cracked wheat porridge and fried eggs. The three sat down to eat, and his parents filled him in about the arrival of their two orphaned cousins. He said, "Aw, gee, Mama, I'll go and help Cara get their room ready. I can put off the study I was going to get done today. My head is like an overstuffed pillow anyway so that I could do with a break." He slid the hard-fried egg onto a slice of thin toast, cooked just as he liked, folded it, and bit into it. His mother watched his lack of table manners and, exasperated, shook her head at him. His father, however, didn't let them pass without comment. "Luke, son, of all my children, you may well be the youngest, but you have the most education; at least you will. Eddie completed five years at Mr Cape's Academy but never continued to university. For you to be the first student enrolled at Sydney University is a feather in your cap, lad. You are the son of an earl; admittedly, I didn't know for four decades, but you must behave appropriately, especially when living at Government House as you will be next year. You may only have a lesser title of The Honourable, but it is more than many others here have. So, please remember your table manners."
The diatribe of his father's correction had taken so long that Luke pushed the last mouthful into his mouth as his father finished. He knew not to talk with a full mouth, so he grinned and nodded.

His mother could see the glint in her youngest son's eye and turned her back to start washing the dishes with a grin on her lips. The conversation was repeated at least once a week, and most mornings, Luke remembered. It was a habit he and his next older brother, Wills, had fallen into when they were little. The pair of them would spend their Saturdays adventuring with a group of local and aboriginal children. The native imps were dark-skinned versions of her own children, even often down to the two deep dimples in their cheeks. They were all lovely children keen to teach and learn from each other. Sal was pleased that her children had all tried to learn some of the local languages and teach their native friends some English. However, it was the water that drew all the young ones. The hot, steamy summer days were perfect for cooling off. After some scares with sharks in the tidal section of the river, they now always swam above the weir. Even at eighteen and twenty, the two boys would sneak down to the weir to swim on hot days. They never went without a bag of hard-boiled eggs and a pocket of paper twists of salt to share with their friends.

Wills was now married and had two children, and he had lived in the lower cottage until recently. Sal was always on hand to help Cathy when Wills was away. She smiled when she thought of her sons' wives. Ed and Wills had married two of Jack Turner's daughters. Jack had arrived with Charles as a convict, and the two had reported about a mutiny and given early tickets of leave. Jenna and Cathy had a middle sister, Vicky, and she had married a Viscount's brother four years before. Harry Harlow and Vicky had lost their first child only months into Vicky's confinement. Since then, they had two more children. Sal froze. A thought had just occurred to her. Although her arms were sudsy, she turned and said, "Charles, Harry and Vicky, Wills and Cathy are in need of maids up at *Roseneath*. That silly Portuguese girl has finally left them and found employment with that Spanish family. Mayhap our girls will be interested in helping them out. They have a nice maid's room, too."

Charles had just taken a long draw of his hot sweet tea, so his reply was to nod assent and raise his bushy eyebrows.

Luke had just finished his porridge. "So, do I go and do the room at Ed's or wait until you talk to Harry?"

Charles thought for a bit, then replied. "I think it will be good for them to be close for a while. Your mother will be at hand, and then we will see what happens. Harry and Vicky will be here for Christmas next weekend, so we'll talk to them then. In the meantime, the ferry leaves at eight, so we have to get moving. Love, Luke can finish the dishes. We only have fifteen minutes before the tide."

Sal glanced at her son, who was nodding in acknowledgement. She wiped her arms and went to prepare for a possible overnight stay in town. Hopefully, the boat would arrive before the four o'clock ferry returned. Any of the girls' excess luggage could come by wagon.

By the time the ferry pulled into the wharf, Charles and Sal were standing in the shade of a big tree just up from the jetty. Even this early in the morning, it boded to be a very hot day. Both being fair-skinned, they burnt quickly. Sal wore a wide-brim straw bonnet that Charles had just purchased for her. The wide brim kept much of the sun off her fair skin. This new design was very practical for the hot summer days. They had no intention of going anywhere in town, so they only packed the bare necessities. One leather hold-all bag sat in the cabin of the small ferry. Only three other passengers joined them, and the vessel cast off the ropes at precisely eight o'clock.

The river's tide had already started rising, so the timetable would again need to be changed. The ferry's access to the wharf was dependent on the tide's height and whether the ferry could run up the river at all. The small steamer ferry's draft was deeper than the government barge's, but the trip was much quicker these days, taking only an hour or two instead of most of the day. The breeze off the water was thankfully moist and quite cool compared to the stinking heat of the Parramatta summer days.

Charles stood at the gunnels with his arms around Sal. They were out of sight of the other passengers, or he would have stood more circumspectly. The amazing love he had for this woman still made his emotions race. Having both arrived as convicts, he first saw her among a line of convict women assembling for assignment. She stood out from them as she had managed to wash her hair and clean herself. Their eyes met, and both froze. Ned Grace was with him, as was Jack Turner; they were walking with Ned as they had just been collected from their own convict lineup. Ned had been told he needed a housekeeper, and his friend, Perry, was looking for a maid. They had been together from that day.

Sal had been accosted on the way down to Ned's cottage soon after she started there. Charles would walk her down to the barracks, then meet her late in the morning and carry Ned's laundry home while escorting her back safely. They had married in February, only weeks after their arrival. Charles had been with her for the birth of all six children. She had nursed him through the year when he had fallen from the barn loft and broken his leg. It still ached and caused him pain. Although he could hide the limp most of the time, Sal knew. Sal always knew. Holding Sal as he was now was also to steady himself. Leaning on her meant he could take the pressure off his gammy leg. She never mollycoddled him but ensured a footstool or pillow was always handy. Every day, Charles brought her a token of his love. Sometimes, it was a beautiful feather, a flower, or a unique leaf. That token was placed in the middle of the kitchen table each day. It was how Sal showed her love and acceptance of his gifts.

Over the past twenty-eight years, Sal had tended to the needs of others. Before they moved into the inn, she discovered a void underneath. This was quickly converted to a hidden room and storeroom. Bunks, a wardrobe of clothing and some underclothing were placed in the drawers there. Word spread through her church group that any woman could come to see Sal if they needed a safe place of refuge. The first beaten woman arrived only weeks after the room was completed. She had a broken arm from the man who had claimed her. She had been violently abused. He had twisted her arm up behind her back, and it snapped. He then rearranged her looks with his fist before forcing his carnal desires on her. How she made it to their door, they didn't know. She could barely stand. The doctor had been brought in and attended to her. She remained hidden for weeks until she healed. Lachlan and Ned reassigned her out of town. Therefore, the doctor had been let into the knowledge of the secret room, and he soon brought more victims of domestic abuse. Ned, of course, had been involved in building the secret room.

Over the years, more and more came for refuge. Ned had a network of safe houses. Over the years, he weeded out the young and innocent convict girls and placed them in these venues before such harm had come to them. A friend's farm was down at Mulgoa, Barnes' farm halfway to Bathurst. There was, of course, Jack and Martha Turners' inn at Emu Plains. One special haven was Loganberry Farm at Yarramundi on the Hawkesbury River. This place was where Martha Turner had first found healing. More than thirty girls had received Hetty Walker's healing care since Martha. Ned sent more and more of them to Hetty; however, the need for convict placements diminished with the cessation of transportation.

From the first shipload of Irish girls that arrived, Sal sent some of the very timid Irish girls to Hetty and Loganberry Farm. Their work making baskets and bee hives was growing. They were sold in various stores, including The Scotch Shop at The Rocks near the wharf. This quirky store sold confiscated grog on behalf of the government. However, they had various other rooms dedicated to the assistance of various charitable groups. Hetty's baskets now filled one room, and another room was filled with ships' ropes and assorted chandlery made by the boys in Ricky English's orphanage. The family had taken an interest in this place soon after it opened. Ricky and Eddie had first met as children at school. Being an orphan himself, Ricky set about helping similar children. His mentor was a fabric importer, and Ricky English had been given the damaged bolts at cost price to finance the orphans. This tiny idea had grown into a fabric emporium and was now used for wholesale and retail. His mentor, John Landon, now had difficulty keeping stock in the store. Ricky's two adopted brothers had been through Howard and Naomi Marlow's boys' orphanage, but both had left early. Neither realised they knew each other from there.

Sal had asked Charles if she could buy a new picnic basket and heard they had double-lidded ones at the shop. As the ferry pulled in near the store, they should have time to do a spot of shopping. They may even be able to get to Ricky's fabric store.

Once the gangplank was down, Charles escorted Sal onto the jetty. The carriage from the Kings Arms Hotel was waiting nearby, and Charles hailed the driver for it to take them to the hotel. They had a standing arrangement at the hotel to use the carriage. Being an earl had a few perks, and using this carriage was one of them. With his gammy leg, he needed all the help he could get.

Mr Stewart found them a room, and even if they didn't stay often, the mere knowledge that the Earl of Coxheath was occasionally in residence was enough to bring in business for the hotel. The main suite upstairs was often vacant, so they settled in there until the carriage was available again to drop them off at the shops.

Word came through from the lighthouse that the *Christina* was running a little late. It would be some four hours before she made the heads. When the notification arrived, Charles and Sal headed off for their shopping trip. The first port of call was Ricky's English Emporium. The building became hot during the afternoon, so Sal was determined to purchase her fabric before her hands became too sticky.

After thirty minutes of choosing a selection of baby fabrics, brushed cotton, and a roll of wide white satin blanket-edging ribbon, Sal arranged for her purchases to be loaded into the carriage. The next stop was The Scotch Shop at The Rocks. Sal had only ever glanced at the many baskets that were now available for sale. Sal had her heart set on her picnic basket, but she fell in love with a small basket that would keep her knitting yarn clean.

Charles left the store with an enormous armload of assorted items. Sal got her baskets, and Charles purchased a long length of rope to make a swing for the children. Eddie had a mulberry tree that was perfect for a rope swing, and Charles was keen to put his tinkering skills to good use. Retirement for him had not been what he expected. Gone was the dawn-to-dusk business of both his inn and the government store, and now he had little to do. He loved tinkering.

They were about to return to the hotel when a livery-clad man approached them. Sal was already in the carriage, and Charles was about to step up when he was waylaid. The man was known to Charles, and his presence always meant that he would need to use his title. The Governor's Aide-de-camp was a nice chap, but this work was not always the sort that Charles liked.

The Aide-de-Camp gave the obligatory bow to the earl. "My Lord, His Excellency was wondering if you could spare a moment or two for an informal chat. Her Ladyship is, of course, included in the invitation." The Aide bowed again and ushered the earl and countess into the government carriage. The hotel carriage returned their shopping to their room. As the Governor's Viceroy, Charles was often called to perform some duty out Parramatta way or further west. For six years, he had been occasionally summoned for some task or another, from the opening of a building to stepping in at a function. Charles hated it, as did Sal, but they stepped up, donned their best clothes, took a deep breath and did their duty. Hopefully, this meeting will not take too long. Sal would leave Government House if word came that the ship had arrived. It was now due at one o'clock. The carriage dropped them at the front door of Government House. The stone porticoed entrance offered much-needed shade. They alighted and were escorted into the governor's office.

The governor, Sir Charles FitzRoy, apologised for dragging them in unannounced. "Charles, I would like to ask if you are interested in being part of the January regatta celebrations."

Charles's heart sank. He had been looking forward to a peaceful day with his family. He was wondering how he would escape the event when Sal intervened. "Sir Charles, as you probably know, we are awaiting the arrival of some of my Irish family. We were expecting the parents and some children. We learnt yesterday that the parents are dead and the two girls are arriving alone. Hence, we have no idea what state they will be in. His Grace, the Duke of Gracemere, arranged passage for them, but other than that, we won't know what is before us until they berth this afternoon." She heard Charles release an almost indiscernible sigh of relief.

The governor nodded understanding. "I did hear of the deplorable conditions many are having to endure. I thank you for assisting with the placement of that shipment of orphan girls that Earl Grey and his cronies sent us. I understand that you managed accommodation for most of the younger ones."

Charles nodded. "Yes, sir, they went to many of Ned's safe houses and some rectories." Charles knew that the governor had pinned Ned down the previous year and given a list of the venues where he had placed vulnerable convict girls. Hetty Walker's Loganberry Farm had taken more than its share, but they had room, and the youngest girls would be safe there. Jack and Bea's farm out on the Bathurst Road also took half a dozen of them. A few were sent to the Laceys at Mulgoa. The Middletons up in the Hunter Valley always needed nursemaids, so four more went to them to train and then find placements. Charles knew the governor had the list. "Sir, these two girls are family and will need us close by. Sal is all they have left, so we need to be nearby for them. Until we know what state they are in, may we ask to be excused from all but urgent cases?" Charles hoped that FitzRoy would acquiesce.

The governor rubbed his nose while thinking. A frown briefly crossed his brow. Eventually, he spoke. "Charles, if you think you can wiggle out of your share of these official duties, I'll be disappointed. However, I will excuse you from this one as I understand this tragic situation, so you win this time!"

Both Sal and Charles visibly relaxed.

The governor chuckled. "Will you have tea? The ship will be another thirty minutes, and my carriage will get you down there in good time." The governor had learnt the Lockleys liked their tea as most colonists did: hot, sweet and black.

Chapter 7   Overwhelming Arrival

The two girls stood on the deck of the *SS Christina*, watching the ship pass through the headlands. The sight was as awe-inspiring as Captain Saunders mentioned. The ship turned slightly southward as she entered the calmer waters of the harbour, and the crew dropped all her sails. The vessel's speed did not diminish much as she was under steam power. She powered on towards a bay on the southern side of the harbour and was soon met by the harbourmaster, Captain Moriarty, who greeted them from the pilot boat. Under his guidance, the *Christina* sided up to the wharf, and soon, the passengers were readying themselves to disembark. The girls had their case packed and were on deck as the vessel cast the thick ropes to the dockworkers, who slipped them onto the capstans on the jetty.

Kerry elbowed Clare, saying, "I won't point, but look at that man over there. He looks just like Uncle Ned. Do you think that is Uncle Charles?"

Clare followed the direction of Kerry's gaze. Sitting in the shade of a covered seat was an elegant-looking couple that looked surprisingly familiar. The lady also bore a striking resemblance to Aunt Christina. She said, "It has to be them; Uncle Ned said they would be here to meet us. He also said that Uncle Charles looked like him." Relief flooded over Clare. For the past months, she had borne the burden of responsibility. All of a sudden, it was just too much for her. She angrily swept a tear from her cheek. Another took its place, then another. Soon, they turned into a torrent of salty streaks running unchecked down her cheeks. Kerry embraced her weeping sister. She also knew the stresses they had both experienced, but Clare bore the brunt as the eldest. Much had been expected of her. If these people were their cousins, then that burden was now lifted. Kerry didn't hear the footsteps approaching. She was too busy comforting her sister. When a caring voice spoke from behind her, she saw a fair-haired lady under a wide-brimmed straw hat.

The lady asked, "Are you two, by any chance, the O'Shane girls?"

Kerry nodded. Clare sobbed harder. She glanced up and met the lady's lovely blue eyes and realised that this lady would most certainly care for them.

Her legs gave way as the turmoil of tangled emotions overtook her completely.

Charles had arrived with Captain Saunders, who, thankfully, was in time to catch her as she fell. He scooped the thin figure and, rather than sit her anywhere, carried her down the gangplank and placed her directly into the waiting carriage. Kerry and their cousins followed in their wake.

Charles and Sal fell behind a little, and he quietly said, "I think we may have some loving to do with these two. They have lost everything, and the elder one has obviously had a tough time coping. She seems somewhat overwhelmed that they made it safe and sound."

Sal nodded her agreement. "We'll get them sorted, and if they are up to catch the afternoon ferry, we'll get them home and settled as soon as possible. Thankfully, they will stay with Jenna and Eddie, but I will be nearby for them." After placing Clare in the carriage, Captain Saunders said he would send their luggage. He left the Lockleys to their family and returned to his ship. The coach took the family to the hotel, and by then, Clare had recovered somewhat. She was able to walk inside herself.

Mr Stewart saw her tear-stained face and took in the situation. "I'll send tea to your suite, Lord Charles." He bowed them in and called for a footman to escort them upstairs.

Charles expected more tears, and he hated weeping females. He may know the reason for them this time, but this did not make them any easier to cope with. He drew a deep breath and went to face the traumatised girls. They were family and now came under his umbrella of responsibility.

Clare, however, had shed the fear of not being met on arrival. This apparently had been worrying her because she was unaware that Captain Santray had sent a letter. With that burden lifted from her far too young shoulders, Clare finally relaxed enough to look around her. "I'm so sorry, Lord Charles, but I have been so worried about how to find you should you not have been here to meet us." Her delicate sniff showed that her tears remained unshed and not too far away.

Charles released a sigh of relief. He knew more would come, especially when it came to the retelling of their story. Sal and Jenna would be at hand by then. For now, they had to get to know each other.

Sal removed her hat and turned so the girls could see her face. "My dear girls, none of the Lord and Lady stuff. We are to be Uncle Charles and Aunt Sal. We are family, and as such, we will be here for you however you need us. When you are ready, you can tell us about the situation at home, but we will wait until you are more settled. In the meantime, we need to make decisions about today. We can either stay here for the night or catch the ferry home. It will only run for a few more years as they are putting a railway through to Parramatta."

The girls' eyes met, and with a barely indiscernible movement of their heads, they decided to leave. "Can we go home, please, sir?" Clare asked in such a way that she was unsure of herself.

Kerry nodded her agreement. "Will Captain Saunders look after our bag?"

Charles's heart had already been touched by Kerry's care for her elder sister. "Yes, dear, Mr Stewart downstairs will see to everything. I'll send a message and tell him to send it by road to Parramatta. We don't have room for you in our cottage, but you will only be across the road at our son's home. They have four little ones."

Clare's face brightened. "Uncle Ned said they have twins the same age as their oldest pair. We spent some wonderful days with them in Cornwall."

Kerry added, "We had brothers and sisters ourselves, but they all died. So we loved having little ones around us." A wave of sadness swept across her face as she thought about her missing family members.

Sal smiled, "Good because there are plenty of little ones in the family. Until you get to know them, you will mix them up. Most are fair-haired with big blue eyes and dimples, just like Ned's imps. Charlie has three, Eddie and Jenna four so far, Liza and Anna have two children each, as does Wills, although there are more on the way. Luke is our youngest, and he's not married, and he's off to university next year." The conversation focused on the Parramatta family until tea arrived. Charles sent word with the footman to send the girls' luggage to Parramatta, and they would catch the four o'clock ferry. That meant they had a few hours to pass before leaving.

Sal thought it might be an idea to drive around town before heading to the ferry. Once they had consumed the sumptuous afternoon tea repast, they gathered up their meagre possessions and left for a scenic journey around town. Sal's shopping and their carry-all bag would be sent with the girls' luggage. They stopped at a few stores and purchased fabric and sewing notions. The girls were both seen eyeing a bolt of fine white lawn fabric as they had not kept any of the stained material, as the others had a greater need. Christina had purchased new undergarments for them in Plymouth, which were the same fabric. They fingered velvets and damask silks but returned to the lightweight fabric twice. Sal noticed and ordered several yards to make new camisoles, drawers and night rails for the girls. She asked, "Can you both sew?"

They both nodded. Making these garments themselves would give them something to do in their idle hours. With an astonishing array of paper-wrapped parcels sitting on the carriage floor, the four occupants circled the waterfront. They drove along the trackway past Mrs Macquarie's Chair in the park east of the wharves. The lush green gardens and foreshore brought gasps of delight from the young Irish girls. They had left a decimated country filled with death and dying. Here was a land of sunlight and greenery. The greens were of a different shade, and the air smelled strange, but they gazed around them, drinking in all they saw. Charles and Sal gave a running commentary of everything they passed. The rum hospital, the mint, a library,

Sydney's Government House, wind and grain mills and numerous other buildings were there. When the carriage dropped them off at the waterfront, the Parramatta ferry awaited them. Their arrival at the ferry wharf was only five minutes before departure. The shops in that area would have to wait for another day. Their shopping was left in the carriage and would be delivered to Parramatta with their case.

The two girls clung together. Sal noticed their nervousness and waited until they were seated on the ferry before motioning for the girls to sit on either side of her. "Girls, I do have to warn you about a few things. Firstly, with Christmas just around the corner, the houses will be crowded with many family members and little ones. It's overwhelming for those who are new. However, although I was a little worried about this, I think it will benefit you in the long run. Everyone knows your family is coming, so they know who you are. With so many people around, you can hide away if you wish. However, everyone will also need to pitch in and help. At this time of the year, it's all hands on deck. Cara and her two girls will certainly appreciate any assistance in the kitchen and babysitting." She paused and wondered if she was asking too much. She noticed Clare's eyes fixed on her face with her mouth open. "Clare…?"

A timid voice replied. "You mean we won't have to sit around like lah-de-dah ladies?"

The lilt in her voice made Sal catch her breath. Her mother had sounded just like that. Sal chuckled. "No, sweetheart, here you can be yourselves. You are both part of the family, so nothing will be expected of you. Take time to find your places; the children will help you settle."

Both girls nodded. "We've always worked hard, Aunt Sal. Kerry and I talked about finding some work. Neither of us is happy to sit around and do nothing." Kerry was nodding her agreement.

Sal smiled at her words. "Let's wait until Christmas is over, and we'll see what happens. I have an idea, but we'll see how things play out. Just relax, settle in and have a bit of a holiday. Babysitting and childminding will be the number one thing we all need to do for the immediate future."

Both girls smiled.

Charles had been chatting with the skipper. "Ladies, as the wind is westerly, how about we all head to the bow and out of the smoke? Sal, how about we introduce these lovely lasses to our beautiful harbour?"

The four stood at the bow for the next two hours and admired the scenery. Charles pointed out various bays, birds, and points of interest.

The time passed quickly, and soon, the watercraft was approaching a wall of mangroves.

Kerry dug at Clare's ribs. "We're going to run into them, Clare!"

Sal heard her comment and pointed out that there was a break in the mangrove trees. The small craft moved steadily towards the trees, and they saw the passage ahead. The trip up the river didn't take long, and soon, they were pulling into the small jetty on the south side of the riverbank.

Two ladies and a bevy of small children were on the grassy embankment nearby. The infants were crawling or rolling on the green slope. Kerry watched a smile spread on the lips of her sister. It was the first genuine smile she had seen since leaving Uncle Ned and Aunt Christina's small children. Kerry slipped her hand into hers, and Clare's grin warmed her heart.

Clare said, "I think we'll be fine here, Kerry. Aunt Sal and Uncle Charles are so like Uncle Ned and Aunt Christina that I already feel at peace."

The welcome from the bevy of fair-haired children did more to relax the girls than anything else could have done.

By dinnertime, the girls had settled into their room and had much assistance in unpacking their case and the parcels they had purchased in Sydney. Eddie and Jenna's twins, Neddie and Tina, were so like Chip and Sarah that both girls often got their names wrong. Tina had slightly darker hair than Sarah, but all the children were a delight. At nearly seven, they were more assistance than either girl expected. Lily, at four, ooh'd and ahh'd over all the new clothes that were unpacked. Christina had packed the first half of the girl's trunk and added so many items that the girls had not seen. Their cabin had little hanging room, and they had only used the top articles and the warm clothing required on board. Christina had included muslin day gowns and cotton sun bonnets packed flat. There were shawls, scarves, wraps, and even some dancing slippers.

"Clare, how will we ever wear all these clothes?" Kerry was astounded by what the children passed out of the shipping trunk. Lily climbed into the big case and passed items out to the waiting helpers. The case was so large that the small child was more than waist-deep in the corner of the travelling case.

Much giggling occurred, and the five children were good friends by the time the case was empty. The five older ones tidied the room, and they had not long finished when a voice called them for dinner.

A knocking tap on their door was followed by Cara sticking her head into the room. "Finished, dear ones? *Dia duit agus fáilte.*"

Clare smiled and replied, "Thank you for the welcome, Cara. Can we help with something?" She knew Cara's words actually meant 'God bless you,' but were said as a welcome.

Cara said, "No, dears, but hello and welcome. I wondered if you spoke Gaelic; I see you do. Dinner is ready, and the roast is being carved now. Come along, little ones, and wash up." Cara led the three small children out of the room, and the two girls followed.

They realised that getting to know the routine would be the hardest.

Tina returned and took their hands. "Come on now. We have an indoor bathroom with running water."

Even wash-up time was great fun. Neddie waited outside the door and then escorted them into the large dining room. The lovely room was home to the most magnificent dining table set with shiny silver cutlery.

The girls gasped in unison.

Sal saw a flash of fear cross their faces, and she came to the rescue. "Dears, I'm sure Ned and Christina had you eat your meals with them in England. Don't worry about the fancy table. It has a story of its own."

The girls nodded mutely.

Sal continued, "We are rarely formal here, and family meals are somewhat rowdy. The children will teach you what you don't know, and please do not be afraid to ask. However, I will say if you are unsure of what implement to use, wait and watch. You will notice that the little ones do the same. We eat here most nights and help with the children, which saves me cooking. Cara, Paddy, and their family often join us, but for tonight, they are having their meal in the kitchen. They have seven children. The two oldest boys are farming out on Windsor Road. They are both married and rarely come to town. The three girls are in town. Maryanne works at Eddie's emporium and is married to Robert, and she was Christina's maid. He is the brother of our eldest daughter's husband, so in reality, they are all extended family. Moira and Shauna live here with Eddie and are the nursemaids when they are here, but they attend school during the day. Then there are their two youngest boys. But I will tell you about Shéamas and Liam later; they are about your ages. For now, take your seats, and we will say grace before we eat."

The meal was accompanied by as much chatting and laughter to make the girls comfortable. The last box they had brought had yet to be unpacked; it contained the cheeses.

After dinner, Moira and Shauna arrived and took the three youngest children off to be bathed and put to bed. This left the girls with the four Lockley adults. Sal seated herself on the settee between both girls. She wished to be close at hand for them. Now would be the time that they needed to share the harrowing story of the past year. Knowing what was to follow would be traumatic, Sal was determined to ease their journey by retelling it. A cuddling hug and a friendly shoulder would do wonders. The saga began to unfold.

The retelling was all that Sal expected and more. Charles, Ed, and Jenna sat in spellbound silence as each family member's trials, traumas, and tragic ends unfolded. What these two girls had endured in the past eighteen months was more than most people would face in a lifetime. Even Eddie, who had not shed a tear in years, found his eyes wet. He caught Jenna's eye and met the tragic smile she gave him. Yes, they would do all they could to ease the path for these two cousins. By the time the household settled down for the night, the girls had offloaded their burdens and distributed most of the mail they had brought with them. They had one more long screed to hand deliver, and that was to Kit Kellow, Jennifer Williams's son. During the evening, Shéamas and Liam Connor were mentioned once or twice. The girls had yet to meet them but knew they worked near Kellow's dairy.

Clare refused to hand over Jennifer's letter to her son as she had promised to deliver it personally along with the cheeses they had brought.

After breakfast, Shéamas and Liam arrived and met the new girls. Shéamas was four months older than Clare and Liam, two months Kerry's senior. At fifteen, the older pair eyed each other warily. Shéamas knew she had a letter for Kit, and he offered to deliver it for her. He didn't want to take time off work to escort her across the fields to their farm.

Clare noticed the teenage boy's rude face. "Thank you, Shéamas, but I promised Jennifer I would give it to him personally. I will do that as soon as possible, as I also have more news and things from home." The large cheese wheels still needed to be delivered. Sal had taken possession of their one.

Shéamas grunted an intelligible reply, swung around, and marched out the door, muttering to himself.

Cara stood watching her second youngest son and his apparent rudeness. "Well-I-never, love. He's not been rude like that before. Never you mind, we'll find some way of working out a way for you to deliver your letter."

Jenna arrived in the busy kitchen and found the two girls helping Cara wash the breakfast dishes. Both were enfolded in oversized calico aprons and were chatting merrily with Cara. "Girls, Mama Sal said she and Dar are coming over later, and we will go for a drive around town. She knows about the letters and cheeses you have from Jennifer, and we'll go via Kellow's dairy. Dar has his nose in the long screed from Uncle Ned, and it will take some days before he's digested all that information, so he won't come. Eddie has gone to work, and the girls will watch the children for a while. They are taking the day off school for me today."

The trip around the town was eye-opening for the two Irish lassies. The horrible, never-ending noise turned out to be an insect called a cicada, and the grey-green of the trees was accompanied by an almost pungent smell in the air as the temperature rose. They learned this scent was the eucalyptus oil from the gum trees that the summer heat extracted from the leaves.

Sal explained that the oils were volatile, and the air almost self-combusted some summers, sending bushfires raging through the scrubby bushland. "In the old days, the local aboriginals used to burn sections of the bush so that there were intermittent firebreaks all the way to the mountains. The regular burning off has decreased significantly since the farmers have cleared much of the area along this wide plain, hence the bushfires.

Although it was only nine o'clock in the morning and the perspiration was already dribbling down the backs of the two girls, Kerry exclaimed, "You mean it gets hotter than this, Aunt Sal?"

Nonchalantly, Sal replied, "Oh yes, dear. Today is warm but not overly hot. When the candles melt in the sconces, and the birds fall out of the trees with the heat, you know it's a bad day. Some summers, even the flying foxes fall dead from their roosts."

The girls looked at each other in horror about foxes with wings.

Sal continued, "It will probably only get to about eighty degrees today, but we often take shelter in the basements when it tips over one hundred. Even then, the space heats up with so many bodies. We have no ice here and no safe place for the ladies to swim, but we keep a large hip bath of water in the basement for the children and the big claw foot bath in the washroom full, so we can take a dip and cool off if we wish."

Before they left home, the girls watched as Jenna and Paddy quickly put the stallion into the harness and then reversed him into the buggy shafts. The awesome beast nuzzled Jenna's cheek and all but kissed her as he did so. Jenna chuckled. "It's hard to believe that many are fearful of the black giant. He's a warmhearted animal but will protect us if someone tries to hurt us. Come and meet him." Jenna had made the girls stroke both sides of his muzzle and let him sniff in their scent. After each, he threw up his head and whinnied. It was like he was saying hello and accepting them as family.

She provided the girls with large straw sun hats and parasols that kept the sun from their fair skins. With a gee-up, she capably drove the magnificent black horse off up the roadway. The small carriage took off up the hill. She saw Clare's gaze on the black stallion. "His name is James, you know. He's the biggest show-off. He has a natural high-stepping gait and needs no tight rein to make him hold his head high. He's Eddie's pride and joy. Some people tight-harness them to make them prance as he does, but James does it because he wants to." Jenna obviously also adored the big black stallion. With him pacing along the dusty roads, they all enjoyed the views.

Sal described what they were passing, saying that they went through the main street of Parramatta and up to the top of town. The journey in the open buggy at least meant that a breeze blew over them, so their perspiration evaporated in the heat. They pointed out Roseneath and that it was a family home owned now by Wills and Cathy. The beautiful house didn't look large from the front but had six main bedrooms and more for staff quarters. They didn't stop, as the house was currently only staffed by one maid and a groom who lived above the stables. The family would arrive in the next few days.

They returned to the town centre, and Jenna turned into a vast grassy area. On the top of this sat a white house. "This is old Government House girls," she said as she entered the grounds.

Sal said, "This time last year, the governor, his wife, and son were heading out to Eddie's place. The horses were too fresh, the beasts took off, and the carriage overturned just near the big tree we passed. Sadly, Lady FitzRoy was killed instantly, and their son sustained minor injuries, but their aide-de-camp, Charles Master, sustained fatal injuries. He succumbed at seven o'clock that night. He was a friend of ours and had recently become engaged. So, our family were heavily involved after the accident. My Charles was one of the first on the scene. Our younger daughter, Anna, had witnessed the accident and come to tell us. It was a day of horrors." She fell silent until they had passed the area. As Jenna drove up the hill towards the lovely white house, Sal continued. "The governor moved to Sydney soon afterwards and rarely, if ever, returns. I believe that there are now termites eating the house from the inside out. It's so sad as we enjoyed many a dinner there."

They passed the now-empty house that sat alone on the hill. The grass was long, right up to the front door. There were a few missing shingles on some outbuildings' roof, and the edifice's neglect in the twelve months was evident to Sal. There was green mildew on the once-pristine whitewashed southern walls, and a pane or two of glass had also been broken. Gone were the bevy of staff usually bustling around keeping everything ship shape. The ghostly house sat neglected, a memorial to the former glory of bygone years.

The white building slowly passed from view as the carriage proceeded along the dusty road. The next thing to come into sight was an odd-looking half-sunken building. Jenna took over the description of this. "Girls, this is where Jennifer Kellow was first assigned. This is the Government Dairy. It was here that she changed the cheese-making history of the colony. She taught Betty Eccles, Captain Piper and his wife, Doctor Harris, and others followed. They learned how to make really good cheeses. Until Jennifer came, the cheese made here was good for convict rations but little else. She refined the process and brought the know-how into the colony. From 1820, it became a sought-after commodity. You could even say that Jennifer spawned the dairy cheese-making industry, which, only twenty-eight years later, is now a thriving business for exports. Sadly, I never met her, but Mama Sal did, and they have stayed in contact. Uncle Ned was still here then, too, and he had been assigned to take particular care of Jennifer, but I suppose you know all that? When her son, Kit, returned, Dar and Mama Sal helped him settle back into the farm. On the way out, Kit met and married his wife, Kitty."

The girls nodded. Ned and Jennifer had related their connection and how Ned had made friends with Duke Felix, who was now Jennifer's brother-in-law and had assisted in sponsoring her in the dual-country endeavour. That was why the girls brought the new cheeses. This was the best way to transport the new culture. It was a long story, but the girls wanted to meet Kit Kellow. He was born here in Parramatta shortly before her fiancé, Billy Williams, arrived. They had married only weeks after Kit's birth. Knowing he was illegitimate, life in England became unbearable, and Kit returned here to take over the dairy.

The girls were still somewhat in awe that they knew two dukes and had a cousin who was an earl. Uncle Charles was in no way scary, as he had enfolded them in a loving hug and warmly welcomed them to the ever-expanding family. Although the Lockleys had six children themselves, Charles and Sal were forever offering hospitality to anyone who needed it. The two girls were merely the latest to be absorbed into their family. Harry Harlow was one of Wills's friends, and when he married Jenna's sister, the middle

Turner sister, he had become like a fifth son.

At the dinner last night, the meal had been interrupted by a lady whose husband had beaten her up. It was now well known to the community that Charles and Sal offered a place of sanctuary for women. The centre cottage, next door to them, was set up as a safe house for such women. For over twenty years, they had managed to keep the presence of their safe room quiet until not long before Eddie had married. Charles had been accused of selling grog on a Sunday. This was a lock-up offence, and he had been taken to court. It was only there that two witnesses stepped forward as character references. One was Rev Marsden, and the other was Rev Cowper. Both knew of Charles and Sal's work and spoke out in court for them. Ned had been prepared to do likewise, but his words as a major did not carry as much weight as the two clergymen. The case, however, outed the secret safe room. Husbands knew where to find their wives, and the space under the inn had been converted back into a storeroom. It did house a large wardrobe of spare clothing, and the bunks remained, but they were rarely used. Since the purchase of the cottage next to Charles and Sal, this had been turned into a women's craft house and workroom for charity. One room was used for stock and storage, and one room was set up for emergency accommodation. With the earl only next door, the abusing husbands were not prepared to meet the chastisement of the illustrious gentlemen, and they kept well away.

The buggy stopped at the most beautifully kept building they had seen since leaving Eddie's house. A tall, well-dressed man appeared and introduced himself as Kit Kellow. His smile was welcoming, and Clare could not help but return it. Although they had not met, it was as though they knew all about him. Kit had been sent to the top schools in England under the protection of his uncle Felix. His unfortunate start to life as the illegitimate son of a baron had in no way stopped the way he faced life. He had used his mother's married name and attended school as Christopher Williams. Only when he neared adulthood did he decide to return to the family dairy here and live in Australia.

Clare had handed over the fat letter from his mother and the cheeses and the next few hours passed quickly. Kit's wife, Catherine, known as Kitty, took Kerry on tour and showed her the ins and outs of cheese making. They had been shown around the dairy, and Clare could see Kerry quickly becoming interested in learning the trade. Clare sat talking to Kit and relayed the news from home. Kit drank in every story as she happily related the activities of his siblings and cousins. He had made no attempt to read or even open his letter. He knew he could ask for more information later as the girls were not leaving town. They stayed for some hours and only made a move to leave when Jenna mentioned that she needed to return home for luncheon.

Chapter 8   Making a New Home

Six months after arriving, Clare and Kerry attended the local school with Moira and Shauna to catch up on their missed education. They were asked if they might like to move to Roseneath and help Wills and Cathy care for the lovely house. Shortly after they arrived, the second maid that had been at the house had left, and the beautiful home sat nearly empty.

It had been a hard decision, but Cathy and Vicky needed someone to assist with caring for the children when they came to visit. This was now frequent. If Harry or Wills needed to head off on a trip somewhere, the families came to stay at Roseneath for the duration of their absence. Neither Clare nor Kerry had wished to leave the loving care of Jenna and Sal, but Shéamas had made living at the house almost untenable. He had taken to teasing Clare with every opportunity he had. He pulled her hair frequently, and he once tripped her up, only to catch her before she hit the ground. He would pinch her bottom or stand too close in a doorway, so she had to squeeze past him. Once, he had even kissed her neck and then sniffed her hair, making inappropriate comments. His actions always occurred when no one else was around, so although she pushed him away, she remained silent about his atrocious behaviour. She did not dislike him, but his actions were immature. Clare did not know what to do, so when the chance to work at the house at the other end of town came up, she took it.

Shéamas was too good-looking for his own good. Before he started the teasing, Clare would blush when he was near, but his recent treatment of her made her uncomfortable. She still liked him, but his treatment of her was borderline insulting. Kerry refused to let her move alone, so the decision was made to take the first step into a new life. Clare had just turned sixteen, but no one realised but Kerry.

Their move to the house in O'Connell Street occurred mid-winter. The buggy was too small for the mountain of possessions they now owned, the inn wagon was harnessed, and the big draught horse was loaded with their large shipping case and numerous bags and boxes of other items they had obtained since their arrival. Jenna and Sal had outfitted them in style. The only other person at Roseneath was Brodie Murphy. He had also just moved in, and at eighteen, he was in charge of the gardens and stables. He was capable and a hard worker, but he only had eyes for Shauna. He was not old enough to marry and had barely spoken to her. But he was always nearby when she and Moira visited after classes. Brodie's interest was gentle and respectful. It was nothing like how Shéamas treated Clare. His rudeness was annoying and downright irritating. His younger brother Liam was showing interest in Kerry. He, too, was gentle and caring. His hand would linger on Kerry's for a fraction longer than necessary, and when he lifted her down from a horse or a carriage, he would keep her a little too close to him. Liam never attempted to kiss or touch her in any other way, and Kerry didn't mind his attention at all, even though his actions were slightly inappropriate. However, both Moria and Clare could see that their sisters liked the men and each other. Cara's husband, Paddy, had already read Liam and Brodie the riot act and forbidden any inappropriate relationship from developing without permission.

Brodie abided by Paddy's decision, knowing that he was too young to marry without permission from his father, Finn, as well as Shauna's papa. He was near her, and therefore, he was content. He hoped he would one day be permitted to approach her father and gain permission to court her. Brodie felt that not much courting would be required.

Clare often caught Shéamas smiling to himself, but he would grin at her and then proceed with what work needed doing. Unfortunately for Clare, Shéamas and Liam were also friendly with Brodie, and the boys began to visit more frequently. Clare often made herself scarce during these times, but Kerry and Liam would be found working together in the gardens or stables while the two older boys were talking.

~

1849 faded into 1850.

The summer that year brought the first bushfires the girls had seen.

Now seventeen, Clare officially finished her education. She saw the affection between Liam and Kerry grow into a new form of contentment for them both. They sought each other out as often as possible and were content to be seen doing the various chores required to keep house. They always remained in sight of either Brodie Murphy or Clare and never pushed the boundaries of propriety. Shéamas, though, continued to torment Clare whenever possible. It was a forced touch when passing something from the continual gentle tugs of her plaited hair, but never enough to hurt her. Occasionally, he even patted her on the bottom. He never missed a chance to annoy her. Clare often flashed her temper when they were alone.

Liam and Brodie would pitch in to do the heavy cleaning and work. Shéamas, on the other hand, became more surly and to Clare's way of thinking, even to the point of obnoxious. Twice recently, he had tried to kiss her, and each time, she had managed to avoid his advances, both incidents leaving her shaken. He was so good-looking that she couldn't drag her eyes from him, but he gave her no respect. Again, his timing was perfect from his point of view, as no one had witnessed his actions.

Liam and Brodie would have called out his behaviour, but neither had seen any of the incidents.

Clare remained silent.

Liam would climb ladders to clean the crystal lamps if Kerry even mentioned they needed doing. He and Brodie would lug buckets of coal and help sweep the chimneys when required. Shéamas just stood and watched her, brooding. Clare knew when his eyes fell lustfully on her. If the others were busy, he would blow her a kiss or manoeuvre himself so he was touching her. She avoided him now as often as possible.

~

One afternoon, late in summer, just before the family arrived, Shéamas arrived early from the dairy. For once, Clare was alone as Kerry and Brodie had gone to stock up on food for the forthcoming week.

Shéamas did as he usually did and entered via the back kitchen door. What he saw horrified him. He had been hoping to catch Clare alone and sit and talk over a mug of tea, but what he saw made his blood run cold.

Clare was pushed up against the kitchen sink and was fighting to be freed from the arms of a filthy man. Shéamas had come to steal a kiss, but seeing the girl he liked struggling against an attacker made him throw caution to the wind. The man was making so much noise, as was Clare, who was crying out in protest. Neither heard nor saw Shéamas as he crossed the room and picked up the cast iron frypan from beside the fire.

With one thwack of the iron pan, the man was soon inert on the floor.

Clare stood frozen, gazing at the fallen man.

Shéamas felt his heart racing, but he, too, could not move. The room was silent but for the tap dripping and crackling of the fire.

Clare finally lifted her tear-filled eyes to his. "Thank you, Shéamas, thank you so much."

Shéamas had no memory of dropping the pan or crossing the room and reaching out for her. However, Clare soon was where he had wanted her to be for over a year. "I couldn't let him hurt you, my sweet girl." He drew her into his arms and held her as she wept. He lovingly stroked up and down her back, and this was comforting. For once, he revealed his feelings. "Oh, my Clare, my dearest girl, I could not let anyone hurt you ever."

Clare's weeping stopped, but she did not pull away from him. His words had stunned her. She had no idea that he liked her. The handsome man suddenly seemed to turn into the man she had wanted him to be.

Shéamas found his tongue now loosened; the words he had bottled up for so long soon flowed. "My dear, dear one, when I came in and found you struggling in his arms, I was ready to explode. You are mine and mine alone, but dear heart, I am not good with words. I don't know how to show you I care and know that I have annoyed you. Tell me you forgive me, dear heart. Please say you care for me, even a little bit."

Both were still looking towards the prostrated figure on the floor rather than each other. The man was breathing and not bleeding, so they did not attend to him more than ensure he remained still. She nodded.

Shéamas felt her head give a gentle nod against his chest. "You mean you don't mind that I care?"

Clare finally lifted her eyes to him. "I don't mind at all, Shéamas. I like you, but I am so confused. I watch Brodie with Shauna and how caring he is to her. I watched Liam with Kerry; he was always willing to help her with anything, and all you ever did was tease me or pull my hair. My little brother, another Liam, by the way, used to do that to me before he drowned. I hurt with confusion, Shéamas." She put her head back against his chest. The smell of the dairy herd was still in his clothing, but the aroma of his shirt was comforting.

He was about to say more when the sound of the cart was heard coming into the yard. Brodie would be needed to help take the man down to the authorities. Clare reluctantly drew from his arms. "I won't kiss you, Clare, but know that I'm here for you. We're too young to be betrothed, but I'll wait for as long as I must."

At his words, Clare's eyes dropped, and she blushed. "Really, Shéamas? You care that much?"

Shéamas chuckled. "Really! Clare, my love, I certainly do." This is not how he expected the visit to occur. The outcome was, however, much better than he could have dreamed. His words had been released and willingly received. His heart was all but dancing. "Go and bring Brodie in and get some rope, love."

Clare left the room with a spring in her step that had been absent for over two years. Even the evil man on the floor and his accosting of her had brought a smile to her face. She almost felt like bending and thanking him, but she passed by him, well out of his reach, just in case he was acting and would grab at her.

Brodie and Kerry had just pulled up when Clare met them at the stable gate. With a quick explanation, Brodie grabbed a length of rope from the stables before heading indoors. The girls set about unloading the stores next to the gate while the men dealt with the problem inside.

Shéamas and Brodie soon had the unresponsive man trussed like a chicken ready to be roasted. They manhandled him outside and dumped him on the grass while they helped unload the huge sacks of food. There were some enormous bags of dry goods, and they rested these against the wall.

They roughly placed the still, unresponsive man onto the cart's bare wooden boards and tied him to the seat's base for good measure. They were still unsure if he was playing them for fools. With him now secured onto the wagon, they promised to return as soon as possible and assist with the food storage.

For once, Clare was bubbling with joy. She explained to Kerry what had occurred and how Shéamas had come to her rescue. Considering the number of times Clare had previously complained about the man, Kerry stood open-mouthed at her sister's obvious delight at the afternoon's occurrence. "But Clare, you hated him!"

Clare shook her head with absolute assurance that she meant her words. "No, I just didn't understand him. I have always liked him, and as you know, I have always said he was too handsome for his own good. He teased me mercilessly, prodding and poking me until I twice slapped him for trying to force a kiss. But oh, Kerry, I was so wrong about him. He said he just was too shy to show he cared the way Liam does for you." Her voice sounded dreamy.

Kerry shook her head, amazed at her sister. It was as though she had not just been violently accosted. A few words and a big hug had banished that from her thoughts. Kerry heard her humming happily as they worked. The stores were slowly brought inside, and only the massive sack of flour, some other bags, and barrels of dry goods were left beside where the cart had pulled up.

The work done, the kettle was soon on the boil on the large stove. Four mugs were placed, ready to be filled with the hot, sweet brew when they returned. Clare had become used to drinking this hot concoction, even on a scorching summer's day.

One hour passed, then two.

The girls wondered what had become of the two men when more footsteps approached through the stable yard. Thinking it was them, Clare flew out the back door only to be met by a uniformed police officer.

He looked at the flushed face of the young lady before him. "Sorry to startle you, miss, but I've come to take your statement. We have the man down at the office, and I need to obtain your report of today's incident to corroborate their story. Mr Shéamas Connor said that you were being accosted when he arrived?" The frown on the officer's face showed Clare that he did not believe her.

Fearful and wondering if this man was, in fact, whom he claimed or if he was masquerading as an officer, Clare reversed back into the kitchen, and the officer followed her. Kerry came to her side, and the officer waved them to take a seat at the table while he took notes.

Once seated on the other side of the table, the man pulled a notepad and pencil from his pocket.

Clare relaxed and proceeded to retell the earlier incident but left out the romantic side of Shéamas's visit. She said he was a family friend coming to assist with the stores, but that was all. Apparently, he had said something similar, although, by the look on the officer's face, Shéamas may have added some more details. She blushed, thinking about the hug and his words.

One of the officer's eyebrows raised, and he looked at her as though he knew she was not revealing everything. "Miss, is there something you're not telling me?"

Clare shook her head, but it changed to a nod. "It's true, sir; Shéamas found me struggling and trying to escape the horrible man. However, after he had knocked the man out, Shéamas hugged me, sir. That's all, nothing more happened, but I was upset, and I've known him for ever so long, and he comforted me. We lived with Uncle Charles and Aunt Sal Lockley's family since we arrived, and Shéamas's parents lived there, too. So I saw him most days. Honest, sir!"

The tear-filled pleading eyes were enough to make the tough officer wish to hug the beautiful girl. "Now your stories tally, so all is well. What you do not know is that the man was black and blue by the time he arrived at my office. He had tried to escape and had managed to get the rope that held him to the cart around young Shéamas's neck.

Clare gasped, and her face blanched and felt faint. "Nooo! Is he all right?"

Kerry grabbed her hand.

The officer jumped up and went to her side. "Now don't you go passing out on me, miss. Your young man is fine; only we had to take him to the hospital to make sure. Young Brodie Murphy gave the beast a left hook, and another followed it to his right eye. When the convict released Shéamas, the pair of them laid him out good and proper, and he came off the worse for his attempted escape. However, both young men are a little war-weary. Brodie has four stitches in his lip, and Shéamas is being held at the hospital under observation. Shéamas's mother and sister are attending to them, and Liam has come with me to finish the work they had left undone."

When Liam's name was mentioned, Kerry's face brightened. The observant officer, too, did not pass this by unnoticed.

The officer said, "Brodie said there are a few bags to be brought in before Wills arrives tomorrow. I said I'd help the lad bring them in; hence, we arrived by the rear entrance. Sorry, miss!" He noticed the girls' astonishment. He explained, "Wills and I were lads together at The King's School. I've known him for many years. I also know what his parents have done for the town." After tucking his notepad back into his pocket, he noted Kerry was comforting Clare, so the officer gave a slight bow and took his leave. He and Liam returned only minutes later carrying an immense bag of flour. A few other items were quickly stored, and the officer took his leave.

The afternoon was not yet over.

Liam had been late, as, without Shéamas, the milking had taken a little longer. He had come as soon as he could. The three of them stood in the kitchen and wondered if they should stay or go and see how the men were.

Carriage wheels were heard on the road outside, and then they stopped. Wills and Cathy had arrived a day early.

As Clare, Kerry, and Liam exited the house, Cathy jumped out and said, "Something has happened, hasn't it?" Clare nodded. Cathy didn't wait for an answer but turned to her husband in the driver's seat. "See, Wills, I said we needed to come today."

Wills nodded. "I know, dear; that's why we are here." In the years he had known her, Cathy's intuition had never been wrong.

As Liam went to the horses' heads, the two girls assisted the children. Aged only three and two, Lukie and Pip were tired, angry and sick of sitting still. Tilda was eight months old and content to coo at everything that went on around her. Her toothy smiles were a delight to Clare, and she dived to claim the baby. "Yes, Cathy, something happened, but it's all sorted. The officer had just left after taking my statement, and we were wondering if we should go down and see the boys. I'll tell you when we get these three sorted."

Cathy ushered her sons inside, and Liam took them out to the backyard for a run and to give the horses some apples and carrots.

Wills drove the carriage around to the backyard, and he and Liam attended to the animals' needs while the three women carried the baby and luggage inside. They chattered while they worked.

Clare revealed the day's happenings, but again, she left out the revelations that Shéamas had made to her.

Wills had just come inside carrying Pip when another vehicle was heard stopping outside. Wills recognised the voice of his parents and went to investigate. Knowing they were not due until the following day, he wondered why they had come. On exiting the building, the sight made him gasp.

Brodie and Shéamas were a sorry sight. Brodie had a line of stitches holding his wounded mouth together, and Shéamas was black and blue with a rope line around his throat. He gingerly alighted from the conveyance and stood somewhat unsteadily. He laughed and said with a lopsided grin, "The other bloke looks a lot worse than we do."

Clare heard Shéamas's voice and came flying out the door and straight into his arms. They were open and waiting for her. "I'm okay, love, truly I am. If you think we look bad, you should have seen him when we'd finished. No one touches my girl and then tries to escape, but, sweetie, he fought like a madman. It turns out he was an escaped convict who had been living in the bush for over a decade."

The embracing couple was oblivious to the stunned stares of the family around them. They only broke apart when Paddy said, "Shéamas, you are in full view of everyone, laddie."

Shéamas's father, Paddy, assisted Brodie from the seat and escorted them into the kitchen. The reins were flicked around the hitching rail, and the group followed Brodie and Paddy inside.

Clare moved from under Shéamas's arm but escorted him inside, away from the prying eyes of a convict chain gang just approaching.

Convict transportation may well have ceased, but chain gangs for road construction were still needed. Many of these men were serving life sentences. These groups passed the house door twice daily, and this gathering of exhausted, bedraggled men was returning to the prison.

As the house's front door closed behind Shéamas, he hoped he would get a chance to hug Clare again. Now that they were out of the view of the convicts and soldiers, Clare turned to him and went into his arms again. She didn't draw close but said, "Are you sure you are all right?"

Shéamas could not believe the change in their relationship in such a short time. His bandaged knuckle brushed the auburn tendrils of hair from her cheek. "I will be fine, love, but I never want to have another day like this. First, I thought I had lost you; then, I thought he would kill me before I could even give you a first kiss." Without waiting for her reply, he bent and kissed her upturned face. "That will have to do, sweetheart, as my lips are a little the worse for wear, but I will see if I can get permission from my father and Lord Charles to see if we can at least court. I'm not permitted to marry until I'm eighteen, but that's only months away, and that is only with my father's permission. I have a good job at the dairy, and I've even been offered the job as the head stockman on the government farm."

As no one had appeared, he quickly kissed her lips again.

Cathy had realised what was occurring in the corridor, but she had given them enough time to have a reunion after their trying ordeal.

Brodie felt sorry for himself while sipping a big mug of sweet black tea with Wills, Liam, and Kerry.

Cathy reappeared and said, "Enough children!" She chuckled. "Yes, yes, I know you are both nearly eighteen, but you are not courting yet, so hands off, please, Shéamas."

Clare stepped back from his comforting arms. "Come on, let's have tea." She took his hand and gently squeezed it as they walked.

Chapter 9   Fire

$\mathcal{T}$wo months after the December day when Clare had been attacked, Shéamas had turned eighteen. He was finally permitted to court Clare.

Charles gave Shéamas consent to ask Clare when she came down for Sunday luncheon at Eddie's house. With all the family around, the new couple would be well escorted by all the children. However, Shéamas grabbed her hand and pulled her to the yard's far corner. He managed to duck behind the trunk of the large mulberry tree in the backyard, and Shéamas stole a proper kiss there. Although taken unawares, Clare found her arms snaking up and around his neck. His kiss deepened as he drew her close to him.

The sound of young giggles above broke them apart. "Why is Shéamas eating Clare?"

Clare almost jumped out of his arms. She was blushing adorably and was now quite flustered. "Oh, Shéamas, that was nice. Really nice," she said softly.

Shéamas's heart was thumping with anticipation. "I came to ask you officially if you would court me. Lord Charles has finally given permission, as has Papa."

Clare was delighted. She was hardly able to contain her joy but asked, "Truly? We can officially be a couple?" She gave a small shout of glee and threw herself back into his arms. "Yes, of course I will."

The children clustered around the new couple, and Liam and Kerry soon joined them. They reluctantly broke apart. Nearly a dozen fair-haired children were running around the yard, and soon, a hide-and-seek game was underway. Climbing the tree was out of bounds. The younger children were paired with older ones, and the afternoon passed with much laughter.

Charles and Sal came over after luncheon and sat under the shade of the big tree. It was nearly as cool outside as down in the basement. As the dishes were done, others meandered outside and joined the happy throng.

Throughout the afternoon, the new couple managed a couple of sly kisses behind the large tree trunk, but after being caught each time, Paddy read the riot act. Shéamas was told to treat Clare as the lady she was.

It wasn't until later that Jenna subtly took them aside and told Clare the etiquette and rules of courtship that Shéamas had the courtesy to look embarrassed. Jenna said, "Clare, in the colony, things are a little more relaxed here than in London, but Shéamas, you should know already that courting does not permit kissing or sneaking away for private rendezvous."

Clare gasped and looked at Shéamas, somewhat guilty. "I'm sorry, I had no idea, Jenna. What are we permitted to do?"

Jenna gave Shéamas a frown of disapproval. She knew full well that he understood the etiquette of courting. "Ahh, well, that's where it becomes difficult. As you live at Roseneath and are now courting officially, Shéamas shouldn't be permitted up there without a chaperone. Kerry is fine to do this, but she must always remain with you. Even Brodie is suitable, but no sneaking off for secret meetings. If this proceeds to an engagement, you will only be permitted to kiss her demurely and even dance with her more than twice at a public dance. Dancing three times once engaged is the maximum limit at a community event until marriage. Family gatherings are different, but we're not planning one of those for a while."

The guilty look that passed between the young couple spoke volumes.

"May I hold her hand?" Shéamas asked Jenna.

Jenna's head shook. Her heart was hurting for them, but they needed to abide by the rules if they were to have a rumour-free romance. "No, not until you are engaged. She may walk on your arm, but you must have an escort."

The look on Clare's face spoke of her sadness. "How long do we have to court for? Are there rules around that, too?" It had been hard to ask, but she, no, they needed to know.

Jenna said, "That depends on your father, Shéamas. Paddy must give you written permission to marry as you are under twenty-one. Even though you are nearly the same age, the legal age for girls is only fifteen. Even though Mama Sal is her cousin, Dar is her legal guardian, as you know. That is why he has given permission to court her. Don't break his trust, Shéamas, and things may well proceed faster."

The couple nodded their agreement.

Although they found it hard for the following months, they stuck to the rules and no longer snuck off for a kiss. Liam and Kerry accompanied them on an evening walk when the families were not staying at Roseneath.

~

The winter months passed quickly.

Summer rolled around, and evening strolls were curtailed by smoke from the surrounding fires. A year passed in a flash, and now drought hit again. Christmas came and went, and in January of that year, a man died in a fire on the harbour's north shore. More fires threatened the towns and villages throughout the settled areas.

The rains stayed away. The air was so dry that Clare's nose bled.

In Parramatta, the first whiff of smoke caused the colony to panic. The previous year had been scorching, and although one fire had already occurred last year, none had threatened the towns; not so this one.

Then it happened!

The event that no one ever wished to see occurred on Saturday, February 6th. No one was sure if it was a cooking fire that escaped or if the scorching hot sun ignited some leaves. However, it started and soon spread.

Bushfire!

From the middle of Parramatta, the pall of acrid smoke was choking everyone.

Children were kept indoors in the already overheated houses. Those who ventured out had their faces covered with damp flannel cloths.

The fire seemed reasonably contained until the early afternoon when a breeze sprung up out of nowhere. With it came more danger. It turned the flames towards town. The grey bushfire smoke turned to plumes of bellowing black, and soon; the wind forced the fires closer to town. Tornados of the black clouds now carried live embers, and the winds carried these closer. As the twisters travelled towards unburnt areas, these soon caught alight, spreading the devastation.

Outlying farms were consumed by the flames one by one. The occupants did what they could to fight the fires, but wet bags and small coopered buckets of water were useless against the ravages of an all-consuming monster hot enough to melt the tin on the roofs.

The few remaining bark huts from days gone by were gone in a puff.

Crops, wildlife, and people perished. Soon, fire vortexes were visible from the top of the Parramatta hills and surrounding areas.

For hours, every able-bodied person, man, woman, and older child thrashed out the small spot fires that started in the long grasses near their homes. Only a miracle could save the town, and the lawless ex-convicts who dwelt there were unlikely to pray for one of those.

The God-fearing families were out in force, alongside the town drunks, the convicts from the chain gangs, and every other body that could carry a bucket from the river and bash out flames with wet hessian bags.

Roseneath was abandoned.

At the other end of town, Clare and Kerry were asked to keep the small children inside, preferably in Eddie's basement.

Down there, it was cool and reasonably smoke-free. However, this meant they had no idea what was happening outside. Kerry took charge of the little ones, and Clare stood watching with Sal and Charles on guard of the extended grassy area that led down to the wharf. Animals normally grazed this area, but lately, they had been allowing it to go to seed so the grass could regenerate. Now, they wished they had thought of slashing the knee-high dead paddock.

Eddie and Jenna's eldest lad, nine-year-old Neddie, was on watch with his nearly eight-year-old twin cousins. The three boys were well-versed in what to do but had never faced a fire like this. Even these strong boys were frightened by the wall of black smoke approaching.

At noon, they needed to light the lamps indoors so they could see. Outside, it was as dark as night, and the air was almost suffocating and the heat overwhelming. Yard by yard and mile by mile, the fire drew closer.

The red glow was no longer just on the horizon; it towered over the town. No one knew how many houses had burned, if the town would survive, or if people had perished.

While watching this trauma, Clare slipped between her cousins and took their hands. "Aunt Sal, can we pray for a miracle? I know God didn't send this, but He can send rain. Can we pray for a storm?"

Over her head, Charles's eyes met those of his wife. "Love, I think that we should do just that."

While holding hands, the three bowed their heads and begged for rain. They were sure that others were doing the same throughout the area.

All three looked up when they heard a shout of fire.

An ember had landed nearby, and the three boys ran to extinguish it before it took over the field. As fast as they hit the grass with their wet rags, another, then another, started. Hot glowing sticks and twigs were falling from above, and soon, the amount of these was getting out of hand. It was raining live embers.

Sal called for Clare and Kerry to join the boys and her in tackling the flames. They had only been at it for ten minutes when Liza's two boys joined them. With eight people now belting at the flames as they licked the tall grass, they now had a chance to win the epic fight. If this area caught alight, the entire town was in danger, let alone the family inn.

Charles was so angry that having re-injured his previously broken leg, he could not join in. Clare saw Sal take a moment and say to him. "Charles, it's up to you to keep the children quiet and safe. Only you can now stop them from panicking." She drew his head down and gave him a big kiss on the lips. "I love you, you big stubborn man. Look after the little ones, sweetheart." Then she was gone.

Liza had joined her father in caring for the children. Seven little ones under seven were a handful for anyone, and Charles was overwhelmed. Although he adored each one, and he could easily have coped with them upstairs, they were frightened in the almost darkness of the basement. All were not crying, and all he could do was hug them. It's what they needed. Soon, all sought protection in his arm.

Liza realised his distress, and rather than join her mother and cousins, she saw that her father needed her there. She brought more lamps and some storybooks and soon had her father reading to them.

With Liza and Charles caring for the children, Clare grabbed her bucket and bag and followed her sister. They had never seen fires like these before.

Soon, the eight of them were black from head to foot with soot, but they managed to stop every spot fire near the houses and inn.

Roseneath had been abandoned to God's care. If it burned, then it burned. But no one lived there permanently except Brodie and the girls. They had come to protect the cluster of family homes. The inn was the lifeblood of the family.

Eddie had already cleared the area around his blacksmith's forge as it regularly had small spot fires from his overheated fire-pit. Eddie's Emporium in town had a tin roof with no gutters and was kept debris-free due to the value of the stock inside. With a stone base, even if any grass did catch fire, it was unlikely that the building would burn. Robbie and Maryanne lived there, and he would be on duty with the other staff, minding that.

The huge fire raged for hours, circling the town.

By three o'clock, the children wanted to have a run, but the air was just too thick. Charles and Liza had their hands full, keeping them from all howling for escape.

Eventually, Sal said, "Fine, let them come upstairs and have a look from the top windows. It will start them coughing, and they will wish to escape back downstairs to the cooler area very quickly."

Her idea worked. The various small children and babies were permitted onto the top verandah to see the smoke themselves. After watching for only minutes, they did precisely as Sal expected. Nine-year-old Tina wished she was out helping her twin brother with the flames, but she realised she needed to help with her siblings. Lily, Kit, Nick, and baby Shannon all required attention. Her cousins, Emma and the baby, Molly Grace, both cried in fear. Shannon and Molly Grace needed feeding, but both were on the breast, and neither mother was nearby. Jenna and Gracie were threshing flames.

Sal eventually boiled some water and gave each a mug of cooled water. Although not nourishing, it hopefully settled them until their mothers' returned.

With the embers no longer falling, the eight weary firefighters returned from the paddock to get a drink and rest. All were sure their fight was not over yet. They went inside to have a long, cool drink when an almighty crack was heard.

Mugs were abandoned as they fled outside.

Had a tree fallen?

In the minutes since they had gone indoors, the temperature had dropped, and the smoke had lightened in colour.

Charles soon joined the group on the back verandah and asked, "Was that lightning?"

Sal didn't care that she was filthy and he wasn't. She snuggled to his side. "I think Clare's prayers have been answered, love."

Sure enough, the air around them was soon peppered by sooty raindrops. The hum of the droplets hitting the stable's tin roof was followed by a torrential downpour, followed by sheets of water.

The group sought shelter from the new torment and watched the debris come floating down the river as it rose.

With no chance of fire overwhelming them now, they each took turns cleansing themselves and having something to eat.

For an hour, the rains kept coming.

Soon, the sky lightened again, and the sun peeped through the darkened clouds. By six o'clock, the sky was clear, and the sun shone above as though to say, "See, I'm still here."

Charles and Liza permitted the children to come and watch the storm. When the rain stopped, the two babies were again awake and screaming for nourishment. With no milk at hand, Liza mashed some cold roast pumpkin and fed it to each child. Although their eyes were wide open, neither refused the gooey morsels placed into their screaming portals.

Orange mashed pumpkin oozed from their mouths, and they both cooed with delight at the unexpected consistency. Neither had ever had solid food before, and the other children were currently gorging themselves on sultana cake with lashings of butter.

Kerry and Liza managed to bathe and bed down all the children. Once the little ones were asleep, thoughts turned to the other weary firefighters. None knew where they had been fighting, but they had prayed for their safety.

The group of tired and weary adults were soon brought home on the back of a firefighter's wagon. None were injured, but all were filthy. Jenna and Gracie fed their sleepy babies before falling asleep in their soiled clothes.

Over the coming week, stories of many near escapes were reported. Many homes were lost, but there were stories of miraculous rescues and fires jumping overhead. No one seemed to have perished, but the houses, barns, and farms would take a long time to recover. No one would forget the trauma of the day.

Chapter 10 Courting Danger

*T*he week before Shéamas's nineteenth birthday, Paddy finally gave his approval for them to become engaged.

Shéamas had been promoted to head stockman at the Government Dairy, and this brought the promise of the cottage on the farm. He didn't move in, but in the spare hours, Clare, Kerry, and the ladies of the family set about redecorating it. They made blue gingham curtains and put cheesecloth on the windows to keep the numerous flies away.

The date for the wedding was set for Easter Monday, 21st April 1851, as all the family would already be coming together to celebrate that event.

Clare had a lovely muslin gown that Christina had purchased for her, which she had not worn. She also had the one she had made for the fabric purchased on the voyage out here. She was tossing up between the two dresses. She finally chose the lovely gown Christina bought for her in Plymouth. Sal purchased satin slippers to match.

Jenna and Cara had made a garland base, and all they had to do was pick fresh flowers and add them the day before.

Banns had been read, and the cottage was awaiting them. The family arrived for Easter, and the yard at the Jolly Sailor Inn was made festive and ready for the nuptial feast on Monday.

The Good Friday service was sombre, and the congregation left the morning service to spend a quiet day at home.

The children's laughter was hushed, and the day's topic was the events of so long ago with Jesus. Wedding plan discussions were put on hold until after three o'clock.

Tick tock, tick tock… the hours passed slowly.

At three, the large clock in the hallway chimed its resonating gong. Charles stood and quietly said, "It is finished!"

Everyone sombrely echoed with, "It is finished, indeed."

These words were said every year and were the final words of Christ on the cross.

With the words now spoken, the children gave a sigh of relief and were soon heading outside to run and play.

After the biblical discussion all morning, Clare and Kerry understood these words referred to the death of Christ on the cross over eighteen hundred years before. The meaning of Jesus's sacrifice and that He had taken our sins onto His shoulders when He died and rose again had been revealed to them not long after arrival. Sal had not inundated them with knowledge, but her faith and gentle beliefs in eternal life were fully explained. Her simple acceptance of the words of the Bible and that they were all true opened their eyes to a different side of the church and what it really meant. Kerry had felt the same. Life for the two girls was wonderful.

At home, they had spent most days on their farm digging potatoes with their father; here, they had duties, but they were minimal. Life was good.

Clare was looking forward to being married, keeping the house for Shéamas, and then becoming a parent if God blessed them with children.

Although they had gone to church at home with their parents, Father Patrick's services were in Latin. As children, his sermons did not make much sense to them as they didn't understand the language. Church services were an ordeal. Since they had come to live in Parramatta, the words of the Bible began to make sense. Services were in English, and the sermons brought the Bible to life. The Lockley family lived Jesus's words, and they made sense.

Charles's mother, Lady Elizabeth, and her second husband, Richard Childs, had taken the girls aside and explained their Christian faith. Richard was headmaster of the Female Orphan School, and Lady Elizabeth had the ability to make complicated things easy to understand. The girls adored her. Consequently, over the years, their faith had grown.

After Jenna's warning on the day that Shéamas asked to court her, they never slipped away again. Until they were engaged, he never did more than give her a chaste kiss on the cheek in view of his parents. Even their kisses after their engagement only occurred with someone waiting for them. He had never encroached more than he should, but Clare would see him watching her, and when their eyes met across a room, he would blow her a kiss and smile.

Shéamas had to help with the afternoon milking as some of the usual helpers were having a holiday over the Easter week. "See you at the cottage at four, sweetheart. I'll ensure that the dairymaid, Lavinia, who was permitted to stay in the cottage over the weekend, has gone. She said she only needed it for a night or two." He leaned over and gave her a quick kiss of farewell. He was running late and didn't delay his departure. The family knew this dairymaid had stayed a night or two in the empty cottage.

Liam followed and arranged to meet at the cottage when the milking was done.

At a quarter to four o'clock, Eddie and Paddy harnessed the two buggies, and the adults headed to the head stockman's cottage to take up some food for the future newlyweds' pantry. They drove past the abandoned Government House and noticed some new equipment piled in its backyard. It looked like work was about to commence on the repairs.

When they arrived at the cottage, they heard raised voices emanating from inside. Eddie, Charles, and Paddy made the ladies wait until they discovered what was happening. The three men hopped down the short path to the cottage.

The door was open, and Shéamas was inside arguing with the young woman who had been given permission to stay for the weekend while he was staying at Eddie's place. She was supposed to have gone.

The three stopped at the front door and were horrified at what they heard.

The teary female voice said, "But you are the father, Shéamas. I didn't do this to myself. You must take responsibility for your actions."

"How the hell can I be the father? I've never placed a hand on you." Shéamas's face was red, and the men could tell he was furious.

The lass had her hands on her hips and spoke quite rudely to the other occupant. "This is your responsibility, Shéamas. Permitting me to stay in your cottage proved to everyone that we have a relationship."

"What do you mean my responsibility? I've never touched you, Lavinia. Why accuse me of your condition? What harm have I done to you? I let you stay here because you said you needed a safe place for a few days. I had no idea you were in the family way, but it's no fault of mine, even if you are! Ask the child's real father." His voice was getting louder.

As it did, Lavinia dissolved into tears. "What am I to do then? Where am I to go? Everyone knows that I'm here and that you come every day. What do you think they will say?"

Shéamas was nearly choking with anger; he spat his following words. "Yes, I come to the farm daily as I work next door, but knowing you were here, I have stayed well away from the cottage since you moved in. I have not visited once since you moved in. I only came today to make sure you had gone."

Charles frowned. He had noticed that she glanced at them before starting her accusations. She had obviously been waiting for an audience, if not a witness. For him as the earl, to be used as a pawn raised his ire. This was one of the ex-convict girls who had served some of her seven years in Hobart, then moved to Melbourne and came to Sydney when her term expired. Charles didn't trust her one bit. She had come with written permission to work at the Government Dairy and learn the trade of cheese making. Finally, having heard her accusations, he stepped forward and exploded with, "Enough! Shéamas pipe down! Lavinia, stop snivelling."

The two young people turned to the earl.

Shéamas respected him, and he hoped that the earl would make her retract her claim. "Lord Charles, help, please. She claims…"

Charles's hand silenced him. "I heard her claims, lad. But now is not the time to discuss this. The ladies are in the carriages and can overhear your words from there. I need to send them home, lad. Ed, Paddy, I'll stay here with Shéamas, and you take the family home, then both return here, please."

Ed and Paddy nodded.

Before he left, Paddy gave his son a filthy look. He stalked out, shaking his head and muttering to himself.

Shéamas saw, and his heart fell. If his own father didn't believe him, what hope did he have that anyone else would? He felt like curling up into a ball and weeping like a small child. He and Clare had resisted any physical touching, as the one time they had been permitted to have a long, deep kiss, both were left breathless with physical desire. Shéamas had lovingly pushed Clare away from him, and both resisted the temptation of similar situations.

Lavinia McKone was reputed to be having illicit relations with an unknown man. She had boasted about such once at work and was overheard by Kitty Kellow, who had arrived unexpectedly from her own dairy. She reported the conversation to her husband, Kit, who then told Shéamas. No one had seen her with anyone, so no one knew who it was.

Charles didn't like standing for long because of his bad leg. He limped to the table, pulled out a chair, and sat. "Shéamas, outside, please, and stay close by. Preferable within view." He took a sly look at the accusing girl and thought he had better protect his own reputation.

Shéamas nodded. Giving Lavinia an icy stare, he did as requested. He stood just outside the open door but kept an eye on what was occurring inside. He was still so angry at the accusations that his breathing took some time to get under control. He heard Lord Charles begin to question Lavinia, but he had dropped his voice so Shéamas could not hear the exact questions.

Lavinia, on the other hand, played her trump hand. "Lord Charles, I accuse Shéamas of fathering my child, and no one can prove otherwise." Her head lifted stubbornly, and her teeth clenched on her lip as she did so. She folded her arms and turned her back on Charles. "Prove me wrong. It's my word against his." She folded her arms in defiance.

Minutes passed, and she refused to discuss anything more.

Charles tried to ask more questions, and she shut him down each time. Charles had not met such a shrew for some time. Thankfully, they had been few and far between in his life. Sal had dealt with many when she had been incarcerated, but that was many years ago. He was sure Shéamas was innocent, but as she mentioned, it was her word against his. If she had burst into tears and claimed that he had ruined her, then he may have doubted the lad, but by her behaviour, Charles knew her to be lying. His eyes were drawn to movement, then sound at the door, and he realised that Shéamas had heard her last retort. The noise was an angry gasp.

Charles hauled himself to his feet and went to speak to the shattered boy. He knew the community would insist that he marry the wench, and Clare would be shattered. As a good lad, he had little choice but to do the honourable thing, even if he was innocent. "Shéamas, I don't know what to say," Charles said apologetically. He knew it was his idea that she stay there.

Shéamas brushed angry tears from his eyes. "I do! She's a liar, sir. I have never touched her, honestly, sir." He sniffed. "Sir, Clare and I have never even done that. I've never been with any woman that way; I don't even know how yet. Father would have my hide if I disrespected a girl like that."

It was as he spoke that Eddie and Paddy returned.

Shéamas turned to his father as he arrived at his son's side. "I didn't touch her, Papa. I have not laid a hand on her ever. Clare will tell you I haven't touched her, and we're engaged."

Paddy held his son at arm's length and stared deep into his son's eyes as though reading his soul. As a child, Paddy had done this often, and Shéamas knew his father could tell when he was lying.

Shéamas's gaze didn't waver.

Paddy smiled, "Son, I believe you." He gave him a quick hug. He nodded and continued, "However, it is her word against yours, son. And therefore, you have no choice but to marry her." Paddy said the words that Shéamas did not want to hear.

A strangled "Noo…" was torn from Shéamas. "I love Clare; I want her as my wife. We are to be married in three days. Lavinia can't make me do it. I won't do it! She can't do this to me, no, to us!"

Paddy drew his shattered son into his arms again. His sobs shook Paddy to the core, but he had no words to take away his pain. He may be nineteen, but a broken heart is never too big to refuse a father's loving hug.

Back at Eddie and Jenna's house, Clare sat numb. No words penetrated her grief. She had heard enough to know that Lavinia's claim would change her life and their future together. After all their abstinence, Shéamas had been caught in the shrew's net.

Jenna brought tea, but it sat untouched.

Cara breezed in and out but had no words either. She was so looking forward to their marriage only three days hence. Now, the wedding was in limbo. She had no doubts that her son was innocent and that all would be well.

Sal sat outside, waiting for Charles to return. She knew the outcome, as Eddie had given her a brief outline of what had occurred. Clare had not heard Lavinia's claim or the way she said it, but she knew Shéamas would need to do the honourable thing for the girl. She doubted if he were the responsible party and realised that the girl would have lied to escape an awkward situation. She waited, knowing the result was a foregone conclusion.

The men did not return until six o'clock. Charles alighted at the verandah next to Sal. His look spoke volumes. His lips were almost grey. Unable to say anything, he just shook his head.

Sal gasped. "Oh no! She won't retract?" She asked so only he could hear.

Charles sat beside her, unaware that Clare had moved to just inside the window behind them. "No, she won't retract. But I sent Shéamas outside, where he could still see us. She told me that there was no way Shéamas could prove the child was not his. Her words didn't actually admit that they had been together. She's lying, Sal, but we can do nothing to make her withdraw her claim. The poor lad has no choice but to do the honourable thing." Charles sighed. "To make matters worse, I believe he's truly telling the truth, thus making it even more painful. Clare must be told and soon. Whatever occurs, the wedding on Monday is off." Charles reached for his wife and drew her to rest against him. "Our young ones have behaved admirably, and now they are being punished by a shrew. Love, I am grieved, but there is nothing I can do. Paddy is with him now. Shéamas almost collapsed, poor boy." The pair fell silent.

Rather than wait to hear more, Clare silently left the room. She collected her shawl and went to see Shéamas. The kitchen was empty, and considering how many people stayed there, the house was surprisingly silent.

Clare went down the back steps and across the backyard to the small cottage next to the stables.

Liam and Kerry were sitting outside the family cottage. They did not need to say that his parents and brother were inside. She could hear Shéamas's voice pleading his innocence to his parents.

Clare knocked and waited. Silence fell.

Paddy opened the door to her.

Shéamas felt ill, knowing he had to tell his beloved they could no longer marry that coming Monday. He realised he had to say something but blurted out his innocence. "Clare, I didn't touch her. I promise I didn't. I've never been with any woman that way. I love you and only you. I have since the day I met you."

Clare ignored his parents' compassionate gazes and went and stood in front of him. She gently took his hand and looked him in the face. "Shéamas, I believe you. I know you well enough to know that you would not do that. You never even tried it with me. Know that I love you all the more for what you now must do. You will do the right thing and marry this woman. This is not just because you must; you will do this for your family. I know you care for me, so do this for me. Shéamas, we can't stop tomorrow from happening, or the next day, or those that come afterwards, but how we deal with today matters. I have learnt that from this wonderful family. I have faith that this is the path God wishes us to walk. Shéamas, trust that He is never wrong." She pulled off the ring she had worn since he placed it there months ago. Without saying more, she took his hand and carefully placed the golden circle in the palm of his hand. Another symbol of their vow to each other should have joined it only days later. Now, they would sit together and remain unworn. She was sure Shéamas would not give her rings to this woman.

His fingers closed over the ring, and he opened his mouth to say something but was stopped.

Clare placed her fingers on his lips. "Shéamas, be a good father to the innocent child, whomever it belongs to." She reached up and kissed his cheek. Without waiting for further conversation, she turned and left. Rather than return inside the big house, she walked out the back gate.

Liam and Kerry saw her leave, but she didn't even acknowledge their presence. They presumed she was going to the river's edge as she often did.

The grassy field across the road was just down from Charles and Sal's cottages. All signs of the recent fires were gone. There was a large fallen log under a large tree and a larger one by the river's edge. Clare was often found sitting on one or the other of these seats. However, when Clare carefully shut the gate, she turned towards the main street rather than go to the river. At church that morning, she had overheard a conversation between one of the visitors and one of the street boys. She knew from his words that the visitor was staying at Rear Admiral Duncan Inn. This was Bill and Molly Miller's inn on the main road. Her attention was drawn as his accent was similar to her father's. She intended to ask Molly if the man was still there. If so, she would ask to speak to him as he had said he was looking for staff. If the Irishman were still there, she would ask if she could take one of the positions he was offering. She needed to leave, and it would be better if Shéamas had no idea where she was.

Her quest was successful.

Molly showed Clare into the sitting room and asked her to wait while she sought out the visitor.

The Irishman, John Moore, owned a farm about eighty miles further up the coast. Molly sat just out of earshot but left the sitting room door open.

Mr Moore joined Clare a few minutes later.

He bowed on entry. "Good evening, Miss…"

Clare gave her name: "O'Shane, sir, Clare O'Shane! I have come to ask a favour, sir. I overheard you are looking for staff for your farm. I need a job quite urgently."

Mr Moore started when he heard her name, then he frowned. "I was looking for men or lads, miss. I need staff to tend my orchard and milk my cows. I live alone and have no wife or children, so a lone unmarried woman would cause problems." He remained standing and listened with a frown on his brow.

Clare was desperate; she needed to leave as soon as possible. "Can I not be your milkmaid? I know about cows and the dairy industry. I was to marry a dairy stockman and have learned the skills required. Please, sir, I won't cause any trouble. I need to leave town. Molly knows me well and can vouch that I'm a good girl. Please, sir, let me come. Give me six months or even three, but please let me come with you. I really need to leave town now." She was horrified to realise her eyes had filled with tears.

The kind Irish voice asked, "Why the urgency, Miss O'Shane?"

Clare swallowed, hoping her voice would not fail her. "I was due to marry on Monday. Banns have been read, and all is in readiness. However, another has claimed that she is carrying his child. Although I believe him, he has no recourse but to marry the liar. He is an honourable man and will do what is required. I cannot stay, sir. I cannot see my beloved in the arms of another. Ask Molly; she was supposed to be coming to our wedding." She managed to explain fully before her voice failed. "Please, sir, let me come," she pleaded. "I need to leave."

The girl begged so hard that the man reconsidered. "You really know about dairy work? Can you make cheeses?"

She nodded slowly, "I know how to make soft cheeses, and I know the theory of making hard cheeses, but I've never made any, only watched. I know you need rennet and a cheese room to be successful, though."

He smiled, "Your honesty is good. If you had said you could and then failed, I would have sent you packing. Cheese is not an overnight product unless you eat the soft stuff." He saw Clare nod her agreement. "Now, tell me where you are from. You have an unusual lilt to your Irish accent that is familiar, as is your name."

Clare realised she had passed the first barrier when he seated himself in a comfortable armchair on the other side of the room.

She said, "Sir, my sister and I are all that remains of my family. We lost our parents and five siblings during the years of famine in Ireland. We lived on the shores of the bay in County Kerry, not far from Tarbet. But we had not always lived there. Before that, we were in Avoca for about half a year with Papa's family, but Kerry and I were born in London. Aunt Sal Lockley is my parent's cousin, and the Lockleys are our only family left."

The frown on the man's brow deepened. "Did you say Avoca? In County Wicklow, Ireland?"

Clare nodded. "Papa had family there, but we only stayed for a few months. We moved to County Kerry onto our own farm, which was away from people, the same vindictive people who caused my parents so much hurt. You see, Mama was not a Catholic, and that made things difficult for us."

This time, Mr Moore nodded understanding. "I cannot believe that you once lived in my hometown. You see, I am from Avoca and have named my farm here after the area." He paused, thinking hard. "O'Shane, you say, was your Papa's name Kieran?"

Clare's face broke into a beaming smile. "Yes, sir, that was his name. He was murdered for a few shillings. Mama died in childbirth at the end of the same month in 1848. Being the only ones left, we continued their plans and came to live with Aunt Sal."

He sat watching her face as he thought. "Kieran's girl from Avoca, eh? I met him years ago." His thumbs twiddled. "Fine, I'll give you a trial. Three months, and we'll revisit the position."

Clare was delighted. "May I ask that you say nothing about this to anyone? I wish to vanish. It will be easier on Shéamas if I am not here. I have already spoken to him. I promise I will leave a letter for Aunt Sal, Cathy and my sister, but please say nothing to Molly."

He felt like he was entering into a conspiracy, but he nodded his agreement. "Fine, but I leave at dawn. I need to get home, and it's a long trip. I have two young lads that are coming too. I have a maid's room in the house, but the boys will be in the staff quarters in their own building."

She nodded vigorously. "Thank you so much, sir." For the first time all day, she smiled.

He stood to leave. "Remember a dawn departure. Where do I collect you?"

She was over the moon. "Do you know Roseneath up on O'Connell Street?"

It was his turn to nod.

"I'll be waiting under the tree at the front of the house." Her grin showed her joy.

He was about to leave when he turned and asked, "I don't suppose you can cook, too?"

She once again nodded. "I'm quite a good cook, sir. Can I do that, as well?"

Mr Moore smiled and nodded. "Miss Clare O'Shane, I think we have an agreement. I shall see you at dawn."

Clare waited until he had entered his room and shut his door before going into Molly. She gave her a hug of thanks and said that he had once lived in a town where they had, and he had known her father. She did not mention that she was leaving with him.

Molly had a letter in her hand, and she was obviously in the middle of reading it. She asked no questions but returned Clare's hug. "Are you heading home, dear? I'll call Sam, and he can walk you back." She was obviously distracted by something but did not elaborate.

Sam soon appeared, followed by his younger sister, Ellen. Although she was a few years older than Clare, they were friends. Ellen's presence would be as a chaperone for them. Sam was recently married, and after the day's happenings, Clare was delighted that Molly had thought of her reputation. She wondered if the news had already reached Molly's ears. However, she said nothing. There was no mention of seeing her over the weekend, being at church, or at her wedding.

Clare tried to chat naturally, but Sam was full of the news that his wife was soon to have a child. The three avoided any conversation about Clare or even the wedding.

The mile walk was accomplished quickly, and the siblings made their farewells and returned home.

Clare set to finding a bag and writing the letters. On the walk, she had decided not to let on where she was going. None of the Miller family had asked, and she didn't volunteer the information.

She intended to vanish. She knew the tears would come but had no time for them now. She quickly packed her bag and placed it out in the stables. She sat down to write the letters and then dressed for bed. Her stomach rumbled, so after preparing and eating some bread and butter, she crept into the crisp linen sheets, where she cried herself to sleep.

Chapter 11 The Lady Vanishes

The Kitchen door at Eddie's house crashed open. Shéamas rushed in. "What do you mean she's not here? Did she not come back inside an hour or more ago?" Shéamas may well have to marry another, but his love for Clare had not died.

Liam had gone outside looking for her to join the family for dinner. He now trailed in after his brother, and he entered in an almost panic.

They had caught a large amount of bream the day before, and these were cooked and ready to serve for the Good Friday meal.

Liam said, "Shéamas after she left you, she went for a walk out the back gate. Kerry and I saw her go, but we were called to mind the children soon afterwards. We haven't seen her since. I have no idea if she even returned."

Shéamas sought out Eddie, who was in his office. "She's vanished, Eddie. I can't find her anywhere. Liam said he had not seen her since she left our cottage."

Eddie had an open-door policy for his office, so if the door was open, you could enter; as his door had been slightly ajar, Shéamas barged in. He was doing the books from the day before. Not that he liked working on Good Friday, but because they had gone to church the evening before and celebrated the Maundy Thursday Holy Communion, he'd not done yesterday's books. On return from the evening service, he and Jenna had retired early. With the happenings of the day, his books had not been done. He put his pen back on the stand and gave Shéamas his full attention. "Gone, what do you mean gone?"

Shéamas threw himself onto the settee in the room, "Gone as in she can't be found. She gave me my ring back, Ed. Liam and I searched everywhere. As if she doesn't have reason to leave me, but Eddie, where could she be?" Shéamas swiped his arm across his eyes. "Bloody women! You can't do without them, but I want to throttle one and hug the other, and I am no longer permitted to do so. Life stinks!"

Ed came and sat next to the grieving groom.

Clare may no longer be getting married, but Shéamas realised he had no choice but to submit to society's demands.

Shéamas said, "I may have to marry Lavinia, but I will not live with her. There was no rule anywhere that said I needed to do so. Our marriage will never be consummated, of that I am sure. I will remain celibate."

Ed did not touch on that topic. That was for Shéamas to decide, but he thought staying away from his legal wife was a good idea. "Shéamas, tell me where you have looked."

Shéamas proceeded to list the venues. All her haunts had been checked: the logs, Charlie's inn, and even Charles and Sal's back verandah and garden. She could not be found.

Eddie said, "She could have walked home, you know. Have you checked Roseneath?"

Shéamas's shaking head made Eddie say, "Ask your papa to saddle James for me. I'll go and check." As he spoke, he made for the door. He was still in his best clothes and would need to change. His black stallion would relish an outing.

Shéamas stood and followed him out the door.

For another hour, everyone searched along the river.

Clare had all but vanished. Kerry was clinging to Liam and almost bouncing from foot to foot.

"She can't have just gone. Where would she go?" Shéamas was beside himself with worry, and nothing anyone could say would ease his anxiety.

Paddy even gave him a shake. "Control yoursel' boy. You're no good to her if you drop from apoplexy. We're all doing our best to find the gel. She can't have gone too far."

Shéamas's reply gave insight into his mood. "I'd rather die from apoplexy than marry that hussy living in my cottage. I'll delay the nuptials for as long as I can. The child may well be born with my name, but I shall never touch the wench." He stormed off for another check along the river and into the various tracks into the mangroves. His only light was an oil lantern that didn't cast much light. He wondered if she had thrown herself in the tidal shark-infested river. Her release of him so lovingly had broken the final thread of his tortured emotions. He wept as he hunted for her.

~

While the family was searching for her, Clare was at The Rear Admiral Duncan Inn with Molly Miller and meeting John Moore. She realised that the family would be worried, but she needed to escape the untenable situation she now found herself in. By the time she arrived home, Ed had been and gone from Roseneath.

Sam and Ellen had returned home without seeing anyone. Clare was unaware that the search was now concentrating on the river and sat to write her letters.

With the letters now written and her bag safely stowed for a quick escape tomorrow morning. Clare extinguished her light and went to bed. Nightmares disturbed her slumber, but at dawn, she was up, dressed and waiting for the wagon to collect her. She had not heard the family return and knew that they would check her room sometime that morning and find her letters on her bed. As the clothing she was taking was packed, all the drawers and wardrobe were now almost empty. Kerry's room contained what she had not packed. The only gown that remained was the one she would have been married in. She left her wedding finery in her room.

The trundling wheels of the wagon hardly paused as it passed. Clare was up and on it before it came to a stop. She wanted to be out of town before anyone else was awake and around. She had motioned for silence, and not a word was spoken.

Clare was unaware that none of the family had returned home. All had stayed at Eddie and Jenna's place, searching through the night. No one had checked her bed and had therefore not realised she had slept there.

Wills had brought Cathy and the children home for a change of clothing at seven o'clock. Cathy checked her room and found a letter for her on Clare's bed, another for Sal and one for Kerry. Calling for Wills to wait, Cathy checked the wardrobe and drawers. Seeing them nearly empty, she realised she needed to call off the search of the river. She gathered an armload of children's raiment and returned to her brother-in-law's house with the news that Clare had left rather than killed herself.

The journey back to Ed's was made at some speed as Shéamas had mentioned that he would swim the river to see if she had fallen in and been caught on a submerged log. Wills knew that he had to stop him. They arrived back at the jetty to see Shéamas about to enter the water. Wills called, "Shéamas, stop! We have news."

All eyes turned to the approaching vehicle, and Shéamas came at a jog. "What? Where is she?"

Cathy didn't reply but handed him her letter, knowing Sal had yet to read it.

His eyes fell onto the neatly written screed, and he read the words. It took a second read before he realised she had left no hint of her direction or whom she had left with. "Gone? Cathy, who could she have gone with?"

Cathy didn't know and said as much.

Kerry came close, listening to his words, and Cathy handed her the second envelope. Kerry opened her short epistle and sank onto the ground as she read.

Roseneath
16th April 1851

My dearest Kerry,

I know you will be safe with Aunt Sal and the family, but I must leave. Please know that I, too, am safe. I have gone with the promise of paid employment, which will at least be useful. I am no longer in town as the job is some distance away. I will give no details about my direction or of where or who I have gone with. I wish Shéamas all the best in his life, but I cannot remain to see him married to another woman. My love for him means that I hope he somehow finds happiness. I believe him and know that she is lying. However, I know him to be honourable and will do the right thing in society's eyes. I have not written to Shéamas as I saw him last night and told him myself. I will not tell you where I'm going but know that I am safe.

My darling sister, you know I love you, and I would not leave you except that I know you are safe there. Tell everyone not to worry and that I love them all. I will write in a year or so. I pray that you will find happiness with Liam. Marry him with my blessing.

Your loving sister

Clare.

Kerry's watery eyes met Shéamas's. "She does not wish to be found, Shéamas. She has gone to get a job out of town." She handed the letter to the man standing over her.

Again, he read the words before releasing a howl of frustration and anger, which echoed along the riverbanks.

The noise brought the family close.

Word of Clare's safety soon spread, as did the information about her leaving town. Shéamas sank to the ground and wept with relief. She was not dead, and hopefully, one day, she would return.

With no need to check for her body in the river, everyone returned to Eddie's house to consider the next move in the saga.

Lavinia still needed to be dealt with. The minister needed to be informed that there would be no wedding on Monday, and the arrangements for the post-wedding celebrations needed to be cancelled. Thankfully, there were still many of the family to feed who had come for Easter so that the wedding food would be eaten.

The wagon proceeded northward along the Old Northern Road to Wiseman's Ferry.

Clare sat on the back in silence. She had not even introduced herself to her travelling companions. Mr Moore had warned the occupants to keep quiet until the vehicle had left the town precinct, but even as the last building faded from view, the conversation did not start. Clare's mood seemed to be infectious. The two young lads who were on the wagonload of stores were as equally morose as she was. She had no desire to converse with anyone, but as they would have nearly a week at walking pace, they had time to get to know each other better then.

The two horses that pulled the loaded wagon plodded along with their heavy burden. The bags of flour, grain, and other items were sitting in the back under a canvas cover. Clare didn't care about them, her companions, or anything else. As they reached the outskirts of Dural, tears were sliding down her cheeks unchecked. She had given up brushing them away, so they just dripped onto her skirt, leaving a growing wet patch.

Half an hour later, the horses were given a drink at a trough. The three passengers finally took the opportunity to introduce themselves.

Clare's eyes were red from crying.

Dave Fisher and Glenn Worboys were the two teenage boys that Mr Moore had employed to work his farm. The lads had been in trouble with other local lads, and the magistrate told them to find a job out of town. The magistrate introduced them to John at church. As friends but orphans, the two wanted to stick together. This job suited their needs, but both said they were leaving their lady loves behind, and neither lad was happy about that. It was this that had been the reason for the fight.

As Mr Moore stepped down from the wagon, he said, "Okay, you three, all of you are leaving broken hearts behind. You have that in common, so you will know exactly how the others feel. All I ask is that you are not only kind to one another but that there be no hanky-panky between you later. Boys, you will need to look after Miss O'Shane. We have a family connection in Ireland; therefore, she is my cousin."

The two boys looked at Clare and nodded in agreement. "Will do, Mr Moore. We'll treat her like a sister."

John Moore smiled. "On the plus side, she can cook, so we should eat better than I have been."

With the horses having been given a drink, the wagon set off on the dusty road.

The heat of the day was now climbing, and Clare wished she had brought a parasol of some sort. She had left it on the hook behind her door. The poke bonnet with a mob cap back gave some protection from the sun, but the heat was burning her neck. Rather than pulling up her shawl, she reached up and let her hair down. Her almost strawberry mane of hair fell in a cascade and sat on her back, bringing some relief to her neck.

Mile by mile, the terrain seemed to grow drier and drier. By noon, they had just passed through Forrest Glen farm and were a little over halfway to Wiseman's Ferry. After the experience with bushfires last year, they were all careful with sparks by not throwing away bottles.

John Moore planned to stay the night at the inn in town and then take the day's first ferry across the river.

At dusk, they were approaching the riverside village. The trip to this area could easily be accomplished in a few hours by coach and four or on horseback, but with a fully loaded wagon and only two horses, he was taking the trip easy. He was in no hurry to get home, and he decided to use this time to get to know his three new staff members.

Clare had pinned her hair up under her hat as they entered the larger village of Wiseman's Ferry. After a day of sitting in the full sun, she wanted a wash, but she was hopeful of a hip bath in her room. She had taken her share of Uncle Ned's money and planned to pay for a better room at the inn. She wondered about the night's accommodation, and her interest was piqued when she heard him order three rooms.

John Moore said at the check-in counter, "One of the better back rooms for the lady and two front rooms for the young men and me."

She was to be given one of the best rooms.

They settled in and arranged to meet in the dining room at seven o'clock. Clare ordered herself a bath and went upstairs to wait. She had placed the bulk of her money into her personal hygiene bag as she knew no self-respecting man would ever touch such things. Men seemed to have an aversion to anything that could be associated with women's monthly blood loss or personal hygiene. Once, when the house had been robbed, the valuables had been missed, as Cathy had their money stored in a leather pouch with her underclothing amongst her drawers and camisoles.

Now clean and rested, Clare went downstairs to join the men. Only her new boss was there.

John stood as she entered and held out a chair for her. "Clare, before the boys join us, I will claim the friendship with your father to all and sundry. It will protect you on our journey and into the future. I did meet him and your mother, too, as they stayed in a cottage at the back of my parent's farm. If they are the same people, they are distantly related. I wondered why the name was familiar, but the more I thought about it, the more it came back to me. If I remember correctly, they were a mixed-marriage couple that had married in London, against their family's wishes. I gather you and your sister were born there? I think that's what you mentioned?"

Clare nodded but remained silent.

Mr Moore nodded. "I first went home after I had left the army, and I was looking for somewhere to settle. I returned again a few years later. I remember your father being a nice chap. Your mama was expecting a child if my memory serves me correctly."

Again, Clare nodded. "Liam was born in Tarbert, but he drowned in June 1847. Papa was murdered a bit over a year later; then Mama died in childbirth three weeks after he died. There were three other little ones, and the starvation or illness took them when the blight hit." She related her losses in such a matter-of-fact way that his heart went out to her.

He continued to probe. "So there is only you and your sister left?"

Clare nodded. Tears were not far away, but she realised he needed to get the story straight if they were to be believed. The fact that they had met years ago in Ireland brought her some comfort. It was good to talk about some familiar places with him. Aunt Sal had never been to Ireland until recently. Clare knew this man had met her family and was distantly related.

Clare wondered what the years ahead would bring. She had tied all her dreams into her life with Shéamas; now, he was not to be included and pulled from her grasp at the last moment.

John Moore saw a wave of melancholy pass over her face. "Clare, I was wondering if you called me Uncle John and that it might give you another layer of protection. As I told you before, I have no wife; you would be the only female on the farm. If I claimed the relationship with you, it may well suffice." He saw Clare frown.

"Sir, I think there is a much closer relationship as Papa said we were with cousins when we were staying in Avoca. We were living in the cottage belonging to one of his cousins. Grandmother, his mama, was a Moore, so we must somehow be more closely related. I know of a cousin named John but did not know his surname. He is our closest male relative, but we didn't know where he was. It must be you." Clare was racking her brain to remember what her parents had told her.

John Moore's face brightened considerably. "You know, I think you are correct. I remember my mother saying something about my father's relations. I have not had much to do with them since I joined the English army at the age of seventeen. On my short visits home, family connections were not discussed. I had no idea how Kieran was connected. It's nearly ten years since I met them. I remember he was a few years younger than me, and your mother was younger than him. Am I correct?"

Clare nodded again.

He lay back in his chair and relaxed. "Then, starting today, Miss Clare O'Shane will become Clare, my young cousin. I shall be Uncle John, and no one will raise an eyebrow at the impropriety of you living with me at the house as I must, therefore, be your closest male relative. If I ever meet Sal, I will enforce the relationship."

Until now, she had not addressed him as anything, so the boys had no idea that the moniker was new. She said, "Father Patrick mentioned that Papa said there was a closer cousin than Sal, and Father Pat knew his name was John."

The two boys joined them, and they went into the dining room. They enjoyed a hearty meal of steak and vegetables, followed by peach cobbler and custard.

The first time she used his new name was towards the end of the nearly silent meal. As the boys left, she asked, "Uncle John, what time do you wish to leave, please?"

The gaze of the two young men fell onto her, and both mouths dropped open. She saw Dave dig Glenn in the ribs with his elbow. He whispered not so quietly, "See, I told you she must be related, or else she'd have a chaperone. He must be her close relative and, therefore, her legal guardian."

She murmured, "He is." Clare dropped her head and smiled to herself.

He would now become her protector.

John replied with a sly smile. He had heard the comments and knew he was correct in protecting Clare in this way. "Dawn again, young ones. Sleep well. Clare, lock your door, please, pet. I want no one breaking into your room." Clare stood to leave, his voice carried across the dining room.

Others turned and looked at the lovely young lady dining alone with three men. Some were puzzled, but her comment announced her relationship with the older man. She replied, "Thank you, Uncle John. I will." They fell back to eating their meals and minding their own business.

With their cover now established, Clare tipped her head to say goodnight, then left for the safety of her room. At his suggestion, she turned the key in the lock after she entered. She thanked God for leading her to the only other relative she knew of in the world.

She hoped sleep would come. Last night, she had only slept for a few hours and was disturbed by bad dreams.

~

The ferry crossing the following morning was an experience in itself. The vessel that carried them across the river ran on a thick guide wire that ran over a huge wheel. The vessel had fold-up ramps at either end for the assorted vehicles to board it. They were among the first in the queue, as it had overnighted on their side of the river.

The horses stood with their heads drooping until the ferry arrived. They moved onto the ferry when John flicked near their rumps with the tip of his whip.

The crack of the leather thong made them gee-up. With a lurch, the heavy wagon took its place at the head of the barge.

Seven other vehicles joined them.

The ramps were pulled up, and the ferry started its crossing.

The river water sloshed against the side of the almost water-level barge for the fifteen minutes it took to cross the Hawkesbury River.

The ferry slid up the muddy embankment, lowering the front ramp.

With a tip of his hat and a wave, John negotiated their exit and took off up another dusty road. He was in a jovial mood. He was determined to cheer up the trip somewhat; he said, "Well, my young ones, we have a few long days before us. We'll sleep rough for a few nights before we get home. But let me tell you about my farm."

Chapter 12 Towards a New Beginning

*J*ohn proceeded to tell them about his land and a bit of his story.

"Sit back and get a bit of history of both the farm and me. Clare knows some of this already, but you will all have the same information. Ask questions if you wish, but hopefully, I will cover most things."

The informative story began with Clare sitting beside John and the two boys behind on the flour bags. John's soothing voice took Clare's mind off her hurting heart. With John talking, she only had to sit back and listen.

"I was born in 1803 in a small town called Avoca in Ireland, where I was Baptised a Roman Catholic. Clare knows of it as she lived there for a while on our farm. The town was named after the rivers that intersect there, as it means a *meeting of the waters*. When I was seventeen, I enlisted with the English and fought without sustaining any major injury. However, on returning home, I could not settle. Not to mention that I was not that welcome because of the religious bigotry and all that. Now, at twenty-six, I undertook a long journey of discovery and found myself at a beautiful beach that no one had yet claimed; by now, it was 1830. A fellow countryman had settled in this area, and I had gone to stay with one for a while. I requested a land grant, and it was given on condition that it be surveyed first." He smiled at Clare.

She realised that the dates were wrong. "But you said you met us on your farm in Ireland. Did you go back for long?"

He gave a quick chuckle. "Yes, dear girl, I did. I completed my voyage of discovery while the paperwork was being sorted out. My cousin is married to the daughter of a convict ship captain, John Coghill. Robert Maddrell and his wife, Elizabeth, live down at Braidwood. The government said my land would take time to survey, so as I was not in too much of a hurry to get back here, I went home to Ireland. It was on that trip when I met your family, Clare. You lived in a cottage at the back of my parents' farm. Having fled to London due to religious persecution. They, like me, were seeking refuge from the bigots who did not believe that there was only one faith and one true

God."

Clare nodded.

John said, "The pathway to find God may vary, but they could not see beyond their snobbish noses. Kieran and I, that's Clare's papa, agreed on many things." His eyes rested on the girl beside him. "You and your sister were such adorable imps that I felt like getting married and having some of my own. However, that was not to be. No Irish lass would marry a turncoat as they saw me, so I left." He did not elaborate on that comment. "That would have been about 1838 as I returned here after saying my farewells to my family for what I thought would be the last time. I did not know where Kieran had taken his family. I now have you three heart-sore folk accompanying me on this journey, but that is a story for another day."

He coughed to clear his throat before continuing. "Now, where was I? Oh yes, in Ireland… I stayed until about the time your family left. They went to western Ireland, and I returned to Australia, hoping my land would be ready for me. I had been gone about eighteen months, and on my return, the survey still had not been completed, but it was imminent. I asked if I could start preparing the ground, and the authorities approved my doing so provisionally. I did not tell them that I already had a tiny shack built on the headland. During my absence, the foundations for my larger house were done. They said no compensation would be given if I farmed outside my six-hundred-and-forty-acre boundary. That is one square mile, but the land doesn't really fall into neat blocks. On my return from this trip from home, I came prepared with an assortment of fruit trees and numerous vine cuttings. I found that the grassy hillsides were perfect for the vines and soon had them growing. In my absence, local lads had been employed to clear the designated farm area. There is a large flat area below where my new house now stands, and it was for cropping when it was fully cleared. I dug into the sandy soil and found good fresh groundwater so I would not need to water the crops. I only have to fertilise them. Then there are the fruit trees I had brought with me. I had them in barrels so I could keep them potted until I was ready to plant them. Some had already had a first small crop."

Dave asked, "Did they all survive?" To which John nodded.

Glenn added, "What sorts, sir?"

John chuckled. "Patience, lads. I'll get to that. Now, where was I?"

Clare said, "The survey, Uncle John."

John smiled a thank you. "Ahh, yes, the survey! Well, they were slow about doing that. I didn't get the paperwork until September 1840, and by then, much of the land I wanted on the main headland was already cleared. With my friend's help, I employed some local lads from Kincumber to clear the shrubs off the flat area. He oversaw the farm in my absence." The horses had almost stopped walking as they approached a steep section of the road. "Dave, hop out and take their heads, will you? We may have to do this a few times over the steep section of this trip. You two will have to share this job.

In one section, you all may need to walk with them. The same goes for a few of the downhills. Clare, even you will have to get out for one of those. There's a bad one going down the escarpment in a few days, and I want no one but myself on board in case the horses cannot hold the load."

Getting the horses to tug the heavy wagon up the hill took time. It was an hour before John continued his story. The road wound along the river as it headed eastward.

The story continued as they headed to Singleton's Mill for the luncheon break. "When I returned from my somewhat extended jaunt, the local lads had done their job well. The most easterly headland was nearly cleared, and the area I had chosen for the house was also ready for construction to begin. All the felled trees had been kept, dried, and were being slabbed. The first place I built was a smallish cabin at the back of the farm, but the termites ate through that quickly, and it burnt down a few years later. I moved the house position so I could see the sea. The new house faces northeast and overlooks the crop area. The lads had cut the cedar trees and she-oaks from the headland and moved them to the hill where I wanted to build. Every one of the logs that were used for building the house was milled onsite. There is a delightful variety of timbers in this area. All the various sorts of gum trees have their own strengths and weaknesses. I also discovered a stand of local cedar trees that the termites don't seem to eat. These were scattered along the lake's foreshore, along with a few wonderful swamp mahogany trees. Ahh, you don't want to know all about the timbers, but Clare, you will, in particular, see the various colours of the timbers I used."

On and off for the remainder of the morning, he spoke lovingly of the beautiful house created from waste wood, as he called it. There was a small roadside store at Gunderman, where they purchased a few small items; then, they travelled a little further to Singleton's Mill for the night.

The old water mill was housed in a timber-clad building. The mill had been water-driven and used to grind grain to make flour. A small stone wall constructed into the river doubled as a jetty, diverting the tidal currents past the water wheel. Now abandoned, the outbuildings were little more than a mail depot for the outlying farms. The two-story timber building had a few planks missing, and dead grasses surrounded it. Although the mill had long since closed, the name remained because of the stone jetty. A few settlers remained in the area, and the river postman left their mail in the old mill building.

The dirt and dust had dried John's throat, and he wanted a tea mug. "We'll make this a bit of a longer stop as I'm parched, and I want to boil the billy." On a wide grassy spot beside the river, he pulled the wagon off the road and hobbled the horses so they would not walk away. There was plenty of feed nearby for them. He couldn't release them from the traces but let them graze at will. The wagon weight meant they could not go far hobbled.

Glenn poured water into a bucket they carried for the purpose. A large coopered barrel was full of water for their journey. It seemed to the boys that John did not drink alcohol. They had not heard the rattle of bottles or felt any other barrels of ale. It was water, tea, or they went thirsty.

Clare was content with either. She had become used to the hot, sweet brew that the Lockleys served. Milk was an option, but it always needed to be brought in, especially for her. She had recently tried the black brew with some light honey, which had made a world of difference.

The three men quickly assembled the makings of a fireplace. Soon, the billy was sitting in the flames, heating. Once boiled, Clare removed it with a stick, threw in a spoonful of tea leaves and swirled around to draw. She was amazed that cooking here was very similar to cooking back home in Ireland.

Clare had already taken the opportunity to investigate what was under the canvas and soon had the mugs, tea, and a damper loaf purchased at Wiseman's Ferry. She also found a box containing butter, jam, and honey and placed these onto the wagon's tray. Soon after arriving, she had learnt that the ants could smell food even before children.

Food would be prepared and served from the back tray rather than on the ground; it also meant they could stand to serve themselves. After sitting down all day, this was good. She had quizzed John about what other foodstuffs were on board. He had quickly shown her what was there. Beside the water barrel were a large bag of potatoes, a smaller barrel of salted beef, some bags of dried peas and a bag of rice. The wagon had much more food, but these were the easiest to access. The first thing Clare did was undo the top of the potato bag. She chose four large potatoes and proceeded to prepare them for the evening meal. She had noticed an enormous cast iron camp oven amongst the cooking implements and dug that out.

She had no idea that she was humming as she worked. Her mind had returned to the last big potato that Kerry had found on the day their mother had died. However, the loss of her mother was not what was on her mind.

While John sipped his hot tea, he watched her work. The four large potatoes sat on a rock beside the fire, and he wondered what she would do with them. He watched while she stood with her hands on her hips, surveying the area. Her face showed delight, and without a word, she walked over to an exposed embankment and dug into the wall with a stick. She had found clay, and although they were experiencing a drought, the embankment's proximity to the river had kept this shaded cliff moist.

John watched as she encased the potatoes with the clay and put them into the fire around the billy, which she had refilled and put back onto the coals. He knew they would not cook in the time they had to stay there and said as much.

Without explaining, she asked, "Uncle John, may I use the camp oven too?"

He nodded. "Use what you wish, Clare; it is all for us to consume."

She then started collecting large handfuls of dry grass. This went into the camp oven. Only then did she sit down and drink her tea. It was now cool enough to sip without burning her lips. She sat staring into the flames, lost in her thoughts. The man noticed her facial expressions but said nothing. The odd tear escaped, and then she looked up and caught John's gaze on her.

She gave a wan smile but said nothing. Slapping her thighs, she jumped up. With the aid of two sticks, she dug the solid clay balls out of the fire and left the four of them to cool slightly. She removed the billy from the fire with the same thick stick, added more tea leaves, and then fitted on the lid. She carefully carried it to the camp oven and surrounded it with dry grass. One by one, she added the potatoes around the billy, covered them with more dry grass, and then put on the camp oven lid.

John had moved, but he'd not taken his eyes from her movements. "Okay, explain, Clare, explain all that."

She did. "The fire sets the clay and starts the cooking, and the billy and grass will keep the heat in them. By the time we stop tonight, they will be cooked. Praties became so precious at home during the famine that we didn't dare just put them in the coals any more. This way, they come out perfect. But it also means that the billy will stay warm for afternoon tea. We will have a warm mug of tea without boiling the billy."

John looked at her with a stunned look on his face. "Well, I never. Lass, I think having you in the house will be wonderful."

They used another billy to pour river water on the fire and extinguish it, leaving the circle of rocks in place. In the dry weather, a single spark could mean death for them all. So, they pulled the logs away from the coals and doused the red coals until they were cold and black. Once content that the fire was safe, they loaded up and trundled off.

The journey was long and arduous but interesting to the three young people. John settled back for the next leg of their journey. "Well, folks, the next stop is Spencer. It's a few hours upstream. It used to be known as Fernleigh, but at some stage, they changed the name to Spencer. I have a feeling that was about the time that Lord Spencer died, but in truth, I have no idea."

The three young people learned they did not need to reply. The older man rattled on with his descriptions of the area.

Clare's mind turned to Shéamas, and her mood sank. Tomorrow was Easter Day, and the day after should have been her wedding day. She shook her head, thinking of her mother's saying. She murmured it, unaware she said it aloud. "You can't stop tomorrow." She fell to thinking about home. That also made her sad. She didn't know John had overheard her.

After Singleton's Mill, the road turned northward as they curved around an inlet. The mill was on an isthmus with water on both sides, and the river doubled back on itself. The Hawkesbury River was wide, but small inlets were along both edges. The colour of the water changed from a dirty brown in the fast-running areas to a greenish-blue in the quieter sections. The bush along both sides of the river was thick with tall timbers that were a saw-millers delight. All were surprised that no one had felled the saleable timbers along the roadside. Other than small clearings every now and then, the bush remained untouched. On the other hand, the jutting isthmus and flat areas were cleared and cultivated, and various houses and cottages were dotted along the roadway. This itself meandered in the least direct route but passed every nook and cranny that had a residence constructed close by. None knew if the road had come first or the cottages. But the trip through the overhanging river branches along the dusty road was cool in the day's heat.

John kept a stream of conversation going, and occasionally, one of the three young ones chipped in. He had not asked any of them a single question, and they wondered if he ever would. Clare had already told him her story, and he knew that she didn't want the boys to know about her heartache. The two boys remained tight-lipped to their own backgrounds. All Clare knew was that there was some trouble and they had to leave. John obviously knew their history, but he had not let on.

Spencer was their overnight destination. They would stop early so Clare could prepare their meal. John's mouth was already salivating over the thought of a hot potato with lashings of butter melted on it. Like Clare, these foods were one of his favourite treats. She had found a bag of onions, and as they passed a cow and calf, she had stripped off a couple of pints of milk and planned to use this for their meal.

They had eaten the damper they had purchased at the last stop, so Clare said she would make another one. An early halt would allow her to cook before the darkness fell, and they needed sleep.

Mid-afternoon, they paused while Clare passed out the mugs of tea from the camp oven. It was still hot enough to drink without much complaint. With nothing to eat, the stop didn't take long.

John had met one of the new residents of Spencer on the way into town the week before. James Crossland had only moved into town the year before, and he said that John could camp on the riverfront whenever he liked, but he suggested moving back a little as the wildlife also liked access to the water. John had set up camp in a clearing about fifty yards from his house when southbound. It was this destination for their night's camp.

They drew the wagon to a standstill and choked the wheels before unhitching the horses. The poor beasts threw their heads up in relief. The loaded vehicle had sapped their strength, but as the evening cooled, they were hobbled, rugged, and permitted to wander. Again, the horses grazed on the native grasses and drank from the buckets Dave and Glenn had filled for them.

James Crossland had collected some dead wood and left it in a big pile for campers. John used a flint to start the fire. Clare set about preparing their evening meal. John opened the barrel of salted beef and extracted a hunk of gooey meat from the briny water. "If you can make this palatable, I'll double your pay."

Clare chuckled. She had learned to love corned beef and the white sauce that Jenna made for it. She had helped make it numerous times over the years. However, doing it over an open fire was a little more complicated, but she would do her best. Having fresh milk to make it with was a delight as it would make it creamy. Cara used water and flour, and it was bland. Jenna's food had an extra zing, and although the sauces looked the same, they tasted vastly different. Clare had often asked her the secrets of making food taste good. It was usually just frying the ingredients in butter before it was left to cook through. The caramelisation of the onions or browning of the meat added another level of taste. Clare set to work cooking.

John fished out a cutting board from the wagon, plus some sharp knives and a large, flat wooden stirrer. Knowing where the cutlery and cooking implements were, she ransacked the back a few more times.

The dinner was of corned beef, covered liberally with a creamy white onion sauce, clay-baked potatoes and mushy peas. This was followed by billy-boiled honey-sweetened rice pudding cooked with milk. The tasty meal filled the boys and earned praise from John.

"I can't believe you not only made that palatable but also delicious. And that rice pudding is to die for, Clare. I've never had rice as a dessert before, but I like it."

She beamed at the praise. The boys had hardly spoken her name, but Glenn said, "I agree, Miss Clare; I've eaten my fill, and for a seventeen-year-old, that's something rare." He clapped his hand over his mouth, realising that he'd inadvertently given away the lie about his age.

John noticed the error, and both his eyebrows flicked up. "Seventeen, eh? Thought you said nineteen. I suppose you aren't orphans either?"

Dave glared at his friend. "No sir, that bit is true, but we are only seventeen. We're just big for our ages. I grew up at the orphanage with Mr Marlow till I was ten, then went to live with Glenn." He didn't await a reply. "Miss Clare, I agree with Glenn; filling two growing boys takes a mighty fine cook. I'm stonkered, miss."

Clare looked puzzled. "Dave, what is stonkered?"

Dave was relaxing, holding his mug of tea. His youthful grin was a sign of his being relaxed. He said, "It means I'm full, Miss Clare. Can't fit in any more. My par used to say it when I was a wee tacker. He was Scottish, and it was a saying over there. He died last year, sir, and Mama, two years before that. She died in childbirth."

Clare quietly added, "So did mine!"

Glenn said, "Mine too, but my dar ran out on us before I was born. So it was just Ma and me. So I 'spose I'm not really an orphan, but she couldn't keep me. I kept in contact with the Marlows. I got no idea where my dar is. Mama's bub wasn't his."

Clare didn't answer. She didn't want sympathy that her father had been murdered for a few small coins. She met John's eyes, and he gave her a small smile, which gave her confidence. "Uncle John, do we have enough water for a quick wash? You and the boys swam while I was cooking, but I wondered if…."

John interrupted her. "No need to ask, dear; use what water you like. We can replenish that at Mangrove Mountain. One of the farms up there has a lovely spring with cool, clean water. James has to be careful here as he only has rainwater, so don't use any from his tanks. Wait until dark, though, dear; it will give you more privacy. We'll all stay at the fire until you are ready. Oh, and by the way, you will be sleeping on the cart, and we will be around the fire, just so you all know your place."

Clare did as suggested and waited until it was dark before having a thorough wash in the warm water. Now clean, she redressed and attended to the camp oven to rescue her soda bread. At home, they had cooked bread in the coals, but the camp oven made a beautiful, clean loaf of bread. She tipped it onto a large square of linen and wrapped it so that it could cool slowly.

With the fire stoked against the cooling evening, the men settled down on the grassy bank, and Clare climbed onto the flour bags, and they slept.

On waking, John's stubbly beard was visible, and the two youths showed evidence of patchy fair whiskers. Clare wondered what she should feed them for breakfast when John mentioned a bag of rolled oats next to the flour. Within a short time, the last of the milk was made into a creamy porridge and sweetened with more honey. She had made up more than they could eat, so before they set off, she added some flour and cooked them as little oat cakes that they could nibble as they drove. She knew the boys would now eat whatever they were given, so she suggested that they prise off all oysters visible on the rocks while the tide was out.

Clare called to them, "Eat any that break open, as we can't keep them fresh. Only bring back the whole ones; whether they are stuck together or on small rocks doesn't matter."

While cleaning up after their meal, she was stowing the utensils she had used when the canvas moved. She sprung back and squealed. John abandoned the boys and was by her side in an instant. "Clare, what's wrong?"

She had frozen as the canvas was still moving. She pointed, and he could see she was shaking. "There's something under there."

John could see something under the canvas as the entire thing moved towards them. "Move, Clare, and quickly!" She did. She hitched up her skirts and ran. About twenty feet away, she stopped and turned to see John flick back the canvas sheet. Unable to stop herself, she let out a bloodcurdling scream. A nine-foot leviathan, at least three inches thick, slithered across the bags she had slept on all night.

John was undecided if he should kill it or just let it go. The decision was made for him when Clare fainted. He needed to attend to her. He called for the boys to watch the slithery beast while he made sure it did not come to investigate the now prostrated girl on the grass.

The two lads came at his call. They ushered it away from Clare and the campsite with fiery branches.

Clare slowly came around to the sound of excited voices as the boys watched the snake head quickly into the undergrowth. She realised that she was half lying in John's arms. "Oh, I'm so sorry, Uncle John. I'll never get used to those horrible beasts. Uncle Charles showed me one on the river bank at Parramatta, and it was nowhere near the size of that thing." She sat up and shivered. "Can we leave here now, please? So much for being Easter Day!"

John smiled, "We're Irish, Clare, neither of us like snakes. Blame Saint Patrick for that." He chuckled. "I believe the locals here eat them. I've heard that they taste like chicken, but that is one meal I forbid you to serve me unless we are starving."

His lighthearted comment made her chuckle. "I'm fine now, sorry for my weakness. I've nearly finished packing up; then we can go. Can you check if there are any more?" When the boys returned to the oysters, she said to John, "I was supposed to be getting married tomorrow, so this is not a good start for me. Everything has gone wrong." She turned away before he saw the tears falling, but she wished he had given her a fatherly hug. She didn't see the sadness cross his face or the compassion he felt for her. He would have liked to take her in his arms and give her a platonic, comforting hug, but that would not have helped her at all. He couldn't fix this.

They were on the road again less than an hour later. It had taken time to harness the horses and break camp. The boys had found about thirty-five large oysters, and she would make a light batter and fry half for dinner that night. For the rest, she would sit in the fire and let them cook in their own juices. The shop at Gunderman had some eggs, and John had purchased four. They crossed the river at Lower Mangrove by carefully negotiating the rickety, low-level log bridge. It had no sides and consisted of two giant trees that had been felled across the creek, and then split logs had made a road of sorts. The four wagon wheels clattered as the horses plodded their way across. Having had a late start, they stopped for luncheon at the cemetery in Lower Mangrove. The area was kept well-scythed, and the soft green grass of the graveyard was inviting. The last time she had been in a cemetery was to bury her mother and sister. However, Father Patrick's church grounds looked nothing like this; this area was cool and inviting. All she could remember about that day four years ago was the many mounds of soil and no grass.

She shivered at the thought and set about preparing food for the hungry men. The oat cakes had gone, but they had been eaten with delight. She went to bed that night and wept. She should have been waking to get married tomorrow. Now, she doubted if she would even ever see Shéamas again.

On waking, Clare had found a tree for her morning ablutions. Today should have been her wedding day, but she had woken up in a cemetery. How appropriate, for it was just how she felt, dead inside with a heavy heart.

The day proceeded much as the day before. The horses had a climb before them, so they didn't tarry over their meal. The fire to boil the billy was small, and rather than do the potatoes the way she had that night, she planned something different. They set off again, having boiled the billy and set it in its nest of dry grass in the camp oven. The warm tea mid-afternoon had been a delight the day before and meant they didn't have to stop for long. The wagon moved so slowly that calls of nature meant whoever needed to find a tree would hop off, relieve themselves, and catch up when they were done. The horses plodded on.

From Greengrove, the road steadily rose. They had now left the creek and were heading uphill. They found a safe spot further north for their night stop.

That night, dinner was oysters, cooked as fritters and natural, and slices of potato slathered in butter and baked in the camp oven. John had also produced a chunk of delicious cheese. She melted thin slices on top of the potato. Although the boys asked for more rice pudding, she could not provide it as they had no milk. But she had an idea. She made something sweet for their dessert. The treacle dumplings went down better than the rice pudding had. Again, she had never cooked these in a billy before, but they tasted good. Once she had a real kitchen, which John assured her he had at the house, she would cook for them until they rolled out of their dining room chairs. Cara had taught her well.

The next day's destination for luncheon was Mangrove Mountain; from there, they would hope to get through Mangrove Mountain, and once up on the plateau, they should be able to move a little faster. The orchards on the plateau were a delight to drive through. The wagon stopped just out of Central Mangrove for the next night, and the air was much cooler up on the range. There was still no rain in sight, and although the nights were cooler, they still slept without any coverings.

The following day was the beginning of the downhill run to the coast. John had to hold the horses back in some spots as they wanted to trot, and he knew they could not stop if they came to a slope. "From here, there will be sections that we will need you two boys at the back with ropes, and Clare, you and I will be walking the horses down. I carry chocks for the wheels to give the beasts a break, but Peats Ridge Road is very dangerous to traverse with a heavy wagon. The bridge at the bottom is even worse than the one at Lower Mangrove but of a similar design. Unfortunately, few use this one, so it's not as well maintained. However, we have little choice as the only other option is even worse."

Chapter 13 Liam's Plan

While Clare was waiting for John Moore to collect her, Shéamas was on the way to work. He had never wept as much as he had last night, so his eyes were red and puffy, and his mood was sour. After reading the letters from her, he realised she was right. However, he would not sit back and accept the situation. He may have to marry the girl, but he had decided that with many children dying at birth, he would delay the wedding until she had produced a living child. That was, thankfully, six months away. He had yet to inform his father, but he would not be pushed into an early marriage.

The cows came at his call and were soon in line for milking. He led them down the dusty road and towards the milking shed. Liam and the rest of the girls from the gaol were awaiting them. The boys had worked here since childhood and knew each cow by name. He had only been three when Betty Eccles died, and although he had never met her, he knew all about her. When Shéamas was six, he started working at the dairy, mucking out the milking shed. Each docile beast had their own personality and responded to the names they had been given. Most wore bells, and each rang with a different sound. Eddie had made these years before for the herd. The flimsy fencing was often falling over, and if a cow had a bell, it could be heard wherever it wandered away.

Liam was not surprised that Shéamas had not waited for him this morning. They usually walked to work together. "Hey Shaé, you all right?"

Shéamas shrugged his shoulders in reply, nodded, and then shook his head. "What do you expect?"

Liam understood. "Anything I can do?"

Shéamas's eyes were already watering, "No, just keep that woman away from me, as I'm likely to kill her!" He was about to walk away when he turned to Liam and said, "And you keep clear of her too, or she'll get her claws into you as well." He wouldn't put anything past Lavinia's evil.

Liam was shocked, "Cor, but she's got what she wanted, hasn't she?"

A flash of a smile crossed Shéamas's face, "No, not yet. And she will be waiting for a blooming lot longer than she thinks before she gets me. I will not marry her until she produces a living child. She may well be able to force me up the aisle, but I will dictate the terms of when. And if she thinks that I will be a complacent husband, she had better think well about her claim! I still wish to marry Clare and only Clare, and I will do whatever it takes to shake off this whore." With a leafy switch that he carried, he flicked the rump of a cow who had stopped to graze.

Liam grinned, "Lavinia's not going to like that, Shaé."

Their eyes met, and they both smiled. "I know, eh? I haven't told Papa yet, but he will agree because he knows I'm telling the truth. Also, I'm not going to live with her. I was going to leave her in the cottage, but I will make her move into Eddie's servant room under Papa's eye and under lock and key to curtail her activities. I will move into our cottage as it's the only place I can feel close to Clare."

Shéamas had started work at the Government Dairy when only six. Liam had joined him a couple of years later. They had lived in the cottage with a woman who had taken Betty Eccles's place as the senior dairy maid. Cara and Paddy had not been reassigned to Eddie until shortly before the house was finished. That had been in 1843, and Shéamas had been at the dairy for nearly a year. Liam had started there as soon as his parents moved to Parramatta. The boys had come for Sunday dinners until they moved into the stables accommodation with their parents. Moira and Shauna had moved into the small servant's room and later up to the nursery. This was the room Clare and Kerry had first occupied. The thought of limiting her activities brightened him up, and Liam saw him smile.

Liam frowned. "Hey, Shéamas, what are you thinking. 'cos I know that look, and it means mischief."

The grin that met Liam's was puzzling. "I'm just thinking about what Eddie and Jenna will say about my idea and how to stop her whoring ways. She'll have to mend them, or she will be cast out. I do not doubt that she's still seeing the child's father, but I have no idea who it could be."

Liam nodded. "I think we should do a stakeout, don't you, Shaé?"

This time, Shéamas's smile lit up his eyes. "I think you are right, Liam; if we can catch her at it, then...." They had arrived at the dairy, and she walked out of the cottage swinging her hips provocatively.

Shéamas's good mood vanished in an instant. Liam could handle the herd for a bit. He turned and walked into the milking shed. He refused to talk to her.

By mid-morning, they had finished the milking and cleaned up. The milk had been stored and loaded onto the wagon for consumption in the various homes and at the soldier's barracks. Once the wagon was loaded by the boys, Lavinia came out and stood with her hands on her hips and watched them go. They noticed that Cyril Phipps tipped his hat to her and raised a hand in farewell. Knowing he was married with seven children and another on the way, they were a little surprised at his friendliness.

Thankfully, the others did not see the look that passed between the boys. They chatted to Cyril as usual, asking about each of his children. They wondered about his friendly greeting with someone whom he should not even know well. This would need watching.

When he returned home, Shéamas took his father aside, and they sat under the mulberry tree discussing the situation. Once seated with their mugs of the potent, hot, sweet brew of tea that Cara made for them, Shéamas said, "Papa, I have made a decision. I may be required to marry the wench, but I will not be forced into it too early. I may even have Banns read and not marry her until the child is born."

Paddy remained silent but nodded in agreement.

He continued. "If the child dies or she miscarries, then I will not go through with it. I give you a fair warning about that. I love Clare and only Clare. I will never touch another woman." Shéamas's eyes lifted to gauge what his father's reaction would be. He was surprised to see his toothy grin.

"Ohh, Shéamas, I do like that. That will teach the little baggage to accuse you. I know you too well, son. You know I would box your ears if you disrespected a girl like that. You caught that punishment a few times for teasing Clare, but I knew you would do her no real harm as you care for her too much."

Shéamas nodded. He sat thinking about how he would suggest his plan for her accommodation.

Paddy took a swig of his tea and said, "Spit it out, lad." He saw a flick of concern on Shéamas's brow.

"Well, Papa, if I have to marry her, I will not live with her. But to stop her whoring, I wondered if she could live in the servant's room here at Eddie's place. I refuse to live with her and will not consummate this union. If I can't have Clare, I will not have anyone. Lavinia will have my name and, therefore, be under my authority. I will not permit her anywhere without me, or one of us, accompanying her. If she thinks I'll be a complacent husband, she had better think again."

He and Paddy sat deep in thought. They were about to go back inside for a refill, but Eddie came to join them. He carried a tray with three mugs of steaming tea and a plate full of cake. They greeted him and ran the idea by him.

Rather than answer that question, he said, "I've just been chatting to Liam, and I like his idea. Shéamas, we all know you are telling the truth. She arrived with the reputation of being a light skirt, but the cards are dealt, and now we have to sort out what we will do."

Shéamas looked puzzled and replied, "Huh?"

Eddie sat where he could see his friend's face. Eddie grinned. "I've been talking with my Dar too. Liam mentioned he suggested doing a stakeout. Shéamas, if we can get you out of this, we will. However, to pacify her, I suggest you go through the motions of planning your nuptials, if only to silence her and keep her off guard. I also agree that you should delay as long as you can. Babies can be lost at any stage, and then you could call it off. In the meantime, if we can lull her into betraying who she's been cohabiting with, they may relax their guard, and we may discover who it is."

Shéamas beamed at Eddie. "You mean you believe me too?"

Eddie was shocked. "Of course I do, Shéamas. I've known you since you were six, and other than teasing Clare, you have never been mean or lied to any of us. I've seen Paddy box your ears for your miss-endeavours, and you know the consequences of your actions. Cause and effect and all that."

Shéamas nodded.

Eddie continued, "Well, she doesn't! I do not trust her as far as I can kick her, and trust me, I want to do just that. Lavinia McKone is as untrustworthy and slippery as an eel."

"And...?" Shéamas questioned hopefully.

Eddie smiled at Paddy, then Shéamas. He had not had a chance to mention this to him, but he and Jenna had sat up discussing the conundrum the night before. He said, "And then, Liam suggested we set a watch on her in a week or so. Possibly even employ a child to sit and watch over her activities surreptitiously. See who comes and goes and how long they stay. Surely, whoever the father is will still be around because now she thinks she has you in her pocket. I'm hoping she will let her guard down a bit. I'm guessing the man is married already; otherwise, she would have forced his hand."

Paddy and Shéamas both gasped.

Shéamas uttered, "Cor! I never thought of that, Ed."

Paddy was grinning wickedly. "Add me to the watch list, Ed."

Eddie relaxed as he lay back on the bench seat. "I think we'll be tripping over each other to do that, Paddy! We'll catch her out, Shéamas."

Shéamas nodded. "Now I know you are on my side; I will, Ed. But don't trust me near that shrew. I told Liam to make sure she stayed away from both of us. I was about to ask Papa to act on my behalf and make the required arrangements. He knows my thoughts and the timing."

Ed frowned at the words. "Try to be patient, Shéamas. However, that's not our only problem, as we have no idea where Clare has gone. Jenna and I have been looking all morning. She's vanished. She wasn't on the Mail as it didn't run on Good Friday, nor did the ferry to Sydney. She may have hitched a lift with someone, but no one has seen her, nor did anyone see her leave. Kerry said most of her clothes were missing, so she packed her things herself. There is only one gown left. Jenna brought it back here and put it in her wardrobe." He paused before saying, "It was the one she was to wear on Monday. That entire ensemble was the only thing left."

Shéamas gave a half smile. "When the shrew is exposed, I shall take Clare's clothes while searching for her. I'll find her, Ed. I'll marry her and then bring her home. I'll never let her go again."

Paddy put a hand on his son's shoulder. "I'm sorry, son. I should not have made you two wait so long."

By the time the discussion ended, their tea had long since been drunk, and the cake consumed.

Liam stuck his head out the door and was called over. The four remained in the shade, discussing their plans for tailing Lavinia.

With a light at the end of the tunnel and it not being a speeding locomotive, Shéamas had brightened. Knowing that his family and friends fully supported him gave him confidence. "Papa, Clare has a funny saying that her mama used. When things went wrong for them in Ireland, Kerry told me she would stand up, shake her skirts and say, 'Well, I can't stop tomorrow from happening. So I shall get on with today and make the best of it.' I heard her say it once or twice but didn't understand what it meant. Now I do."

Paddy smiled at his second youngest son. These two boys were good lads. They had both worked hard and made a good life for themselves. Neither had been in trouble at all, and both had stayed away from the troublemakers in town... and there were plenty of those.

~

Easter Saturday finished with the boys returning home from the evening milking. The milk was set aside for the cream to rise overnight, and they would skim the cream off to churn it into butter tomorrow after church.

All the empty milk containers had been returned from the Female Factory, hospitals, and barracks and washed up for reuse. Quite a few of the women were serving life sentences, but most loved the work. Others had come to learn how to make cheeses. It was a good life for them all.

Kit Kellow's mother, Jennifer, had worked at this dairy for some years, and Kit had been born during that time. She had brought the skill of making good quality cheeses to the colony. Within a year after her arrival, the price of cheese had doubled, and her products were in demand. She had taught Betty Eccles, Dr Harris, Captain Piper and a Scottish couple the secret skill of making delectable food. Others had come, and she had willingly taught them how to make the plain cheeses. However, she had kept the secret of the first quality ones to herself. Kit knew and made the top quality product that was now mostly shipped home for sale in England. The government dairy made the soft curd cheeses, but they left the hard blue-veined cheeses that took years to mature for Kit's skilful hands.

Clare and Kerry had often gone to Kellow's dairy to learn the skill and technique of making cheese. Clare had been shown how to make the flavour and culture from the cheeses she had brought from Cornwall. The Government Dairy still only made quick-to-mature cheeses, like ricotta and cottage varieties. Jennifer had shown Betty Eccles the technique for making plain cheese, as well as fresh cheeses, which needed little more than lemon juice or vinegar. Betty worked at the dairy until 1835, when she died there. She was reportedly over one hundred years old. The chimney in the dairy was perfect for smoking the ricotta, adding a depth of flavour that even Kit's dairy could not replicate.

Cara taught Clare to make a delicious creamy casserole, to which Jenna added herbs and flavourings as Shéamas liked it so much. He knew that Clare had learned to cook various dishes, especially for him. He loved eating the beautiful creamy cheese sauces and desserts.

~

Easter Sunday came and went with the usual family gathering over luncheon. All the extended family gathered in Eddie's house's backyard for a sumptuous repast of spit-roasted lamb. This year, there was more food than people as the wedding fare was brought out for consumption.

Molly and Bill Miller were supposed to come for luncheon, but they sent a message to say that one of their patrons had taken ill and they would drop in for a while mid-afternoon.

Shéamas and Liam had done the early morning milking and gone straight to church for the morning service. They returned to the dairy to clean up after the service was over and arrived in time to eat.

When Bill and Molly arrived, the boys were about to head back for the afternoon milking.

Molly asked, "All set for tomorrow, Shéamas? Are you nervous?"

Shéamas shook his head. "It's off, Mrs Miller. I can't explain, but Ed will. I can't talk about it." He didn't wait for her to ask more.

He heard her say, "Clare didn't say anything on Friday night. She came for a visit late in the afternoon."

He swung around to face her. "What time, Mrs Miller?"

Molly's face screwed up while she thought. "Um, about four, I think; she stayed for a few hours chatting to a guest, and then Sam and Ellen walked her home. Why?" She found she was talking to thin air. Shéamas had vanished.

Shéamas went directly to Ed, who was chatting with his father. Shéamas stood next to Ed and anxiously changed his weight from each foot.

Charles watched his frustrated movements. "Shéamas, What's up, lad?"

Shéamas's eyes flicked from Charles to Eddie's. He directed his comments to Eddie. "She spent a couple of hours at the Miller's Inn on Friday Ed. That's where she was. I bet she met someone she knew, and she's gone with them."

As he knew that Clare had vanished, Charles questioned him. "She, you mean Clare?"

Shéamas nodded.

Charles said, "Did Molly say who it was she saw?"

Shéamas shook his head. "I didn't ask, sir." He replied to Charles, then said, "Ed, I have to go to work. Can you find out all you can? And Ed, please let them know why the wedding is off. They don't know; I couldn't tell them."

They were a step ahead as they had already started moving towards her. Ed nodded. He put a caring hand on his shoulder. "Go, Shéamas, leave it with us. You have enough on your plate. You can no longer be seen hunting for Clare, but be assured we will leave no stone or lead unfollowed." Ed shooed him away.

Shéamas saw Liam waiting for him, and he realised they should have left some minutes ago. For Shéamas, that shift at the dairy was the longest he had ever done. He could not wait to return home to see if there was any news about Clare.

In the end, Liam said he'd finish up and told his brother to clear out.

When the last broom was cleaned and left to dry for tomorrow, Shéamas took off at a run.

The one-and-a-half-mile track was completed in minutes. Admittedly, much of it was downhill, but he was hardly puffing on arrival. He arrived calling for Ed. As he all but swung through the kitchen door, his mother pointed him towards Ed's office. "Go easy, lad." She wanted to enfold her son in a motherly, caring hug but knew he was keen to hear the interview's outcome with Molly.

"Thanks, Mama. At last, we know she was all right. I imagined her sitting under some tree and weeping." Shéamas bent and quickly kissed his mother before going to find Eddie.

Eddie was waiting for him. He heard his entry and greeted him with a smile. "Come in, Shéamas; I have a bit of news."

Ed settled on the settee next to the unhappy man. For the next half hour, Ed related his conversation with Molly and also his chat with Sam and Ellen. "Shéamas, Clare said nothing to any of them. She did not seem upset or distracted. In her words, Molly said that Clare asked for the Irishman from church. Do you have any idea who that would be? Molly apologised, as she had been reading a letter from her mother, and she was distracted. She had a full house, but she pointed Clare to the sitting room, and the man from room four joined her there. All she can tell you is that his name was Moore and that he came from out of town. They don't keep a register of people who stay, so they have no idea where he lives. All the patrons but two left at dawn on Saturday morning."

Shéamas groaned. "She has no idea where Clare is, then?"

Ed explained. "Shéamas, we are none the wiser as Moore is a common name. However, it does give us a starting point. As Dar is an earl and he is also the Viceroy, he can get access to the census that was taken about twelve years ago. At least we have a name; it may contain a country of birth. Dar needs to speak to Governor FitzRoy about some official things; he will be in Sydney on Tuesday and will delve deeper."

Shéamas nodded his understanding. Now, at least, they had a clue. He wasn't happy that she'd gone off with a strange man.

Eddie felt sorry for the innocent young lad. None of this was his fault. Tomorrow should have been his wedding day. "It will take time, Shéamas, but you must leave this to us. If you get involved, it won't look good. Be assured we will leave no stone unturned to return our cousin."

~

Over the following weeks, snippets of information were revealed.

Firstly, Charles found that a land grant was issued to a John Moore about twenty miles north of Sydney as the crow flies. It was on the coast, but the area was very remote, being over eighty miles by road. He was the closest but also the most difficult to get to. There were three other possibilities, each in a different direction: one on the South Coast, one in Bathurst and one up north of Newcastle. There was no country of birth listed. The four men were yet to be traced, and even then, Clare may not be with them. No one reported seeing any man by that name in town recently.

Liam had found that one of Kit Kellow's sons, Logan, was prepared to watch over Lavinia. At twelve, he was already a familiar site on the farm. He was often over near the Government Dairy buildings petting the cows, so Lavinia would not notice if he were there more often than usual.

By the end of June, Logan had discovered who was sneaking around in an area where he should not have been.

However, they could not act yet!

Chapter 14 Arriving in Avoca

*T*he wagon set off from Central Mangrove and headed down the steep hill towards Gosford. Peats Ridge Road was a nightmare; they would all need to walk with the horses. The boys walked beside the wagon and were ready with a thick branch to use as a chock. Four big rocks were on the back if they needed something more substantial. The journey down took all morning, and they reached the rickety bridge just before noon. Before the crossing, there was a clearing off to the right. John pulled off here with a sigh of relief. One big hill was done, and another to follow. "Lunchtime, young ones! We'll stop for no more than one hour as we have yet to do another climb. Depending on the horses' stamina, we can camp another night or go down into East Gosford."

They had a hasty stop, leaving less than forty-five minutes after halting. They made the climb with relative ease and decided to make the descent and stay at the bottom of the hill. "There's a lovely camping spot further out of the village. It's out on a peninsula." Once more, John chattered on about their surroundings. Clare tuned out. She didn't care about the state of the roads, the rickety wooden bridges, or dead people. She should have been on her honeymoon with Shéamas, and all she wanted to do was cry. John realised that she had fallen silent. He saw her brush a tear or two away, and he reached over and squeezed her hand. "Where we're staying should suit your mood, dear girl. Tonight is in another graveyard. I don't need to go this far off the road, but there is a nice spot at the end of the road I wish to show you. Will that help? Admittedly, it was only this year that a friend of mine was buried here, but I believe there are a few others in unmarked graves."

Clare gave a watery chuckle. "Yes, Uncle John, it will suit admirably."

Determined to cheer her up, he said, "You know that funny saying of yours, 'You can't stop tomorrow?' Well, here's another one for you; 'You can't change yesterday'." He coughed to cover her sniff. He turned to check that the boys were sitting at the back and out of earshot. "Clare, you have your life in front of you. Don't waste your life thinking of what could have been. Use the time here on the farm with me as healing time before you return home. We'll arrive tomorrow, and your life will start afresh. Do you understand? Stay as long as you wish, but don't plan that you will stay here forever. Make a life for yourself, have beautiful babies and enjoy a full life."

Her freckled face and big brown eyes searched his face. He could see she was close to tears, but she held them back. She was not what you would call beautiful, but she had a loveliness that took one's breath away. Clare nodded. "I just need time, Uncle John. I know that Shéamas and all my family will already be looking for me. I left no hint of where I was going. I only said I was safe and didn't even know you were related then."

John wouldn't reveal his personal life to the girl but said, "We all have regrets. With what you survived in Ireland, you have reason to fight to live. Yes, your heart is broken now, and you are not alone in that, either. Even the boys have those. Clare girl, get through one day at a time. And let tomorrow care for itself. It's what that saying of yours means, you know."

The camp at Point Frederick was another lovely wide grassy spot right on the end of the point. They had passed by a few houses along the way, and one or two occupants waved to John, but he did not stop and chat. Clare cooked a meal for them but put little effort into it. Her heart just wasn't in it tonight. John had called this a down-day. He was not wrong; she only wished to weep for her lost love. At dusk, as the tide was out, John had sent the boys off for a scout around. "Boys, take a bucket and see if you can find some oysters, will you? There are none at home, and they will keep for a day or so if they are whole. Fill the bucket if you can." He watched them scamper off as if on an adventure. "Clare, come for a walk with me; I wish to show you something."

She stood and followed him towards a new grave. He stood looking down at it. "I don't know who this one is for as it looks recent, but I would like to be buried nearby, my dear. Do you know that you are my closest relative in this land? I have a male cousin, Robert, who lives down south, as I said earlier, but when I die, will you see that I am buried here?"

Clare gasped. "Are you ill, Uncle John?

John spun around to her. "Oh no, lass, I'm in fine health, but no one else nearby. I turn fifty in a few years and must think about these things. For you to appear now is a Godsend to me. You may have been surprised when you heard my accent, but no more so than when I heard your name. We share blood, Clare. Will you do this for me when needed?"

The spot next to this grave was overgrown. She nodded her assent. "Here? Why here, Uncle John?"

His lips turned up in a half smile. "Peace, Clare, it's where I feel closest to God. I'm not devout, but I care for my fellow man. Like your family, I left Ireland under a religious cloud. I lean more towards the

Protestant beliefs than the Roman Catholic as I wouldn't say I like the trappings they have added to their faith. God, I love dearly, but I dislike religion intensely. I certainly call myself a Christian. This is a Church of England burial ground. There is one at Kincumber, which is closer to my home, but this one has two bodies of water, too. None of that is important to God. Denominations are man-made things. Our earthly bodies are just a husk and will turn to dust." He paused as if thinking deeply, and after a few moments, he said, "However, my time fighting my own countrymen made me realise many things, the most important of which was that denominations are irrelevant. There are no Catholics or Protestants in heaven under those tags, but there are faithful believers. Those names are merely tickets we place on ourselves. I remember having a conversation with Kieran about this, and he agreed. Freedom of faith was one of the reasons I returned here. Here, I can be me. I believe in God, and all that faith entails, don't get me wrong. I believe that we need to be the best we can be on this earth. I believe in repentance, forgiveness and eternal life. That's why I took the Justice of the Peace role at the governor's request. I don't know why he chose me, as he knew little about me. I can issue legal chastisement and enforce the law, but hopefully, I also administer justice for the wronged innocent people. I try to be fair in my judgements, I do what I can for others, and I've seen enough killing to last more than one lifetime." He glanced down at her. "War does that to a man, lass. Still, many years later, my nights are broken with nightmares or bad dreams, and the farm I chose is as far as I could find from civilisations I could get, and yet still have people reasonably close at hand. My farm is named after Avoca at home, as a lake meets the sea there. So it's a little like the meeting of the two rivers at home. Not that the lake here is open often because it takes quite a bit of rain to make that occur."

Clare had listened with interest. Thinking of his request, she said, "I'll do it for you, Uncle John, if I can, but I hope that is not for many, many years yet." She moved quickly and gave him a big hug. "I don't want you to die, Uncle John. Not for a long, long time. I don't know what I would have done if you had not brought me with you."

Her actions towards him were surprising. He said quietly, "I'll try to stay alive for you, lass, until I see you happy again." He felt her head nod against his chest. He wished he had a daughter like her.

The wagon moved off at first light. This was to be an easy day for travel with few hills. John said they should arrive at Avoca late morning if the nearby punt was working. John knew the tides here were hours later than they were at sea. Thankfully, the tide was high enough, and the punt quickly moved across the creek. The loaded wagon was soon on its way through the mangrove-lined track and would turn away from Erina and head towards Kincumber. Soon after exiting the punt, Clare glimpsed two shacks built on the water's edge. They were so close that you could easily fish from the verandah. In awe of the stilt-like construction of the buildings, she said,

"Uncle John, would those two houses not flood?" She was peering through the mangrove trees and saw various vessels anchored in the creek.

John didn't take his eyes off the narrow track. "Probably Clare, but they have survived thus far. I think they belong to some of the boat builders. I'm not quite sure."

They passed various boats in assorted stages of construction. Some large boats had masts visible over the trees. One was easily visible just near their turnoff. It was a three-masted boat almost too big to even take the corner to near the punt. Glenn and Dave had been discussing the boats, too. Dave asked, "Sir, how do they get such large ships out of the small creek?" They, too, had seen the ships under construction.

John smiled at his question. "I asked that myself, Glenn; I believe the water level is high on a spring flood tide to float the boats out. The king tide is something that occurs once or twice a year. The boat builders know when they are due and plan the launches accordingly." They turned south into the road towards Kincumber. Someone had painted a road sign that pointed in the direction of the coastal road. The two-wheel track meandered through the farms, orchards, and shacks. Soon, the wagon was travelling towards a long, straight road, and a small church was visible at the end.

John pointed out the new St Paul's Church of England church. As he had done for most of the journey, he gave a rundown of the building. "This church was built in response to the needs of the area. There is a much larger Roman Catholic one at South Kincumber, but fewer Church of England people are here. This new building, St Paul's, only seats about fifty, but it's adequate for the local families. I worship here when I can, but the services are not weekly. More often than not, I forget what day it is when I'm on the farm." He chuckled. "Since the governor saw fit to make me a Warden and Justice of the Peace and Magistrate of the district, I manage to remember when I'm required for court duties, but days seem to blur into each other a bit, so I've missed the odd session."

The boys gasped. They had no idea that John was so well respected in the district. John mentioned that his fruit trees were not just citrus, as expected. None had ever seen banana trees or even tasted them. The three young folks traversed the last three miles with rising excitement. All were now pumping John for information. He pointed out who owned which farms. They passed the Humphreys, Pickett, Davis and Frost farms. Names were reeled off as they passed their farms.

Coming over a small hill, John paused the vehicle. "Well, dear ones, we are here. This is the beginning of my holding. It's one square mile, according to the map, but it goes from the left down that creek to the sea. The boundary is up the middle of the lagoon, which we will soon pass. Now take a deep breath; you will smell the salt in the air." John flicked the reins, and the horses lifted their heads and took off. They knew they were nearly home and had lifted their pace a little. John pulled back on the reins to slow them. "Oh, and the difference between a lake and a lagoon is that a lagoon sometimes opens to the sea, whereas a lake does not. My old cabin that burnt down overlooked the lake and faced west, but the new house faces north and overlooks the lagoon. The main stables are still near the old house, but I have turned it into a tack room and carriage house."

The track headed down to the flat from the small hill, then wound along the lagoon edge. They could see the water through the paperbark and she-oak trees. The potholed, rutted track was like an arched bower and was cool in the day's heat, but it was a rough ride. The horses turned again, and the route headed eastwards. John had the boys hop off and lead the horses over the deeply rutted route. Then, they continued at a snail's pace, dodging potholes. Another narrow path headed off to the right, and John explained, "That's the old entrance to the farm, and although I still use it occasionally, I don't do much to maintain it. My beef cattle are up in the valley over there." He pointed to the south, but all they could see were trees. They kept heading straight ahead. The she-oak trees were predominant and lined both sides of the handmade path. The swishing of the sea breeze and the salty air was comforting. The trees sounded like they were whispering a welcome.

Again, John narrated their journey. "You all know that bridge at the bottom of Peats Ridge Road; when I decided to make a shortcut here and fell some trees, I made my own version. As I showed you, the road used to go right around that arm of the lake. Well, I built this…" In front of them was the most incredulous-looking contraption that could barely be called a bridge. Four giant trees have been felled and spanned the short distance across the narrow opening of the lake. John had placed long planks on these but no horizontal cross ones. The planks lay the length of the fallen logs, thus making the bridge only passable for a dual-horse vehicle or a single rider. There was a void in the middle of the logs. "Boys, one of the jobs I need to do is to place cross slabs on these so the deck is more stable. As my old house was at the back of the lake, I used to go the long way, but the new house is nearby. This saves a lot of road maintenance needed on the longer loop road. Since the last two burnt my cottage, I won't have convict here."

The wagon trundled across the logs and turned again. The horses needed no steering as they turned southward and headed towards a large house on the hill. The vehicular entry to the house was at the rear, and there was an assortment of outbuildings. One rear building had a long, narrow verandah that faced west. Various doors opened onto this, showing that it contained individual rooms. John pointed to the most substantial of these dwellings, the one with the verandah. "Boys, that will be your accommodation. You will share it with two other lads, but they are out on the farm. As I said before, I have no house staff, and Clare, you will be in the maid's room inside the house. My room is at the other end of the house. During harvest time, I employ more local boys, and I have one of the local ladies come and clean the house weekly. Clare, you will be occupied with the dairy cow and cooking."

He saw Clare nod, but she remained silent. "Clare, is this what you expected? Are you disappointed?"

Clare looked aghast. "Oh, no, Uncle John! It's much bigger than you led me to believe. I was wondering how I would keep it clean, cook and do the dairy all by myself, that's all."

John chuckled, "Oh, so I keep the cleaner then?"

Clare nodded, "Oh, yes, please, at least until I find my feet. I'll see how I manage. She might need the money, too."

By the time the boys were settled in their new quarters, two other lads had appeared. The four strapping lads soon had the stores unloaded and were chatting as though they had known each other for years. The opened bags of potatoes, rice, and flour were moved into the large pantry. The remainder of the unopened dry goods were taken into a small stone storeroom near the house's back door. Clare found her room light and dry, if somewhat stark, but it was hers and safe. She was also at the end of the house that was closest to the sea. She could hear the waves breaking on the shore and was itching to investigate the area. She fell to her knees and thanked the Lord for bringing her somewhere safe and that John was her missing relative. He had been a needle in a haystack, and God led her to him. A breeze blew in through the window she had just pushed open. The salty air reminded her of home. It was a long time since she had smelled the sea, and the scent reminded her of all the sad times and losses. The estuary at Tarbet had been tidal, and her daily swims to wash had left the family salty, but they had smelled much better. She stood looking at the view of the beach. The elevation of the house gave a beautiful vista down the mouth of the lagoon. She could see a thin bar of sand blocking the lagoon entrance. It was while she was lost in thought that John discovered her. He offered to accompany her for a walk down to the beach, but she felt guilty and asked if they could postpone it until the following day. She knew that work needed to be completed, and she also had to prepare a meal for everyone and had no idea what was available. Shaking off her melancholy, she tackled her immediate problem. Food for six was urgently needed. They had consumed the last of the damper, but she thought she could whip up some savoury scones and serve them with some eggs that sat on the bench. She wondered how long they had been there and sat them in some water to see how high they floated. Realising they were fresh, she whipped up an omelette.

With requests for more treacle dumplings, the appetites of the five men were finally sated. John sent Glenn and Dave to do the dishes, as the other two lads had been working all day, and Clare was handed a mug of tea and told to sit on the verandah and enjoy the sunset. Twilight was descending, and the day closed in. John called from inside for Clare to get her wrap. "Come on, all of you; we're going for a walk. We need to stretch our legs." He headed out the back door and waited. This seemed to be the main entry into the house. From there, you could see straight through the house to the front verandah. The five young ones followed him as he wandered down the sloping embankment. This was obviously a much-used shortcut to the beach as it was well-worn. The two lads who had been working all day were Tom and Bill. No sooner than they had reached the flat, Bill turned to his friend and the two new lads and said, "Swim chaps? Beat you in!" He took off down the flat and headed towards the lake entrance.

"If they go in the water, we will stay well away, Clare, as they have no swimming attire." John knew they had no other clothing. They would be stripping off as he usually did. John was somewhat jealous but could have a dip in the morning. Clare, as yet, did not know her way around the area. John had her on his arm, watching until the boys were well out of sight. "The twilight won't last long, so we will only walk to the water's edge tonight."

Seeing that Bill had taken the boys into the lake rather than the sea, he said to Clare, "I'll have just enough time to point out the area. Tomorrow, you will have time to look around more. I will harness up the buggy in the morning and take the three of you to show you my boundary. Across the lagoon to the north is not my land. I can only keep you safe if you stay within the borders of my farm." He fell silent as they walked, wondering how to broach a delicate subject. "Clare, I should not have brought you here. I realise how wrong I was. There will be comments about you living alone with five men, and I will not have your reputation tainted by innuendo."

Clare chuckled. "You forget, though, because, in reality, I am your ward now, Uncle John. I have been thinking about this myself. I am old enough to be your daughter or niece but am not yet twenty-one. Kerry and I are related to you, and also we are orphans. She is with other relatives, all of which is true. However, by law, you are indeed the closest male relative, as Aunt Sal is a female. If anyone wished to say anything, tell them you promised my father. No one but us will know anything different. Kerry would have been too young to remember meeting you. I only vaguely remember our time in Avoca in Ireland."

John looked at the lovely girl with surprise. He nodded, saying, "So that will remain our cover story, then?"

Clare nodded. "Yes, please, then we are both safe. But it's the truth, not a cover story. " He flicked her cheek, just as he had once done to his real niece in Ireland when he left. It was lovingly done with no threat or intent and showed his care.

~

Life on the farm settled into a smooth routine. Glenn and Dave found they fitted in well to life with the trees and animals. Bill had previously only milked the cow to ease her udder. With six to now feed, Clare stripped half of her milk, leaving enough for her calf. The chickens were producing eggs a-plenty, and she found an upright cobweb-covered butter churn in the store room. Although John had no cheesecloth, she did find a few yards of fine muslin. This would be adequate for the ricotta cheese but would take longer to drain.

Soon, Clare had the kitchen producing all sorts of delectable foods. On the first Sunday morning after their arrival, a church service was to be held at the small church in Kincumber. The wagon was harnessed, and the six set off for what John and Clare knew would be an inquisition. They had spent the evenings on the verandah talking of their memories of Ireland and their homes. Clare revealed the horrors of the famine and how her father had eked out an existence for their family. She told of the seaweed broth her mother had made and the death of each of the children. Each revelation was followed by a long period of silence and reflection.

In turn, John spoke of some of his experiences in the war. "I'll not give much detail, Clare, but even now, so many years later, I rarely manage an undisturbed night's sleep."

They had come to know each other's stories well over their shared reminisces. On Sunday morning, Clare was easily passed off as John's ward. She would cook for the men and earn her keep, and no one even raised an eyebrow. Clare was in her element, having a large kitchen with every modern convenience that could open and shut. The men were well-fed, and although Clare had initially agreed to do the milking, she had been content to let Bill do the morning strip of Bessy, the cow. She produced more than enough milk for their needs and her calf.

Over the following months, the bull calf fattened quickly. He was sent off to market, and Bessy was put to a bull for her next calf. This meant that for some months, they had little to no milk.

Clare mentioned this to John and, having become used to the delicious fare she served them, a fat brown cow soon arrived from the herd on the back hills. The mottled, long-horned beast was obviously used to being handled as she submitted to milking quickly. Someone had inserted a large ring through her nose at some stage, making leading her easy. As Bessy's milk dried up, the new cow, whom Clare had named Trixie, submitted to being milked. Her milk did not have as much cream as Bessy, who was a Jersey cow, but there was enough to make butter and a little soft cheese. Being less creamy, her milk became the base of many rice puddings, custards, and numerous other sweet desserts they all enjoyed. The chickens supplied numerous eggs, so bread and butter pudding was a treat they all loved.

Clare's thoughts often turned to Kerry, Shéamas and the family in Parramatta. She missed them all, but as John had wisely told her, "You can't change yesterday, and I can't stop tomorrow." Clare had no intention of leaving her new home. She was safe and comfortable, if somewhat heartsore. At least here, there was no one pushing themselves on her. She didn't want to look for love. It hurt too much.

Chapter 15 Shéamas's Joy

*L*ogan Kellow's effort had more than paid off. The information he gathered meant they could now set up their sting.

At Eddie's insistence, Shéamas knew nothing of their discovery.

Cyril Phipps was seen entering the cottage before collecting the evening load of milk. His visits were as regular as clockwork.

Logan began watching how often the wagon was left tied to the hitching post and timing the man's stays. Each one was at least half an hour. The man may have had an excuse to be there in the mornings as he collected the milk. As a father of so many, he may be giving Lavinia fatherly advice, but not every night. However, since she had moved to Eddie's house the month before, Cyril now had no reason to be in the cottage at all, and neither did she. Shéamas now lived at Roseneath with Brodie.

After Logan mentioned his initial observations to the family, Eddie moved Lavinia into the servant's room sooner rather than later. If Lavinia snuck away to meet Cyril at the cottage, there could be no excuse for either of them to be there.

Unaware of being observed, Lavinia was followed by Moira and Shauna, who had occasionally started visiting their brothers at the dairy. Lavinia was none the wiser as they kept their distance.

If anything happened between the illicit couple, they needed to be caught in the act by more than one person, preferably someone high-up and not one of the family; only then could Shéamas escape her clutches.

~

Over the next month, Cyril and Lavinia were carefully watched. Logan kept a diary of their visits and reported to Liam each day. Logan found that on Thursday afternoons, Cyril would arrive even earlier than usual.

Shéamas was still kept ignorant of her activities. He needed to be totally oblivious to any revelation so his reaction would be genuine. Word had spread through town that Shéamas would now marry Lavinia, not Clare. No one gave the reason, but many guessed. All saw how sad he had become.

Being unaware of Lavinia's actions, he became quite morose. He avoided any contact with her. His heart still hurt. He had resisted moving to the cottage as he had been able to avoid Lavinia at Ed's house. However, he did more to Roseneath with Brodie and Kerry. No matter whom or where he asked, no one had heard from Clare. Unbeknownst to him, a plan would soon unfold. Since Lavinia had moved, Cyril had curtailed his visits to only once a week, but the venue was the same, although their duration was now a little longer.

On the first Thursday in July, everything was ready. Lavinia was six months along in her confinement and, as such, said she was now unable to work, so she should have been ensconced at Ed's house. On this particular day, Charles, Eddie, and his eldest brother, Charlie, planned everything to the minute.

Governor FitzRoy, Charles, and Charlie, the Assistant Viceroy, were routinely inspecting all the government buildings in the town. At ten minutes to four, they arrived unannounced at the door of the dairy cottage, the last building on the governor's list. They had just finished the dairy inspection and found everything as it should be. Charles noted the presence of the milk wagon and smiled.

The governor walked in unannounced as he had done at the previous venues. He had presumed the cottage to be vacant, as it should have been. Being a good dancer, his footsteps were light, and his entry was silent. The sight that met the governor's eyes made him freeze.

There was a couple almost caught in the act of having illicit relations in a supposedly empty, government-owned building. The female was partially clad, and the man wore no trousers. Their intentions were obvious, and as they had not heard the governor enter, their actions did not stop. The man was about to climb on top of her as he pulled aside what remained of her undergarments. Little was left to the governor's imagination. He was dumbfounded at what he witnessed.

The moaning of carnal delights was quite audible. Charles heard their sighs of rapture from outside. Within moments, they would be *in flagrante delicto* if not interrupted immediately.

The governor was about to say something when Charles and Charlie appeared at his side. Behind them was a fourth visitor, one who knew the cottage well. After thanking Logan, he sent him home. Charlie met Shéamas outside the dairy. Knowing what was about to occur, Charlie dragged Shéamas unresistingly into the cottage. He entered, hard on the other men's heels.

Charles and Charlie were fully aware of what the governor would find. Both knew that Shéamas's situation would soon be resolved, and it was not of his making.

Shéamas, however, was stunned at finding Lavinia in the arms of another man, thrilled but shocked.

The governor was about to say something, but Shéamas pushed past him and verbally exploded. The angry groom's response was as genuine as Charles and Charlie had hoped. "You brazen little hussy! So this is the father of your child. No wonder he can't marry you. He has seven children already, with another one imminent. If you think you can hoodwink me into marrying you now, then forget it. No wife of mine will be found cuckolding me even before we marry. This engagement is over, not that I would have married you before the child was born anyway. But I shall have my ring back right now."

Lavinia hastily pulled a sheet over her partially clad body. She tugged off the cheap ring he had been required to give her.

Cyril dropped to the floor beside the bed, hoping to hide his partially clad state and his physical reaction to her state of undress. The interruption had deflated his manhood quickly.

On hearing Shéamas's words, everything changed. As Lavinia threw the ring back at him, verbal pandemonium ensued. Her foul-mouthed diatribe soon filled the room, and the vile, filthy words made the governor and Charles retire from the cottage.

Charlie stood beside the twice-insulted groom to support him.

Lavinia shrieked like the whore that she was and tried to attack Shéamas; she was attempting to kick and claw at him. All the while, she was screaming at him that she would sue him for breach of promise. Her breasts were hanging out of her unbuttoned undergarment.

Shéamas remained calm and watched her actions without responding.

With the governor now gone, the trouser-less, Cyril at least had the decency to grab her around the waist and try to curtail her ranting. She had been a more than willing participant to his attentions, and when she had fallen with child, he had wondered if he should continue his visits. Her allure was more potent than his will, and their illicit liaison continued unabated. With Shéamas used as the scapegoat, Cyril did not curtail his visits until she had to leave the cottage. His wife was large with child and had been unwilling to acquiesce to sate his desires, so Lavinia received his ardent visits with glee.

Once calmed, Cyril's desire for her had undergone an amazing transformation. He had never seen a female fighting and clawing so viciously. His bit of fluff had turned into a wildcat. His wife was a quiet and complacent woman who knew of his philandering but realised he would always return to her bed. He had never seen a woman in such a violent rage, and she disregarded her lack of clothing in front of these men. Her breast bounced delectably as she repeatedly attempted to attack Shéamas.

Seeing that Cyril now had her under some control, Charlie said, "Meet us outside when you are both decently clad." He then ushered Shéamas outside to wait for them to dress. Cyril knew he now had to face the governor and Lord Charles. He was not looking forward to that interview.

Now quietened somewhat, Lavinia was given some privacy to cover herself appropriately. She was still muttering angrily, but she knew she had to explain herself.

Charlie warned Shéamas to remain silent and let the governor deal with the situation. If he did, things would go better for him.

Shéamas nodded with a huge grin on his lips. The end was nigh!

~

Within a week, Lavinia was placed on a ship to Moreton Bay and told that she was never to return to Sydney or Parramatta. Shéamas and the Lockley family each gave her five pounds, and armed with more wealth than she had ever had, she set off to see if she could entrap some poor man into marrying her before the child was born. They had no doubts that she would pass herself off as a widow.

Shéamas, Charlie, and Liam escorted her to Sydney to ensure she boarded the ship they had booked.

As the steamer cast off, a shout of glee was heard from the wharf. Shéamas cheered, saying to his brother and Charlie, "Now I can hunt for Clare guilt-free. I will find her and marry her as soon as I can." Unbeknownst to Charlie and Liam, he had no intention of going home with them. He had said his farewells to his parents as they left. They presumed that the duffle bag he carried had been for Lavinia. However, it sat at his feet. He and his father had long talks about how and where Shéamas should start his search, and with the four names they had, they decided that the one on the south coast was a possibility as it was new dairy country. As Clare knew this, it was where he would try first. He was to catch the southbound steamer and would hopefully hunt around the Milton area for her. If there were no trace of her there, then Bathurst would be the next stop, as there were dairies there too. The other two places were up north. One was an obscure place on the coast just north of Sydney, but getting there would take a week by road. Shéamas intended to hunt for her until she was found. He handed some letters to Charlie as he moved to the other jetty to catch the southbound steamer. "Thanks for helping with this, Charlie. You know how much Clare means to me. I shall find her if it takes years. The letters are for Kerry and your parents. I told the governor that I would not return to the dairy, and he was kind enough to give me a reference. Your father has explained the situation to him. He even told me I always had a job there if I wished."

Charlie nodded. "I figured that this was what you would do. I brought you some funds from the family. Clare is our relative, so please accept it on our behalf. If you need more, do not hesitate to let us know. Bring her home, Shéamas. Do it for us all."

Liam hugged his brother, and Shéamas charged him with caring for Kerry. If all turned out as planned, the two boys would marry the sisters. With a spring in his step, he boarded the coastal steamer and went to find his cabin. Charlie and Liam were hard on his heels. Once his bag was stowed, they made their farewells in private, and the two made their way ashore. As soon as they left, the gangplank was hauled aboard. The ropes were brought on deck, and the belch of smoke from the smoke stack soon trailed behind the departing vessel. Shéamas had never been on a boat in the open sea, and by the time the ship had reached Sydney Heads, he was burleying the fish with his luncheon. He was still grinning through his distress as this was all for gain. He was free from the cloying tentacles of the evil woman, and he would find Clare if it took years. His heart was once again light.

His arrival in Ulladulla was after a torturous journey on the heaving seas. He was determined that all future travel would be with his feet firmly planted on the good, dry land. It would take a full day resting on the grassy banks of Narrawallee Creek to overcome the illness that had overwhelmed him. The steamer had pulled into the relative calm of the bay and offloaded him onto the pilot vessel with the mail. On landing, Shéamas threw himself on the beach and groaned.

The pilot looked concerned, and once he had secured the boat, he came to see his passenger. "Eh, laddie, are you okay?"

Shéamas shook his head. He felt as though he was going to die, and the sand beneath his feet felt like it was moving. Shéamas managed to utter, "Cor, how do you do this day in and day out?"

"You get your sea legs soon enough." The pilot helped him to his feet and steadied him. "Where are you heading, boy?"

Ignoring the question with a shrug, Shéamas asked, "How long does it take for the land to stop kicking?" He turned and vomited bile. It was all that remained in his stomach.

The pilot commiserated with the young man. "Come have a mug of tea, and we'll talk. I gather you have a destination of some sort, but we can discuss that later."

Shéamas nodded in reply. With the mailbag over one shoulder and Shéamas under the other, the pilot moved slowly towards a waiting buggy. Though hobbled, the horse had been left to wander; it didn't take long for the pilot to have it in the shafts, and they returned to his house.

By the time the fifteen-minute drive was completed, Shéamas was not feeling as dizzy. "Where are we, sir?" He was now able to take stock of his surroundings. They were pulling to a road that turned along the lee of a headland; Shéamas saw a house overlooking the bay. "Oh, what a lovely location! What beach is this, sir?"

The pilot smiled. "This is Narrawallee Headland, and that is my house. The area was first settled here, so the headlands have been cleared of timber. From here to Milton, the valleys are now being used for dairy herds." He noticed Shéamas brighten at the mention of both Milton and dairy. "So, how about you tell me why you are here?"

Shéamas did. "I don't suppose you know anyone named Moore or if a young light, red-headed lady has appeared in the past months."

The pilot grinned, "I'm guessing the lady is your quarry, and she may have travelled with Mr Moore?"

Shéamas nodded. He didn't like how that sounded but replied, "Yes, sort of! She is my fiancé, and she fled due to a big mix-up. I have letters from her family explaining everything to her, and I seek to let her know that the mess is now sorted. However, I need to find her first. All we know is that she possibly left with someone named Moore to work for them. Four men fit our category, and we hope she will have travelled with one of them. If not, we are stumped."

The pilot nodded his understanding. The lad was a lovesick groom, and he had no idea where she had gone. His lips pursed before he said. "Charles Moore has not left the area in months, and no single females are here for miles. If so, this will mean another sea voyage for you, laddie."

Shéamas was shaking his head. "No! No, never again! No more ships for me. I don't care if it takes me weeks, but I'm going overland. However, I'll find this chap first and make sure for myself. Thankfully, my next destination is Bathurst, and no ships go there. I promised her sister I would find her and bring her home. Even if she no longer wishes to marry me, her family wants her to return."

The pilot saw the mournful look that crossed his face. He felt sorry for him. "Well, until you feel better, you are not going anywhere. I am to sort and take the mail up tomorrow, so I will take you to Moore's place, and you can ask him yourself. There are timber wagons and store drays that travel the Bathurst route, but it's a long way. Are you prepared for a couple of weeks roughing it?"

Shéamas nodded. "I'd do anything to find her. You see, I love her."

~

As expected, Shéamas drew a blank in Milton. He did have time to view some of the incredible dairies in the area in the guise of looking for Clare, but he was soon on his way to Bathurst to seek the next Moore on his list.

From Milton, the timber wagon headed northwest. The wagoner took his load of dressed timber up a steep track up what looked like an unnavigable escarpment and onto the plateau on the mountain range. Somehow, they made it unscathed. There were some touch-and-go areas where the narrow track had fallen away down the side of the mountain pass. The wagon wheels only just fitted on the remainder of the so-called road. Once up on the plateau, the going was easier. They had to follow a two-wheel track that led into a seemingly endless scrubby bushland.

Bathurst was over two hundred miles away, and with no accommodation *en route,* nights were spent sleeping around the fire to keep out the cold. Frosts were now nightly, and the weather was colder the further west and higher they travelled. Night after night, mile after mile, they drove further away from the sea but hopefully closer to Clare.

Chapter 16 Avoca Sunrise

A sight that intrigued Clare was the skeletal remains of the shipwreck. She discovered that the *Sir Robert Peel* had been a troop ship that had run ashore in the middle of a foggy stormy night five years earlier. The vessel had rammed the land so hard onto the beach that her back had broken, and the ship had been written off. No one had died, but two men had been injured.

The evening after their arrival, John retold the story of the stormy sea-fog-swathed night of January 17, 1847. They had looked around the wreck earlier that day, and after dinner that night, the four sat on the verandah while Bill and Tom did the dishes. They had lived through the saga and had heard the retelling often. They chose to do the washing up rather than sit through the tale again.

John described the horrors of that storm and of the day after when they discovered the wreck. He forbade anyone to climb on it, as the timbers were now rotting. But more than that, nails and bolts were sticking out of the wood, and they were dangerous. He relaxed in his cane chair, which was placed so he could watch the bridge to his house. No one ever came, but he liked the view rather than the rolling waves. It was more peaceful.

Clare moved another one of the comfortable cane chairs from inside and set hers facing the rolling breakers. Dave and Glenn relaxed on the floor and leaned against the railing. The sound of the waves rolling up the beach reminded her of Ireland and home. Even the sadness of her past in Ireland was easier to think about than her lost love. However, tonight, even that was far from her mind. They all settled down to hear the story of the wreck.

John took a long draught of his hot, sweet tea. "Right, oh, now, for the excitement of the night in question. Let me set the scene. For the three days prior to the big storm, there had been a sea fog so thick that I had never seen the like since I left Ireland. At times, you could barely see your hand in front of your face. Then, on Sunday, the bad weather set in. Gale-force winds and gusts lifted off the shingles on the new roof; the sea fog was replaced by such heavy rain that visibility was nil. The *Sir Robert Peel* was a reasonably new three-masted ship that had only taken four months from London. It had already dropped off troops in Auckland and was returning to Sydney. I didn't know about the wreck until dawn when I heard voices approaching the house. The foul weather drowned out all other sounds. By then, all the passengers and crew were able to land safely. Along with twenty men of the 58th regiment, six were from the 22nd regiment; there were officers, a corporal and sergeant, the crew, the captain, a regimental doctor, Doctor Clifford, plus one woman and a child. Only one of the crew and one of the soldiers were injured. Unable to walk, I had to get the boys to harness the dray and bring it down to collect them." He took another draw of his tea. "Captain Champion stood looking at what had been his pride and joy. The ship was sitting high and dry by this time as the tide had gone out, and her keel was broken in half. She was way beyond rescue, and her position on the beach made salvage unviable. The poor man looked as though he could have wept. I'm sure he did when no one could see. I'll never forget the haunted look on his face." John paused.

Clare had seen the ship's remains, and the keel was still visible in the sand. "So, no one was killed?"

John shook his head. "Nope, not one!" He continued his retelling. "Well, I didn't have either food or room for so many extra people, but I knew they could stay at the lumber yard in Terrigal. Plus, it was far more protected, so ships came in easily. The boys and I harnessed the second large dray, loaded some aboard, and took them by road to the bay to the north while the others walked along the beach. The lake was not yet open, so that way was accessible. The boys led them over there. It took a couple of days for the storm to blow itself out. Within a week, reports of the wreck had been taken to Sydney. From then, I wasn't involved much once I had delivered the passengers, but a vessel called the *Thistle* soon arrived with assessors, and the ship was declared a write-off and strolled of reusable items. The crew and soldiers had already removed all the luggage, personal property and cargo. Virtually nothing was lost."

Glenn was intrigued. "Sir, the ship is now a skeleton; what happened to all the timbers? If it were only five years ago, surely they would not have rotted in that time."

John chuckled. "Trust you to notice that, young man. Well, once they wrote it off, I had a broken ship plopped in the middle of my beautiful, pristine beach. No one would shift it, so it was up to me if I wanted it gone. I do not waste things, so I would not just burn the nearly new timber. Over the years, the boys and I have been stripping off the planks and taking them up the hill to enlarge the small cottage I first built overlooking the beach. One day, I plan to turn it into a holiday cottage or something."

Dave wiggled closer to Glenn, allowing Tom and Bill to join them on the verandah. When settled, he asked, "So, is that still a plan, sir?"

John nodded. "One day, but for now, I would like to get the orchard ship-shape and the bananas growing properly, and then we'll tackle a new top for the bridge. Clare, I have decided that Bill will continue to do the morning milking, and you can concentrate on the cooking and dairy work after the milk is brought in. If you can manage the afternoon one, he won't need to leave the farm early."

They sat discussing the division of labour as they now had extra hands to help. John added, "One thing I must tell you is that I go to town most Wednesdays as I'm on duty for the Bench."

Clare looked puzzled. "Bench, Uncle John? What's that?"

John smiled at her question. "I told you I am a magistrate, dear. It is the day I meet with my fellow magistrates and hold court. So I will be away from the farm one day a week." He already charged Dave and Glenn to watch for Clare when he was away; now, he did the same for Bill and Tom. "Lads, Clare is my cousin. She is under my protection here, but you are to take care of her while I'm away."

The four heads nodded their understanding. John wasn't done yet. He knew that in years gone by, some shady characters had come to his farm in retaliation for some sentence he had handed down to them. For her safety, he said, "Clare, dear, on Wednesdays, I do not wish you wandering around the bay or farm alone. Do I make myself clear to you all? You four are to guard her for me." He saw a look of shock pass over her face. "It's not the tribal people I am worried about; they are wonderful. Pemma and Bagarou would protect you if needs be, but there have been rumours of some escaped men from old road gangs living in the scrub to the west. However, I have recently heard of a few thefts and attacks in the local area. I need a promise from you, Clare, please." He waited until she assured him that she would stay close whenever he was not on the farm.

The following morning, after chores were sorted, Glenn and Dave were taken to the farm, where the two older boys showed them what work was needed. Clare settled into her new life.

~

A month after arrival, they had all walked to the recently cleared headland for an evening walk. To everyone's delight, they saw something that amazed them. Directly beneath the point and close to the shore, a whale was wallowing in the warmer, shallow waters. As they watched, they thought it must have been harassed and attacked by sharks as the water around it went red. However, it did not take long before they realised they had just witnessed her giving birth. The baby whale was nudged to the surface by its mother, and within minutes, it was swimming around with her. The pair moved a little further out into the deeper water.

For the next two weeks, the pair stayed close to shore. The group was delighted to see the baby grow. Then, one morning, they were gone.

Clare loved churning the butter. She didn't, however, do it outside in the shed or the dairy. She cleaned up the dusty churn she had found and carried it out onto the verandah. This churn was hand-cranked barrel rather than upright, and she could sit in her chair and watch the waves break on the beach. The time passed quickly, and the swoosh of the cream soon turned into a slosh of the separated butter and whey. After a few more turns, she would carry the barrel into the kitchen, turn the fresh butter onto the marble slab and shape it into a pat. She kept the whey to cook with. The house had an underfloor cool room, and although it was not that cold, it was usually cool enough to keep the butter pats from melting off a marble slab.

The orchard trees were pruned over winter, and the cow dung fertilised the orchard. However, they still struggled to thrive in the coastal soil. The crops did well, as there were now extra hands to keep them all in tip-top shape. The boys began to cut the timber to make planks for the bridge.

~

The winter passed with no frosts, and the fire's warmth was all that was required to keep the whole house warm. The stone fruit was now being harvested. All the damaged or bruised fruit was dried or bottled and stored for their use throughout the year. The perfect fruit was sent to market and sold.

As spring arrived, so did the whales on their southern journey. They were a spectacle in the bay again, but there was more than just the mother and calf this time. They breached and frolicked before moving southward again. They were gone as fast as they had arrived.

Spring also brought the march of the little penguins. They were seen coming ashore at dusk, moving up through the sandy beach, and waddling out of sight through the flattened area near the creek. Their barking noises in the waves sounded like puppies playing.

John pointed out these new sights and sounds to Clare and the four lads on their regular evening walks.

Often, Clare would stand and watch the waves breaking as the boys harvested food from the rocks. Having grown up eating what they could forage, Clare was a dab hand at turning whatever they found into a delicious meal.

October brought rains so heavy that the lagoon filled in one night. After just one evening of torrential rain, they found the lagoon had burst open by itself the following morning. This was a great event, and as soon as the milking was done, everyone went to watch the gush of lake water meet the sea.

The boys wanted to swim in the rushing water until John pointed out something that made them all stay well away from the torrent.

John grabbed his shoulder. "Dave, don't jump! Wait until the wave breaks and see what's waiting for the fish."

The silhouettes of three large sharks were clearly visible in the morning light. The four boys immediately lost any desire to surf the channel.

Within a week, the seas closed the opening, and the farm run-off was already beginning to refill the lagoon.

When it closed up again, hundreds of black swans arrived from an unknown place and settled on the water. Within weeks, fluffy grey cygnets were seen swimming beside their parents.

John taught the young folk how to beach fish, and as the evenings warmed, the six of them would head to the southern end of the beach and cast their lines into the rip. The receding water would carry their baits out beyond the breakers, and more than one fish was usually carried home in triumph. They caught many varieties, from large jewfish to bream and flathead, as well as sea salmon and other sorts. All were delicious. The group rarely came home without a feed. Various items were used as bait, and although the boys favoured the larger-sized morsels, Clare chose the limpets that were abundant on the rocks. These stayed on her hook well, and the fish seemed to like them. Although her fish were smaller, they were more numerous. She rarely returned home without at least two, but usually more.

One afternoon, Glenn had taken a bucket to collect bait from the rocks, and she accompanied him. The others would follow later to help collect abalone as it was due to be a very low tide, and the seas were calm. Foraging the rocks could only be done at low tide as they were fully submerged when the water came in. Clare had come to know the wonderful array of shells and foods that could be found there. Having spent much of her youth on an estuary, she knew how to make the seafood and shellfish delicious. She cooked many rice, seafood, and seaweed meals found during her gleanings of the tidal rocks.

On this day, she saw a small octopus. She poked it to make sure it was alive, and it coloured up with sapphire blue circles. She was about to pick it up when she felt her hand pulled away from it. She looked around to see who was nearby, wondering if the tribe had returned and snuck up behind her. No one was within sight. Again, she reached out for it; this time, it was as though a voice said, "Don't touch it!" Surprised, she again looked around, and Glenn, although the closest, was now on the far side of the rocks. With plenty of other things in her bucket, she decided to leave it alone and ask Uncle John about it later.

Her decision was wise. On returning from their foraging trip, they took their bountiful harvest to the kitchen, where they sorted food from the bait. John was always interested in what they had found and came to investigate their harvest. He kept the shells they found.

Clare wondered how to go about telling of her strange experience.

She decided to wait until the boys had gone. She said, "Uncle John, I found a small octopus with pretty blue rings that appeared when I prodded it. It would have been just the right size for bait, but when I went to pick it up, I was sure someone had pulled my hand back from it; however, no one was near me. Then I went to grab it again, and this time, I heard someone say, 'Don't touch it!' But again, no one was nearby me."

John looked at her dumbfounded. "Are you sure none of the local aboriginals was close at hand?"

Clare was sure she was alone. "No, I was totally alone. I know Pemma can move silently, but I have not seen them this week. As you said, I stayed close to the beach, but Glenn was within sight of me but a long way away. The others were collecting the abalone on the big rocks around the point. No one else was near me at all."

John paused, "I can't believe I'm going to say this, but I think you heard a word from above. Clare, those little ones with the blue rings are apparently deadly. If you are lucky enough ever to go foraging with the local aborigines, as I was when I first arrived, Bagaroo and Pemma told me never to touch them unless you know what you are doing. They collect them and flip them inside out, which kills them instantly. But they pull out the poison sack and throw it away, then cook them on a stick. Never touch an octopus smaller than your hand; only get the boys to pick up the larger ones. They can bite, too, but are not deadly. I have shown the boys how to kill them. Will you promise me this?"

Her eyes were huge as she listened to how close she had come to picking it up. Clare nodded vigorously. "They are really deadly?"

John came around and gave her a fatherly hug. "They are, dear. We will thank the good Lord for protecting you." His heart was calming from the shock she had given him. He had not considered warning her or the new boys of this danger. This girl had become like a daughter to him. He was twenty-eight years her senior and had stepped into the place of her dear departed father.

The tenuous connection had not been questioned by anyone. The four boys innocently vouched for the platonic relationship and also mentioned that Clare was working for her keep.

The housekeeper, Ann Christopher, had also befriended her, so she quickly shut down any rumour she heard. Gossip was quickly silenced.

In the intervening months, Clare's heartache had eased a little, but her thoughts often turned to Shéamas and the life they could have had together. A tear escaped every now and then, but she tried not to dwell on her melancholy. More than once, John had heard her say the words she had first voiced on their trip north. Only now, they had changed a little. Her words today made him smile. "I can't stop tomorrow, and I can't change yesterday, but I have today, and I'm going to make the best of it."

The phrase her parents had said often scrolled through her mind, and

Uncle John's words followed.

~

As the days lengthened, the local group of aborigines returned to their springtime foraging grounds. Bagaroo and Pemma brought their children to meet Clare, collect some tea and flour, and bring them some honeycomb as a trade.

Earlier, Clare had found mounds of opened pippy shells, and she realised that the fireplaces on the grassy foreshore were from their encampment. She now stayed well away from this area. She had already met some of the other women from the tribe, and John had taught her how to say hello in their language. He often traded with the men, and in the right season, they would bring him one or two large bunya pine nuts to turn the seeds into nutty-flavoured flour. He swapped axe heads, knives, or whatever they needed for whatever they could supply him. He also provided the children with clothing and often a blanket or two.

As expected, the tribe camped in the flat area at the south end of the beach near where Clare had found evidence of fireplaces. These lovely, quiet people never caused any problems; quite the opposite. Consequently, Clare was encouraged to befriend the tribe's girls. One in particular became a friend. Bagaroo was often waiting for Clare, surrounded by children. Her man, Pemma, would be seen sitting in the distance with his spear at hand should it be required. His thin and wiry frame looked as though it would break.

Soon, the girls timed their visits to the rocks so they could work together at low tide.

On this particular day, it was the last week of October, during the lowest tides, and the waves seemed to be coming from the south. This meant Clare could collect some abalone to make fritters for their dinner. She arrived with a bucket and knife and planned to collect six large shellfish for the fritters and some smaller ones to fry as a crispy topping. She had collected only two when the girls from the tribe joined her. They were prizing off limpets and collecting whelks. She had seen them cook these in the coals of their fires. They waved to each other and got back to work. Being heavy with child, Bagaroo was collecting the small black and white periwinkle shells.

Clare saw a particularly large abalone shell and had her head down, prying it off the rock, when she heard a shout. One of the girls was pointing out to the sea. Clare realised a rogue wave was approaching her, but slippery rocks surrounded her.

It caught her before she could get to safety. The bucket had been placed on the top of the rock shelf, and it was safe, but she was caught in the wash and tumbled over the rocks by the power of the incoming foamy water. She managed to keep her head above water as she flipped onto her back, but that meant her legs were dragged over the sharp rocks and barnacles as she was carried inshore.

The wave forced her through the rocky opening and onto the larger rocks. She could feel the pain as the jagged edges dug into her back, hands and legs as they were being cut and scraped.

As the wave receded, she grabbed the top of a big rock and clung tightly. She was winded and in shock, but nothing seemed broken.

Moments later, she saw many bare black feet appear at her side. Although not seriously injured, Clare's legs were bleeding badly, and her flimsy shoes had been washed off. One of the girls grabbed them from further up the rocks. She was about to attempt to stand when Pemma, who had been watching the women forage, arrived at her side. He hoisted her up in his sinewy arms.

Pemma's near-naked body was solid muscle, and he easily carried her slight frame.

She automatically wrapped her bleeding arms around his neck, knowing he would take her to safety on the beach.

He did and deposited her on the embankment; then, he gabbled something to some of the older children nearby.

They fled at his instruction.

Other girls arrived with her bucket, knife and shoes. The wounds on her hands and legs were now beginning to throb.

Bagaroo sat beside her and wrapped her arm around her waist, drawing her close for comfort. The girl was naked but for a groin cloth of sorts. Her baby stomach protruded over the crotch tassel.

Clare didn't care about her friend's state of undress. She hurt all over. The shock of what had occurred began to sink in, and her tears began to flow.

Bagaroo enfolded the drenched and bedraggled Clare in a careful hug. She said, "Help come soon; you wait."

Chapter 17 Unexpected Visitor

*T*he children returned with handfuls of assorted items. Clare recognised the green moss from the creek and saw that one child had two lemons from John's trees. Another child had a roll of what looked like a grey bandage. She had no idea what they would do with the moss but knew the lemon juice would sting.

Pemma had moved away slightly, but he stood guard. Another of the girls took some moss from the child, then she rolled Clare onto her stomach and lifted her skirt. Bagaroo, still beside Clare, said, "Good medicine, but this bit hurt."

Now half-lying in her lap, Clare submitted to their ministrations, turning to Bagaroo for comfort. The moss was used to scrub the wounds of the bits of grit and shell embedded in the cuts. That was followed by the sting of the lemon juice squeezed directly into the cuts. The juice hitting the raw flesh was agony, and she could not help but cry out. Her hands felt like they were on fire, but she knew their treatment would stop the infection. She used lemon juice herself for cuts and understood its healing benefits. One deep cut was bleeding profusely and needed binding. Some moss was placed on it, and the grey bandage held it in place. She discovered later that this grey stuff was dried eel skin.

As the throbbing of her wounds made her feel light-headed, she wondered how she could walk the mile home along the sandy beach. Her feet hurt too much to put her shoes back on. No sooner did the idea enter her head than Pemma hoisted her into his strong arms again. The unusual troupe of mostly naked young people headed up the beach towards the house. Clare expected she would be too heavy for the wiry man, but he hardly varied his pace for the entire distance, including up the rise to the house. The women and older children followed, carrying the various implements, including his spear. One girl had even collected the large abalone that Clare had seen, plus more and carried a dozen or so of these delicacies along with Clare's knife and shoes.

Pemma did pause for the others to precede him up the grassy slope to the house. He carried his burden effortlessly and, once there, placed her carefully on the chair on the verandah.

John appeared from somewhere quite breathless. He must have been outside somewhere when the children called him. Her bedraggled state and the torn and bloody gown made him gasp. He exclaimed, "Oh, Clare dear, what happened?"

Clare was close to tears. "I was caught by a big wave, Uncle John, and they were nearby and helped me. Pemma carried me here, and Bagaroo and the other girls brought my things."

He could see her hands were cut to pieces, and rather than take one to bring comfort, he stroked her cheek. A large bruise formed on her brow, and she had some small grazes on her other cheek. He knelt beside her, "Oh, my dear girl, are you terribly hurt?"

Unable to speak, she nodded because the tears were very close to falling again, knowing she would weep if she spoke.

John saw that Bagaroo was about to lift her dress to check the wounds, and he said he would go and find bandages. His heart was racing as he stood. He ran his hand over her damp hair. "Bagaroo and Milbah will get you sorted, and then she can help you change." He left the girls to clean Clare up properly. John went and collected his medicine kit. He had purchased a new cleansing agent when he was in Parramatta. He visited the hospital to ask about the latest infection treatment, and the doctor mentioned a chemical called Sodium Permanganate, but the medic called them Condy's Crystals. John had purchased a small bottle of them and was about to put them to a big test. He had used some on a small cut to see if they stung, and the solution had not done so, but his wound did not infect. Clare would be lucky if she could get through this with no infection. He made it up as the doctor had instructed and was again surprised at the vivid pink colour. He wondered if he should attempt to treat Clare himself or wait for Bagaroo to do it. He hesitated when he realised that if he did not, Clare would be unable to reach some of the gashes on the backs of her legs. Swallowing his nerves, he returned to the verandah.

Bagaroo had done all she could and had silently left with Pemma and her friends. Clare was alone with him now, and he had no choice but to bathe her wounds himself. Realising this solution would stain quite badly, he covered her gown with a towel and treated her hands first.

The warm, hot pink solution soon coated her hands, her lower legs, and one deep gash on her thigh. John had made her hitch up her skirt and do that one herself. He had turned his back so she would not be embarrassed. Her knees were also grazed, but not as deep as she expected. Most of the injury was to her back and legs.

With the indignity of the treatment done, he now needed to bandage the bleeding cuts. This was done with a modicum of embarrassment by both of them, but they had little choice. A tear or two of hers fell onto his hands as he worked. She was soon swathed in the dressings, and he carried her to bed. She managed to get her torn gown off and night rail on by herself, as thankfully, Bagaroo had undone what remained of her gown. She climbed into bed and lay on the side that had mercifully escaped injury. Her back was bruised but not cut. Then, the shock finally set in. The bed shook as she felt chilled, and also she wept. It was her first real bout of tears in some time. But today, it had all become too much for her to cope. Her emotions overflowed.

John heard her and brought in some blankets.

When Clare awoke some hours later, the sounds of a female voice met her ears. "So, you say the poor lass was badly cut up?" Clare sighed with relief. It was Ann, the lady who came to clean the house. She was not due for a few days, so John must have sent one of the boys for her.

Clare heard John say, "A wave caught the poor lass, and she has been badly banged up."

Clare then caught her reply and almost wept again, but with relief. "I brought a few things so I can stay and nurse her."

Ann Christoper was an angel. Like Pemma, her wiry frame belied her stamina. This dear lady had a warm heart. Clare loved her. For her to come when Clare most needed a woman nearby was wonderful. Clare tried to sit up in bed and cried out in pain.

Ann came to her aid moments later. "Oh, dearie, you have messed yourself up good and proper, haven't you?" She checked the bandages and saw that one had oozed through the wrappings. Clare was teary from pain. She nodded assent. "Well, don't you mind, little one, I've come to stay for a few days. It will be like a holiday for me with only the six of you to feed." Ann bustled around tidying the room.

Last night, Clare had dropped her gown on the ground and left it there. She gingerly picked it up and checked it over for spiders. She saw that there were various rips that she would need to repair when her hands improved.

Ann gently sat on the edge of her bed and carefully drew the weeping girl into her arms. "Don't weep now, dearie. I'll stay until you're back on your feet."

Clare had not had a hug like Ann's since Sal had comforted her on the day her world fell apart. She had fled the following morning. Now, her shoulders hurt where they had crashed into the rocks. She ached all over. In the time she had been asleep, the pain seemed to have seeped into her entire body. She ached, and the cuts throbbed. She realised she would soon be black and blue when the bruises developed. Once Ann treated her again, Clare had finished her tea.

John brought in a mug of hot, sweet tea, more clean bandages, and a dish of the pink solution. He then carefully lifted her out of her bedroom and placed her in her chair on the verandah. She did not realise her feet were so badly cut up.

~

Ann tended to Clare for three days in a way she had never been pampered before. On the second day, her feet were pain-free enough to walk gingerly around the polished timber floor. She could not get her shoes on but could sit on the verandah and shell peas with her fingertips. The abalone had been kept in the bucket, and the boys had changed the water daily. They could stay alive for some time yet.

After nearly a week of nursing Clare, Ann needed to return home. Unfortunately, it was Wednesday, and John was on court duty. He left early for his trip to the Brisbane Water Courthouse in town. After the milking, Bill took the dray out to harvest some of the early crops. The other boys had already left for work, but Bill assured her he wouldn't be long.

Clare was left to churn the butter. Due to her injury, this simple chore would take her twice as long as usual, as her arms still ached. Then, she had to wash the butter and then shape it into pats once it was done. Thankfully, she was the only one there for luncheon, and Ann had left a fresh loaf of bread already sliced. Clare only wanted bread and butter, and as soon as she finished making the pats, she would eat her snack. Although Clare felt much better, Ann would return to cook dinner for them. However, Ann needed to return home after she had prepared their meal. With a large mug of sweet tea beside her, Clare had settled down with the churn. Because her arms were still sore, she took the job slowly, and the butter would usually start turning after about twenty minutes. Today, mainly because she kept stopping to rest and admire the beautiful scene before her, it took nearly an hour. Once it turned, she put the churned butter in the kitchen for Ann to shape into pats when she returned. She had been going to attempt it, but her hands hurt too much. She couldn't do the final hand wash of the butter because adding the salt would sting too much. One cut was still weeping. She returned to the verandah and sat watching the waves.

Shortly before noon, Clare heard a noise. The boys were all out on the farm as Bill had been and gone again to take the lads their midday meal. John was away at work, and Ann was at her home. Clare was hoping that Pemma and Bagaroo had come for a visit, so she called out, "Hello, I'm on the verandah!" There was no reply. She called again, having just heard a door shut. "Hello! Who's there?" She smelled the intruder before she saw him.

A filthy man stood in the back doorway, blocking her only exit. He wore tattered clothing that had obviously once been a convict's black and yellow coat. What remained of his trousers were shredded and befouled with excrement, and she could smell his breath from fifteen feet away. His grin revealed blackened stumps in his mouth, and as he drew closer, Clare could see that his beard was embedded with goodness knows what. He reeked! So much so that Clare was dry retching before he even approached her.

Knowing she was still unable to move quickly, she stayed seated. She had nothing to defend herself with, and she knew that no one was nearby to hear her yell. Step by step, his filthy bare feet edged closer. Clare remained frozen in her chair, silently praying that someone would rescue her. Her mind was looking for a means of escape. Memories of the other attack flowed through her. She was now panicking about defending herself when a slight movement behind him caught her eye.

As the convict edged closer, John quietly closed the door and flicked the lock. He pocketed the key. Knowing that he was in direct line of sight for Clare, he put his fingers to his lips. He edged towards the fireplace, where he picked up the cast iron poker. Knowing help was at hand, Clare started talking to the man. "What do you want? Food, money, tell me, and I'll get it for you…" She was able to watch John's actions as she spoke.

The convict grunted his reply, "I want all that, missy, but I'll have you too. I need a bit of loving, dearie, and you'll do nicely. Your man won't miss some clothing, but I'll get that later." His very tattered trousers left little to the imagination. They were all but shreds of fabric tied with a rope.

His bare buttocks were easily visible to John as he walked menacingly towards Clare. John was now nearly behind him.

Clare managed to rise and now placed her chair between herself and the approaching man.

John had the poker above his head and swung it like a cricket bat to hit the man's shoulder; however, it slid and hit his neck. The force of the blow sent the convict reeling. With no more than a grunt, he crumpled onto the chair in front of Clare. Clare pulled her chair away from him, and the man slid to the verandah deck, unresponsive.

John dropped the poker and dived at Clare as she collapsed. He eased her into a dining room chair inside and said, "Clare, I have to bind him in case he comes to. I came home early as I knew you would be alone today. When I arrived in town, I heard reports that he was in our area. Did he hurt you?"

Clare shook, but she said, "No, Uncle John, he came in shortly before you did." Now seated in the dining room, she watched the prostrated man's form. A pool of something vile spread around him, adding to the stench. His bladder had emptied on the verandah floor.

After ensuring she was all right, John unlocked the back door. He handed her the poker and said, "Watch him and scream if he moves." He left to find ropes to bind the escapee.

Clare nodded. Her stare was fixed on the unconscious man anyway.

John returned with a length of strong rope. He trussed the man with his hands tied behind his back, and with the same rope, John tied his feet together, then tied them to his bound hands. If he roused, he might be able to roll over, but he could not run. There was no blood, and his pulse was strong. While the man was still unconscious, John went outside again and rang the big bell three times. One long peel meant meal times. Two peels told the boys they needed to return as fast as possible. Three clangs meant they had to drop everything and run back, as something was wrong.

John returned to Clare, pulled up an armchair, and sat beside her. She was still shaking, shocked at the recent occurrence. John questioned her about how she was feeling. "Clare, dear, I had one of your strange experiences. I felt I needed to return as urgently as I could. I also knew I needed to take the back road, so again, I did. When I saw that man stalking you, my heart was in my mouth. I could not let him hurt you, dear girl." He had come to care greatly for this girl in a very fatherly way.

Since she was injured, Clare appreciated his care for her, particularly lately. They heard a noise at the back door and expected it to be the boys. However, a tall, bearded man stood in the doorway. With a cry of panic, she fell to her knees before John and hugged him for security. Clare wrapped her arms around John and hid her head against his chest. She was oblivious to the screaming pain in her cut legs and feet.

John enfolded her protectively, wondering if the second man was also a convict.

The latest visitor's jaw dropped open. Then he noticed movement on the verandah deck. The stench emanating from the prostrated body made him rethink the situation. However, words of shock exploded from him. "What the blooming heck is happening here, sir?"

The angry voice was a delight to Clare's ears. At his words, Clare gasped and pulled away from John. She struggled to her feet and flew to the stranger. "Shéamas? Oh, Shéamas, what are you doing here?" Moments later, she was wrapped in his arms and weeping with relief against his shoulder. "I thought you were another convict. Oh, Shéamas, hold me. That's twice you have appeared when I needed you most." She didn't care that his embrace hurt her shoulders and arms. He was here, and that was all that mattered. He had come looking for her.

John coughed. "I am sorry to interrupt your reunion, but now is not the time for this. Clare, I gather this is your young man?"

She nodded. It took Clare a few moments before she could collect her thoughts. Pulling away from Shéamas's arms a little, she explained, "Yes, Uncle John. This is Shéamas Connor; however, he didn't have a beard or look so scruffy when I saw him last." Clare lifted her face to Shéamas's, and she grinned broadly.

Their eyes met, and he dropped a quick furry kiss on her lips. "I'll explain in full later, sir, but I'm now free, and I have hunted high and low for Clare for many months. However, I notice you have another more immediate problem." Shéamas reluctantly released Clare and approached the filthy man. He had now roused and was fighting against his bonds. Shéamas placed his sandy-booted foot in the centre of the prisoner's back.

The following minutes saw John and Shéamas working together to move the restrained man out the back door. They had each grabbed an arm and dragged him outside. Whether it was urine or liquid excrement that trailed behind him was hard to tell, but it stank. The offensive trail turned all their stomachs. No sooner than they had reached the back door, the other four lads were seen climbing the driveway from the farm.

By now, the foul-mouthed expletives emanating from their prisoner were loud enough to bring the boys running to assist. With six pairs of hands now manhandling the convict, the crook realised that his luck had finally run out. The fight in him was soon gone, and he deflated in surrender; however, his verbal diatribe continued. His freedom was now forfeited, and he knew a flogging would follow; if he survived that, he would not be returned to the road gang as that gave him a modicum of freedom. If he were lucky, he would be sent to the coal mines in Newcastle rather than hung on a gibbet. He called his captors every disgusting name he could think of.

Clare remained well out of sight.

In a short time, the convict had been unceremoniously loaded onto the dray and secured tightly, then tied securely to the seat. After Shéamus's last encounter with such a ruffian, he was not permitting this man an inch of spare rope; the last time, he had nearly been strangled and had to fight for his life. He rubbed his throat as he remembered that incident. This convict was given no wiggle room. He remained hog-tied, and he was now well-trussed to the dray with numerous ropes. Although he had no chance to escape, that did not keep him quiet. To shut him up, John gagged him. The prisoner's foul-mouthed tirade had hardly ceased since he regained consciousness, and Clare retreated inside until the six men had the convict silenced. He would not escape again, and he knew it. Now, he could not even talk.

John returned to explain to Clare that he needed to take the prisoner to the lock-up at Wyoming. However, they turned to the newest visitor and said, "Shéamas, your arrival is perfect. I would have had to take her with us, but I know she will be safe with you. Tom and Bill will accompany me, but Glenn and Dave will stay with you. I will take my gun should he attempt anything. Clare has not yet recovered from her accident, but she can tell you all about that after we leave." He turned his attention to the two younger lads. He said quietly, "Lads, stay close to home for the rest of today as this criminal may not have been alone. He escaped with one other who is still at large. Keep the other gun handy, too, just in case." He heard Clare gasp. "This new young man is Clare's betrothed, at least he was, but we shall sort that out on my return. He is to be trusted to care for her. But stay close to the house in case any other miscreants appear."

Dave and Glenn nodded at the instructions and eyed the newcomer. His scruffy appearance belied his well-spoken words and his obvious affection for Clare. John turned to her and gave instructions for Shéamas's room. "Clare put Shéamas in the room next to me. We shall have a long discussion when I have disposed of this malefactor. He's been on the run for nearly three years now and was seen in the area a few times this week. I heard about a recent violent altercation as soon as I arrived at work. Having spent time in the lock-up myself some twenty years ago, there will be no hope of escape for him once there." A muffled harrumph emanated from the dray.

Clare was not prepared to guess what the smelly man was trying to say. His words had frightened her enough already.

The prisoner had fouled what remained of his tattered trousers again. John looked at the mess trickling again from the man's nether regions. He stepped away from the side of the dray as the ooze crept towards him. He explained his last words. "In 1835, I was unceremoniously arrested for cattle theft. It took three years to clear my name. After that, I was made a magistrate to ensure such unjust situations did not occur again. I spent a few weeks incarcerated in the hell hole this man will be locked up in. He shall not escape again." The convict muttered again before John said, "This chap..." thumbing towards the prisoner, "... is a life convict, done for the murder of an innocent, and he is a nasty sort. He should never have been on a road crew." John knew he had to get moving. "Take care of her, Shéamas, and Clare; stay inside until I return."

Clare nodded. She needed no second warning. She knew Ann had kept the visitor's room clean, and the bed had already been made up after she had moved home. Her hands were not yet healed enough to make a bed. Shéamas came and stood beside her. "You are injured, love?"

Clare nodded. "I got caught by a wave and washed onto the rocks some days ago, but I'm healing." She held up her bandaged hands. "My legs got the worst of it, but I have bumps and bruises everywhere."

Shéamas gingerly slid an arm along her shoulders. "So, I'm a welcome sight?" His perfect teeth showed through his beard as he grinned.

Clare's smile reached her eyes. They twinkled with delight. "Absolutely, Shéamas! I gather our situation is resolved?" She didn't wish to discuss Lavinia in front of the others. John knew the whole story, but the others didn't.

Shéamas again dropped a quick kiss onto her hair. "Yes, love, fully resolved and banished." She snuggled under his arm. They would discuss Lavinia privately, although John would have to be told.

John knew he had to leave but said to the cuddling couple. "Shéamas, until we discuss things, you must first clean yourself up. In the meantime, unhand her, laddie, until things are sorted."

Shéamas reluctantly dropped his arm around her and took a small step away. Slightly abashed, he said, "Yes, sir. Of course, sir." His excitement and confusion at what he saw on entry had made their reunion far from what he expected. He presumed he would need to beg her to forgive him. He had also wondered if she had found someone else in the intervening months. For her to turn to him with glee had been a delight for him.

Chapter 18 More Tomorrows

*T*he four young folk stood side by side as the dray departed. Once it was out of sight, Clare officially introduced the two remaining men.

Shéamas grabbed his bag from where he had dumped it and placed it in his bedroom. The airy room was sparsely furnished, with a bed, nightstand, and washbasin. He noticed hooks along the wall for his clothing and a shoe shelf. He frowned when he saw this.

Clare was sitting on his bed, watching him settle in. She saw his questioning look and explained. "We have big black spiders here, Shéamas, and they crawl into your shoes. The boys get more of them in their quarters than we do in the house, but after the rain, we have had a few. Never put your boots on without checking them first, and don't leave clothes on the ground. Hence, the shelf is for your shoes."

At the bottom of Shéamas's bag sat a special tiny parcel. He would not unpack that until after their discussion. Realising that she should not be in his room, he said, "Come on, Clare, we have a bit of mess to clean up, and with your hands bandaged, you can't do it. Show me where the cleaning things are, and I'll clean up this vile stench."

With her hands injured, she could not sop up the mess the man had left; the three men quickly set about that task. The smell hung inside the house, and every door and window was flung open. Clare found some vinegar, and Shéamas sloshed some over where the mess had been.

Once done, Clare put the kettle on the hob. Shéamas stowed the cleaning bucket and mop, then made the tea. When the boys left to circle the house and check for prowlers, the reunited couple had time to talk over a mug of the hot, black, sweet brew. Shéamas related an outline of the happenings of Lavinia's exposure and his resulting search for Clare. His journey had taken him from Parramatta to Milton, then to Bathurst, north to Taree, and finally, another dreaded boat trip from Taree to Terrigal Haven. He had walked over the headland and then along the beach. He heard the bell ringing while walking up the embankment towards the house and ran up the hill. He arrived unsure if Clare was even at this last stop. He was disheartened at seeing her on her knees and with her arms around another man, and this made him lash out in anger.

One of the first topics of conversation he raised with Clare was her relationship with John.

Clare explained that he was, in reality, related to her father. She said honestly, "He is my closest male cousin."

Shéamas said he understood her willingness to leave with him.

Clare didn't dare tell him that they had not discovered the closeness of the tie until later; however, she promised herself she would tell him sometime later.

The two boys were in and out, getting tea for themselves. After cleaning up the mess outside, they needed to change their clothing. Finally, they left to milk the cows. The dairy was behind the house, so they would be nearby even while they were milking.

Contrary to John's instruction, Shéamas waited until they were alone before turning to her and leading her inside. "My darling Clare, I will explain the full story of Lavinia later, but believe me when I say she is gone. She was caught in bed with her lover by the governor, no less. She was banished to Moreton Bay. So I am free; I came as soon as possible." With no further ado, he fell on bended knee; he proposed again and offered her his ring of promise. "Dear heart, will you do me the honour of becoming my wife?"

As far as Clare could, she restrained her squealing excitement, saying, "Yes, absolutely, Shéamas. Of course, I will."

Standing and drawing her into his arms, he carefully bestowed a loving caress before taking her hand. Here, he was somewhat stumped as her hands were bandaged. Her little finger remained unscathed, so he carefully slid on the token of his love. Her ring was the small package at the bottom of his bag.

She giggled. With her response of her unreserved "Yes," they shared a long-awaited kiss. This was one of great passion, such as he had never given her before. His tight embrace made her grimace and made him realise the painful state of her injuries. He bumped one of her hands, and she gasped in agony. He released his hold somewhat and held her gently rather than crush her to him.

She quickly gave details of her accident and the extent of her injuries. Her bandaged palms showed that they were worrying her, but he could not see grazes and bruises on her legs, but her fingertips were visible. They were now able to be used if she was careful. Shéamas's ring would soon take its rightful place on her ring finger. Clare glowed with contentment. Their relationship had started because of a similar situation.

With Dave and Glenn on guard outside, the reunited young lovers sat on the verandah with some tea, and Shéamas told Clare the entire Lavinia saga. He outlined his horrific boat trip to Milton, then followed that story with the overland journey to Bathurst. His hunt had left him more than frustrated. From there, an extended leg had taken him up the inland road to Taree, followed by the last but shortest leg. Shéamas had swallowed his pride, caught the coastal steamer from Taree to Terrigal Bay, and then walked the final miles. Surprisingly, he had not become seasick on the overnight boat trip.

Those last miles from Terrigal had been some of the hardest, not because of the terrain but the uncertainty of what he would find. Shéamas still had no idea if Clare would be at this Moore's farm, and he walked with a heavy heart. For him to arrive and find her in the arms of another man had made his emotions plummet. Had he taken too long to find her?

Shéamas poured out all his feelings and love for her. He had previously been reluctant to expose his heart in such a way, but in the months that followed, he realised the importance of Clare's presence in his life.

Clare knew that the longer she held back her lack of knowledge of John's relationship with her, the harder it would be. She confessed to overhearing the conversation at church and leaving with a virtual stranger. She knew about a mysterious cousin named John but only discovered that it was this man after they left. "Shéamas, he is truly my father's cousin."

Shéamas gasped but said, "I understand your need to leave Clare. And in a way, it made it much easier not seeing you every day. I'm glad this man turned out to be related, but you knew nothing about him. It was so dangerous for you, my sweetheart."

Clare nodded her agreement to his statement and apologised.

With their stories told, they could now move forward with their lives.

No further convicts appeared.

Ann Christopher returned. As she entered, she caught Clare and Shéamas having a hug. She had walked in unannounced. She sighed and said, "Well, this and better will do, but this and worse won't." The couple fell apart at her words, and they frowned. She had brought a shepherd's pie to put in the oven for the household. She knew of Clare's lost love and greeted Shéamas with very little surprise to see him there, but she made hand movements to separate them. "I gather you are her young man?"

He nodded. Both blushed at being caught hugging.

Ann sent Shéamas to shave off his beard while she changed Clare's bandages.

Shéamas did but decided to leave on a big bushy moustache and sideburns to see if Clare liked it.

Once Ann had prepared the vegetables for the evening meal, she said her farewells and warned Shéamas to respect Clare.

Dave and Glenn finished milking the two cows and setting the dairy to rights. Dave brought in a jug of milk for use indoors and reported that the farm vehicle was crossing the bridge. He raised his eyebrow when he saw

Shéamas's new look.

The trio had returned from depositing the prisoner at the Wyoming lockup; the group stood waiting for his return.

The four boys left to clean the fouled wagon. Only after they left did John formally welcome Shéamas. However, he noted the small ring on Clare's little finger and raised an eyebrow at its presence. "Shéamas, I said we needed to talk first. I'm guessing you've jumped the gun somewhat?"

Shéamas could not believe what he was hearing. He had found her, and now she would be torn from him again? He stammered, "Yes, sir. I'm sorry, sir. I did not realise you meant that, sir." His brow broke out in a sweat.

John was a little disappointed with them. "I did, but we shall discuss that later."

Shéamas felt ill. Having just found her, had he blown his future with her?

Clare and Shéamas set the table for dinner, which Ann had put in the oven for the household. Since his arrival, Shéamas helped where he could, but he was now fully aware that John was Clare's legal guardian and could halt their union should he wish. His nerves showed.

Somehow, he made it through dinner. While eating, he sat opposite Clare but did not converse much with anyone. Although hungry, he toyed with his food, wondering what John wanted to say to him. Could he lose his beloved now? He felt like weeping.

After dinner, he dropped some cutlery while drying the dishes and then slopped the tea on the tray as he brought it out to Clare and John. He hid his shaking hands behind his back. His stomach rumbled.

John waved the other four boys away and motioned for Shéamas to join him on the verandah. A slight odour remained, but the vinegar had helped remove it. John banished Clare to her room for the duration of their conversation and told her to take the opportunity to rest.

Shéamas took his seat in the cane chair that Clare had recently occupied. The warmth of her body on the padding soaked into him. He nervously sipped his tea and burnt his lips without realising how hot it was.

John noticed his nervous state and said, "Shéamas, relax; I'm not here to ban you from marrying Clare, but as it's now October, it's seven months since you have seen her, and therefore, your Banns have expired."

Shéamas's head jerked up at those words. "I didn't know they did that, sir."

John nodded. "Well, they do. When they are called, the couple needs to marry within six months of the final time they are announced. We are well over that period, so now we must determine what to do."

Shéamas nervously asked, "So I am permitted to marry her?"

John relaxed back into his chair and watched the sun hit the tops of the tallest gum trees on the top of Kincumba Mountain. "Yes, laddie, you may, but we must do it legally."

Shéamas relaxed a little more and was now blowing on his tea. He frowned as he had no idea what he could do. "Can we do them again?"

John settled himself into his chair and watched a cow as it wandered down to take a drink from the trough. "We can and will, but are your parents still alive?"

Shéamas nodded. "Yes, sir, both of them."

John met the lad's gaze and replied, "Good, that makes my suggestion even easier. As you are still underage, you will need their written approval to marry, but it's better if they are there in person. It's not just girls who need that, but I presume you know all that?"

Shéamas shook his head. "I know Papa had to fill out some forms, but I didn't realise that was one of them. I am twenty now, sir, but I do not wish to wait any longer." Shéamas's gaze didn't waver until John's face turned aside. He watched the flat area below the house. Shéamas did not wish to wait another year, so he waited without interrupting the man.

John watched as the cow below them lifted her head and low, and then she dawdled back to the herd. John smiled and returned his thoughts to the conversation. "First thing tomorrow, we shall send a letter to your family. They can call Banns again down there. Shéamas, I am suggesting that you marry down at Parramatta. The three of us can travel down in a couple of weeks, and as I'm Clare's closest male relative in this country, I shall fill in the forms on her behalf. As you probably know, for a girl, the legal age to marry is younger. Fifteen, I believe, is normal in London." He shook his head. "I think it's too young, but that's the law. I know all this as I am one of the three local magistrates with permission to authorise underage marriages. Anyway, unless you have a spare three hundred pounds, it costs nothing to do the forms to make sure."

Shéamas nearly choked as he had just taken a mouthful of his tea. He shook his head in horror. "I don't have that sort of money, sir."

John continued as if he'd not just seen Shéamas spit the tea back into his mug. With a half-smile, he said, "You won't need to if you can then marry with all the family attending, and there will be no shred of innuendo of a hole-in-the-wall marriage. The entire town will know that everything is well above board. Including that Clare has been with me; family. With what you have both had to endure, you must do this to clear the air. All the residents of Parramatta will have heard what occurred. It will also allow me to meet Kerry and Sal, both of whom are related to me."

"What?" exclaimed Shéamas as he spluttered a mouthful of his tea. "We would get married at home? Really, sir, you would do that for us?"

John glanced at the young man beside him. "Shéamas, I knew about you before I agreed to take her with me. We sat in the sitting room at the Rear Admiral Duncan Inn, and she told me the pertinent parts of her story. She didn't mention your name back then, and in reality, that was irrelevant. She left because staying would have made it hard for you. Her actions were done because she loved you and you alone. I also knew that she trusted you more than anyone else she knew. That spoke volumes to me. True, we did not realise the closeness of our relationship until later. I have come to more than admire your young lady. She managed to get her sister and herself out here from Ireland unharmed due to her determination and strength of character. I might have even fought you for her if I was twenty years younger. But in truth, Shéamas, her father, was my cousin, and I greatly liked and admired Kieran O'Shane. The family stayed on my family farm for months at Avoca in County Wicklow, Ireland. It was where I first met Clare and Kerry. Although she was only a child, the fact that I remember meeting them stayed with me for some time. Back then, she was nearly always assisting her parents in caring for Kerry, which impressed me even then. Her mother was heavy with child at the time. Clare was the most adorable little girl. Shéamas, take care of her for me. I would not trust her to just anyone."

Shéamas's eyes grew wide. This is not how he expected this interview to go. Thankfully, Clare had already admitted her lack of knowledge to him. The two stories tallied perfectly. He thought he would have to beg for her hand and need to prove himself worthy. He nodded his assent. "Of course, sir. She is my life. I, too, have liked her since the day we met. However, being so young myself, I did not know how to show her, so I stupidly teased her mercilessly. I supposed she told you about that?"

John chuckled and nodded. "Boys often do that, Shéamas. Teenage boys don't always have a lot of sense."

Shéamas grinned in agreement. "I certainly didn't. My little brother, Liam, wants to court Kerry, so you'll have to meet him, too, sir. My feelings for Clare were revealed in a situation similar to today. Another escaped convict accosted her, and I used a frypan to lay him out. He then got the better of me on the way to the lock-up; hence, I tied this one up tightly."

After retelling that incident, the two men sat in companionable silence, drinking the remains of their tea. Eventually, John said, "Go get her, lad, and we'll let her know our decision, eh?"

Shéamas was up like a shot and took the two empty mugs into the kitchen. With a quick wash and wipe, he left them on the kitchen table.

Clare's room was a little further down the corridor, and he timidly knocked on her door.

She must have either heard him coming or been waiting for his arrival as she opened it instantly. Clare was teary. "Is everything all right, Shéamas? Will he permit us to marry?" Her worried face and glassy eyes met his.

Shéamas could not stop himself from reaching out for her and pulling her into his arms. "Oh, sweetheart! Yes, everything is fine. Sir pointed out that the Banns called for us earlier had expired. Come, and he can tell you himself." He dared not stay near her room with her in his arms like she was.

Clare lifted her head to him. She had a gurgle of laughter in her voice as she asked, "So, we really can marry?"

Shéamas again dropped a quick kiss onto her lips. "Yes, love, we can."

She clung to his arm as she walked gingerly out to the verandah.

They returned to John, and Shéamas seated his fragile lady into the seat he had just vacated. He brought out a dining room chair and placed it near hers. The trio discussed the upcoming plans for their delayed union.

After an hour, John said he would leave them and pen a letter to Sal Lockley and the Connors. The groom's father would need to fill out the forms and file them again. His letter to Sal was a little more problematic, as he also had to detail how he was Clare and Kerry's closest male relative, and therefore, it would be him who filled out the forms on Clare's behalf this time. His role as magistrate in Gosford meant that this was one of the regular duties he was required to perform. He knew the ins and outs of the law and was not prepared to break them. Once the letter was done, he suggested Shéamas write to tell his parents about the end of his quest. John ushered him into his office while he spent a few minutes with Clare, ascertaining that her feelings had not changed. Clare joyfully reassured him that she was as sure as she always had been.

The following morning, Tom was sent to Terrigal Haven to deliver the letters to the coastal trader heading to Sydney. He carried the letters for Parramatta in a leather pouch. The Lockleys and Connors should have word of the young lovers by the end of the week.

Shéamas's search had reached a happy ending.

The return vessel brought three long letters, one for Clare, another for Shéamas and a longer one from Lord Charles to John.

Sal's screed to Clare was one of joy; the situation had sorted itself out, and they were happy they would not miss out on a wedding. She gave all the family news from the past months and the information that Banns would have been called once when she read the letter.

Clare grinned as she met Shéamas's eyes over the tops of their respective missives. Kerry had added a paragraph about the joy of their upcoming marriage.

Shéamas's letter also brought news of everyone's happiness at him having found her. He had written to his parents from each town, so they had been expecting news from this last stop. They were delighted that the couple were to be married in Parramatta. Paddy was thrilled and spent half a page expressing such to Shéamas, which made him chuckle. Shéamas loved his father's turn of phrase and found that John reminded him of a better-educated version of his father.

~

Charles's letter to John was read in the privacy of his office, which overlooked the verandah. The young couple were sitting just outside the tall windows of this room. He decided that he would not reveal all the contents to Clare or Shéamas as Charles had written about the inappropriateness of John's actions of taking a girl from her family without at least a note. John agreed and fully intended to acknowledge his actions and apologise in person.

They could see John rubbing his brow. The frowns he directed towards the couple made Clare wonder what Uncle Charles had written.

After dinner that evening, they learned some of the letter's contents when the four male staff members retired to their quarters. Clare made them tea as usual, and Shéamus carried the tray. They sat on the verandah, listening to the crashing of the waves. By now, the bandages were off her hands, and although there was still scabbing, they were healing well. Shéamas's ring would soon be able to take its proper place. Likewise, her legs had scabbed over, and although itchy, they were doing nicely. The bruises had faded completely, and she was nearly back to full health.

Shéamus placed a small tea tray on the table in front of John.

John waited until they were settled before revealing his news. He sat staring into the dark liquid in the mug.

They waited.

Finally, he lifted his eyes, blew out his cheeks and said, "I suppose now is as good a time as any to tell you my long-term plans as it involves you both."

Clare and Shéamas's attention was now firmly fixed on him.

"In my letter to your Aunt Sal and Uncle Charles, I mentioned something that brought a long and detailed reply. I won't go into it, but as you know, I am your closest male relative in this country."

Both nodded but didn't interrupt.

"Well, Clare's arrival made me think about my own future. I have no wife or children. My closest male relative on my mother's side is Robert Maddrell, down at Braidwood. He is to inherit the farm and all I possess at the time of my demise." He saw Clare nod as they had already discussed his first cousin Robert and his role as a magistrate in Braidwood. Therefore, this was no surprise to her.

John paused, then said, "However, as a wedding gift, a dowry if you like, I shall provide a small holding for both of you girls; therefore, if you both are married before I die, you will be secure. My will is written, and that will be enforced at my death. As I did not know of you girls then, you have no mention. Clare also knows where I wish to be buried and the details of that occurrence. I have let Robert and the girls know about that. He is unrelated to them, as he's my mother's cousin."

The pair sitting with him both gasped.

Shéamas started to get up, but John waved him to remain seated.

Shéamas was not to be silenced. "Sir, you don't need to do this. I have ten pounds saved up, and I will find work somewhere."

John had not moved. "Ah, yes, well, that's another thing. After you marry and have a honeymoon, not too long, mind you, but if you are willing,

I would like you to return here and work with me for a year or two. I need the assistance, and Shéamas, your position at the dairy has been filled by someone else. I saw you both notice my frown earlier. You have no job to return to. Clare will always have a room wherever I am, but she will have no further claim on me as a dependent on her marriage. The same goes for Kerry."

Clare was delighted. "Uncle John, how can I ever thank you for everything you have done for me?" She came over and kissed his cheek.

Strangely, Shéamas didn't feel the wave of jealousy that had flashed through him earlier. Now, he just watched her actions with clarity and understanding. He was overwhelmed; they would be given a farm of their own. He was stunned. He had never thought about owning his own farm. He knew that with his money, he could buy a small cottage with a tiny bit of land. But an entire farm? All he could do was blink in astonishment.

Ignoring Shéamas, John met Clare's gaze. "Be happy, love, that's all I ever wanted. You know my story. It has been one of many twists and turns, many of which your papa shared with me. We were similar in many ways." He quickly recounted his background for Shéamas. "I was born and Baptised a Catholic, but I joined the English army in Dublin when aged seventeen. I won't go into why, but if you know Clare's family history or have discussed the religious bigotry in Ireland, you will understand why I chose not to live in my homeland."

The young people both nodded their understanding.

Shéamas replied, "My parents were arrested because of their faith in a Catholic land. They are serving life because they would not renounce what they believe. Papa won't discuss how he came to be transported as I would have thought it was because they're Catholic, not Protestant." He shrugged.

John continued. "After I served my time in the army, again, I will not go into details, but the Bible was correct when it states that brother will kill brother and the persecution of the faith will kill many. I did not expect that persecution to be amongst fellow believers and sometimes my own family. Each stupidly fights over minutia that is not even in the Bible. As I said to Clare earlier, denominations are man-made things. There are no Catholics or Protestants in heaven, just those who believe in Jesus. I refused to join the bigots in saying one is either right or wrong. However, having said that I feel that the faith taught in the Church of England is closer to what I have read for myself in the Holy Scriptures. Jesus was neither Catholic nor Protestant. He was a Jew, and he lived some eighteen hundred years ago. Times may have changed, but not His teachings of love, forgiveness, acceptance, and peace."

John waved his hand as though to change topics. And that is what he did. "Now, to the farms! I want Shéamas to assist the boys here and learn many skills. You need to know more than just the dairy work. A mixed farm will serve your purposes better than focusing on a single beast or crop; trust me, I know. It protects if disease hits one variety of produce. If those folk in

Ireland had done this rather than just growing potatoes, the famine would not have hurt so many, but that is by the by and I have the benefit of hindsight. I have cattle, both dairy and beef, some sheep, a few goats, citrus trees, bananas and vines, not to mention the crops you see on the flat down there."

For a while, John spoke lovingly about his farm. For over twenty years, he had poured himself into the work. He loved this area. Many failures had occurred, but other farmers in the area had learned from his errors. His bananas were surprisingly good. They grew well on the sunny side of the ridgeway track.

After some time describing his vision for his valley, he saw that the young ones' interest waned a little. Chuckling to himself, he said to them, "Fine, I'll hush about my visions for my vale. Now, about our trip to Parramatta…"

For the next half hour, they excitedly made plans for the overland trek. The three would travel by wagon again as John needed to purchase more supplies. He knew he could order things, and they would come by sea, but the journey was more like a holiday. It also meant he had his own vehicle when there. He dearly wished to connect with the Lockleys and get to know his rediscovered family.

By the time they were ready for bed, they had everything sorted.

Shéamus assured Clare that her wedding gown still hung in Jenna's wardrobe. He had intended to take it with him but was now glad he had not.

After a quick kiss goodnight, the three went to bed happy.

~

The weeks passed, and the furniture was rearranged in the bedrooms. The big double bed in Shéamas's room was moved into Clare's and vice versa. Clare's single bed, with its horsehair mattress, now resided beside John's room. A new sizeable triple-door wardrobe arrived on the back of a flatbed wagon. With much huffing and puffing, it was eased through the house and manoeuvred into position in Clare's room.

Clare had only three serviceable gowns with her, so the vast central hanging space was mostly empty. The doors on either side were shelves, and on her side, Clare had the scant remains of her undergarments that had worn quite thin over the months on the farm. She had put the majority of her good clothing in Kerry's wardrobe at Roseneath.

Soon, much of what she owned would need replacing, but that was a concern for tomorrow. She still had Uncle Ned's money as there had been nowhere to spend it. For today, she had clothes to wear and a coat for warmth, as well as a new straw bonnet that had just arrived to keep the sun from her face.

Chapter 19 Bountiful Harvest

A few days before leaving for Parramatta, Pemma, Bagaroo, and their tribe arrived back in the area. They vanished a few days after the accident and now came to show Clare their new child.

The infant was adorable. She had deep dimples in both cheeks that popped when she let out a howl. Bagaroo had these in her cheeks, and they were of evidence now. She passed the baby to Clare.

Bagaroo said proudly, "We come show *gurung* to Missy Clare. Her name, too."

Clare turned to John and asked, "What's a *gurung*, Uncle John?"

He came over to inspect the baby. "You're holding one, Clare. It's a child of either gender, I believe." He stroked the baby's cheek with a hooked finger. The gentle action made the baby girl pull up her cheeks, and the dimples popped again. "She'll be a heartbreaker like you, Bagaroo," He said to the baby's mother, then turned to the father and said. "Pemma, I hope you are proud of your girls?"

The tall, skinny black man nodded somewhat vigorously. "Plenty proud, boss. Bagaroo did good. Little *gurung,* come real quick."

Bagaroo saw a ring on Clare's finger and noticed Shéamas. "He your man, missy Clare?"

Clare grinned as her eyes noticed Shéamas staring at the partially clad pair. "Soon, Bagaroo, we go to marry next week."

Bagaroo's post-baby body was beautiful. Her stomach, which had been round and distended, now only had a slight bulge. Her breasts were full of life-giving milk, and as the baby awoke, Bagaroo fed her without hesitation of being observed by the men. Their two other children had not arrived with them.

Neither Shéamas nor John wished to watch, but they could not tear their eyes from the exquisite scene. Her action was so natural and not at all offensive.

Shéamas had never seen a naked nubile female form before, let alone with such beautiful black shiny skin. To have one appear and stand unashamedly in front of him was far too much to take. He choked out an excuse and went to find something to do until she vanished.

John was used to seeing the unclad tribe, but eventually, he, too, left the women to feed the baby, and he took Pemma to the store room. Shéamas was already there, and the three of them sorted a parcel for the couple to take with them as a congratulatory gift. Pemma produced a string bag under his loin tassel and loaded the goodies. "You good to us, boss."

John wondered what he would trade as they had arrived with nothing. As Pemma put the last of the food in the over-stretched bag, he said. "John, you come tonight down there. *Maugra* on tonight." He made a sign with his hand like a child waving goodbye or crawling. "You bring buckets; we help catch. Eat well tonight. Fire and eat." Pemma grinned in delight.

John nodded.

Shéamas was puzzled. He had no idea what the man had said.

John saw his frown and translated. "A *maugra* is actually an inland fish, but I'm not so sure they have a word for prawn. If the prawns are running in the lagoon tonight, we will be feasting on the most beautiful meal you can imagine, so we won't prepare a meal. We'll need a noon nap as they only run for a while at the new moon and depending on the tide."

Having never tasted prawns before, Shéamas wondered if he would like them.

After luncheon, the small buggy was brought around and loaded with an array of lamps, buckets, an old copper that had obviously been put over a fire on some prior occasion, a selection of nets, and containers of salt, pepper, butter, and loaves of bread.

At dusk, they set off down the hill with the loaded cart. The five young men walked as there was only room for Clare and John in the full vehicle.

When they arrived at the mouth of the lagoon, they saw that a fire had been started by the group of waiting Aboriginals. A huge pile of timber was on the sand nearby, so Clare figured they were in for a long night.

Clare had never noticed a small boat lying upside-down under a stand of paperbark trees with the many hands that now abounded. The boat was soon launched. She saw a large mound under it as it had been flipped over.

Pemma made sure the women were well clear before he and a few others stood waiting with lamps and sticks in hand.

Bagaroo grabbed Clare's arm and tugged her away from the boat. "You come!" She said, making a curving sign with her arm.

Clare had learnt to do what she suggested. She would be as far away as possible if a snake were nearby.

With the swift movements that only the tribal men could do. They pulled back a rolled prawn net, and sure enough, a large black snake was underneath it. However, it was not alone. On the other side of the net were two more, only they were obviously in the process of mating. One looked as though it was biting the head of the other, but his lower section was twisted around the tail of the other one.

With shouts of glee, the three serpents were quickly despatched and would soon be placed in the coals around the fire.

The men were laughing and now spreading out the net. As twilight faded into night, the encampment was made ready for a seafood harvest.

Pemma and Bill half-filled the copper tub with water from the lagoon and sat it near the fire but not on it.

All was now in readiness. The men arranged themselves in order of height. John was in the boat and had the oars ready. The net was tied to the back of the boat. As he rowed out, the net slowly unravelled. It was fed out, and soon, the entire mouth of the lagoon was netted off. When John reached the other side, he was pulled back to shore.

With the tallest man, and this was Pemma, now walking out to the back of the net, the others were at various places along the line. The women squealed with joy as this was now their turn. Clare and a few others stayed on shore, watching the children or readying themselves for the harvest. Bagaroo's sister, Milbah, was the first in the water. Rather than splashing and making a lot of noise, she and about ten others walked in, shuffling their feet and stirring up the sand.

Only about half an hour passed from the boat's launch to the net being hauled in. The net was drawn ashore as the women stirred up the sandy bottom. Pemma was the last out as the net was dragged ashore. The job of the men holding the net had been to keep the top above water and the bottom on the sand with their toes.

The bountiful harvest was soon apparent. Even the children joined in sorting the fish from the eels and prawns. Occasionally, a yell would be made as a bullrout was found and thrown into the fire. Many had been pricked by these devil fish over the years, and they did not want them to breed, so they killed them as quickly as they could.

The numerous buckets they had brought down were soon filled with large flathead, bream, whiting, flounder, and mullet. All the small ones were tossed back to grow bigger. Clare knew that some fish would be flayed open and salted, then left to dry or smoked. Others would be pickled, and some would be made into fish paste.

Various eels were also set aside in a lidded bucket. The tribe would later process them and extract the oil from them. The eel skins would also be preserved and dried. Clare now knew that they used them to bind a sprained ankle or hold on moss, as they did for her wounds, and they were kept and reused.

The prawns and some crabs were scooped into the copper bowl, which was lifted onto the fire. As the water heated, the prawns and crabs stopped moving and changed colour.

By midnight, the feast had been eaten, and the excess was distributed amongst the tribe and the house on the hill. The tired group meandered up the hill, with the two youngest men carrying their share of fish. John and Clare drove up in the loaded vehicle. The following day would be dedicated to preserving them. For the moment, sleep was needed.

~

Two days after the seafood feast, Bagaroo came to say farewell to Clare. She appeared from the back of the dairy and gave Clare a quick hug before vanishing as quickly. Clare stood watching her go. The girls had come from different backgrounds but quickly became good friends.

A few days later, when they were ready to leave for Parramatta, all were pleased that working with the fish was behind them for some time. Clare's hands stank of fish, and she asked John, "How do you get rid of the stink?"

John gave a gurgling chuckle. "Salt and vinegar, dear. Rub them over your hands, and that should do the trick."

As the wagon was nearly packed, Clare raced in and gave her hands a final wash. The wine vinegar certainly smelled better than the fish. The vehicle was virtually empty, so the trip would take much less time.

The extra hands had achieved much on the farm in the eight months since Clare arrived with the boys. Shéamus assisted with the last of the plank capping on the bridge. This now could be traversed by a vehicle with a single horse and much quicker than before.

There had been no further sightings of escaped convicts, but Clare had been happy that John always made sure she was never in the house alone again. Having been assaulted twice by escaped convicts was enough to make her jumpy at every unexpected sound or footstep.

As the vehicle trundled down the hill from the house, Ann Christopher's gig was coming over the newly surfaced bridge. They stopped and chatted, and she assured them she would clean the house and keep her eyes on the property while they were away. She kissed Clare and said she would pray that all would go well for the wedding.

The trip along the dusty road through Kincumber was accompanied by chatter between the three. This was just the beginning of the adventure before Shéamus and Clare.

A couple of months earlier, John had seen a parasol for sale in one of the stores in East Gosford. He had given it to Clare for a belated birthday gift, and she now sat under its shade as they drove. The heat of the late spring weather started a conversation about bushfires. The undergrowth of the scrubby bush they traversed was almost waist-deep with fallen leaves, branches and dead shrubs.

Shéamus noticed John's worried look as they passed around the base of Kincumba Mountain. "There's a lot of dry undergrowth, sir. How long is it since this area burnt?"

John looked at the lad beside him. "Ahh! That's the point, laddie; it has not since I have been here, and the build-up of undergrowth is a big worry for me. If a fire started, it would sweep through to the coast if there was a westerly wind behind it." John fell silent before adding, "It's a big worry, laddie, a very big one, but there is little I can do but keep the areas around my house cleared. On our return, we may prepare for fires this summer. My old cottage burnt in a local fire, but it was riddled with termites."

The track took them along the waterfront as they approached the punt. The tide may not be high enough for the punt to run. John had packed fishing lines on this trip, so they planned to camp near the water as often as possible. They could while away the time fishing if required. Some of the stops along the route were by the Hawkesbury River, and they carried only enough essential stores for three days.

Today, the wagon only had to wait an hour before the punt could carry them across the channel, so they didn't bother fishing. With the lighter cart, the vehicle made it up to the top of the range for the first night. The next stop would be the old water mill at Gunderman, and then the last night was planned to be at Wiseman's Ferry Inn.

The trip went to plan until they pulled off the track at Singleton's Mill. John didn't see the depth of the pothole until it was too late. They had all been watching a school of fish being dive-bombed by birds when the back wheel of the cart crunched into the hole. The reaction of the three on board was instant. The two horses had also jerked to a stop.

"Damn!" John realised instantly that his expletive was impolite. "Oh, sorry, Clare, that was uncalled for." He gave a huff of resignation.

Shéamus hopped down and went to the horses' heads so they would stop trying to pull the vehicle.

It was just as well that they were planning to spend the night there, as the vehicle would not go further. The wagon tray was at an odd angle, and John had to lift Clare off the high step.

On inspection, the wheel was unfixable. The metal rim was buckled, and some wooden felloes were shattered. Four spokes had also broken, and even the hub had a crack in it. They had no spare wheel, and the four-wheel vehicle was now immobilised. It was unlikely that a passing vehicle would come.

After inspecting the damage, John stormed off towards the old mill building, and Clare heard him release a shout of frustration. However, he returned having calmed himself. "Right, oh, young ones," he said cheerfully. "We will stay the night as planned, but the excess food we must leave here. The mill door is open, and we can leave what we don't need. Shéamus lad, how are you at riding?"

Shéamus's eyes flew to Clare. "I can, sir, but I don't wish to leave

Clare here, even with you, and I can't stay either, as we are not wed yet."

John chuckled. "No, lad, I wasn't thinking that. We have two horses but no saddles. Clare, have you ever doubled on a horse? We have to get to Wiseman's Ferry tomorrow night; I can't wait until another vehicle passes, so I propose we ride."

Relief flooded through Shéamus. "Oh, in that case, yes, I have. And Clare has even doubled in front of me. However, that was with a saddle."

John nodded at his answer. "Good, then tomorrow we ride the rest of the way."

They quickly unloaded the wagon, and the bags and stores were removed from the cart. Before the horses were unharnessed, they could pull the now-empty wagon out of the deep hole. The horses were soon unharnessed and hobbled. The wagon was abandoned where it was, and Clare reused the fire pit that they had used previously. Someone had recently added more rocks around it and left a billy hook. The area around the fireplace had been recently scythed, so the grass was low and reasonably safe to sleep on. Clare remembered the giant python from the last visit and was not too keen to sleep on the ground, but she had little choice.

While Clare prepared the camp, John took Shéamus to the waterfront and collected oysters for their meal. He had also thrown out a thick set line and hoped that they would catch something else to eat other than oysters.

Clare had a damper cooking by the time they returned. Dealing with the wagon had taken far too long, and dusk fell all too soon. The oysters and damper had filled them, but hopefully, they would have fish for breakfast. They turned in for the night, sleeping on the ground around the fire.

The crickets and splashes in the water soon lulled them to sleep.

Around midnight, the snapping of a twig made John wake. He lay listening to the sounds and heard nothing. However, moments later, a silhouette of a man loomed over him. He snapped his eyes shut and lay still. His ruse didn't work.

A bony hand shook him awake. "Mr John, you better pull in the fishing line." The words were followed by a grin showing a white teeth line in the moonlight.

John gave a sigh of relief.

Pemma's brother pulled at the hand held out to him. "You caught something big, Mr John. Could be shark, could be fish. Him plenty big!"

The other two had woken by the hushed conversation.

John turned to Clare. "Build up the fire, Clare. Barraboi says there is something big on the line."

That comment moved Shéamus faster than yelling "snake" would have done. His stomach was rumbling as he was not a big fan of oysters. He'd eaten a couple of slices of damper, but he was still hungry. A midnight fish feast would satisfy him greatly.

"Boots on, laddie. We may have to walk over the rocks to bring it in."

John was in the process of lacing up his boots.

Barraboi poked a long stick into the fire, and soon the branch was blazing. He held the fire branch aloft, and the two men followed him to the water's edge. Two more men from the tribe fought for their lives with whatever was on the end of the line. One was knee-deep in the river water while the other held the thick line hard. John and Shéamus watched the battle as the moon rose above the eastern headland.

For over an hour, the battle with the large aquatic creature was passed from one exhausted hand to the other. Eventually, both Shéamus and Barraboi were waist-deep in the river water, and John was able to pull in the massive fish between them so that they could land it. It had somersaulted in the air a few times, and they saw in the moonlight that it was a fish and not a shark. Unwilling to lose it, the two young men decided to try to catch it by its gills. Their ploy worked, and they triumphantly grabbed the huge fish and dragged it out of the water.

The fish seemed to keep coming as they managed to get it to the water's edge. The river ghost fish, as Barraboi called it, was a shade over five feet long. It wasn't until the small group carried it to the fireside that John said, "This is a huge mulloway or river kingfish, Shéamus. I've never seen one before, but I believe they are good eating."

Barraboi was seen nodding. "Very good, Mr John. Too much for you, but feed us good."

John was not averse to sharing his good fortune. Considering that, without Barraboi, the fish probably would have gotten away, he was keen for the tribe to have a feast with the river's bountiful harvest.

Barraboi whistled, and soon, the fire was surrounded by a dozen or more of the tribe. Each came with more firewood. Clare was at a loss regarding how to cook the fish when Barraboi took a coolamon of clay from one of the girls. In a few minutes, the entire fish was encased in clay and placed on the coals of the fire. After a few stories from those who spoke some English, the fish was turned over for another twenty minutes. By the time the fish was cooked, a few other women had arrived carrying sleeping children.

The fish was finally dragged from the coals, and the clay case was broken open. Even with so many mouths waiting to eat the fish, it fed them all with much of it left over. Sated, the enlarged groups soon settled around the fire to sleep for the rest of the night.

With so many bodies sleeping around the warmth, Clare moved closer to Shéamus. They fell asleep holding hands. Hopefully, by the end of the week, they would fall asleep entwined.

Barraboi stoked the fire and again dug John awake. "Mr John, you wake, eat and leave."

When John woke in the pre-dawn light, he found that the tribe had vanished into the bush. He thanked his friend, then stretched and pushed

Shéamus, who woke. He then leaned over and kissed Clare awake. "Love, it's time to get up. We have a long way to go today."

Clare groaned. She was stiff from sleeping on the ground. They were all tired after being up for over two hours during the night. She rolled over and noticed that everyone but Barraboi had gone. With another groan, she sat up.

John handed her a plate of fish and damper. Bleary-eyed, she ate her morning repast in silence. Shéamus and John also ate their fill, and then John gave the remainder of the fish to Barraboi to take to the tribe.

In the time that Clare had taken to wake, John had made arrangements with Barraboi for the tribe to watch over their abandoned wagon and the possessions they would need to leave behind. He told them they could have the food. He also gave them the fishing line and a few spare hooks. Barraboi was thrilled with his trade. Twine they could make, but the sharp steel hooks were a treasure.

By the time the sun hit the horizon, the camp was packed, and the fire was extinguished. The horses' hobbled and the remainder of their possessions, like plates, were stored in the mill, and John adjusted the harness into reins for the horses. Thankfully, he had buckles on these, and it was a simple conversion.

They set off for Wiseman's Ferry on horseback. They had used the wagon as a mounting block.

Clare sat sideways in front of Shéamus. She snuggled into him and wrapped one arm around his waist. Clare cradled a flagon of water in her lap, as John knew there would be little drinking water until they reached the ferry. She said, "I like this; it's so much more comfortable without a saddle."

As he had no stirrups, he could only control the beast with his knees and the remainder of the traces from the wagon.

Although they were riding bareback, they travelled faster than the wagon could go. They reached the ferry for a late lunch. As they had no saddle bags, Clare put some slices of the damper in the clothing bags tied onto John's horse's back.

They stayed at the inn on the other side of the river at Wiseman's Ferry. The mail coach carried them on the last leg of their journey while John's horses stayed at the inn.

Chapter 20 Tying the Knot

*T*he arrival into Parramatta was made with some confusion. Clare wanted to avoid getting off at Roseneath, even though Kerry would be there. Shéamus wanted to go to Eddie's house, and John wanted to book in at Molly's inn. Ultimately, they decided to all alight at the Rear Admiral Duncan Inn and then walk down to Charles and Sal Lockley's place.

Clare knocked on their door and was greeted with a squeal and a big hug from Sal. The welcome they received was one of great joy.

Sal enfolded her young cousin in her arms. "Oh, my dear girl, welcome home. I was so thrilled when I heard Shéamus had found you." Sal brushed Clare's hair back from her brow and kissed her again. She then realised that there were others with her. Before she spoke to them, she called over her shoulder. "Charles, Clare is back with Shéamus." She then turned back to the three at the front door. She took Shéamus's hand. "Thank you for bringing her back, lad."

Shéamus's reply was a big grin.

Charles appeared beside his wife and welcomed the visitors. "Rather than come in here, let's go to Eddie's."

John had yet to be introduced, but he was in no hurry. He had drawn in a quick breath when he saw Sal. The woman could be a younger sister to his father's sister. Even Clare carried a family resemblance, but her hair was more strawberry red than fair, and her skin freckled. He smiled as Clare had more freckles now than when he met her.

Charles noticed John standing at the cottage gate and nodded a hello. He waited for Sal to grab a wrap, and the group walked across the road towards the back entrance of Eddie's house. In the middle of the road, Clare finally introduced John. Charles and Sal welcomed him.

Charles fell behind and touched John's arm to show he wished to talk to him. When Sal had taken Clare and Shéamus's arms, they walked on as Charles slowed his pace. "Mr Moore, I wish to say thank you on behalf of the whole family. I presume she explained the situation?"

John was not used to being nervous, but he was walking with an English earl. He swallowed before replying. "Yes, Lord Charles, she confessed everything but Shéamus's name. Sir, may I ask you to call me John? Therefore, I am related to Clare and Kerry and your wife."

Charles nodded, "I will if you call me Charles. We're of an age and share a family through our ladies. I find that having a title still does not sit well with me. Since my friend Ned left in '42, the discovery of this rod upon my back is uncomfortable, and friends are hard to find."

John looked at the fair-haired gentleman with astonishment. "Sir, I mean, Charles, you do not like having a title?" He was astonished.

Charles was equally surprised at the question. "Of course not, John. It was thrust upon me. I arrived as a convict, so what do you think? Until then, I was content being an innkeeper and living a quiet life. I had my faith and my family. My health is reasonable, although my broken leg from a fall some decades ago gives me grief. When Ned returned to England in '42, he discovered I had been an earl since I was five; I felt like crawling into a hole and hiding."

The two men skirted around the circumstances of their meeting. That would follow. For now, the two loners sought friendship. Charles may have a quiver full of children and many more grandchildren, but he and Sal were content hidden away in their tiny two-bedroom cottage and dressed in old work clothing.

John dropped his voice and said, "Charles, may I say I would have guessed that your good wife was related even if I did not know the blood connection. She could well be my father's sister. My father, of course, is long gone, but Lady Sal is the image of his sister."

Charles gave a nod and said, "Drop the title with Sal too, John. She dislikes it as much as I; she's your cousin."

The two arrived at the back gate and followed the path that the others had. The backyard seemed filled with mini versions of Charles and Sal running around everywhere. They were in time to hear Cara's squeal of joy when she saw her son. Both men chuckled, knowing how that would make Shéamus squirm with embarrassment.

Charles broke their silence. "He'll hate that, and Cara will then enfold him in a big mother's hug. He will dutifully kiss her back, and then he will roll his eyes behind her back."

John now chuckled. "I've only known the lad for a few weeks, but he seems quite sure of himself. I think the months on the journey have matured him somewhat, too. Clare said as much."

The men sat in the shade of the big mulberry tree in the backyard.

Charles got straight to the point. "It was a bad situation for the lad, John. The shew, Lavinia, nearly got away with it. If Shéamus had done what the community expected, he would have married her immediately. Although he proposed to Lavinia as he was forced to do, he said he would hold off marrying her until after the child was born due to his love for Clare. Knowing the death rate of babies at birth, I agreed with him. Of course, Lavinia was caught in a compromising position with her lover before that occurred, and the girl's married lover admitted the child was his. As this occurred in front of the governor, the girl had no choice but to leave the colony. The man was dismissed from his government job and forced to leave town, too. This was unfortunate for his family, as they now have eight children. She was sent to Moreton Bay with her reputation preceding her in the form of a letter from the governor to the commandant of the settlement there. She was lucky Shéamus did not press charges. He had worked hard at the dairy since he was six. He lived with the dairyman's family, but when his parents, who are life convicts, moved in with Eddie, he and his little brother, Liam, came to live with them. That was over ten years ago."

The talk turned to John's offer of a dowry for both girls and his promise to buy them both farms. "Charles, I have no immediate family, and my farm has been very productive. As their oldest male relative, it is my prerogative to supply the girls with a dowry." Once he voiced his idea, he then asked Charles if he would oversee the project. "I thought that while I was here for the wedding, I would look around and see if there was something suitable for them. However, if you know of an available farm that would suit them, I am perfectly content to follow your advice."

Charles smiled at the easy friendship that quickly formed with this Irish ex-soldier. "I do happen to know a place, John. It's on the road to Parramatta, just out of town. I saw it advertised in the paper this morning. I know the farm well. The family don't wish it to go to someone who will not care for their vineyard. It was the passion of the husband. However, they have fallen on tough times. The house and land are for sale, but it has some three acres as a vineyard, and the rest is mixed farming. I believe the house is quite extensive, with some ten-plus bedrooms."

John's eyes lit up. "That sounds good, Charles. They may even be willing to stay on and farm it for Shéamus. It would give them time to save a little money and get back other feet elsewhere. Later, it will also give me a place to stay when I'm in town. Could you arrange an inspection while the young ones are on their honeymoon?" John saw the young couple approaching and dropped his voice as he said the last words.

Charles said equally as softly, "I'll see what I can arrange for Monday."

The men stood as Sal, Jenna, and the engaged couple arrived. Charles introduced his daughter-in-law to John. Eddie was not yet home from work at the forge.

John liked the girl's look, with her honey-coloured eyes and hair. Her face showed her joy of life, and he had already heard her infectious laugh.

"We've just been getting to know each other, love." Charles drew his wife to him. "However, as John is your relative, I suppose I had better bow to your superior claim." Charles gave a mock bow.

John was surprised at the banter between the earl and countess and watched on with the hint of a smile tickling his lips.

Meanwhile, Jenna was watching him. As she did so, she did not notice Eddie's arrival until his hands slid around her waist. Her gasp and giggle showed her delight. She turned in his arms and welcomed him with a passionate kiss.

Eddie's bristly chin grazed her cheek as he kissed her. "Hello, sweetie, I missed you." He had hardly glanced at the others in their backyard as it was for family only. He eventually took notice of who his parents were talking to. One was a stranger, and the other two made him give a whoop of delight. Releasing Jenna, Eddie embraced Clare, then almost shook off Shéamus's hand. Only then did his father introduce him to John. Eddie frowned and then said, "If you're mother's cousin, then we must be about third cousins." His face lightened. "Dar, that's the same as Uncle Ned and you."

Charles nodded. "John is family, son; hence, we're out here rather than sitting stuffily indoors. Mother says start as you mean to go on, so I am." As he spoke, an older couple arrived through the back gate. Charles looked up and smiled, "Speak of the devil!" He waved to his mother and stepfather.

The graceful new arrival smiled at the comment. "I love you too, son." Then Lady Elizabeth ignored him. "Molly told me you were back, dear, so Richard and I have come uninvited for tea."

Eddie said, "Our home is an open door to you, Grandmother."

Charles introduced his mother, Elizabeth, and stepfather, Richard Child, to John. "John, Richard and Mother run the female orphanage school. Richard took over when the government gave it up. Mother kidnapped his bachelor's heart some years ago, and now she shadows him everywhere, or that could be reversed; I'm not quite sure as they always arrive together. The female orphans they produce from that place are the best-educated little girls you will ever see. They are giving Howard Marlow's boys' orphanage a run for their money. Mother started teaching cleanliness, and now she's got them learning Latin, arithmetic and geography." He chuckled. "Rather than turning out milkmaids and laundry maids, the girls are educated enough to be governesses. I was a disappointment to Mother, so she's taking it out on those poor little mites." Charles had the goodness to look embarrassed. He turned to John and said, "I'm here because I skipped school so much I got mixed with the wrong crowd. I came as a convict, as I said. However, I was charged with stealing a sheep. I didn't, but that's another story. It was all sorted by Ned, but it took twenty years to do."

Elizabeth chuckled. "Behave, Charles!"

Charles gave his mother a sheepish grin. "Yes, Mother."

John was beginning to feel at home with this unusual family. He had been accepted without a qualm. He was beginning to grasp who's who when another couple arrived through the back gate. They, too, were fair-haired, and with a glance at both Charles and Eddie, he presumed this young man was another brother.

Again, Charles did the honours. "John, this is The Right Honourable, The Viscount Lockley, otherwise known as Charlie. His lovely lady is Lady Lockley and is known by all as Gracie. You have already met her parents, Bill and Molly, at the Rear Admiral Duncan Inn."

The astonishment on John's face made Charles chuckle. "Your astonishment is no more than theirs when they found out about their titles. They were already wed by then. Our youngest daughter, Anna, is married to Gracie's eldest brother, Tim. Our children in age order are Charlie, Eddie, Liza, Anna, Wills, and Luke. The younger ones all have The Honourable plastered in front of their monikers, and all of us dislike them intently."

The heads around him nodded their sad agreement.

John had not realised the exalted state of his cousin's family.

Charlie broke the silence by saying, "Nice to meet you, John. And welcome back, wanderers. Now that we have the bridal couple back, the wedding is planned for this Saturday. Gracie and I are here to let you know that the usual family party is on down at the inn courtyard, and we've made it open slather for the town as it will do everyone good to see all is settled and above board. Cara has already sorted the food, and of course, we have the Irish band booked for a jig or twenty. George and Bertie Ellis are going to bring their violins. This will be the first family wedding we have had since we moved into Willow Grove. That's our new house, John. So we're all looking forward to letting our hair down."

The group sat in the shade, watching the multitude of children play for some time.

Shéamus's parents, Cara and Paddy Connor, soon joined them to finalise the details of the weekend of festivities.

Charles introduced the groom's parents to John before they all retired indoors for a meal of stew and an enormous mulberry pie with an equally enormous bowl of clotted cream. The simple fare that these titled people ate made John relax even more. For the first time in years, he felt at home. He had yet to meet Clare's little sister, Kerry, but that could wait until the morning.

Eddie suggested that Clare stay in her old room at the house for the night. It was no use going to Roseneath as a new maid had taken her room, and Kerry would be down in the morning anyway to help with wedding celebrations.

After dinner, Shéamus met her at the back door and kissed her goodnight.

John had already left with Charles and Sal. Sal was escorted home, and the two men wandered up to Bill and Molly's inn.

Charles knew they would not have much opportunity for private conversation, so he took the opportunity to ask John about their earlier discussion. "John, are you serious about us looking at the farm next week?"

John could still see him in the dim light. "Absolutely, Charles! I have no other family but Robert Maddrell in Braidwood. He already has enough wealth, so I would like to supply a dowry for both girls. Robert married the daughter of one of the convict transport sea captains who settled in the area. I truly am the girls' closest male relative. Clare admitted she knew of a cousin named John but did not know where to find me. God dealt with that. Only He could find a needle in a haystack. I would consider it an honour to be permitted to do this for them. I will not change my will but intend to see them settled before I die. I will also take the opportunity to tell you that I have asked Shéamus and Clare to come back to my farm for a few years so he can learn the skills of running a mixed farm. Hence, the suggestion for the existing owners to stay on. I believe his younger brother Liam may also be brought into the family if Shéamus is correct. You know them better than I do. Charles, you have my blessing to approve of that union if you think he is right for her."

Charles sighed in the darkness. "I believe so, John, but they are young and not even officially courting.

John replied with one word. "Yet!"

Charles chuckled. "Yes, yet. Anyway, if this is truly your intent, I will be honoured to show you what's available. And as you suggest, the family may be prepared to stay on and run the farm for you." As Charles spoke, they arrived at the inn. He didn't go in as he knew that Bill and he would not have a quick conversation. He would catch up with his friend tomorrow. Charles made his excuses and headed home to Sal.

~

Friday morning, Kerry knocked on the back door as soon as the sun was up. Liam had brought the news that Clare had returned with Shéamus, and she couldn't wait to see her. Kerry left Roseneath before dawn to walk the twenty minutes to see her sister. She could not stay long as Wills and Cathy were due to arrive with Harry and Vicky and all their children.

John had yet to meet Jenna's two younger sisters, but having heard that about them over the months, he had worked out that Wills was one of Eddie's younger brothers and Harry was Wills's business partner. Those two couples lived at Emu Plains. Charles let drop that Harry also had a minor title. John had given up trying to work out which children belonged to whom. He just smiled and enjoyed the organised chaos that was going on around him. This family was vastly different from his peaceful life at Avoca, yet he was enjoying every moment of belonging to such a dynamic family. It was ordered chaos and mayhem.

Charles had taken him for a long morning walk along the river edge, and they tried hard to keep out of the way of the numerous wedding discussions that seemingly were occurring in every room.

During the afternoon, Charles escorted John to meet the Reverend Henry Bobart. Paddy and Shéamus accompanied them, and the four men made sure the appropriate paperwork was in order. Charles's arrangements were perfect, but Reverend Bobart took the opportunity to thank John for giving permission for the young couple's union. He was fully aware of the previous unfortunate situation.

Henry turned to Charles and said, "Sir, I probably won't get to thank you tomorrow, but Charlie said the after-party is again for the community. After what these two have endured, I think it is an excellent idea. The town will see that all is now as it should be."

Charles thanked his friend. He had one special guest who would be in attendance, and only he and Sal knew about it. The governor was coming.

~

Saturday morning, dawn broke with a shower of rain.

Clare was up early and washed her hair.

The bridal couple had been kept apart the day before due to the Connor's superstitions.

Clare had no idea that Cara and Paddy were so superstitious. Although Shéamus no longer worked at the dairy, he was sent to Kit Kellow's farm for the day to keep him out of the way. He arrived home after dinner with Kit's family and went straight to bed. Thankfully the wedding was to be at ten in the morning. Clare didn't think she would cope if she had to wait any longer before she saw him again.

Jenna woke Clare with a mug of sweet tea, sat on her bed, and gave her some motherly advice. After the fiasco with Lavinia, Jenna was sure they had not been intimate. As Clare's mother died long ago, Jenna took the role upon herself and gave Clare some instruction as a mother would typically give her daughter before marriage.

Clare drank in all the information and knew she would not have long to wait before discovering much of this for herself. She knew from Bagaroo that such intimacies were enjoyable. Once back on the farm, Ann and Bagaroo were the only women nearby.

The morning hours seemed to drag by slowly. The chaos the children caused passed the time.

Eventually, Clare was dressed, ready, and waiting for Kerry to appear in the sitting room. In the silence of the room, her mind turned to her parents. She had come across an item that Kerry had handed her yesterday morning. The limpet shell on the twine had been the only thing she had left from her father. She thought it was lost years ago, but Kerry had kept it safely all this time. It sat in her pocket. With that thought, soon she was overtaken by sadness that neither of her parents could be with her on this special day. She was teary. She pulled out the shell and fingered it while wiping tears away.

John saw the state she had worked into and knew Kerry was not the person she needed. Only Shéamus could comfort her at this time.

John knew the lad was nervously sitting under the mulberry tree and waiting for his parents and siblings. He summoned him and explained Clare's melancholy. John hardly recognised him. His face was clean-shaven, and his hair and sideburns were trimmed. He was dressed as a gentleman of fashion in tight-fitting buckskin breeches and a gold damask vest with a fawn tails coat. The lad could have passed in any society. For him to be the son of Irish political prisoners made John smile. He loved this new land. Hopefully, their new farm would one day give them a start in life that he didn't have. His parents had not precisely cast him out, but his presence made life difficult for them. He was not much younger than Shéamus when he left home and joined the enemy army. He served there for nine years, and when he left, he couldn't settle and decided to see the world. That was when he saw his beautiful Avoca Vale with a private beach. He had spent some time traversing the coast on a coastal trader steamship but had stopped in the Kincumber area as some fellow countrymen named Humphreys, Davis, and a few others lived there. He had fallen in love with the area, which was now home.

However, the nostalgia for Ireland still stirred his heart. Paddy's thick Irish lilt was a delight to his ears. Mid-afternoon, another Irish family arrived and settled in the backyard. These people were Brodie Murphy's family from Emu Plains. Finn and Maureen were also Protestants and escaped before being arrested. He discovered that Finn and his extensive family were behind Murphy's Spuds. A product that he knew well and purchased as often as possible.

Shéamus snuck into the house under John's protective eye. The groom didn't take Clare into his arms but slid his arm along her shoulder.

For some minutes, she barely acknowledged his presence. "I always wanted Papa to give me away. I wanted Mama to see me on my wedding day, and they are not here, Shéamus. I miss them so much."

Shéamus turned her to face him. "No, sweetheart, they are not. But God sent you John and Lady Sal, not to mention all the rest of your blood family here. Your parents planned that this was the family you would live with. You did what your parents wanted and brought Kerry here. They would have been so proud of you and everything you have achieved, including leaving me. Doing that, you found Uncle John. We both believe that God controls our lives and know that the Bible tells a story of the other Lazarus, who can see his brother on earth. Trust that your parents know that we will get married today. Darling, it is what would have occurred even if they had been here."

Clare now had her head on his chest. She nodded, and he bent and kissed the top of her head.

Shéamus knew he needed to make her laugh. "Cheer up, love; in an hour, we will be married; that is unless Mama finds me here, then I might be a corpse instead." It worked. His words brought the desired watery gurgle of laughter.

She said, "Go, sweetheart; I will see you in church. Thank you."

As Shéamus left, he nodded thanks to John, who had stood at the door watching their interaction.

John said nothing but squeezed Shéamus's shoulder as he left the room. He turned and watched as Shéamus left the way he came in, by the back door. He was about to go into Clare when Kerry came down the stairs. "Hello, sir. Is Clare ready?" She had not entirely become used to calling him her Uncle.

John put his finger to his lips and said, "She's a little upset your parents are not here for her today."

Kerry nodded her understanding; her hands were holding an old shawl. "This will help; it was Mama's. I just wanted to say thank you for standing in for Papa today. It even makes a difference to have someone who knew our parents with us today."

John already liked this young girl. At seventeen, she was wise beyond her years. John felt a lump in his own throat. He had never expected ever to walk anyone down the aisle for a wedding. He would not miss this day for anything. He was delighted that Clare had asked him rather than Charles. He would one day repeat it for Kerry.

She gave a nod to John and went to join her sister.

Again, John stayed within earshot. He heard Clare's gasp and saw her throw her arms around her sister. "Now Mama will be with me after all."

Clare wore the lovely gown she had made with the tiny potato-like flowers circling the hem. The shawl was their mother's lovely lightweight one that Kerry placed around Clare's shoulder. Rather than let it drape like an everyday shawl, she tied it in a knot at the front. Kerry then enfolded her weeping sister in her arms. After a while, she said, "If your eyes go puffy and ugly, then Shéamus might leave you at the altar. I know you are to marry for better or worse, and with two attacks and that woman, I hope that all the worst will be in your past. But, if you walk up the aisle leaving a river of tears, you will have everyone wondering what he's done to you." Kerry could see John's surprised face at her words. "Uncle John may also object and not wish to walk a wet mop up the sanctuary; he might abandon you too. So cheer up, or I will have to tickle you or something drastic like that."

Clare gave a wet gurgle of laughter. "I'm not really sad, Kezzy. Uncle John has been wonderful; having him is like Papa is here. He knows everything and even remembers us as littlies." She caressed Kerry's face. She had not used her nickname for her since they left Ireland. "It all just crashed in on me today, Kez. I so want to be with Shéamus, but I don't want to leave you here alone."

It was Kerry's turn to giggle. "I'm not alone, Clare; I have Liam, Aunt Sal, and all the rest of the family, as well as now Uncle John. Come on, let's get you married." She whispered, "Uncle Charles won't let us court until you are wed." Unbeknownst to Clare, John had walked in and stood behind her.

"Oh, he said that did he? I'll have to have a word with him later today as Clare will be married by then." John's eyes twinkled with mischief.

Clare could see him holding back a smile, but Kerry looked horrified. It was what Clare needed. She couldn't hold in her laughter. "He's joking, Kerry. Uncle John has already spoken to Liam and Paddy. Probably to Uncle Charles, too, if I know him." Her face now shone with happiness. "You might be courting by tonight, sweet sister."

Kerry swung around to the man, who was now walking to take his place beside Clare. "Really, Uncle John?"

He flicked the tip of her nose as he smiled. "Really, Kerry! I'd say it's a sure bet. But as you said, let's get your sister married first, eh?"

The three of them had heard the rest of the family leave via the front door. Eddie had already told him that Charlie would drive them to the church in the coach as Paddy was the groom's father and would need to be seated with Cara before they arrived. The house had fallen silent while they had been conversing.

John ushered the girls out the front door to the waiting carriage, amazed that a viscount would be their chauffeur. He chuckled at the absurdity of it all.

~

A gasp was the first warning Shéamus had that Clare had arrived. Then, the conversations in the congregation ceased.

Liam was standing beside him, and to calm him, he made him chuckle by retelling their old antics. He dug him in the ribs and said, "Turn now."

Shéamus turned and saw his lady love silhouetted in the archway of the church door. John's easily identifiable figure stood beside her. Shéamus's bitten lips curved into a big grin. She had arrived and was about to come to him.

The music started, and the room was filled with a joyous hymn from the out-of-tune organ. Tiny shafts of sunlight came through the roof, which still had hail holes from a hail storm and tornado of long ago. Tiny dust motes were caught in the sunbeam, and it looked like fairy dust was playing around Clare as she walked. All Shéamus cared about was that Clare had arrived. He had no idea what music was playing; he didn't really care. What he wanted was Clare, and soon, she would be his. He held out his hand, and she came to his side.

Chapter 21 A Safe Haven
Five Years Later, 1856

$\mathcal{T}$he heat was so overwhelming that the candles melted in the sconces, and the wax and tallow dribbled onto the floor.

Pemma, Bagaroo, and their tribe appeared laden with their possessions. Even Barraboi was there with his wife, Milbah, and their children, plus the other boys, now grown, who had helped pull in the big fish years ago.

Pemma stepped forward and said, "Mr John, we come to stay in a big cave on rocks. We bring everything and all the tribe. Boss, soon all burn. You bring good stuff to the cave, too. We care while you go away. We might lose a big house, but you live, we live. Build again another time."

John's frown showed his concern. "You really think there will be a bushfire?"

Pemma's head was shaking. "Not think, Mr John, me know! The smell is in the air. Bush not burn for longga time, and now too much dead leaf. Him bush, burn big-time now." Pemma's hand met in a clap and then lifted and parted to infer a big fire. "Mr John, you leave all gates open and move cows and horses to the beach when you go. We care for them."

John's brow was now beading with perspiration. "Oh no, Pemma! That bad?"

Pemma nodded. "Real bad, boss!"

John had learnt that the tribe knew what they were talking about. He had been concerned for the farm for some time. The undergrowth was just too deep. They had burned off the headland around his original cottage over winter, and the weeds there needed clearing. They had to leave for Kerry and Liam's wedding in just three days. It was on that coming weekend. Shéamus and Clare were to take over the running of their own farm and they were sad as John would be left alone on the farm. He had arranged for some of the local boys to come and help, but he would again be alone in the big house. Clare felt terrible, but she knew it was time for them to leave Avoca Bay and start their life on their own farm in Parramatta.

Dave and Glenn were long gone, and Bill and Tom married local girls and had their own families nearby. They still came in to work three or four days a week most of the year, but as bean farmers, they were busy harvesting.

John had been doing the farm books while he listened for noises from the currently sleeping boys. Two small children, aged four and two, were asleep in the room next to his. The boys, Kieran Patrick and John James, known as Johnny, were his pride and joy. They were the closest he would ever get to grandchildren. To have one named after him was even nicer. Clare was in the dairy with their youngest, Gráinne Joy, which meant Grace Joy. Joy was the image of her mother, including her rosebud lips and Clare's strawberry-blonde hair. She was even destined to have some of Clare's freckles. The boys took after their father. Both could milk a cow and also the nanny goat that had wandered onto the farm the year before. John had taken it into the impound in Gosford to see if anyone came and claimed it. The nanny goat produced a kid during her time of confinement, and John offered to keep them at home where the owner could claim it if they ever turned up. After a year, the goats were still there. Johnny adored the kid, and it followed the toddler around the yard. Last week, John had even found the child trying to smuggle it inside.

John told Pemma to follow him to the dairy while the boys were asleep. The four discussed the situation there while Clare and Shéamus continued to milk. There were only two cows, but they were trying to get them done before the children awoke. Joy was asleep in her basket in the corner. The voices did not wake her, but she stretched, made a whimper, and then settled again. These two cows would be moving to the new farm in Parramatta with the young family. They were to travel by the coastal steamer from Terrigal Haven in three days.

John glanced at the sleeping angel and smiled. He loved this family so much. He knew that the trip to Kerry and Liam's wedding meant that he would be alone at the house from now on. It was something he did not relish. However, he didn't tell Clare, as he was sure they would stay if he voiced his concern.

The day was spent packing everything they could. Most of their possessions had already been sent by hired wagon, and they were awaiting their arrival on the new farm. Liam received the goods, and since the previous owners had gone, he arranged for their stock to be fed and the vines tended.

Pemma suggested they use the tribe members to carry as much as they could down to the beach, or better still, for all John's possessions to be placed on the rocks. While they packed, Barraboi and Pemma started taking some of the goods to the backyard dray. Bag after bag was carted to the beach shack.

Shéamus and Clare spent a three-week honeymoon in this tiny cottage that John built on the southern headland. In the week after Shéamus and Clare had married, Tom and Bill had finally enlarged the shack overlooking the beach with the last of the timbers stripped from the wreck of the *Sir Robert Peel*. The cottage had a single bedroom with a large sleep-out off to the eastern side. There was a double-sided fireplace between the kitchen and living/dining room. They had used it often over the years, and it was set up with bedding for the family. The cows had grazed the new grass down as low as they could, and Pemma doubted this shack would burn. As the headland only had a few she-oak trees along the cliff edge, he was pretty sure it would survive. However, the main home was cedar-built and surrounded by shady trees. These were a danger to the house. The cedar was dry and would burn quickly.

Numerous loads were packed and moved from the homestead. Most of Clare and Shéamus's things were taken straight to Terrigal Haven to await their departure later in the week.

The first waft of smoke was seen on the western horizon just before sunset. The large group stood on the beach as they delivered the last load and watched the spectacular glowing sky. The plume of smoke seemed far away, but a westerly wind was blowing, and they had seen cinders and significant chunks of leaf ash landing on the beach throughout the day.

As they walked back towards the big house, John and Pemma were in deep discussion. "We'll be fine in the big house tonight, Pemma. We won't need to stay in the cave tonight."

Pemma was adamant. "No, Mr John, you come now. Big fire come this way quick. Be too late to leave later; you come now, or you die." He grabbed John's arm. Determined that he would not remain alone.

Shéamus hated fires. He had spent many summer days in his young years fighting the flames, and he saw how fast they moved. Now, as a father of three, he sided with Pemma. "Sir, if you don't mind, I'd rather spend a cold night in the cave and be safe rather than need to flee in the middle of the night with three small children. Sir, we need you with us. Please come."

John looked around at his family. They were his responsibility now, and he realised Shéamus was right. With a deep sigh of resignation, he said, "Fine, but I'm taking lots of blankets. Last time you dragged me down there, I nearly froze." Before they shut the door, John looked back at the polished cedar extension table in the middle of the vast dining room. He had purchased it when Clare had said she was expecting her first child. It was like he was saying goodbye to his life. He was sure the fire would come nowhere near his farm, but for Pemma to come and evacuate them worried him. He accepted the tall native man's wisdom. John walked around the house, closing all the windows and doors. He picked up a toy one of the boys had left on the floor and stuffed it into the last bag to be removed.

Bagaroo had arrived by this stage, and the situation was out of his hands when she walked off with baby Joy in her arms. Clare followed her with blankets, pillows and some clothing filling the baby's basket. She was also going to the cave. Shéamus had already said they would sleep there tonight. John watched them leave, and after closing the back door, he reluctantly followed the path back to the beach. He, too, carried more bedding.

By the time they reached the cave, twilight had faded into night. They needed to negotiate the foot-wide gap and jump up to the ledge to reach the vast cavern. It was barely visible in the gloomy light.

The westerly wind had not dropped as it usually did at nightfall. The ash was now falling thick and fast, and a live ember could occasionally be seen drifting past the opening. As they were in the lee of the cliff, the wind let the cinders fall onto the rock platform and Shark Island just beyond the cave entrance. John had sent down a drum of kerosene and a few lamps in one of the first loads. Bagaroo had lit one of the lamps. With the help of their friends, the family scrambled across the fallen boulders to the back of the cave.

The young boys had been passed across the gap and were carried to safety to join the tribe's children. Bagaroo had easily negotiated the gap, and Joy had once again fallen asleep.

Soon, the thirty or more people were settled and eating some of the supplies that had been sent down in the first dray load.

The sound of the breakers washing into the cave was loud, and being unused to the proximity of the water, they didn't expect to sleep much.

John was right about one thing: the heat in the house had been intolerable, but the chill of the salt spray in the cave made the family huddle under the blankets for warmth. The many children of both colours were on a shelf at the back of the cave and quickly fell asleep huddled together.

Clare lay cuddled up to Shéamus, and they eventually drifted off to sleep.

John sat quietly, chatting with Pemma, Barraboi, and some older men. After some time, they, too, settled for the night. The blankets had been shared around, and many were snuggling under them. Others had kangaroo or possum skins to sleep on and under. Still, the chill permeated deep.

Joy woke for a feed sometime after midnight, and Clare was surprised to see how light it was. However, the light was red, eerie, and casting moving shadows. She elbowed Shéamus, but she didn't need to explain anything as he sat up. He drew her to him and kissed her hair.

The fire was in their valley. Pemma had been right.

The calm of the night was soon gone as the roar of the fire above their heads exploded into the night.

John stirred and was about to go and investigate when Pemma grabbed his arm. "No, Mr John! You stay here. Tomorrow, we all go and see what's left. You go now, you die."

The roar overhead meant that most of the adults were now awake. The noise of the flames sounded like an explosion. There were crackles, bangs and thuds as they heard trees engulfed by the advancing disaster. Embers were like fireworks and fairy lights falling onto Shark Island just outside the cave.

Pemma did not let go of John's arm. "You stay now; go later. You go now. Mr John, you die if you go now."

John sank back down again, knowing there was nothing he could do. He eventually said, "I'll stay, Pemma." A whimper sounded behind him. John turned to see Clare tending to the baby. Shéamus sat beside her with his arm casually slung around her shoulder. At least they were safe. Even if the house burnt, he would still have them. He'd already lost one house to fire, and the new house he had built was much better, but could he start all over again? Thankfully, he still had his houses in East Gosford. Most were rented, but one was vacant.

From the back of the cave, they could see burning branches falling from the cliff face. The sea had quieted overnight, and the large embers sizzled as they hit the gently lapping water. The rocky island, a short distance offshore, was easily visible in the eerie glow of the fire.

Inside the cave, all were silent. Each knew the valley they would find in the morning would vastly differ from the lush but somewhat thirsty farm John and Shéamus had lovingly tendered. Knowing there was nothing they could do but pray, they settled back to rest.

John lay on the rocky ground smiling. He thanked God for his native friends. Clare had quickly learnt to trust the Aboriginal skills and their vast knowledge. Even though he had made friends with them, it had taken many years of initially tense interaction before the hand of friendship had been extended to him. The provision of the boat and net one prawning night had done it. He had willingly shared his catch, and they had become friends around a shared campfire. As he settled back to sleep, he thanked God that he had listened to Pemma.

At dawn, a falling tree woke them. It crashed down the cliff face and onto the rock platform. The sky was a bright red in the predawn light, and the air was thick with smoke and falling blackened embers. As the sun rose, the red turned to a vivid purple. The yellow orb continued its passage, and the sea released its hold on the sun as it exploded into a new day.

The roaring of the fire from above was now absent, and only the sounds of the waves hitting the rocks met their ears. The gulls were screeching loudly, and other birds' chirps, including kookaburras, soon laughed at the start of a new day.

Pemma said, "Safe now, boss."

John was unable to wait any longer. He was up and out over the rocky floor before the other had even rubbed the sleep from their eyes. John was turning around the point by the time Shéamus negotiated the gap in the rocky ledge with Clare. The children were left with the tribe. As the tide was now high, he had to wait until the waves permitted him across the gap. He followed as fast as he could and was close enough to hear John's gasp of horror.

"Oh no! Good Lord, why? It's gone, all gone!" John was leaning into the rock wall and almost gasping for breath as he rounded the corner.

Shéamus caught up to him and lifted his eyes to see the horrific sight. The charred trees and burned farmland were expected; the carcasses of blackened cattle, burnt wallabies, and other native animals scattered along the beach. The sight shocked him into silence. They would all be dead if they had stayed on the beach as John wished. The heat had been so intense that it had killed the animals that had taken shelter in the sea.

Shéamus asked his benefactor, "Sir, what do you wish to do?" He paused and added, "I shall come with you and see if anything remains, but this…" he waved his hand over the scorched land in front of them. "…this is total devastation."

John had got his second wind. "I don't imagine anything will remain, laddie, but let's go and survey the damage, eh?"

The two scrambled over some fallen charred trees and emerged to see that everything was black. Even the larger clinker-built boat that lay upturned on the sand was now a burnt-out hull. Here and there, a green treetop remained. Smoke still oozed from the trunks of many of the banksia trees that lined the foreshore. Knowing fallen trees would probably block the track, they walked along the soft, once-golden sand on the beach. Their feet left cream hollows in the soot-covered sand.

Walking towards the lagoon opening, they saw that a few of the trees along the edge of the waterway had missed the ferocity of the flames. Some were singed, others unscathed. They soon saw that the fire had carved a path across the hilly boundary at the back of the farm. Hardly anything had escaped the ferocious wrath of the terrifying calamity that had befallen the area. The crop on the flat area near the bridge had thankfully been harvested and sent to market only the week before; the stubble now hosted a few of the wallabies that had somehow survived the catastrophe. John presumed they had been in the lake.

John could hardly bear to lift his eyes to his house. He knew it would be gone, but he did not want to see it.

Shéamus stopped walking. Gone was the expansive verandah, and gone was the welcoming kitchen, where many conversations had taken place around the kitchen table rather than the formal dining room table. Gone was the comfortable big feather bed and mosquito net that Clare had made for them from cheesecloth. All that remained was the charred skeleton of what had once been their home. Shéamus blew out his cheeks. There were no words to cover what he felt. In his peripheral vision, he saw John finally turn and look at where his beloved home had once stood. Shéamus knew that if he felt bad, then John would be even worse. He walked to John's side and laid a hand on his shoulder. "We'll stay, sir. We'll help rebuild."

John shook his head. "No, laddie! I'll not start again, not here." John wanted to say more, but the words stuck in his throat. "With you going, I'll not rebuild. I shall move into Springfield into my house there."

Shéamus saw his eyes glistening in the morning light. "Then come and stay with us and help us get on our feet. I wanted your advice anyway, but I knew you have responsibilities here." He paused momentarily before adding, "But now, sir…." He did not need to put his thoughts into words. There was nothing for John here for many months.

As they drew closer, they saw that the staff quarters at the back of the house still stood. Clare's rosemary bush had somehow been overlooked by the ravaging flames. Even the tiny stone storeroom remained. As they drew closer, they saw that the solid frame held up the charred timbres that had once been the roof, windows and rooms. The timber top of the big cedar table still smouldered on the dining room floor. They didn't enter as they were unsure if the floor would hold.

Knowing they had yet to check if any stock survived, they kept walking. They followed the blackened, ash-covered track from the back of the house to the orchards. Presuming they would find that nothing had survived, they knew they still had to look, just in case. From a distance, they could see the banana crop was now merely smouldering stumps. The citrus trees were ghostly skeletons, dead cattle were scattered over the farm, blackened, and some still smoked as the fire had stolen their lives. Amazingly, the stable building had also escaped the inferno. As they drew near, they heard the bleating of the nanny goat and her kid where they had taken refuge in the building. All the gates had been opened, and the stock and horses were free to roam. How she had found her way inside amazed them.

They had not seen the horses' bodies, and John hoped they had fled along the beach to Terrigal. They entered the stables to find John's two white steeds munching on the hay in their feed manger; they were completely unconcerned. Both whinnied a hello as the men entered. One had a burn on his rump, and the other was covered in ash, her tail singed.

Knowing there was no feed for them anywhere else, John and Shamus forked down what remained of the fodder from the loft above. The native animals would need to eat, and John would probably need to send his horses and goats to Parramatta with Shéamus and Clare. His words about not returning hit hard, but he realised he meant them. He didn't wish to be here without them anyway. He didn't have the heart to start again. He didn't want to be alone. They were his family, and he would miss them.

They had just finished forking down the last of the fodder when they heard voices.

Bill and Tom came to see how they fared. Bill and his family lived near the bush, and Bill and his family stayed at Tom's farm in Terrigal. Thankfully, the fire had missed that hamlet. The men knew every inch of this farm, and after noting the burnt house, they followed the footprints and came to check on the stock. They were surprised to see hay floating out of the stable door and to find both horses; the stray goat and her kid were all alive.

Nothing else could be rescued or salvaged.

Tom said, "Sir, why don't Bill and I take the horses to my farm? The goat can come too if she has a mind to. I think she may have originally belonged to my papa. She was an escape artist and broke down so many fences that he was pleased to see the back of her."

John's face brightened. "Thanks, lad. Put some salve on the burns, too, please."

Tom produced a glass tub of his lineament from the shelf on the wall of the stable. He cleaned the burn, smeared it with the cream, then dug into a pouch and covered the wound with cheesecloth. The burn looked like a burning branch had swiped the gelding. It wasn't too deep, and the horse barely flinched as he was treated.

John knew Tom would care for his beloved horses; having them cared for was one thing he would not have to worry about. He forced a smile onto his lips, but he felt anything but happy; he was gutted. What would he do with himself now? At fifty-three, he didn't want to start over again. He had poured his life into the farm and his home; now, it was all but gone.

From outside the stables, they could see a few small patches in the gullies that had escaped the ravages of the natural disaster. There was absolutely nothing John could do for the farm, but could he turn his back on it? It had been his life for over twenty-five years. It needed time to heal.

The four men meandered back to the remains of the house in silence. There was nothing to do there, but John needed to sit and think about his future. He felt numb and knew it was the shock. He stood and looked back over where his banana crop had been. He didn't know some of the others from the cave had arrived until he felt Clare's hand slip into his.

She rested her cheek on his shoulder. "Uncle John, I'm not taking no for an answer. You are coming to stay with us for a while. It will take months for the grass to grow again here, and there is nothing left that Bill and Tom can't handle." She had seen them with Shéamus as they walked around scavenging the precinct for anything useful. The dray sat unburnt behind the house. They had meant to put it into the stables but had no time. As various items and tools were found, they were placed on the cinder-covered vehicle.

John dropped her hand and slid his arm along her shoulder. "Sweet Clare, I think that you are right. I will send a message to the courthouse with Tom. They will need to reassign my cases for an indeterminate time."

Clare looked up at the man who had given her away five years earlier. "Uncle John, you were there for me when I needed you. Let me be permitted to repay you for everything you have done for us. You know your room is ready and waiting there. Come and stay with us until you work things out."

As she spoke, some of the tribal girls arrived with the children.

Bagaroo carried Joy, and the boys were being held tightly by one of the other girls. They dropped the girl's hand and ran to John. Kieran arrived first and was bubbling with excitement about the devastation of all he knew. "Unca John, youse said you didn't want us to leave, but now it's not us leaving, but you. Youse gonna come and live with us, please."

Little Johnny put his arms up to be lifted, and John could not resist. The small boy's small arms slid around John's neck, thus comforting him. "Come live with us, Unca John. Prease!"

The begging tone of the younger boy's voice broke through John's hurting heart. "Clare, you really want me?" He didn't expect her reaction.

She chuckled. "Of course, Uncle John. You have given us so much already. Thanks to Pemma and Bagaroo's warning, we saved quite a lot of your things. Also, the honeymoon cottage on the hill is still intact, so we can all stay there until the ship sails."

John's eyes flew to hers. "Your cottage made it through? How? I didn't dare look as I presumed it had gone too! Pemma doubted it would burn, but I didn't trust him again. He said something about salt in the wood."

Clare smiled at his surprise. "The cows have eaten the grass so low around the house that the fire seemed to jump over it. It survived along with the feather mattresses that Pemma's boys moved. We can thank our good Lord for that as well as them. We will sleep there in comfort tonight, and tomorrow, we will catch the ship as planned, only we won't return for some time. I presume Tom will care for your horses?"

John nodded.

She continued. "Then we will load up the dray with everything here and take it all with us. Uncle John, take your time getting back on your feet. You gave me the same thing: time. You didn't push me and waited until I was ready to make decisions for myself. I'm merely returning the favour. You will always have a room with us. You see, I love you! You are the father I lost far too young. You are my family."

John bent and kissed her forehead. "It looks like I'm moving to Parramatta. Then I may go and stay with Robert for a while."

Clare reached up and kissed his sooty cheek. "I hope you stay for a long time, as we will need your wisdom."

John's face remained passive. His heart still hurt, but he said to Clare, "Many years ago, I took you at your word and brought you here. You and the family have been a balm to my hurting soul. I had never missed what I did not have until you came. You showed me just how much I had given up. I will come, Clare, but I won't stay permanently with you. I have no idea what is before me or if I will return here to the farm."

Clare's grin lit up her face. "As long as you know, you will always have a room at our place."

~

The following day, the coastal steamer collected the family from the small jetty in Terrigal Haven. The day after the fire, the entire Bouddi tribe helped load the big dray, and they carried the rest of the personal items along the beach and over the headland to await the family's departure. John told them to help themselves to all the food left in the store room and whatever was in the cottage overlooking the beach. He realised that their food supplies would be gone, too. Bagaroo and Clare made a tearful farewell to each other. The two girls had grown close over the nearly six years since they had met.

Pemma, John, and Shéamus also bid farewell. Barraboi stood back and just grinned. He was often on hand to assist with various tasks and even learned to milk a cow. Pemma's goodbyes were more emotional than Bagaroo's tears. He placed his hand on his heart, and then he put the same hand on John's heart. They had learnt much from each other, and their friendship would last the separation. "We see you by 'm' bye, boss."

With the last of the luggage loaded from the dray, they farewelled the family from various points around the harbour.

Pemma vanished, but young Kieran saw where he had gone. Bagaroo put her fingers to her lips. She bent to kiss the boy and said softly. "You show Pemma to Mama when ship leaves. Pemma's way to say goodbye."

Kieran nodded. He was close to tears as he had to say his own goodbyes to his tribal friends. The children had grown up running around naked and playing in the pools and waves together. The boys were fluent in their dialect. Bagaroo loved Clare's boys as much as she did her own children.

The farewells were now over, and the ship cast off its ropes. Clare stood between Shéamus and John, each holding a child.

Tom, Bill and their wives stood on the wharf to wave. The Bouddi tribe members were a little further up the hill.

Only when the family hunted for Pemma did Kieran show them that Pemma was standing on top of The Skillion headland. They could see their friend had his spear in his hand, one foot propped on his knee. As the ship rounded the point, the family waved their final farewells.

Pemma gave a salute, mimicking the way John had shown the boys.

John knew this was honouring his time served in the English Army. He saluted back to his friend.

Pemma held his hand in salute until the ship sailed to sea. John returned the tribute.

All too soon, the headland faded from view.

Sydney was only a few hours away, but the seas were growing. There were other passengers on board, plus a selection of stock in pens on the deck. With the land now out of sight, the family went to sit in the cabin below.

Chapter 22 More Wedding Plans

*J*ohn's best suit was pressed and waiting for him. His wedding finery had arrived from the farm the week before. The fire had burned the area north of Broken Bay and completely missed Parramatta.

Liam made sure everything was in order for the upcoming nuptials. Now twenty-one, Paddy had eventually permitted his youngest child to propose to Kerry. This also meant that John had transferred ownership of a new farm for the newlyweds to live on.

Two years earlier, Charles had heard that the farm next to Shéamus and Clare's was for sale. John had purchased it, and they had put in tenant farmers. As Paddy said, he would not permit Liam to marry until he turned twenty one, but they knew they only had two years to wait. When the wedding date for Liam and Kerry was set, John sent word to the tenants to vacate a month before.

John only told Liam after they announced their engagement. Liam was delighted and set about getting their new home into order. The extra work of refurbishing the cottage kept his mind from the momentous day. Therefore, Liam was busy on his new farm, sourcing and overseeing furniture placement in their house.

Charles and Sal had not long returned from England. They had left only days after the double funeral of his mother, Elizabeth, and her husband, Richard. The deaths had left a large hole in Charles's life, and John's presence would fill the void left by their deaths.

With the family's impending arrival *en masse,* everyone was lending a hand to prepare the Jolly Sailor Inn courtyard for the post-wedding party as they had done for Clare.

Everyone knew that fires had circled Gosford, but no one knew if anyone had lost property. Thankfully, the farms and towns south of the

Hawkesbury River had been spared this time. All knew that news would trickle in over the following weeks about how all the outlying farms survived.

When the family arrived on the afternoon train from Sydney, the welcoming party knew that something was dreadfully wrong. The two carriages that met the procession carried the travellers directly to Eddie's house. There, Sal and Charles Lockley awaited them. Once afternoon tea had been consumed, the horrific saga of the past week unfolded.

In the intervening years since Clare's wedding, John had often come to stay with Eddie rather than at the inn, and his friendship with Charles had grown with each visit. He usually came with Clare and Shéamus, but occasionally, he came by himself and left them in charge.

The bedraggled family had arrived two days before the wedding.

With the fire consuming his farm, John needed to unload to Charles and seek his wisdom on what to do.

Charles saw John glance his way a few times throughout the afternoon. When they had finished the tea, he turned to his friend and asked, "John, care to stretch your legs?"

John was up like a shot, and the men were gone before others could offer to join them.

They had barely made it through the back gate before John said, "Charles, I am all undone. My farm was my livelihood and my source of income. Thankfully, I have some money from the crops I sent to market, but I have little money put away for a rainy day. I have nowhere to live, and Clare has offered me a room with them, but I'm at a loss as to where to stay and what to do. I have houses in East Gosford, but they are tenanted. They bring in a pittance."

Charles looked at his friend, somewhat shocked. "You have no funds at all?"

John shook his head. "There was no bank up there, and I only have what wasn't burnt. But Charles, I'm not talking cash; I have some gold coins tucked away, and they are safe enough, but they will not give me an income. It will take some years for the farm to regrow."

Charles nodded his understanding. At least John had the girls and the wider family for support. He released a sigh, then said, "I'm sorry about the farm, John, but you must trust that God can see the big picture in all this. You would have been up there alone, and that is not good. Yesterday is gone, and tomorrow is not here, so we only have today. We must make the most of what we have. Take up the offer of a room with Clare and help the two young couples settle into their farms. You could not have done this if you had your own place to care for, not to mention your work as a magistrate."

John was surprised at Charles's counsel. "You think I should stay?"

Charles chuckled. "I know little about farming, so asking for my help would be useless. I can run an inn. I brew a decent cider and make a potent ginger beer, but I leave the milking to Sal and the children. I like horses, but call in the experts when they get ill." Charles looked almost embarrassed at his admission. "Offer me a rolling drunk swagman to deal with or a cantankerous cow, and I'll take the drunk any day!" He gave another chuckle.

John grinned. "On the plus side, Charles, it would mean I could have a few more chats with you and a few other fellows I'm getting to know here."

They walked in silence for a while before John added, "You know, Clare has a funny saying that Kieran and Gráinne used to say. I added my own bit to follow it. I heard her say an extra bit once. Clare says, 'I can't stop tomorrow from happening.' I added, 'And you can't change yesterday'." He blew his cheeks out and said, "Now I will add, 'I shall get on with today and make the best of it'. Charles, I shall look forward to my unexpected holiday here and see what door God will open for me. I will stay for a while, but eventually, I will return to clean up the farm, even if it is to sell it. If I rebuild, I won't live there again. The cliff cottage survived the fire, as did the stables, staff quarters and storeroom. The house can be rebuilt, and I will install one of those new tin roofs this time. I think it was the shingles that caught fire. The cliff cottage has a tin roof."

The men walked for a while before returning to the house. The family had to settle into their new home and sort out who was sleeping where.

Charles said that Liam had cleaned out the previous occupant's things, and it was ready for them.

The family who had sold it to John had only stayed for a year before moving south. Charles had placed in tenants, and they had tended the vines but little else. Charles said to John just before they arrived at the back gate. "John, both farms are going to need much work. You being here with them will be a Godsend for the young ones. You know you are loved, but now you are wanted and needed too. Stay as long as you can and get them on their feet. Your farm is not going anywhere and will not grow anything for some time. Bide your time here and be useful to them. Dear friend, you need them as much as they need you."

John could not answer. For the first time in many years, he had found a home where he was both welcomed and wanted. The overwhelming realisation was that hearth and home were not bricks and mortar or timber and shingle; they were family and faith. He had all of those here, as well as a good friend in Charles.

As they reached the kitchen door, John said, "Yes, Charles, I will stay. I will set them on their feet before I move on. You are all family, so I will let you know my plans before making any decisions. I foresee many discussions."

~

The wedding day dawned with mist rising from the nearby creek. Clare was up early with baby Joy and cooked breakfast for everyone before Shéamus returned with the cows' milk. The sunbeams flickered through the gum leaves as the sun rose. It was a glorious day for a wedding.

Liam arrived for breakfast, and the family planned to dress and prepare for the ceremony at their house rather than at Paddy and Cara's minute cottage.

The day's excitement was infectious, and laughter soon echoed through their new home.

The farmhouse was bigger than John's house, and the children were delighted that they had so much flat ground where they could play outside. John's house had been built on a hillside, and other than the beach, the grassy verge around the lake had been the only cultivated flat area. Here, the house paddock was large, and there was evidence that sheep had been in to keep the grass down. Knowing that short grass was safer, as snakes had no cover, they planned to continue to do this. Short grass also meant that the fire had not burnt the honeymoon cottage. They had all learned a lesson from that.

The wedding service was at ten o'clock, and they were all waiting on the borrowed wagon and ready to leave by half past nine. Clare ensured Joy had been fed, carrying spare napkins and two changes of clothing for each child. The babe lay asleep in her basket, and Shéamus gently placed her on the wagon's flatbed.

John gee'd up the horse, and they set off to St John's church.

Shéamus glanced at his brother and saw his forehead beading with perspiration. He knew that feeling well and soon had his little brother laughing. "Liam, many pearls of wisdom have been taught to us over the years, but one has stuck with me. When we were going through all our troubles, someone told me that when you pull a loose thread in your past life, you don't know how it will affect your future. It may well pull it tighter, or it could unravel it completely. I'm sure Kerry has told you of the phrase her parents used, 'You can't stop tomorrow.' That is true, but you can use today wisely. Today, your new life will start, and it will be a good life, Liam. Kerry has waited for you long enough, and if Papa had not been so mean, you could have been married years ago. However, there is much you have learnt over those years, and now you are wiser and will make a better husband."

Liam looked shocked. "I'm sure you are a great husband, Shéamus."

His brother chuckled. "I wasn't, Liam. I was only nineteen when we married, as you know, but those months I spent looking for her made me realise many things. One was that I needed to grow up quickly. You were always much more mature than I was in that way. Liam, be the wonderful man that you have grown into. Be true to yourself, and be true to Kerry. We will always be here if needed, and there will be times when you both need a time-out. Come to us or go milk a cow, but never storm off like I used to do. Clare would worry about me, which made things worse when I got home." He was speaking quietly, but Clare could hear his words.

Their eyes met, and a secret smile passed between them. They had had the occasional angry word with each other. Clare said, "It's true, Liam. Aunt Sal also told me never to go to sleep angry with each other. That has been good advice. If, or should I say when, we have something to discuss over a disagreement, we stay up late but never go to sleep angry with each other." Again, they shared a smile.

Liam watched their rapport and realised that they had a bond that tied them securely to each other. He and Kerry would work hard to build that, too. With that thought, he realised that they had arrived at the church. His nerves were gone, and he would have a wife and a new future in less than an hour.

There was a buzz of welcomes from the others already at the church. Liam was brushed down by his mother, and his father straightened his cravat. The youngest Lockley sibling, Luke, had been married only a few months ago, and they were already expecting their first child. Luke lightheartedly joked about the size of his wife already. He said, "Although she is only five months along, she is already waddling. This could be you two next year, Liam; I wonder if Ellen is expecting twins. It's the family failing, you know. You are lucky you don't have the Lockley blood in you."

His chuckle made Liam's jaw drop. "Cor, Luke. Twins, eh?"

Luke's cheeky grin made Liam smile.

Luke tapped Liam's hat onto his head. "Come on, lad, let's get you hitched!" He beckoned Shéamus and pushed them both towards the church door.

Luke had seen the family carriage drawing near, with Kerry and his father on board. With the boys now out of sight, Luke ushered the carriage to a stop.

John handed Kerry out and gasped. The young girl he had met five years ago had bloomed into a beautiful young lady. "Kerry, you are a delight to my eyes and heart. For me, to have to give you away is both sadness and joy. If it had been to anyone else but Liam, I may not have given permission. However, he is a fine, upstanding young man."

Kerry brushed away a nervous tear. "Thank you, Uncle John…" She threw her arms around him. "…for just everything. For you being here, for the farm, for looking after us and for being family!" She kissed him and then said with a cheeky giggle, "Now I've claimed you, can you give me away?"

He flicked her nose as he had done when she was tiny. "Yes, sweetie, I would be proud too."

The ceremony progressed without a hitch.

Liam was seen to brush away a tear, and Shéamus heard him sniff.

They said their vows with loving intent, and soon, they were signing the register. Liam's hand slipped down to clasp Kerry's. For the first time, he leaned in and said, "My darling wife, I love you so much."

Reverend King heard him and gave him a strange look. Liam took the hint and dropped Kerry's hand; however, he didn't move away from her. With a grin towards the minister, Liam offered her his arm, which she willingly took. They went to stand at the steps in the sanctuary. There, Reverend King introduced them as Mr and Mrs Connor.

Kerry beamed at her new name. They walked down the church aisle to the congregation's cheers and applause.

As soon as they were out the door, Liam pulled her into his arms and soundly kissed her. Shéamus and Clare were hard on their heels and stood on the lookout for them. Soon, all were on the way down to the Jolly Sailor for the festivities. The Irish band climbed and set the theme for the day with their fiddles and songs. They knew George and Bertie Ellis would serenade them later with a classical rendition of something on their violins, but for the moment, they were setting the mood for their friends by playing an Irish jig.

The foot tapping soon turned into dancing. The December day was thankfully kind to them and was not overly hot. The festivities continued into the night. Soon, the couple were collected by a carriage and were on their way for a week in Sydney at the King's Arms Hotel. It was the best place to stay, and Charles had pre-booked and paid for their luxury week. He had done the same for Clare when she married.

~

Life on the new farms settled into a smooth routine, and after six months, John felt that he had guided the boys enough and left them to visit his cousin in Braidwood. Robert had heard about the loss of John's house and had written to him, inviting him to come. After sitting on the invite for a week, John mentioned it to Clare over breakfast. Clare was feeding little Joy when he casually said he might accept his cousin's offer for a while.

He was gone by the end of the week. John knew that he would be unlikely to leave at all if he left it any longer to go. The two young couples had brought a new understanding of love to him. In Gosford, he knew he was known as a cranky Irishman, but those who called him so had not lost two houses to fire had not been locked up for something he had not done. He felt he had a right to remain cranky with them. John felt that as Kerry was now expecting her first child and Clare had just confessed that she was carrying their fourth one, now was a good time to go. He would hopefully be back by the time Clare's baby arrived. John headed south to Robert's farm and planned to spend some time renewing his acquaintance with his mother's side of the family. However, on arrival in Braidwood, he found that Robert was just about ready to leave for the Victorian goldfields and wanted him to come. With no other plans, John decided that a diversion to the diggings in Ballarat would be a good distraction until regrowth occurred after the fire. The reason for the visit was to reconnect with Robert, and that did not need to be on a farm. With an unexpected spring in his step, John set off on an unexpected adventure. He wrote to Charles to let him know of the journey, just in case the girls needed him.

As the girl's growing conditions progressed, new staff were hired, and soon, Christmas approached again.

Kerry and Liam were now proud parents of Patrick William, Rick, as he was known, was an adorable dark-haired, blue-eyed cherub. Clare's baby was due at Easter, and they had heard from the Victorian goldfields that John hoped to return around that time.

John's arrival occurred while Clare was in labour. He had been delayed, and this time, he did not travel empty-handed. A wagon load of furniture arrived soon after he did, and it was soon sent on its way to the honeymoon cottage. He only stayed until the newest baby was baptised. Cara Clare was nicknamed Cassie and given a small gift from John. He had already given Kerry, Clare, and Joy their presents. Each small velvet bag contained a small gold nugget on a chain. However, their bags included three more cleaned but unset nuggets weighing about an ounce. At £10 per ounce, that was a fortune in gold.

Clare was delighted but said, "Uncle John, you can't afford to give us this. You need it to get the farm back in order." She offered the three precious bags back to him.

John gently pushed her hand away, "Sweet girl, this is but a sample of the blessing God sent Robert and me. I left here knowing I was loved and wanted, but still dejected. I had lost heart and went to talk things over with Robert. I found he was setting off on a journey to try his luck on the gold fields. I will not go into detail, but I have enough to rebuild the farm from scratch if I wish. Will you come and see it when it's done?"

Clare giggled, then nodded. "Of course, Uncle John. We would love to come back, but not to live. With Kerry and Liam next door, we can assist them with the baby and their farm for a while, then come for a holiday. They can go up when we return. We have Kieran in school, and Johnny will follow him soon."

John chuckled. "I didn't mean to live, sweet girl, but for a visit, be that long or short. Two Bible verses sustained me on the journey south. However, their meaning still took months to really sink in. Psalm 34 verse 18, *'The Lord is nigh unto them that are of a broken heart; and saveth such as be of a contrite spirit.'* The sentiment is repeated in Isaiah and many other passages. The Isaiah reference is from chapter 61, verse 1 *'The Spirit of the Lord God is upon me; because the Lord hath anointed me to preach good tidings unto the meek; He hath sent me to bind up the brokenhearted, to proclaim liberty to the captives, and the opening of the prison to them that are bound'.''* John met Clare's loving look and added, "Clare, it took me months to realise that I was the one who was broken-hearted and the one the Lord was tending. I have been content to lock myself away from the bigots and unjust authorities, but you broke through those barriers and forced me to live again."

Clare placed a caring hand on his arm but remained silent.

John adored these two girls. Their actions spoke volumes. He smiled and said, "I told you why I became a magistrate, didn't I?" The lifted eyebrow on John's brow inferred he wanted an answer.

She blushed, then said, "Sort of, but it was the day the man attacked me. I wasn't really listening. Too much occurred at once, and I was still in pain from the wave accident."

John took a long draw on his mug of black tea. "The head of the police locally, Mr Faunce, arrested me in the middle of the night. I had enough time to dress but nothing else. Having no idea why I was being apprehended, I had no time to grab any evidence. I was taken with two others from the farm and held in the lock-up in Wyoming. It truly is a hell hole and is inescapable. It is just punishment for men like that filthy criminal who attacked you, but it took three years before Donnison, Bean, and I could prove our innocence. Due to that incident and the lack of a fair trial, we demanded that things change. The result saw me exonerated, and I received a pitiful compensation, which I used to pay off outstanding creditors. I'm embarrassed to say my temper often got the better of me back then. I had not even been permitted to access my bill of sale for the so-called 'stolen cow.' I was presumed guilty and treated as a criminal because I was Irish, hence the fiasco with the goat."

She said, "I did wonder why you were so worried about it."

John continued, "Faunce originally used some excuse of hunting for a gun supposedly stolen by one of my convict labourers. He found nothing as nothing had been stolen." He took another long draw of his tea. "In the end, I was fined one blooming farthing, and I'm not even sure what that was for as I was found innocent of all charges. Captain Faunce had to pay court costs, and he also had to print and pay for a public apology to be printed in the newspaper. I feel it must have been because I was Irish, but I shall never really know. And there was no reason that I knew of for Donnison and Bean's arrests." He drained the mug and sat staring at the tea leaves in the bottom. John shook off the memories and continued his story. "Life changed after that, as I had a purpose once again, but I was somewhat people-shy. Then I made the fateful trip to Parramatta to get supplies and find new non-convict staff." He reached out for her hand. "When I left the army, I could not return home as I had hoped. I was not welcome. To meet your family in those few weeks that I spent visiting my family was a miracle. Clare, I had merely floated through life before I met you here. Then Shéamus came, and I thought I would lose you to him, but he was willing to stay and learn from me. In the years since I have been drawn into such a wonderful family, I'm tempted to stay here and relish what you all have to offer, but I need to return to the farm and see if it can be resurrected. I shall return here often as I know you will welcome me."

Clare didn't know what to say. She felt horrible that he would be alone, but she needed to stay with Shéamus and the life they had made together.

John only stayed for a few weeks before heading northward to his farm. He had been gone for nearly a year and hoped that the burnt areas would have adequate regrowth to restock by now. Hopefully, Pemma and Bagaroo would still be around to be some company.

Chapter 23 Honeymoon Cottage

Over the following months, irregular letters arrived telling them about the rebuilding plans. John had decided to enlarge the construction so that there would be enough room for both families to stay if they wished. It would be double the size and have eight bedrooms. As the fire had scorched all the timber on the farm and nearby, John had to source logs from elsewhere, and the construction of the larger building took far longer than expected. Tom and Bill found new helpers and teams of bullocks towed in logs that were dressed on site. They felled some huge trees that needed splitting, hewing and dressing before any building could start. Plus, the old burnt-out shell needed to be removed before the new house could be erected in its place. John had been tempted to torch the remaining shell but didn't. The cedar uprights were still strong.

As the workers each had their own farms, the construction could only be done when harvesting or their farm work was over. The old house had been constructed with convict labour, but that was no longer available. Consequentially, John was frustrated with how long it was taking. The honeymoon cottage was all well and good for a few nights; he was lonely. The companionship of the sea was no longer enough. He missed the girls. Pemma, Barraboi, and the tribe reappeared occasionally, and John sent through messages of greeting from Bagaroo to Clare.

Clare and Shéamus came for a visit with the children and stayed at the old staff quarters. They were amazed that some of the burnt trees in the orchard had survived. Some of the bananas had regrown, and a few had bunches setting. However, the Connors didn't stay long.

After more than a year of isolation in the cottage, John found alternative accommodation in East Gosford village. The tenant in his bigger house, 'Springfield', finally moved, and he decided to move into town. Another Irishman, a French polisher and cabinet maker, Andrew Lenehan, had purchased a block diagonally across the road, and the two got on well. John wrote to Clare, saying that he was safely settled in town and would let them know how the house construction progressed. He mentioned that he had no plans to return to Avoca because he was too lonely. However, he would not sell it. He focused on growing bananas and also had stock.

~

1860

John's house was still incomplete. He had come to stay in Parramatta for a fortnight every few months, but his work as a magistrate now kept him in Gosford. When he was given a Wednesday off, he would come. He had all but given up trying to finish the house as he had decided that living closer to people was better for him. It was within walking distance of the church, and he had made some friends there. He still went to stay in the honeymoon cottage when he had enough of the maddening crowd. He tried hard to control his temper, but people's petty problems often ate away at his resolve, and he needed to escape.

As the girls settled on their farms and their families grew, he knew they could not come for more than short stays. They had nine children between them, and he knew more would follow. He was content with his short visits and exhausted when he left Parramatta's vibrant but extremely noisy households.

The seasons brought droughts and flooding rains alternated with fires and the ravages of illnesses. After one bout of severe illness, John thought his time was drawing nigh. He caught an infection in the lungs and required the doctor to attend to him daily. His weight had ballooned from living alone, and his health suffered. He was now paying the price.

Clare and Shéamus came for a quick visit with their latest baby, and knowing they were coming, John rallied by the time they arrived. Their visit inspired John to fight and overcome his illness, and soon, he could meander on gentle walks to the waterfront at East Gosford.

Clare challenged him about his diet. In the following months, the walks grew longer, his strides were quicker, and his overall health improved as he lost the excess weight. He shelved his whiskey and turned back to tea. He returned to work as a magistrate and set about repairing his farm. He could again make it through the one full day a week in court without needing a noon nap.

~

Three years later, 1863

Clare received an invitation for their family to come and stay. However, the visit also celebrated John handing in his magistrate's hat. He wrote, "I'm retiring, sweet girl. I turned sixty last month and need to concentrate on finishing the house. It's been over six years since the fire, and I still have no proper home to call my own on the farm. I need to hire a team to finish what I started before I'm too old. My health has improved, but I still have the occasional funny turn. I may never move back there, but at least I could put in a tenant farmer and get some income. As I have always said, Robert or his son will eventually inherit it all, but until that day, the honeymoon cottage is yours to use."

Over the years, various branches of the family came as often as they could. Sometimes, it was just the men for a working bee; sometimes, it was one or the other young families. Charles and Sal even occasionally came for a short trip for companionship for John. They, too, met and loved Pemma and Bagaroo and their extended family.

Clare noticed that John was slower and less agile on each visit. "Uncle John, won't you come and live with us? Your room awaits, and we'd love to have you."

Each request was met with the response of, "Knowing I'm wanted is enough, love."

He would play with the children and tell them about Ireland. He was the grandfather they didn't have. Kerry and Liam's numerous children adored him as much as Clare's brood. As each was born, another bag of small nuggets was presented to them.

Shéamus and Clare wondered how much gold the men had found, but they dared not ask.

~

John relished calling upon Charles Lockley, and on his last visit to Parramatta in 1864, Charles admitted that the doctor had told him he needed to take it easy. Charles said, "I have passed on most of my jobs to my sons. But I know my time is shortening."

John had noted a slightly blue tinge to Charles's lips and was surprised to hear that this was a symptom of a bad heart. He had noted his own lips of a darker hue than Charles's. He didn't say anything to Charles about his own poor health, but he knew it was time to take Clare and Kerry back to his farm together. Plans were made, and both families would stay for a couple of weeks on this visit. The house was finally finished; it was the first time they could all be under one roof. The dairy cows on both Parramatta farms were taken to Kellow's dairy next door for the duration of their break, and some of the younger Lockley boys would keep their eyes on the farms. The Kellow boys would tend to the other animals on the farm.

After Christmas, the coastal steamer carried the two young Connor families northward to John. Tom collected them from The Haven wharf at Terrigal and took them to the farm. He had already collected John from Gosford and stocked the pantry the day before.

Tom and his wife Susanna lived in Terrigal and had been overseeing the stock and banana plantation. Having originally thought all the orchards were dead, the fire had refreshed the soil, and the banana plants on the ridgeway road had bounced back well. The bulk of the citrus orchard had not been replanted, but some old surviving trees still produced a saleable crop.

Some blackened tree stumps were still visible, but the scars of the ferocious fire had all but faded. That night and the roar of the flames from nine years before still haunted them, but thanks to Pemma and the tribe, they had survived unscathed.

The tribe currently resided in the grassy camp at the beach's southern end. They were safe from persecution on John's farm and had access to fresh water and abundant food there. Bagaroo welcomed Clare with giggles and a big hug. Both were in their thirties now and were mothers many times over.

It had been thirty-five years since John had first met these kind and loving people. Bagaroo had not even been born. Many elders had died, and Pemma was now grey-haired and one of the oldest in the group. John had not realised he was so much older than Bagaroo, who had aged very little.

Pemma and Barraboi had been young boys when he first met them. Bagaroo had come from another tribe across the Hawkesbury River and came only a few years before Clare. Pemma had kept her hidden. They already had two babies before John met her. The small tribal group had kept their eyes and ears open for John and hoped for his permanent return. Pemma's greeting by putting his hand on his heart, then on John's chest, made John pause and look at his friend somewhat strangely. Normally, Pemma just saluted with a big grin plastered on his ebony black lips with his pearly white teeth showing. Not so today; he looked worried. He stayed close by John's side for a time, then vanished. Some hours later, he returned with some leaves smeared with something and handed a fragment of a leaf. He gave this to John and told him to chew it. "You chew him up good, Mr John. Make you feel better. Tastes bad, but good for you."

John nervously placed the substance in his mouth and chewed. He had tried Pemma's home remedies before and knew that they often worked. Today, he didn't wish to try. He already knew his heart was not behaving as his doctor had told him so already. It was why he wanted this visit to occur. He had something to give the girls before he died. His tongue pushed the leaf to the cheek, but he pretended to chew.

Satisfied that John had taken the medicine, Pemma turned away to greet Shéamus and Clare. As he did so, John spat out the bitter leaf and hid it in his hand. However, his mouth was somewhat numb from the goo that had been on it. It stuck on his inside cheek.

The group settled into their rooms, and soon Clare and Kerry had a meal cooking. John had stocked up on the basics, and Pemma and Barraboi had brought some mullet they had netted. The scant meal of damper and fish was eaten and shared with delight. Bagaroo and Barraboi's wife, Milbah, stayed with their children, but the remainder of the welcoming tribe returned to their camp.

The following days were a delight to the four families and John. Each day, Pemma presented John with another gooey leaf, and most of the time, John managed to repeat the trick of spitting it out. However, he was feeling much better. Twice, Pemma made sure that he had chewed it.

The week-long break was drawing to a close. When they woke up late one morning, Pemma and Barraboi had gone hunting. John sent Bagaroo and Milbah off with all the children to play on the beach. With them gone, John suggested that the five of them head up the headland to the honeymoon cottage.

John said, "I have something for you all, and I've been waiting until I can get you all alone. There are things in here that are yours, Clare, and I would like you to remove all your possessions and treasures from here when you leave this trip."

The walk up the gentle hill exhausted him, and he sat on the grassy embankment, regaining his breath. The cottage now had a small verandah along the front, and they noticed a small door had been added under the building. John pulled a large key from his pocket and held it out to Shéamus. "Laddie, this unlocks that small hatch. Inside are two chests, and they are heavy. Liam, your brother will need assistance to remove them this afternoon, but all of you must go in now and have a look." John was still puffing as he turned and watched the four young ones enter the dark cellar-like room. He knew what they would find as he had stored the two boxes there with Pemma's help. He sat patiently, waiting for them to reappear.

Clare arrived first. She plopped herself down on the grass next to him. "Do you know what's in those boxes, Uncle John?"

He grinned and nodded. "It's why they need to be moved. It's the reason you are all here together. There are fourteen hundred gold coins in each box. Robert and I had a good find and decided to get it converted into coins. Well, we swapped our finds for equal weight in coins. The fixed price of gold is £10 per ounce, so it was a straight swap for gold sovereigns. Robert and I hid his share on his property at Braidwood, and this is my share. I have had fun spending some of it and am keeping some to live on. The balance of what I am keeping will go to Robert or his family with my estate."

Kerry and the girl's husbands joined them. John nodded to them and motioned for them to sit around him. Kerry took her place on the grass on the other side of him. John said, "Boys, this money is for the girls and their children. Please understand that if something happens to them and you remarry, your future children will not get a share of this."

Both boys nodded their agreement. Shéamus said, "That's fair, sir."

John saw the nods and continued. "Nor is it to be spent on the farms unless you are in dire need. None of you are mentioned in my will; therefore, we can keep the knowledge of this gold quiet. Robert has enough, and we have hidden his share on his farm. If I put it in writing or change my will, you will become targets for all the gold diggers of the colony." He looked at the girls and said, "Your Uncle Charles knows of my windfall and that I am giving it to you two girls. It is for your children, as I will not be around as they grow. You can discuss investing it somehow with him. I won't expand too much about his experience, but you already know the family was closely involved with the gold finds in Bathurst. Wills Lockley started his emporium chain because of his share of his bountiful find, so you can also consult him as well. Eddie worked hard for his money and will help if you ask. But do not waste it or blab about it. This is to educate your children as best you can. Charles's youngest boy went through university, and who knows where Luke will end up. I believe he wants to start a logistics company to help his brothers." He paused, then said, "Shéamus, Liam, this country has so much potential; make sure your children have all the opportunities you all never had. Lads, your father and I have often talked about our life in Ireland. Never pine for what you don't know. Ireland is no longer the place of happy dreams and lush green valleys. Do not hanker to return as it is no longer that idyllic place of our childhood. As your wives will tell you, the famine decimated the land, which will take many decades to recover fully. Make your lives here and be happy. Certainly, go for a visit if you must, but never move back there." The four young ones hung on his words. John turned to Clare and said, "Clare, do you remember your parents' words? 'I can't stop tomorrow'."

Clare nodded, as did Kerry.

John smiled at them. "I know you do. And, no, we can't stop tomorrow, but we can do other things. With this bounty, I can help make your tomorrows more comfortable. Our attitude to situations can change, but hopefully, with this money, your futures and those of your children will be assured. Your tomorrows will hopefully be wonderful." John paused, looking at the four dear young ones around him. "I have a confession to make, dear ones. My time is short for this life. My heart is failing me. I need you to take all that is yours this trip, as this will be the last time you will be here." He noticed that Clare's face had crumpled in grief. Tears soon trickled down her cheeks. He drew her to him. "Dear sweet girl, I have had a good innings, and you four have made my final year's good ones far better than I probably deserved. This money is merely one way I can repay the love you freely gave to me, for I won't be here to pay for things myself. There are more nuggets for future children, and the balance of them is to be divided between you two girls." Both girls leaned into his side.

Clare murmured, "I don't want you to die, Uncle John."

John gave a choked chuckle. "I'm not that keen on the idea either, but there are some things in life that one has no choice over. I know my heart is warning me that it's not happy, so my dears, I am saying my farewells in my own good time. I am now getting my things in order. But dear ones, it's also why I will not stay on the farm alone. I may only have a day, a week, a month or even a year. Only the good Lord knows my time." Clare's sob cut him to the core. She clung to his arm, and he could feel her tears soak through his sleeve. His heart was full of compassion. He had stood as a surrogate father to both girls and hated delivering the news, but he knew they needed to know. They had chosen wonderful life partners who would stand beside them through their lives. John gave them some time to adjust to his news before saying, "Lock up the room now, lads and let us meander back home. You two can bring the dray back this afternoon and pack those two boxes along with anything from the cottage you want. Take the set of cane chairs, too, as they will remind you of all the many times we spent chatting on the verandah. Thankfully, we moved them here before the fire." He put out his arms to the boys so they could assist him to stand. "Pop inside the cottage with the girls and have a quick look through now. I will meander down the hill and wait in the shade." John waved them away.

The four Connors did as asked and caught up to him before he reached the beach. They enjoyed their walk along the hard sand of the lower tide. They collected their children from Bagaroo, and the group wandered back to the new house along the grassy foreshore.

After luncheon, while the girls stayed with John and the children, the two boys took the dray and cleaned out the honeymoon cottage. They were leaving in two days, so they left the loaded dray in the yard when they returned. It was loaded up but covered with a sheet of canvas. The new furniture in the house would stay for whoever leased the farm. They had taken the four large cane armchairs, a small round table, a few smaller items, and the two metal chests containing the coins. John had given them padlocks, and both chests were now secured with large brass locks; the key from these hung around the girls' necks.

At dawn on the last full day, Clare was up before everyone else and went for a pre-dawn walk to say her farewells to the beautiful beach. She dressed in the dark and pulled on the first gown she touched in the dim light. It was a long-sleeved white gown that she usually kept for church. As there was no minister in the area at the moment, she did not need to wear it. She had forgotten she left it out to pack. She didn't care what she wore and pulled it on. Once dressed, she crept out of the house before everyone was awake.

She had reached the beach's southern end when the sun touched the horizon. The golden orb almost sizzled as it rose from the sea. The predawn light displayed a golden purple reflected in the high tide water captured by the small rock pools. As Clare watched the sky brighten. She prayed that John's tomorrows would last for a long time. She didn't wish to leave him at all, but that was not what he wanted. She remembered the first time they visited the cemetery at Point Frederick. They had been there many times in the years since. She knew that he had made arrangements with the gravedigger and had chosen the plot where his body would lie unmarked for eternity. She wondered who would visit his grave in years to come. Would someone who lived on his farm remember him? He refused to tell her exactly where the plot would be. She remembered her grief. John took her aside and gave her the words of comfort that had stayed with her ever since. Her parents' words came to her once again, and John's encouraging words of the other day returned. She repeated them aloud. "I can't stop tomorrow. I can't change yesterday, but I can use today as best I can." She was about to turn to go when Bagaroo appeared beside her.

Bagaroo's arm slipped around her waist. "Mr John, him go soon. Him not come back here, will he?"

Clare's native friend had seen John's health was failing. "He's dying, Bagaroo. He asked us here so we could say our goodbyes in private. He made us clean out the cottage."

The near-naked Bagaroo took Clare's other hand and stood together to watch the sun climb higher. After a few minutes, Bagaroo said, "Good Clare! Do you take his heavy boxes, too? Mr John got Pemma and Barraboi to move them under the cottage. No use to us, but he gave us some anyway, just in case. We keep it for our little ones. They grow up in a new world to us."

Clare nodded. "Yes, Bagaroo, we've taken the boxes. Send word to us if you ever need us. You are always welcome to come to us, too, should you need a safe place." The girls hugged each other before they parted. Clare watched her friend leave and then turned towards the water.

Clare saw Shéamus coming towards them as the sun was fully up. He stopped some distance away. With her gown hitched up above her knees, Clare walked barefoot on the wet sand. No one but her husband was in view; it was the last time she could do this.

Shéamus waited for her to come to him. He had heard her leave and followed her to ensure her safety. He remained some distance away until the sun rose, then wandered down to the beach to join her. He knew she was saying her farewells. He knew she needed to do this her own way. She needed space, and he had given her that, but he would always be there. Twice, he had arrived when she was in danger. He had never forgotten the horrible feeling of almost failing her. Because of John, they had so much more than Shéamus could have provided for Clare and their children. All else was a blessing from above, and that included finding John. Once again, God had it all worked out years before their meeting. They had trusted Him, and it had all sorted beautifully.

The time they had with John here on the farm were good years. Even the months on the road searching for Clare had matured him and made him think deeply about what she meant to him. It also strengthened his faith. He had learnt the meaning of the word cherish. And that meant that he had to give her space and the freedom to be herself. Only then could she bloom. She had done just that.

He watched her silliness in kicking the waves and the salty droplets catching the morning rays that soaked her best gown. She twirled with delight in the morning stillness and revelled in just being alive. Her mane of luscious, burnished red hair was loose, adding to her feeling of freedom.

As she drew closer, he held his arms out to her, and she ran into them. He was her tomorrow, and that would never change. He would be her rock for all the days that would come afterwards. They had each other, and for them, that was enough.

Chapter 24 Another Tomorrow

On the morning of their departure, they drove John back into his house in East Gosford called 'Springfield'. He did not wish to see them sail away, so they said farewell after seeing him inside. Shéamus then drove them to Terrigal to catch the afternoon coastal steamer home. Bill and Tom met them at the jetty and helped load their possessions onto the ship. Tom would take the dray and horses home. They were now his unless John needed them again. They waited until the vessel cast off and left the small harbour.

Clare looked towards The Skillion, hoping to catch sight of her indigenous friends. It was as empty as her heart felt. Saying goodbye was horrible! She gulped back her sadness. Tears blurred her vision.

The steamship headed south but was unusually close to the shoreline for some reason. While Clare kept her eyes on the Terrigal headland, Shéamus nudged her to look at the Avoca headland just above their honeymoon cottage.

Every member of the Bouddi tribe stood lining the still-denuded headland. All were shouting farewells and waving joyously.

Clare waved back just as vigorously. She giggled at the shocked faces of the other passengers. She gleefully returned the waves of nearly-naked friends, as did the rest of the family.

Shéamus slid his arm around her waist, not only because he wished to be close to her but also for her protection, as she was not holding on to anything.

Clare spoke softly to her husband as she waved. "That was another thing that Uncle John taught me. The first time I met them, I was so fearful of them. They are so black and so different to us. He explained to me that we all bleed red and that they are the same as us inside. We have the same feelings of sadness, joy, and pain. I learnt not just to trust them but to love them, too. Bagaroo is my best friend, and I won't see her again. Uncle John and Papa both left Ireland because of religious bigotry, but racial bigotry is the same. There are good and bad people in both races."

Shéamus moved again and slid both arms around her as she continued to wave. As the wave height grew, he needed to hold on with both hands. She leaned back against him as he held the side railings tightly.

Clare continued, "I probably won't ever see Uncle John again, Shéamus, but I'll never forget him. In a way, I can almost even thank Lavinia because, without her, I never would have left Parramatta and never would have found him. We knew he existed, but I didn't know his last name or where he was. I should have guessed it was Moore, but I didn't know, nor did Father Patrick."

Shéamus bent and kissed her neck. "I, too, can thank him for keeping you safe for me. I love you, Mrs Shéamus Connor. Remember that always."

As the headland was now out of sight, she twisted around and wrapped her arms around her husband's waist. "I love you too, husband mine."

He silenced her inviting lips, much to the delight of the onlookers, who gave a whoop of delight and a cheer.

Clare blushed and hid her face in his shoulder.

~

More tomorrows

Each month, a letter would arrive from John.

Many started the same way.

My dearest girls,

Well, it seems the good Lord does not want me yet. I get to write another screed to my dear ones...

Then, it would go on to describe how he had spent his time over the past month and the news about any exciting cases he had heard.

Clare and Kerry often wrote about the children's antics and the happenings on the two Parramatta farms. They had invested the money in the bank and set up accounts for the children.

Life was good. With the profits of their farms, Shéamus and Liam had each purchased a new large carriage from Jim Leslie out at Emu Plains. Jim was married to one of Charles Lockley's cousins, and he refurbished coaches. The double family had grown out of the small barouche and gig they had owned. Now, they could travel in safety and comfort.

~

In June 1865, another letter arrived, containing an interesting bit of news.

John wrote, "*My dear, dear girls,*

Did you hear that a Great Northern Rail line is planned? I don't think I will be here to see it completed. But that dratted medicine of Pemma's seems to make me feel better. I have no idea what is in it, and I don't think he would tell me if I asked. Mind you, I'm not sure if I wish to know. I dare not let the doctor know I'm reluctantly using it. Its foul taste is beyond unpleasant. But the dratted stuff works.

Tom comes to collect me once a week, and we make the trip to the farm where Pemma resupplies my medicine weekly. You may be interested to know that I have found

tenants for the farm, and they will soon take over its management. I have let Robert know, which will make his taking over the estate much more manageable. Take care, dear ones. As usual, hug and kiss your children for me. Know that I love you all,
    'Uncle' John."

Clare stood at the kitchen door, leaning against the frame. She had read the letter, and her mind returned to the lovely bay's first views with the skeleton of the ship sitting on the beach. She didn't hear Shéamus come in but felt his arms slide around her. Rather than tell him her news, she took his hand and placed it on her stomach. She had not yet told him that they were to have another child. This seemed to be a good time.

John's letter slipped unnoticed to the ground as Shéamus spun her around. He said, "Do you mean we are to be blessed with another child? Really?"

Clare's beaming smile confirmed his question. However, she said, "Yes, my love, but if this one is a girl, may we call her Jane after Uncle John's mother? This is one tomorrow I do not want to stop." She laid her hand on her stomach to caress the growing bump. Their children would have a future because of Uncle John. They were determined to teach them to love and accept a person for who they were, not their skin colour or what they believed. This was one tomorrow they were both looking forward to.

Point Frederick, East Gosford ca 1900.
Cemetery is on the point where the bush is.

John Moore is buried in an unmarked grave at the end of Point Frederick Peninsular.
He died in his Springfield house on 10th July 1865.
His cousin, Robert Maddrell, inherited everything.
He leased the farm out, and it was eventually sold.

Clare and Kerry are, of course, fictitious.

John Moore and Avoca Beach

The details about John's birth and army service in my story are accurate. He was born a Catholic, became a member of the Church of England, and fought with the English army against the Irish. John found the land in Avoca in 1830, but it was not surveyed for another ten years.

It is unknown if John Moore ever returned to Ireland at any stage, but he may have. However, he did go to the Victorian Goldfields, possibly with his cousin Robert, as he was missing from the Central Coast for this period. He then returned to the Avoca area. He resumed his duties as magistrate, and he died in Springfield on July 10th 1865. He is buried in an unmarked grave at Point Frederick at East Gosford and is listed as one of the pioneers on the memorial at the cemetery.

Portion 44

Little documentary evidence has so far been located regarding the history of this property. It was granted to John Moore in 1839, but he may have taken ownership earlier, in 1830 (Dundon, 1980, p. 42). The property was named *Avoca*, after a region in Ireland (Dundon, 1980, p. 42). A plan from 1831 shows a structure on the property, but it is likely that this illustration was a later addition to the plan (Figure 14). It is possible that the property passed into the ownership of Charles Byron Ives; *(however, when John died, he left it and his even blocks in East Gosford*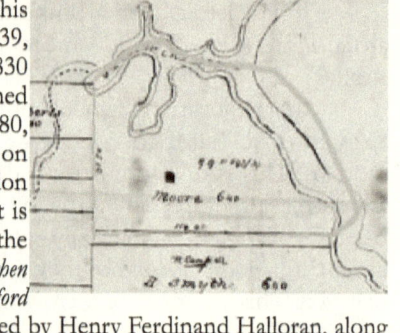

to his cousin, Robert Maddrell.) It was later acquired by Henry Ferdinand Halloran, along with other neighbouring properties (Parkinson, 2009, p. 305). Halloran began subdivision and sale in 1920, but it was not until the late 1940s and 1950s that the sale of the lots took off (Parkinson, 2009, p. 307). By 1954, a number of roads and tracks had been laid out, including most of those followed by Five Lands Walk, and houses had been built on most of the lots along the beachfront and several of the others to the west.

https://www.historicalencounters.org/he/avoca-beach/
https://www.facebook.com/centralcoastfhs.org.au/posts/john-moore-esq-c1803-1865-pioneer-settler-at-avoca-beach-moore-was-a-retired-arm/1815614745268584/
https://www.centralcoastaustralia.com.au/info/towns/avoca-beach/

John Moore's story of Avoca Beach and the Bouddi people

The land claimed by John Moore belonged to the Bouddi tribe, a small tribe associated with the Dharug/Guringai Tribe of the Hawkesbury River area. Like most other tribal groups in the area, the Bouddi were itinerant. I have invented the interactions, as none are recorded.

John Moore was born in County Wicklow, Ireland, in 1803 to John and Jane Moore, who were Catholics. John enlisted in the English Army in Dublin in 1820, aged 17, which fits his history. It is known that John Moore of Avoca indeed served in the British army and, at the age of 26, left for Australia. In 1830, aged only 27, John selected the Avoca Beach land. He called it Avoca as the name Avoca means meeting of two waters. In Ireland, two rivers meet; here, it is a lagoon and the sea. The area has been referred to both as Avoca and Avoca Bay. It is now Avoca Beach.

John's chosen land was not surveyed until 1839, and his farm was 640 acres or 1 square mile. The southern boundary road is where Boundary Road now is. I do not know who Smythe was, as he is not mentioned in any of the records I have seen, but then again, I have not looked much at him.

In 1835, John purchased some cattle, and sometime in the next twelve months, the brother of the person who sold them accused John of cattle theft. The court case involved two other local identities, Donnison and Bean, which took three years to sort out. John was acquitted as he was eventually permitted to produce his bill of sale. For some weeks, he was confined in the nine-foot square vermin-infested lockup in Gosford (probably in Wyoming). The case eventually went to the highest court in Sydney. After this, John was made a magistrate (along with co-accused Mr Donnison and Mr Bean), as within a short time, the governor had asked him to be a Justice of the Peace in the Brisbane Water area. He seemed to have a squeaky-clean reputation other than this incident, but he was known to have a bad temper (I can understand that after his poor treatment by the local police). He was quickly elected as one of three magistrates who were able to permit minors to marry.

(Extract: See the full story- https://trove.nla.gov.au/newspaper/article/252653489? searchTerm=moore%20v%20Faunce)

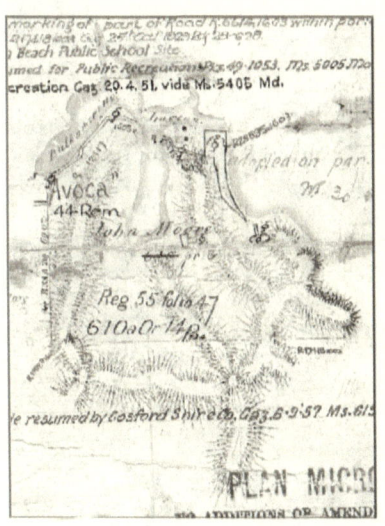

By the time John received his survey in Sept 1841, he had already cleared his land and built a house along Cape Three Points Road or The Round Drive now (near the school). According to the old map, it was down towards the school but across the road and up the hill a little. For my story, this first cottage was burned down by two of his assigned convict workers (FACT). I have moved his new house to a later building site on the headland overlooking the lake. This house was a much later building, although something was built in this area by 1841, as both buildings appear on the map (FACT). There was some building on the lake peninsular, and I have made that into John's new house for my story. A fourth building was on the South Headland overlooking the beach. There is an old house still there called Hunter's Hill. In 1941, when my grandfather purchased this hill, the house was old even then (FACT). There were rumours that some of the Sir Robert Peel shipwreck timbers were used to construct some of these buildings. In the late 1850s, probably around late 1856, John Moore's main house burnt down (FACT). I presume it was in bushfires, but there is nothing mentioned in newspapers about his loss. It may have been a local fire. By this time, he had been a magistrate in the area for over fifteen years.

John had left the farm to Robert Maddrell, his first cousin from Braidwood. John's mother had been Jane Maddrell before her marriage. However, there must have been a friendship between them for John to have left Robert his estate in his will.

I have written that Robert and John were in Victoria gold mining together, but this is only a supposition. John was missing from his farm while Robert was in Victoria, and it was known that he'd gone to the gold fields. A story of 3000 gold coins being buried at Robert's house in Braidwood has never been found. (therefore, I have added an equal share for John in my story, but that is purely artistic licence.) John owned seven town blocks in East Gosford (FACT), and I presume it was in one

197

of these that he may have called 'Springfield'.

After John's second house burned down in about 1856 (his first home had been burned some ten or more years earlier), after the second fire, he went to Victoria to hunt gold for some years. He had been short of funds, and the farm was mortgaged. John was still serving in his judicial role in 1860, but less than five years later, aged only 62, he died in Springfield and is buried in an unmarked grave in the Pioneer Point Frederick cemetery at East Gosford.

John sadly died of a stroke without being mentioned by anyone. His death was marked by a mere two lines in the newspapers, saying John died on July 10th, 1865, aged 62. His burial is not registered in church records, as there was no minister in the area for a year (Dec 1864 to Dec 1865). Thomas Battley read the service at his funeral, as there was no minister in town. It was, therefore, not recorded in the funeral register.

At the time of John's death, the farm was mortgaged to Robert Aspinall. The mortgage was then passed on to two others, Cox & James, in 1872.

Some years after John died, the pioneer Tom Davis leased the farm. After Tom took over, he felled the timber, moved it across the lake and up tramway road in North Avoca, and shipped it out from The Haven at Terrigal. I have no idea if Tom ever worked for John or even knew him, but I have made it so in my story.

By 1904, someone named Mrs Robinson was letting holiday accommodation in Avoca at the rate of £1/5s per week. That price included the use of a boat and meals of fresh local food. In 1907, BATT, RODD, and PURVES, Ltd. put the entire 640-acre farm up for sale.

Henry F. Halloran purchased the farm and planned to subdivide it. However, the local farmers and other residents complained, as they did not want the subdivision to proceed. In the meantime, the boarding house had been purchased, and he expanded and upgraded it to what became known as Avoca House (photo below). It stood for over 100 years on the headland facing north to the lake.

Info from:-*https://trove.nla.gov.au/newspaper/article/263763062/29491653*

Mrs Robinson's Guest House turned int Halloran's Guest house

Original Staff quarters behind house.

John Moore's original Stables and a later water tank.
Photo ca 1911

HISTORICAL RECORDS
OF THE
CENTRAL COAST
OF
NEW SOUTH WALES

THE BRISBANE WATER CASE 1837-8

ney **Gaze**

AND

NEW SOUTH WALES ADVERTISER.
ESTABLISHED THIRTY-SIX YEARS.

SATURDAY, MARCH 24, 1838.

APOLOGY.

MOORE v. FAUNCE.

IN consideration of Mr. Moore abandoning the action brought against me this Term, I agree to pay all the costs due by Mr. Moore to Messrs. Unwin and Want, in this action; and I further authorise Her Majesty's Attorney-General to make the following apology in open Court.

That Captain Faunce acknowledges his error in sending the search warrant to Mr. Moore's house, and admits that it cannot be justified, and Captain Faunce regrets Mr. Moore should have suffered any inconvenience, and acquits him of all blame in the transaction.

(Signed)   A. T. FAUNCE.
March 16, 1838.

Collected Records of the District of Brisbane Water to 1891 Published by the Gosford District Local History Study Group.

Captain Faunce's apology to Moore after a three-year court case.
The case was big news locally, and eventually, the three men, Moore, Donnison, and Bean, became upright men of standing in the local community. All have streets named after them in Gosford.

Authors Note:-

I was born and grew up on John Moore's farm at Avoca Beach, so I knew his name from early childhood.

One stormy night in the 1960s, an old man came knocking and looking for his cattle. My parents discovered that this man had worked for Tom Davis and had lived in the old house, which remains to this day (2024).

In my story, it is called the honeymoon cottage. A member of my family still owns it. I do not know if it was built from the timbers of the wreck of the *Sir Robert Peel*, but the cottage was certainly in existence about this time, as it is on various maps and a photo taken in 1903. This wreck is why Peel Street in Avoca Beach was named.

All of Avoca was clear-felled, and signs of a big bushfire ripped through this area. Another one struck in 1968, and I remember the terror and noise. I heard that the last of the Bouddi tribe were gathered on Copacabana Beach in the 30's and taken by boat to Sydney. I do not know if this is true, but I know that they interacted with the local farmers for decades. I still visit John's memorial at the Point Frederick Cemetery.

Sara

In 1840, John Moore owned seven town blocks in East Gosford.
By 1860 he owned one block on the corner of Wells and Holden Streets.
He died in "Springfield" on July 10th 1865, and this could have been the
name of his house.

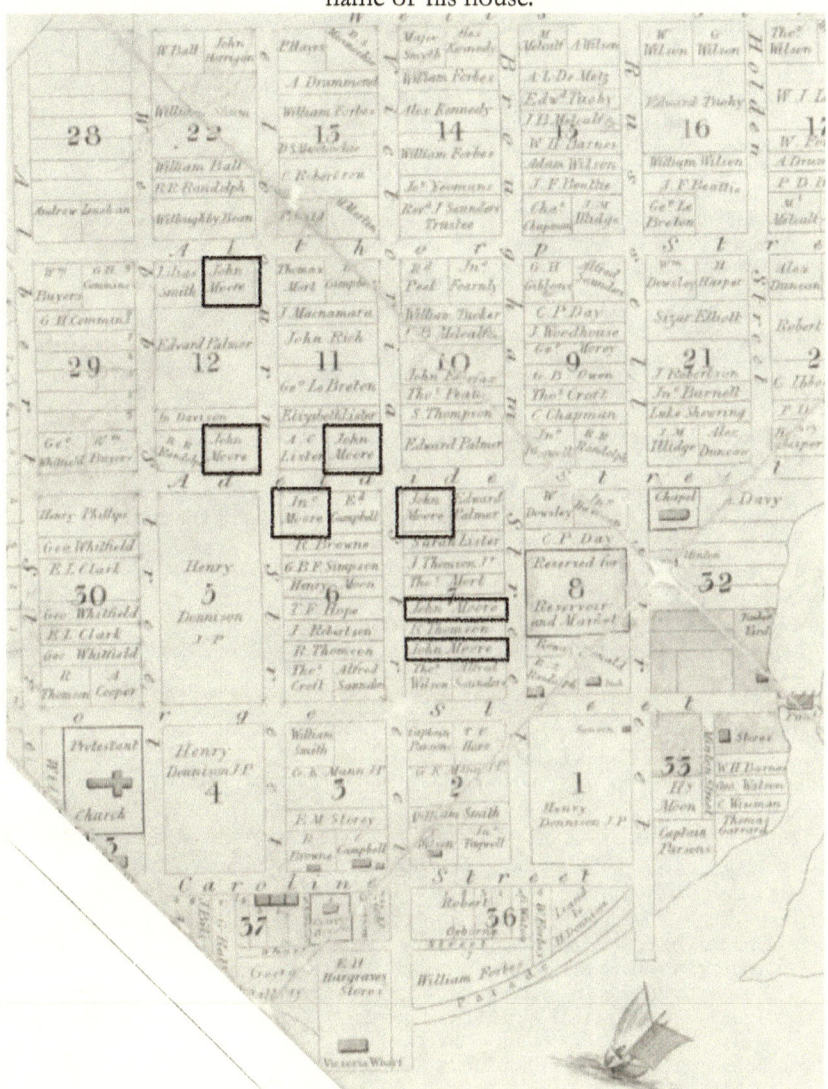

Andrew Lenehans' blocks in the top left of the map are interesting. He was a
French Polisher in Sydney who made much of the furniture for the
Government House in Sydney for Governor Darling.
Andrew's brother Michael married my great great aunt.
The Lenehan's were also Irish.

Characters

Kieran O'Shane's grandparents *(Eamon (Edward) and Nioiclín(Nicola) O'Shane.*
B 1810 *(his mother was a Moore, cousin to John Moore's Father)*
died August 1848
Gráinne McCarthy *(daug of Sal Lockley's older bro, Eamon McCarthy) (1st cousins)*
B 1812
died August 1848

    1 Clare O'Shane   *Sailed 1848 on Lady Kennaway*
    B 1834 m 1851 **Shéamas** Connor b 1832
    2 Kerry   *Sailed 1848 8 on Lady Kennaway*
    B 1836 m Dec 1856 **Liam** Connor b 1835
    3 Liam,
    B 1838 (drowned) June 1847
    4 Mary
    B 1840 died Dec 1847
    5 Kathleen
    B 1844 died Jan 1848
    6 **Patrick** Anthony (Paddy) -
    B April 1847 died May 1847
    7 **Tara** stillborn in August 1848

Edward, (**Ned**) Duke of Gracemere (aka Major Ned Grace)
M 1841 **Christina** Meadows
Children 5, 1 Chip, 2 Sarah, 3, Liam b 1845
4 & 5 Charlotte & Isabella (charl & Izzy) twins born in Jan 1847 in Parramatta

Jennifer Kellow m Billy Williams
Isla Kellow b 1802 - M 1822 **Felix**, Duke of Shesham b 1784
 Children 5
1/ Rupert, b23; 2/ Karensa (Kerry) b25 3/ Tristan b29; and 4/ Rosen (Rose) b 29 5/ Edward
Felix b 1842

<u>Charles</u> John Lockley
b March 1800 and d 27 April, Easter 1870
 Dad John Lockley m Mum Elle Staverly d 2/9/1855. M2 Richard Childs d 1855 3rd Earl of
Coxheath
M Feb 1820 **<u>Sal</u>** (Sarah Shannon) **McCarthy** d early 11 Jan 1896 aged nearly 96 (Dar and
Mama) '<u>Jolly Sailor</u>' Sal's mother:- Shannon McCarthy *parents Eamon (Edward) and
Nioiclín(Nicola) O'Shane. Ireland*
6 children

    1 **Charlie**   m 5 Nov 1842 **Gracie** Miller
    2 **Eddie**   m 4 Dec 1841 **Jenna** Turner
    3 **Liza**   m 6 Nov 1841 **Bertie** Ellis
    4 **Anna**   m 5 Nov 1842 **Tim** Miller
    5 **Wills**   m 14 Feb 1845 **Cathy** Turner
    6 **Luke**   m 2 Aug 1856 **Ellen** Miller

William (**Bill**) **Miller** b mid-1797 and d 1884
m Jan 1819 Mary **Molly** Ross b 1800, (daug of Ellen and Sam Ross) d 1884 '<u>Rear Admiral
Duncan</u>'

    #1 **Tim**othy Jerome b 25/3/1822 (lawyer)   m 1843 **Anna** Lockley b 24
    #2 Grace Letitia (**Gracie)**   b Jan 1824   m 1841 **Charlie** Lockley b 20
    #3 **Sam**uel William b 1828   m 1851 Isabella '**Belle**' Ellis
    #4 **Ellen** Mary b 1830   m Aug 1856 **Luke Lockley**

Paddy and Cara Connor, Political Irish life convicts (Eddie's servants)
 Two older married sons living on the Windsor Road
 Maryanne m **Robert** Ellis - 3 children
 Moira 16 b 1828 m **Connor** Murphy 6 children (Luke & Ellen)
 Shauna 14 b 1830 m **Brodie** Murphy 4 children (Wills & Cathy)
 Shéamas b 1832 m 1851 **Clare O'Shane**
 Liam b 1835 m Dec 1856 **Kerry O'Shane**

George and Charlotte **Ellis** - Father is a Sadler/leather goods in Parramatta
 1Albert George (**Bertie**) b 1820 m **Liza** Lockley
 2Robert (**Robbie**) m **Maryanne** Connor
 3Amelia (**Milly**) m **Marc** Turner (Jenna's brother)
 4Isabella (**Belle**) m **Sam** Miller (Gracie's Brother)

John (Jack) **Turner** b 1800 Transported 1820 d 1886
M 1820 **Martha** Turner (*née Alexander*) Arms of Australia Emu Plains, d 1886
 1 Marcus (**Marc**), b 1820 m Dec 1843 **Milly** Ellis
 2 Alexander (**Alex**) b 1821 m **Mary** Parker saddler
 3 Jennifer Martha (**Jenna**) b1823 m Nov 1841 **Eddie** Lockley
 4 Victoria (**Vicky**) b 7/1825 m 29/12/44 **Harry** Harlow
 5 Catherine (**Cathy**) b June 24, 1827 m 14/2/1845 **Wills** Lockley
 6 Nicholas (**Nicky**) John b 1830 m April 1863 **Betty Ellison** b1838
 7 Malcolm (**Calum**) William b 1832 bapt Jan 1833 m

Dave Fisher and **Glenn** Worboys
Bill & **Tom** - local lads. John's farm hands
Pemma m **Bagaroo**
Barraboi, *Pemma's brother,* m **Milbah**

Real People

Governor and Lady FitzRoy (& her death in the accident)
Charles Masters - Aide who died in the carriage accident.
The various sea captains and the ships listed are all correct.

John Moore

 b Co Wicklow Ireland 1803, to John and Jane Moore (Catholics)
 d 10th July 1865 Springfield, near Gosford.
 Buried at Point Frederick Cemetery, East Gosford (in an unmarked grave)
 Listed on the Pioneers memorial in the cemetery there.
Robert Maddrell, John's cousin (John's mother was Jane Maddrell)
 Robert's wife, who was the daughter of Captain Coghill (also his gold, never found)

Mr Willoughby Bean
Mr Henry Donnison
Mr Hely
Captain Faunce
The Langland's family on the *Lady Kennaway*
The mass of Irish girls leaving Ireland.
 Earl Grey's sonship of the 4000+ Irish orphans who emigrated to Australia and Canada.
Tom & Susanna **Davis** of Terrigal
The ships leaving various ports, including the *Lady Kennaway, Christina,* etc all correct

Bibliography

John Langlands Obit
https://oa.anu.edu.au/obituary/langlands-john-17089
The Coastal steamer *Christina* left Melbourne for Sydney on the 7th of 1848. Arriving 16 Dec 1848. Others regularly ran up and down the east coast of Australia, resupplying the various towns & ports.

John Moore
https://en.wikipedia.org/wiki/Avoca_Beach
Halloraan's Subdivision of Avoca Beach
https://www.facebook.com/photo.php?fbid=4233464020065299&id=450101245068281&set=a.453074078104331

Wisemans Ferry
https://en.wikipedia.org/wiki/Wisemans_Ferry
Aboriginal peoples on the Eastern Central Coast - *especially Avoca Beach*
https://www.yourvoiceourcoast.com/sites/default/files/2020-06/FOR_RELEASE_-_REDACTED_ABORIGINAL_AND_HISTORICAL_ASSESSMENT-__Five_Lands_Walk_Assess_BY_AHMS.pdf

Sir Robert Peel wreck at Avoca Beach - 17/1/1847
https://trove.nla.gov.au/newspaper/article/12890119
https://trove.nla.gov.au/newspaper/article/94445168
http://oceans1.customer.netspace.net.au/nsw-wrecks.html
Sir Robert Peel. Troopship, 724/610 tons. Built Great Britain, 1847; reg. London. 'One of the finest vessels to have sailed to the colonies'. Captain Champion. Ashore and lost in Avoca Bay, near Cape Three Points, NSW, 17 January 1847. In hazy weather, she ran onto a sandy beach, where she remained upright, allowing the passengers and crew to reach safety in daylight. The steamer Thistle reported her predicament and returned to offer assistance. - Captain W. Campion]

Terrigal - History of the Area by Liz Parkinson (hardcopy 2003)
Verbal information and reference sources - Gwen Dundon 2023
1840 East Gosford Map- John Moore had seven blocks in East Gosford.
https://collection.sl.nsw.gov.au/record/74Vve4755Mbl/ak7ldD0gePPxX

If you loved this book, these are similar.
(All are stand-alone stories)
A First Fleet Convict Story 1788
A First Fleet story with the descriptions taken directly from the Journal of Doctor Author Bowes Smith who was the doctor on board the Lady Penrhyn.

Gentle Annie Soames
Her dreams lead to unexpected outcomes. An Australian First Fleet story.

Annie Soames is a girl beloved by the community but not afraid to voice her desires. That leads to trouble, illicit love, and a world turned upside down.

Oliver Quilpie, the recently married Marquess, discovers his arranged union is not to his taste; he is drawn to his wife's companion. Unfortunately, he is unable to keep his hands off her. For revenge, Annie mimics his every move while riding but is dressed as a highwayman. However, she had now fallen in love with him. This action finally leads to her arrest and transportation to a faraway land.

After some years, Oliver's wife dies, and his thoughts turn to Annie. He seeks to find her, but she has vanished. He is horrified to discover she was transported to New South Wales as a convict on the *Lady Penrhyn*. He follows with a shipload of supplies on the *Kitty*. Will Annie want to see him?

ISBN 9780645441574   ISBN ebook 9781923097063
July 2024

The Hunter to Macquarie Collection 1795-1822
When Upon Life's Billows
Sydney 1795-1821 - Governor John Hunter

Captain John Hunter was born to a life at sea. The wind blows where no man knows, and John is caught up in the tempest. Although wrecking his ship, the *HMS Sirius*, in 1790, he became the second Governor of the rough and filthy penal settlement of New South Wales. He always seems to be in the wrong place at the wrong time, trusting the wrong people.

Helena Rosedale is not a typical female convict. She fights tooth and nail to stop the men from abusing her. She gains the name of Helena the Hellcat.

Crispin Milroy is alone in the world and one of the new Governor's security detail. Can he win the fair lady's heart? Life in 1795 in Sydney Cove is raw at best. Food is scarce, and disease often ravages the settlement. Life throws everything except death at these three, yet somehow, they survive. Why does John trust this young couple when others betray him?

What trials must Helena and Crispin endure to make their new lives in this raw town bearable? How can John ease their path?

ISBN: 9780645783339   ebook ISBN: 9780645783346
Coming 2025

Saddler's Song
London 1790s to Parramatta 1840s

George Ellis is a tanner's son living on the outskirts of London. When disease takes his family. Alone and hurting, he seeks to find a new life for himself. Hearing from a friend about the possibility of setting up a business in New South Wales, he sells up and leaves all he knows. His beloved violin is his most valuable item, and his talent for making beautiful music is hidden from all but a few.

Ben Parker is a saddler, like George; he is also alone in the world. Ben also sells up to move to the new colony. The two young men meet and combine their skills to start afresh in a new world. During the journey out, George's skill as a violinist is revealed. On arrival, they find accommodation with a family with many lovely daughters. Two of these girls steal their hearts, but how will the business survive in an animal-starved land where access to leather is limited? What is the saddler's song?

ISBN: 9780645783353   eISBN: 9780645783360
Coming 2025

Tuppence to Pass
London 1800s to Parramatta 1820s - Governor Lachlan Macquarie

Josh Callan is a London lad who makes the best of the life that has been dealt to him. Stealing from the man who killed his father gives the family a change of direction. Josh is arrested, but the judge belittles him, saying he's not worth tuppence. He is transported to the penal colony of Sydney as a convict just as **Governor Macquarie's** term starts. He proves his worth and falls on his feet, becoming the Governor's groom and confidante.

Life in the Colonial town opens opportunities they could never have dreamed about in England, but can Josh find his niche?

Where will this strange friendship take Josh and his family?

ISBN: 9781923097070   eISBN: 9781923097087
Coming 2025

His Majesty's Pageboy
London to Emu Plains, Australia, in the 1800s

Jack **Turner** was born into a life of pomp and privilege that was not rightfully his. He was brought to the royal court for his own protection. By the age of ten, he was King George the Third's pageboy and known as Lord John. For years, Jack roils against the immorality of society and the shallowness of people; then, he meets an unspoiled young girl amongst the mire of humanity whose purity stands out. He is unable to pursue her before his life hits a wall.

Martha **Alexander** is the daughter of a wealthy shipping merchant. She has been presented to London's second tier of society, where she meets the young man of her dreams. She is expected to marry well, and Lord John sets her heart fluttering. However, her father's drinking shatters her future. He was made to sign all his possessions away while drunk, unknowingly including his daughter. Refusing a forced marriage changes her life. How do these two end up as convicts in Australia?

Paperback ISBN 9781923097308   eISBN 978192309792
Coming 2026

Fist Full of Holey Dollars
Sydney Cove 1810+

Captain **Rudi Greenwood** finds himself in a land where alcohol is money and rules are often overlooked in the search for wealth. While on duty, he assists a couple after a carriage accident, and this incident changed his life.

When Governor **Lachlan Macquarie** approaches Rudi for ideas about improving the roads, a seemingly casual remark sets in motion a series of events that not only alter Rudi's life but also have far-reaching implications for the entire colony. In an attempt to tackle the prevalent alcohol problem, a new currency, the Holey Dollar and Dump is introduced, posing a significant challenge for the free settlers.

Can Rudi stand against his peers and bring about change in this unruly penal town, or will he cave in to temptation like his peers and line his own pockets? What has he done that makes him hated by the exclusives and free settlers in the colony?

Paperback ISBN 9781923097407   eISBN 9781923097414
Coming 2026

Far From the Whispering Sheoaks
Set in Australia in the 1817+

Fanny **Little** was in the wrong place doing something she thought was legal. Her actions saw her arrested, tried, and banished. She was assigned from the female prison to ex-soldier Gordon McKenzie and soon found herself in a despicable and humiliating situation of being sold in the public marketplace.

Phil **Bentley** is a man running from his jealous uncle, and he finds solace in a secluded farm half a world away. With the community on their side, can Phil save Fanny from Gordon's vile abuse? Why is their relationship destined to court controversy? And who is Jas? Why does Gordon wish to harm the child? Will they ever escape the shadows that are chasing them?

Paperback ISBN 9781923097315   eISBN9781923097322
Coming 2026

Bound Down in Iron Chains
Set in Australia in the 1818+

Howard **Marlow** is a studious and honest London bookkeeper. When he is asked to help a friend's brother do his bookwork, he unknowingly helps a crime gang. He is arrested, convicted, and transported. On arrival, Howard is assigned to the boy's orphanage with a possibly crooked soldier in charge. He is asked to use his skills to decipher the bookkeeping entries that make no sense. He discovers his love for the affection-starved boys at the orphanage.

Naomi **Buckingham,** a convict girl, is thrust into the harsh reality of the orphanage alongside Howard. She is assigned to the orphanage, but it is far from the refuge she had hoped for as the supervisor is a man who harbours no respect for women. With no one to rely on but the new accountant, she grapples with the question of trust.

Naomi is the key to breaking the bookkeeping code, cracking the case wide open. Can Howard use his brains to save them both? How do they become involved with some of the worst criminals in the penal colony of New South Wales?

Paperback ISBN 9781923097353   eISBN9781923097360
Coming 2026

Unlikely Convict Ladies Trilogy 1792-1840s

Dancing to her Own Tune

Co-authored by Sheila Hunter and Sara Powter

Sydney 1790s to England 1830s

Annie White is released after serving seven years as a convict in Sydney. She gets a visitor who, with his help, she can start a baking business. She is then asked to assist another sick man, **Sam** Corbett. Annie nurses him back to health, and a relationship develops. They settle into a life together, barely making ends meet; she realises she's expecting a child. Sam has his past laid bare and must adjust to the revelations. They both must face their accusers and find that the answers to their questions are not what they thought. Their life experiences seem to cling to them, and unable to shake them off, they end up back in England. They must face their ghosts and discover they are not who they think they are. How can they turn their anger and spite into love and forgiveness? The Dance of Life goes on.
ISBN 9780645110715   ISBN9780645110722

Long-listed in the Historical Fiction Company Competition 2022

Amelia's Tears

Parramatta 1828 – England 1840s

Amelia Westaweller awaits her assignment in the Parramatta Female Prison. Forced to leave the relative safety of gaol, she is assigned and now faces her worst nightmare. A foul man claims her and makes her life a living hell. Then, her world goes black. A glimmer of hope arises when she hears from her brother, Jim, who has enlisted a friend to help her. She writes to Jim, pouring out her heart and telling him of the horrors of her new life. He encourages her to stay firm in her faith. All she can do is pray. When Major **Ned** Grace, her brother's friend, enters her life in Parramatta, he starts to ease her path. Things have changed, as now she has a child in tow. How can Amelia forge a new life for herself? What man could want her with her background and a child at her side? Who is the gentleman who turns her tears of sadness into tears of great joy?
ISBN: 9780645110739   eISBN: 978-0-6451107-4-6 Hard Cover ISBN 979-842061-7953

A Lady in Irons

England 1800s - Parramatta 1808+

Katy Harrington is mourning the death of her husband after he died in a shooting accident. Barely coping, she awaits the birth of their child. If it's a girl, she must hand the family home to her husband's brother. The day after giving birth to a daughter, she and her daughter are left on the side of a road. She collapses and is found by someone she thought had died in a fire ten years before. **Perry White**, badly scarred himself, nurses her back to health. They marry and move in with her widowed friend, Mary.
After some years, she discovers her husband and friend in each other's arms. Now living in a love triangle, she flees. Grasping the only straw available, she intentionally gets arrested and is sent to a colony far away. By doing this, her marriage can be annulled.
What happens in the Colony is different from what she expects. Governor Macquarie comes to her rescue, but what of Perry and her children?
ISBN: 9780645110784   eISBN:9780645441505

The Convict Birthstain Collection 1820-1840s

NO MORE, MY Love

Hunter Valley, NSW 1820s

Jess Elkin is distraught when tragedy ravages her family. She becomes the victim of a carriage accident and is nursed back to health by the driver, **Marcus Ryan**. Marcus was not expecting to fall in love. Yet, when Jess's fortunes suddenly turn for the worse, Marcus must decide how far he will go to pursue her. As time passes in Newcastle, Australia, Marcus must take a business trip and is taken by pirates. Jess is left wondering if her will keep his promise to return to her… Will she ever see him alive again?
ISBN: 9780645441536   eISBN 9780645441581

Long-listed in the Historical Fiction Company Competition 2023

The Vine Weaver

Hawkesbury River area 1820s+

New Beginnings and Old Threats

In the 1820s, Australia, **Joel and Hetty Walker** live on a secluded farm on the Hawkesbury River, which becomes a healing haven for the protection of young convict women. A series of events brings **Fran Rea** to Hetty's attention, and she is taken to the farm. Fran and Hetty develop a cottage industry under the compassionate eye of farmhand **Hector Macdougal;** Hector's loving words change lives. It is to him that Fran turns when threatened.

The vines now must draw them close to survive the future revelations, and of those, there are many.

ISBN: 9780645441512   eISBN: 9780645441529

Long-listed in the Historical Fiction Company Competition 2023

https://amazon.com/dp/0645441511   https://amazon.com/dp/B0C6Z552Y2

The story continues in Scotch at The Rocks…

Scotch at The Rocks

Glasgow, Scotland, early 1800s to The Rocks, Sydney 1830s

Orphaned children Brodie Stewart and Heather Anderson live on Glasgow's streets. Although hungry, somehow they survive and keep out of trouble. Heather finds a job and looks to be settled; things go pear-shaped for them both. Eventually, they marry by declaration, yet even that gets messed up, and they are both arrested soon after they make their vow. In 1838, they were transported to Sydney as convicts. Heather arrives within weeks of Brodie, and they are assigned close to each other. They are now living on the docklands in Sydney, called The Rocks. They now have to forge a new life halfway across the world from their homeland.

Adventures abound, and Brodie gets press-ganged. While he's away, Heather's life changes and soon, she's officially selling Scotch Whisky at a shop in The Rocks.

You can take a Scot out of Scotland, but where did the Scotch come from?

ISBN 9780645441550 ebook 9781923097001 Large Print 9781923097254

Waiting at the Sliprails

The Bathurst Road 1830s

A Convict's Tale

Bea Dawes's term of conviction nears an end, and she has few options other than marriage to a stranger or going on the street.

Jack Barnes, the hired drover, wants a wife. Bea accepts his offer; then, she discovers that he could be gone for months, leaving her alone with **Billy and Netty**, part of the tribe of an Aboriginal tribe who live on his secluded farm. Bea learns to love her husband and also this wonderful aboriginal couple. Drought ravages the farm, and Jack must hit the long paddock with the flock. In his absence, a visitor arrives, threatening to destroy everything she has worked so hard for. Can Bea touch her heart? Can she cope? Will the drought ever end? And when will Jack return?

ISBN: 9780645441543   eISBN: 9781923097032

August 2023

Winner of the Spring 2024 PenCraft Award, for Christian Historical Fiction

Convict Shadows of the Past

Two Jennifers, two hundred years apart

Jenny Kellow is eight years old when she learns of her convict family history. Then discovers that she was named after a convict from nearly two hundred years ago. Her grandfather's stories inspire her to dig deeper into her ancestors' convict past. From her grandfather, she hears stories of bushrangers, convicts, and life in the infant colony of Parramatta. She sets about retracing the footsteps of her convict great-great-great-grandmother to honour her. Jenny's search starts with microfiche back in the 60s, and she learns about the small tin mining town in Cornwall and the production of a cheese that sets London afire. She discovers her ancestor, **Jennifer Kellow,** has brought these cheese-making skills to Parramatta, where she taught others her craft. Echoes of the past can still be heard if you know where to listen.

Who was the first Jennifer, and what does she have to do with cheese? Why is she so elusive? Did Jenny's ancestor, Jennifer, ever see those two small crosses carved into the bricks of the Female Factory? Would Jenny ever find out her ancestor's story?

ISBN: 9780645783315   ISBN ebook 9780645783322

A NaNoWriMo 2022 book winner

January 2024

In Defence of Her Honour

London 1800s to Parramatta 1819

Will the real man of quality please stand up?

Bill Miller was raised and educated with the sons of the family. The youngest, Bert Edison-Browne, had been his best friend. However, jealousy intervenes when Bill's excellent schoolwork curtails their friendship. He wins a scholarship and enters Oxford University. When Bill's father dies unexpectedly, Bert insists that Bill take over as butler, but it's more to oppress him. Bert's jealousy grows and festers. Now looking for a way to rid themselves of their new butler. A ruckus ensues, and Bill is arrested for assaulting Bert.

Molly Ross is the housekeeper's daughter, and she will vouch for him. It's too late; Bill has been arrested and is soon sentenced to be transported. With Bill gone, Molly now fights to defend herself from Bert. After hitting him with a pan, she, too, is arrested and sent to Sydney. Bill and Molly arrive with letters of introduction and compensation from Bert's father. Soon, they will be running the best inn in Parramatta with an endorsement from the governor.

ISBN 9780645441567   ISBN ebook 9781923097049

April 2024

I can't stop Tomorrow

Irish Famine 1840s to Avoca Beach, Australia

Escaping bigotry and prejudice in Ireland, the O'Shane family lives on a secluded farm on the west coast of Ireland. The potato blight soon decimates their farm. It's always darkest before dawn, and the two remaining girls cling to the hope of a new life. With the kindness of strangers, the eldest girls, **Clare** and **Kerry O'Shane**, head to their cousin, Sal Lockley, in Parramatta, Australia.   A new, wonderful life awaits them both. **Shéamus Connor** is the annoying teenage boy who reluctantly draws Clare's affection. However, living in a convict town means ruffians abound.

John Moore is a bad-tempered and troubled Irishman who is content to live alone on another secluded farm until he discovers Clare and two other lads need rescuing.

Can John protect her from the pain inflicted by an evil world?

Can Shéamus find his lost love who has fled?

ISBN: 9780645441598   ISBN ebook 9781923097056

October 2024

Madeline's Boy

England 1830s to New South Wales 1840

A red-coat soldier's tale

All is not straightforward when money and titles are involved.

Madeline Brougham is asked to care for her best friend's orphaned son when his life is in danger. **Chip Downes** is the pawn between a greedy, unscrupulous uncle and his inheritance. Maddie must do everything she can to keep him safe, including moving halfway around the globe to take Chip to his guardian. Major Humphrey Downes is a soldier in the penal colony of Sydney. Humphrey's best friend, another soldier, **Major Tim Hinds**, meets Maddie, and with the support of these two men, a chase around the colony ensues. Will Maddie and Tim be able to find happiness together?

Can the three adults keep Chip safe until he's old enough to claim his inheritance?

ISBN: 9780645783308   ISBN ebook 9781923097094

Dec 2024

Jam or Marmalade for Tea

England 1820s to New South Wales 1825 (Governor Brisbane Era)

Martha Hamilton is the eldest of four orphans struggling to survive on their own. Caught stealing, she is tried, convicted, and transported to New South Wales. With her family gone, she becomes despondent. Life holds no meaning for her, and the ocean waves look inviting.

Captain Guy Manning is a frustrated and injured redcoat soldier returning to Sydney to take up a new assignment. He notices Martha trying to jump overboard and rescues her. How do two cats bring them together?

A convict ship is no place for romance, and she's far too young anyway, isn't she?

Can Guy save her and forge a life together for them? What connections does he have to try and save her siblings? Why is marmalade important for their future?

Paperback ISBN 9781923097933   eISBN9781923097285

A NaNoWriMo 2023 book winner

October 2025

Unshackled Lives

Set in England & Australia in the 1800s
Australian historical fiction of early colonial days

Ned Lockley is the second of four sons of the Duke and Duchess of Gracemere. As his mother's favourite, his childhood years were blissful, but he needs to grow up and quickly.

A whirlwind romance is followed by a loved one's betrayal. The emotional turmoil that follows is hard for Ned to cope with, especially in the midst of a collapsing, immoral society.

Ned can't stay as even his family is falling apart. His mother's words to remain true to himself and his faith make him leave everything he knows.

How does Ned end up in New South Wales in charge of placing female convicts?

Will he ever find happiness or discover who Charles is?

ISBN 9781923097377   eISBN 9781923097384   LP ISBN: 9781923097391

A 100-year, six-part Australian Colonial series

The Lockleys of Parramatta 1800-1900

Hands upon the Anvil

A blacksmith's life and love are more than work
Parramatta 1830s

Eddie Lockley's parents were transported for their crimes. Can a steadfast lad rise above his origins and guide others to succeed in a land of opportunity?

Ten-year-old Eddie longs to help his mum and dad. Living in a convict town with his family, the keen youngster has been working with the local blacksmith since his sixth birthday. But when a lieutenant doesn't stop abusing his older brother, the young boy yearns for the day when he can stand up and end the torment. Though he's thrilled when his mentor offers to send him off to learn his letters, Eddie fears he won't be around to watch his sibling's back. But as he takes on the biggest adventure of his life, the brave believer soon discovers God is looking out for everyone he loves. Does this young man in the making have what it takes to change everything for the better?

ISBN 9780994578235 Ebook ISBN 978-0-9945782-5-9 Hardcover 9798496177368
https://amazon.com/dp/0994578237 https://amazon.com/dp/B08TB51L19

Out Where The Brolgas Dance

Gold is found, and so is love
Parramatta 1840s
How can a question change so many people?

It's the 1840s, and discoveries across the Blue Mountains continue. Major Mitchell's new road is complete, and towns are planned and being built. Abundant land is available for those who want it. Eighteen-year-old **William "Wills" Lockley** has laid a solid foundation for a respectable career as a blacksmith, but the Lockley lust for adventure flows deeply within his veins. He dreads the monotony of work at the blacksmith's forge and yearns for adventure in a new frontier. Wills meets six Englishmen (*Coping with what is now known as PTSD*) who have the means to make his dreams come true. What they discover changes the Colony and their lives forever. Gold fever ensues. While in the West, Wills must deal with an uncertain romance. Does Cathy even want him?

ISBN 9780994578242 Ebook ISBN 978-0-9945782-6-6 Hardcover ISBN 9798755445504
LP ISBN 9781923097155
https://amazon.com/dp/0994578245   https://amazon.com/dp/B08T6NS3XX

Diamonds in the Dirt

Diamonds, love and money… but there is much more to life.
Parramatta 1850s

Luke Lockley, the youngest Lockley son, has completed University, and his life has no direction. No job, no money, and no love. Desperately alone, he prays for guidance. How can Luke trust that God has a plan for him if he can't even find a job? He does the only thing he can … he prays. Within a week, life has changed … oh, how it has changed as his brother Wills turns up with a suggestion. Would Luke be interested in joining the expedition with John Evans? **Reverend William Clarke** needs assistance on a Government Mineral Survey. The challenge, adventure and finds are life-changing for many. However, it gives Luke meaning, purpose and direction. The condition of his heart problems also takes a turn. Can he walk away? Will she wait for him?

ISBN:9780994578273 Ebook ISBN: 978-0-9945782-8-0 Hard cover ISBN 979-8788011141
https://amazon.com/dp/099457827X   https://amazon.com/dp/B09NH1MLXZ

The Earl's Shadow

Who or what is the 'shadow'? How does it affect so many?

Parramatta 1860s

Charles Lockley is the Earl of Coxheath. He spent his youth as a convict in Parramatta and had no idea he was an Earl. He had minimal education and few social skills. His eldest son, **Charlie**, is no different.

Now faced with his own mortality, Charles has to work out how to live the remainder of his life after a near-death experience. He is called to step way out of his comfort zone in London. His action will change the world for many. The echoes from the past still haunt Charlie. London is calling the family, and they can't postpone the trip. How does the Cobb and Co. coach driver **Jim Leslie** fit in? And precisely what is *'The Earl's Shadow'* that he speaks about? What happens if the 'Shadow' is gone?

ISBN: 9780645110708 Ebook ISBN 978-0-9945782-9-7
Released June 2022
https://amazon.com/dp/0645110701   https://amazon.com/dp/B0B158SKSK

Once a Jolly Swagman

An old black Billy Can contain the secrets of an incredible life

An Australian Historical Novel

Set in 1870s Parramatta and Kent, UK

Rick Lockley, battling his family's expectations, runs away to find himself. **Jack**, a jolly swagman, takes him under his care. Even after years together, Rick knows little about the old man.

On his death, Jack leaves Rick his precious billy can; the contents reveal Jack's identity. Stunned, Rick must travel to England to finalise Jack's wishes. There, he uncovers Jack's life of love, betrayal and a link to his own family. Rick also discovers there is much more to learn about this enigmatic man.

ISBN 9780645110753   Ebook ISBN 978-0-6451107-6-0
Released Sept 2022
https://amazon.com/dp/0645110752   https://amazon.com/dp/B0B5JN1WCV

Jonty's Journey

Gems, Love, Artists and a Golden Lion

Australia and South Africa 1880-1902

Sydney Jeweller Jonty Evans' passion for gems takes him to Africa at a volatile time. He finds the diamonds he wants and is given a lion cub. Jonty is all but kidnapped. His experiences in the Transvaal plunge him into questioning everything he knows of life. Soon, nightmares haunt him. (Now known as PTSD.)

On return home, he nearly messes up his love life with **Lottie** before it even starts, and he struggles to settle. Lottie's father, **Luke** Lockley from Parramatta, takes him in hand and points him to someone who can help.

Jonty is then recalled to Africa as a liaison and reconnects with his lion, Chimbu, when he saves the life of his security detail. His life journey introduces him to the most amazing Heidelberg artists, politicians, poets, rebels, and the scapegoat soldier Harry Breaker Morant. Can Jonty bury the past and regain the peace he's lost?

ISBN 9780645110777 HC ISBN 9781923097124   Ebook ISBN: 978-0-6451107-9-1
Released Feb 2023
https://amazon.com/dp/0645110779   https://amazon.com/dp/B0BLJ7ND1Q

Sheila Hunter's Australian Colonial Trilogy 1840s
Co-Winner of 1999 NSW Senior Citizen of the Year, In the Year of the Senior Citizen

Mattie
The Story of an Australian Convict Child
An Australian Historical Story inspired by real Life.

An orphaned child, Mattie is convicted of petty theft, sentenced to seven years, and sent to Australia. She meets another convict woman who, at her death, gives Mattie a chance for a new life. She makes the most of everything that comes her way, earning her freedom, falling in love, marrying, and becoming a mother. But life is not kind to her.

She meets bushrangers, moves to the gold fields in Bathurst, and starts a store. Yet she is the kind of woman who made Australia what it is today. Can she survive alone in a man's world? A remarkable woman who breaks down all her barriers.

(Mattie's story continues in The Lockleys of Parramatta - bk 4 & 6)
ISBN 9781503252370 & ebook AISN BOOTTEDBTO
(The story continues in The Earl's Shadow & Once a Jolly Swagman)
Released 2015
https://amazon.com/dp/150325237X   https://amazon.com/dp/B00TTEDBT0

Ricky
A boy in Colonial Australia

Ricky English and his mother immigrated from England to join his father in the new Colony of Sydney. Upon arrival, there was no sign of his father. Ricky's mum uses the tiny amount of money they brought to get lodgings in a run-down building. Things go from bad to worse when his mother dies; he is thrown out of the rooms, and the caretakers confiscate all their possessions.

Ricky lives on the streets of Sydney Town as a street waif. Ricky finds safe places to sleep and befriends freed convicts who can help him survive. One day, he encounters a lost child and helps reunite her with her family. These people try to help him, but he insists on doing things his way because of his stubbornness. However, he has found a mentor and confidante. The story follows him through his life. He survives and turns his life around, helping others along the way. ***(Will's story continues in Jonty's Journey)***

Paperback ISBN 9780994578211   Kindle ASIN: B00MLYN6IG
Released 2014
https://amazon.com/dp/1500770574   https://amazon.com/dp/B00MLYN6IG

The Heather to The Hawkesbury
Four Scottish families brave a new life in a strange land.

Mary Macdonald and husband **Murd** and family; her brother **Fergus** MacKenzie; sister-in-law **Caro** MacLeod; cousin **Alex** Fraser and all their families who have had to emigrate from the Isle of Skye during the "Clearances."

The story follows the four families from Scotland on the ship out to the NSW colony in the 1850s. Mary does not cope with the changes and losses that occur in the first months in the colony. The other women in the family rely on her, and she nearly crumbles. The families struggle together through accidents, losses, trials, floods, and hard work and forge a strong bond with their new country. Trials, tribulations and triumphs see the four families make a firm mark in their new homeland. The immigrants from Scotland helped make Australia what it is today.

ISBN 978994578228   ebook AISN B01A21JYWQ   Large Print ISBN1533473641
Available on Amazon/Kindle & Large Print
Released 2016
https://amazon.com/dp/1503251438   https://amazon.com/dp/B01A21JYWQ

Sara's Author Bio

Sheila Hunter and Sara Powter were a passionate mother-and-daughter team of amateur genealogists. While working together on their family tree, Sheila and Sara made many captivating discoveries. The greatest of these was finding four convicts, and these four had very different perspectives. They were sent to Australia from 1792 to 1814 during the height of Convict transportation. Before her *passing* in 2002, Sheila adapted some of these histories into enchanting stories, her Australian Colonial Trilogy. Sara later had these published. A fourth she left unfinished, and this inspired her to finish it. However, before she did, **The Lockleys of Parramatta** were created. The first two in the series were completed before she completed 'Dancing to Her Own Tune' for her mother. (*Sheila wrote the first 30k words*)

Vividly living through the Colonial Era, these books delve further into the theme of overcoming adversity in Colonial Australia and how it developed, the demise of the Convict system and the discovery of mineral wealth.

Sara intricately weaves accurate, archival data and a charming narrative to create a series of tales of faith, love, loss, and redemption.

And so, two hundred years after her family arrived in Australia, Sara continues the Australian Colonial stories started in **Lockleys of Parramatta,** followed by the **Unlikely Convict Ladies** Trilogy. **The Hunter to Macquarie Collection** and **The Convict Birthstain Collection** are all stand-alone novels. More Historical Fiction books are to follow... as they are already in the editors' queue.

See Sara's web page to keep up to date with more stories.
With an online store available for a signed copy of Sara's books.
www.sarapowter.com.au   *(Australian Postage only)*

Feel free to email me at
saragpowter@gmail.com

BOOK BUB
 https://partners.bookbub.com/authors/6273615/edit

FACEBOOK https://www.facebook.com/profile.php?id=100063887262514

UNSHACKLED LIVES is **FREE** with a newsletter signup.

Amazon Aus QR

FREE Newsletter signup
From my web page.